DOVER • **GIANT THRIFT** • EDITIONS

Three Soldiers

JOHN DOS PASSOS

DOVER PUBLICATIONS, INC.
Mineola, New York

DOVER GIANT THRIFT EDITIONS

General Editor: Paul Negri
Editor of This Volume: Joslyn T. Pine

Bibliographical Note

This Dover edition, first published in 2004, is an unabridged republication of the work originally published in 1921 by George H. Doran Company, New York. The Introduction is Heywood Broun's review of *Three Soldiers* that originally appeared in *The Bookman*, December 1921, pp. 393–94.

International Standard Book Number: 0-486-43467-2

Manufactured in the United States of America
Dover Publications, Inc., 31 East 2nd Street, Mineola, N.Y. 11501

*"Les contemporains qui souffrent de certaines choses
ne peuvent s'en souvenir qu'avec une horreur qui paralyse
tout autre plaisir, même celui de lire un conte."*

STENDHAL

Introduction*

Heywood Broun

Apparently the war is still too much a part of life to be accepted unqualifiedly as a field for literature. It is so much easier to cry "Pro German" and "Bolshevist" than to discuss art forms, that *Three Soldiers* (Doran), this novel of the reaction of certain characters to the A.E.F. [American Expeditionary Forces], has not received much consideration without taint of political and economic feeling. There are those who think that John Dos Passos ought to be sent to jail and others who hail him as the first of native authors to tell the truth about the war. We are not disposed to class the book either among lamentations or revelations. It does not seem to us a book which may fairly be accepted as a starting point for generalizations about the army. It was not written to be read by a Congressional Committee or anything like that. "Prove it," some few critics have asked, which seems to us just about as ridiculous as if the reviewers of another day had greeted *Tom Jones* with cries of "Add it up" or had demanded of Zola that he demonstrate the square root of *La Terre*. Mathematics ought not to enter into the consideration of *Three Soldiers* any more than politics. It is not important whether there were ten men in the army like Andrews or ten thousand. We feel sure that there must have been at least one, which is ample for the purpose of any artist. Nothing which has come out of the school of American realists has seemed to us so entirely honest. There is not an atom of pose in the book. It represents deep convictions and impressions eloquently expressed. Indeed the eloquence sometimes carries the writer a little

*Excerpted from "A Group of Books Worth Reading" by Heywood Broun published in *The Bookman*, December 1921, pp. 393–94. Brooklyn-born Heywood Broun (1888–1939) was a popular columnist for *The Tribune* and *The World*, and the author of dozens of short stories, articles and essays for, among others, *Harper's*, The *Bookman*, and *The American Mercury*. He was also a passionate and outspoken advocate for the underdog, believing that journalists could effectively fight for justice with the power of the pen. In 1933, he founded the American Newspaper Guild.

beyond the province of realism. There is at times a little more lyricism than is quite compatible with life in the army or elsewhere. Yet it is captious to deplore the occasional imaginative excesses, since nothing but imagination has enabled Dos Passos to reduce so vast and diffuse a thing as the American invading army into a definite personality. The army is the chief figure in the story. When the novelist asks us to meet and regard it there may be many who will object that an old friend has changed beyond recognition. That does not matter beside the fact that Dos Passos has brought the millions into such definite shape that we are enabled to get close enough to the huge affair to look squarely into its eyes.

Contents

PART ONE

MAKING THE MOULD

I

The company stood at attention, each man looking straight before him at the empty parade ground, where the cinder piles showed purple with evening. On the wind that smelt of barracks and disinfectant there was a faint greasiness of food cooking. At the other side of the wide field long lines of men shuffled slowly into the narrow wooden shanty that was the mess hall. Chins down, chests out, legs twitching and tired from the afternoon's drilling, the company stood at attention. Each man stared straight in front of him, some vacantly with resignation, some trying to amuse themselves by noting minutely every object in their field of vision,—the cinder piles, the long shadows of the barracks and mess halls where they could see men standing about, spitting, smoking, leaning against clapboard walls. Some of the men in line could hear their watches ticking in their pockets.

Someone moved, his feet making a crunching noise in the cinders.

The sergeant's voice snarled out: "You men are at attention. Quit yer wrigglin' there, you!"

The men nearest the offender looked at him out of the corners of their eyes.

Two officers, far out on the parade ground, were coming towards them. By their gestures and the way they walked, the men at attention could see that they were chatting about something that amused them. One of the officers laughed boyishly, turned away and walked slowly back across the parade ground. The other, who was the lieutenant, came towards them smiling. As he approached his company, the smile left his lips and he advanced his chin, walking with heavy precise steps.

"Sergeant, you may dismiss the company." The lieutenant's voice was pitched in a hard staccato.

The sergeant's hand snapped up to salute like a block signal.

"Companee dis . . . missed," he sang out.

1

The row of men in khaki became a crowd of various individuals with dusty boots and dusty faces. Ten minutes later they lined up and marched in a column of fours to mess. A few red filaments of electric lights gave a dusty glow in the brownish obscurity where the long tables and benches and the board floors had a faint smell of garbage mingled with the smell of the disinfectant the tables had been washed off with after the last meal. The men, holding their oval mess kits in front of them, filed by the great tin buckets at the door, out of which meat and potatoes were splashed into each plate by a sweating K.P. in blue denims.

"Don't look so bad tonight," said Fuselli to the man opposite him as he hitched his sleeves up at the wrists and leaned over his steaming food. He was sturdy, with curly hair and full vigorous lips that he smacked hungrily as he ate.

"It ain't," said the pink flaxen-haired youth opposite him, who wore his broad-brimmed hat on the side of his head with a certain jauntiness:

"I got a pass tonight," said Fuselli, tilting his head vainly.

"Goin' to tear things up?"

"Man . . . I got a girl at home back in Frisco. She's a good kid."

"Yer right not to go with any of the girls in this goddam town. . . . They ain't clean, none of 'em. . . . That is if ye want to go overseas." The flaxen-haired youth leaned across the table earnestly.

"I'm goin' to git some more chow. Wait for me, will yer?" said Fuselli.

"What yer going to do down town?" asked the flaxen-haired youth when Fuselli came back.

"Dunno,—run round a bit an' go to the movies," he answered, filling his mouth with potato.

"Gawd, it's time fer retreat." They overheard a voice behind them.

Fuselli stuffed his mouth as full as he could and emptied the rest of his meal reluctantly into the garbage pail.

A few moments later he stood stiffly at attention in a khaki row that was one of hundreds of other khaki rows, identical, that filled all sides of the parade ground, while the bugle blew somewhere at the other end where the flag-pole was. Somehow it made him think of the man behind the desk in the office of the draft board who had said, handing him the papers sending him to camp, "I wish I was going with you," and had held out a white bony hand that Fuselli, after a moment's hesitation, had taken in his own stubby brown hand. The man had added fervently, "It must be grand, just grand, to feel the danger, the chance of being potted any minute. Good luck, young feller. . . . Good luck." Fuselli remembered unpleasantly his paper-white face and the greenish look of his bald head; but the words had made him stride out of the office sticking out his chest, brushing truculently past a group of men in the door. Even now the memory of it, mixing with the strains of the national anthem made him feel important, truculent.

"Squads right!" came an order. Crunch, crunch, crunch in the gravel. The companies were going back to their barracks. He wanted to smile but he didn't dare. He wanted to smile because he had a pass till midnight, because in ten minutes he'd be outside the gates, outside the green fence and the sentries and the strands of barbed wire. Crunch, crunch, crunch; oh, they were so slow in getting back to the barracks and he was losing time, precious free minutes. "Hep, hep, hep," cried the sergeant, glaring down the ranks, with his aggressive bulldog expression, to where someone had fallen out of step.

The company stood at attention in the dusk. Fuselli was biting the inside of his lips with impatience. Minutes dragged by.

At last, as if reluctantly, the sergeant sang out:

"Dis . . . missed."

Fuselli hurried towards the gate, brandishing his pass with an important swagger.

Once out on the asphalt of the street, he looked down the long row of lawns and porches where violet arc lamps already contested the faint afterglow, drooping from their iron stalks far above the recently planted saplings of the avenue. He stood at the corner slouched against a telegraph pole, with the camp fence, surmounted by three strands of barbed wire, behind him, wondering which way he would go. This was a hell of a town anyway. And he used to think he wanted to travel round and see places.—"Home'll be good enough for me after this," he muttered. Walking down the long street towards the centre of town, where was the moving-picture show, he thought of his home, of the dark apartment on the ground floor of a seven-storey house where his aunt lived. "Gee, she used to cook swell," he murmured regretfully.

On a warm evening like this he would have stood round at the corner where the drugstore was, talking to fellows he knew, giggling when the girls who lived in the street, walking arm and arm, twined in couples or trios, passed by affecting ignorance of the glances that followed them. Or perhaps he would have gone walking with Al, who worked in the same optical-goods store, down through the glaring streets of the theatre and restaurant quarter, or along the wharves and ferry slips, where they would have sat smoking and looking out over the dark purple harbor, with its winking lights and its moving ferries spilling swaying reflections in the water out of their square reddish-glowing windows. If they had been lucky, they would have seen a liner come in through the Golden Gate, growing from a blur of light to a huge moving brilliance, like the front of a high-class theatre, that towered above the ferry boats. You could often hear the thump of the screw and the swish of the bow cutting the calm bay-water, and the sound of a band playing, that came alternately faint and loud. "When I git rich," Fuselli had liked to say to Al, "I'm going to take a trip on one of them liners."

"Yer dad come over from the old country in one, didn't he?" Al would ask.

"Oh, he came steerage. I'd stay at home if I had to do that. Man, first class for me, a cabin de lux, when I git rich."

But here he was in this town in the East, where he didn't know any-body and where there was no place to go but the movies.

"'Lo, buddy," came a voice beside him. The tall youth who had sat opposite at mess was just catching up to him. "Goin' to the movies?"

"Yare, nauthin' else to do."

"Here's a rookie. Just got to camp this mornin'," said the tall youth, jerking his head in the direction of the man beside him.

"You'll like it. Ain't so bad as it seems at first," said Fuselli encourag-ingly.

"I was just telling him," said the other, "to be careful as hell not to get in wrong. If ye once get in wrong in this damn army . . . it's hell."

"You bet yer life . . . so they sent ye over to our company, did they, rookie? Ain't so bad. The sergeant's sort o' decent if ye're in right with him, but the lieutenant's a stinker. . . . Where you from?"

"New York," said the rookie, a little man of thirty with an ash-colored face and a shiny Jewish nose. "I'm in the clothing business there. I oughtn't to be drafted at all. It's an outrage. I'm consumptive." He splut-tered in a feeble squeaky voice.

"They'll fix ye up, don't you fear," said the tall youth. "They'll make you so goddam well ye won't know yerself. Yer mother won't know ye, when you get home, rookie. . . . But you're in luck."

"Why?"

"Bein' from New York. The corporal, Tim Sidis, is from New York, an' all the New York fellers in the company got a graft with him."

"What kind of cigarettes d'ye smoke?" asked the tall youth.

"I don't smoke."

"Ye'd better learn. The corporal likes fancy ciggies and so does the sergeant; you jus' slip 'em each a butt now and then. May help ye to get in right with 'em."

"Don't do no good," said Fuselli. . . . "It's juss luck. But keep neat-like and smilin' and you'll get on all right. And if they start to ride ye, show fight. Ye've got to be hard boiled to git on in this army."

"Ye're goddam right," said the tall youth. "Don't let 'em ride yer. . . . What's yer name, rookie?"

"Eisenstein."

"This feller's name's Powers . . . Bill Powers. Mine's Fuselli. . . . Goin' to the movies, Mr. Eisenstein?"

"No, I'm trying to find a skirt." The little man leered wanly. "Glad to have got ackwainted."

"Goddam kike!" said Powers as Eisenstein walked off up a side street, planted, like the avenue, with saplings on which the sickly leaves rustled in the faint breeze that smelt of factories and coal dust.

"Kikes ain't so bad," said Fuselli, "I got a good friend who's a kike."

They were coming out of the movies in a stream of people in which the blackish clothes of factory-hands predominated.

"I came near bawlin' at the picture of the feller leavin' his girl to go off to the war," said Fuselli.

"Did yer?"

"It was just like it was with me. Ever been in Frisco, Powers?"

The tall youth shook his head. Then he took off his broad-brimmed hat and ran his fingers over his stubby tow-head.

"Gee, it was some hot in there," he muttered.

"Well, it's like this," said Fuselli. "You have to cross the ferry to Oakland. My aunt . . . ye know I ain't got any mother, so I always live at my aunt's. . . . My aunt an' her sister-in-law an' Mabe . . . Mabe's my girl . . . they all came over on the ferry-boat, 'spite of my tellin' 'em I didn't want 'em. An' Mabe said she was mad at me, 'cause she'd seen the letter I wrote Georgine Slater. She was a toughie, lived in our street, I used to write mash notes to. An' I kep' tellin' Mabe I'd done it juss for the hell of it, an' that I didn't mean nawthin' by it. An' Mabe said she wouldn't never forgive me, an' then I said maybe I'd be killed an' she'd never see me again, an' then we all began to bawl. Gawd! it was a mess. . . ."

"It's hell sayin' good-by to girls," said Powers, understandingly. "Cuts a feller all up. I guess it's better to go with coosies. Ye don't have to say good-by to them."

"Ever gone with a coosie?"

"Not exactly," admitted the tall youth, blushing all over his pink face, so that it was noticeable even under the ashen glare of the arc lights on the avenue that led towards camp.

"I have," said Fuselli, with a certain pride. "I used to go with a Portugee girl. My but she was a toughie. I've given all that up now I'm engaged, though. . . . But I was tellin' ye. . . . Well, we finally made up an' I kissed her an' Mabe said she'd never marry any one but me. So when we was walkin' up the street I spied a silk service flag in a winder, that was all fancy with a star all trimmed up to beat the band, an' I said to myself, I'm goin' to give that to Mabe, an' I ran in an' bought it. I didn't give a hoot in hell what it cost. So when we was all kissin' and bawlin' when I was goin' to leave them to report to the overseas detachment, I shoved it into her hand, an' said, 'Keep that, girl, an' don't you forget me.' An' what did she do but pull out a five-pound box o' candy from behind her back an' say, 'Don't make yerself sick, Dan.' An' she'd had it all the time without my knowin' it. Ain't girls clever?"

"Yare," said the tall youth vaguely.

Along the rows of cots, when Fuselli got back to the barracks, men were talking excitedly.

"There's hell to pay, somebody's broke out of the jug."

"How?"

"Damned if I know."

"Sergeant Timmons said he made a rope of his blankets."

"No, the feller on guard helped him to get away."

"Like hell he did. It was like this. I was walking by the guardhouse when they found out about it."

"What company did he belong ter?"

"Dunno."

"What's his name?"

"Some guy on trial for insubordination. Punched an officer in the jaw."

"I'd a liked to have seen that."

"Anyhow he's fixed himself this time."

"You're goddam right."

"Will you fellers quit talkin'? It's after taps," thundered the sergeant, who sat reading the paper at a little board desk at the door of the barracks under the feeble light of one small bulb, carefully screened. "You'll have the O. D. down on us."

Fuselli wrapped the blanket round his head and prepared to sleep. Snuggled down into the blankets on the narrow cot, he felt sheltered from the sergeant's thundering voice and from the cold glare of officers' eyes. He felt cosy and happy like he had felt in bed at home, when he had been a little kid. For a moment he pictured to himself the other man, the man who had punched an officer's jaw, dressed like he was, maybe only nineteen, the same age like he was, with a girl like Mabe waiting for him somewhere. How cold and frightful it must feel to be out of the camp with the guard looking for you! He pictured himself running breathless down a long street pursued by a company with guns, by officers whose eyes glinted cruelly like the pointed tips of bullets. He pulled the blanket closer round his head, enjoying the warmth and softness of the wool against his cheek. He must remember to smile at the sergeant when he passed him off duty. Somebody had said there'd be promotions soon. Oh, he wanted so hard to be promoted. It'd be so swell if he could write back to Mabe and tell her to address her letters Corporal Dan Fuselli. He must be more careful not to do anything that

would get him in wrong with anybody. He must never miss an opportunity to show them what a clever kid he was. "Oh, when we're ordered
overseas, I'll show them," he thought ardently, and picturing to himself
long movie reels of heroism he went off to sleep.

A sharp voice beside his cot woke him with a jerk.

"Get up, you."

The white beam of a pocket searchlight was glaring in the face of the
man next to him.

"The O. D." said Fuselli to himself.

"Get up, you," came the sharp voice again.

The man in the next cot stirred and opened his eyes.

"Get up."

"Here, sir," muttered the man in the next cot, his eyes blinking sleepily in the glare of the flashlight. He got out of bed and stood unsteadily
at attention.

"Don't you know better than to sleep in your O. D. shirt? Take it off."

"Yes, sir."

"What's your name?"

The man looked up, blinking, too dazed to speak.

"Don't know your own name, eh?" said the officer, glaring at the man
savagely, using his curt voice like a whip.—"Quick, take off yer shirt and
pants and get back to bed."

The Officer of the Day moved on, flashing his light to one side and
the other in his midnight inspection of the barracks. Intense blackness
again, and the sound of men breathing deeply in sleep, of men snoring.
As he went to sleep Fuselli could hear the man beside him swearing, monotonously, in an even whisper, pausing now and then to think of new
filth, of new combinations of words, swearing away his helpless anger,
soothing himself to sleep by the monotonous reiteration of his swearing.

A little later Fuselli woke with a choked nightmare cry. He had
dreamed that he had smashed the O. D. in the jaw and had broken out of
the jug and was running, breathless, stumbling, falling, while the company
on guard chased him down an avenue lined with little dried-up saplings,
gaining on him, while with voices metallic as the clicking of rifle triggers
officers shouted orders, so that he was certain to be caught, certain to be
shot. He shook himself all over, shaking off the nightmare as a dog shakes
off water, and went back to sleep again, snuggling into his blankets.

II

John Andrews stood naked in the center of a large bare room, of which
the walls and ceiling and floor were made of raw pine boards. The air

was heavy from the steam heat. At a desk in one corner a typewriter clicked spasmodically.

"Say, young feller, d'you know how to spell imbecility?"

John Andrews walked over to the desk, told him, and added, "Are you going to examine me?"

The man went on typewriting without answering. John Andrews stood in the center of the floor with his arms folded, half amused, half angry, shifting his weight from one foot to the other, listening to the sound of the typewriter and of the man's voice as he read out each word of the report he was copying.

"Recommendation for discharge" . . . click, click . . . "Damn this type-writer. . . . Private Coe Elbert" . . . click, click. "Damn these rotten army typewriters. . . . Reason . . . mental deficiency. History of Case. . . ."

At that moment the recruiting sergeant came back.

"Look here, if you don't have that recommendation ready in ten min-utes Captain Arthurs'll be mad as hell about it, Bill. For God's sake get it done. He said already that if you couldn't do the work, to get somebody who could. You don't want to lose your job do you?"

"Hullo," the sergeant's eyes lit on John Andrews, "I'd forgotten you. Run around the room a little. . . . No, not that way. Just a little so I can test yer heart. . . . God, these rookies are thick."

While he stood tamely being prodded and measured, feeling like a prize horse at a fair, John Andrews listened to the man at the typewriter, whose voice went on monotonously.

"No . . . record of sexual dep. . . . O hell, this eraser's no good! . . . pravity or alcoholism; spent . . . normal . . . youth on farm. App-ear-ance normal though im . . . say, how many 'm's' in immature?"

"All right, put yer clothes on," said the recruiting sergeant. "Quick, I can't spend all day. Why the hell did they send you down here alone?"

"The papers were balled up," said Andrews.

"Scores ten years . . . in test B," went on the voice of the man at the typewriter. . . . "Sen . . . exal ment . . . m-e-n-t-a-l-i-t-y that of child of eight. Seems unable . . . to either. . . . Goddam this man's writin'. How kin I copy it when he don't write out his words?"

"All right. I guess you'll do. Now there are some forms to fill out. Come over here."

Andrews followed the recruiting sergeant to a desk in the far corner of the room, from which he could hear more faintly the click, click of the typewriter and the man's voice mumbling angrily.

"Forgets to obey orders. . . . Responds to no form of per . . . suasion. M-e-m-o-r-y, nil."

"All right. Take this to barracks B. . . . Fourth building, to the right; shake a leg," said the recruiting sergeant.

Andrews drew a deep breath of the sparkling air outside. He stood irresolutely a moment on the wooden steps of the building looking down the row of hastily constructed barracks. Some were painted green, some were of plain boards, and some were still mere skeletons. Above his head great piled, rose-tinted clouds were moving slowly across the immeasurable free sky. His glance slid down the sky to some tall trees that flamed bright yellow with autumn outside the camp limits, and then to the end of the long street of barracks, where was a picket fence and a sentry walking to and fro, to and fro. His brows contracted for a moment. Then he walked with a sort of swagger towards the fourth building to the right.

John Andrews was washing windows. He stood in dirty blue denims at the top of a ladder, smearing with a soapy cloth the small panes of the barrack windows. His nostrils were full of a smell of dust and of the sandy quality of the soap. A little man with one lined greyish-red cheek puffed out by tobacco followed him up, also on a ladder, polishing the panes with a dry cloth till they shone and reflected the mottled cloudy sky. Andrews's legs were tired from climbing up and down the ladder, his hands were sore from the grittiness of the soap; as he worked he looked down, without thinking, on rows of cots where the blankets were all folded the same way, on some of which men were sprawled in attitudes of utter relaxation. He kept remarking to himself how strange it was that he was not thinking of anything. In the last few days his mind seemed to have become a hard meaningless core.

"How long do we have to do this?" he asked the man who was working with him. The man went on chewing, so that Andrews thought he was not going to answer at all. He was just beginning to speak again when the man, balancing thoughtfully on top of his ladder, drawled out:

"Four o'clock."

"We won't finish today then?"

The man shook his head and wrinkled his face into a strange spasm as he spat.

"Been here long?"

"Not so long."

"How long?"

"Three months. . . . Ain't so long." The man spat again, and climbing down from his ladder waited, leaning against the wall, until Andrews should finish soaping his window.

"I'll go crazy if I stay here three months. . . . I've been here a week," muttered Andrews between his teeth as he climbed down and moved his ladder to the next window.

They both climbed their ladders again in silence.

"How's it you're in Casuals?" asked Andrews again.

"Ain't got no lungs."

"Why don't they discharge you?"

"Reckon they're going to, soon."

They worked on in silence for a long time. Andrews started at the upper right-hand corner and smeared with soap each pane of the window in turn. Then he climbed down, moved his ladder, and started on the next window. At times he would start in the middle of the window for variety. As he worked a rhythm began pushing its way through the hard core of his mind, leavening it, making it fluid. It expressed the vast dusty dullness, the men waiting in rows on drill fields, standing at attention, the monotony of feet tramping in unison, of the dust rising from the battalions going back and forth over the dusty drill fields. He felt the rhythm filling his whole body, from his sore hands to his legs, tired from marching back and forth, from making themselves the same length as millions of other legs. His mind began unconsciously, from habit, working on it, orchestrating it. He could imagine a vast orchestra swaying with it. His heart was beating faster. He must make it into music; he must fix it in himself, so that he could make it into music, and write it down, so that orchestras could play it and make the ears of multitudes feel it, make their flesh tingle with it.

He went on working through the endless afternoon, climbing up and down his ladder, smearing the barrack windows with a soapy rag. A silly phrase took the place of the welling of music in his mind: "Arbeit und Rhythmus." He kept saying it over and over to himself: "Arbeit und Rhythmus." He tried to drive the phrase out of his mind, to bury his mind in the music of the rhythm that had come to him, that expressed the dusty boredom, the harsh constriction of warm bodies full of gestures and attitudes and aspirations into moulds, like the moulds toy soldiers are cast in. The phrase became someone shouting raucously in his ears: "Arbeit und Rhythmus,"—drowning everything else, beating his mind hard again, parching it.

But suddenly he laughed aloud. Why, it was in German. He was being got ready to kill men who said that. If anyone said that, he was going to kill him. They were going to kill everybody who spoke that language, he and all the men whose feet he could hear tramping on the drill field, whose legs were all being made the same length on the drill field.

III

It was Saturday morning. Directed by the corporal, a bandy-legged Italian who even on the army diet managed to keep a faint odour of garlic about him, three soldiers in blue denims were sweeping up the leaves in the street between the rows of barracks.

"You fellers are slow as molasses. . . . Inspection in twenty-five minutes," he kept saying.

The soldiers raked on doggedly, paying no attention.

"You don't give a damn. If we don't pass inspection, I get hell—not you. Please queeck. Here, you, pick up all those goddam cigarette butts."

Andrews made a grimace and began collecting the little grey sordid ends of burnt-out cigarettes. As he leant over he found himself looking into the dark-brown eyes of the soldier who was working beside him. The eyes were contracted with anger and there was a flush under the tan of the boyish face.

"Ah didn't git in this here army to be ordered around by a goddam wop," he muttered.

"Doesn't matter much who you're ordered around by, you're ordered around just the same," said Andrews.

"Where d'ye come from, buddy?"

"Oh, I come from New York. My folks are from Virginia," said Andrews.

"Indiana's ma state. The tornado country. . . . Git to work; here's that bastard wop comin' around the buildin'."

"Don't pick 'em up that-a-way; sweep 'em up," shouted the corporal.

Andrews and the Indiana boy went round with a broom and a shovel collecting chewed-out quids of tobacco and cigar butts and stained bits of paper.

"What's your name? Mahn's Chrisfield. Folks all call me Chris."

"Mine's Andrews, John Andrews."

"Ma dad uster have a hired man named Andy. Took sick an' died last summer. How long d'ye reckon it'll be before us-guys git overseas?"

"God, I don't know."

"Ah want to see that country over there."

"You do?"

"Don't you?"

"You bet I do."

"All right, what you fellers stand here for? Go an' dump them garbage cans. Lively!" shouted the corporal waddling about importantly on his bandy legs. He kept looking down the row of barracks, muttering to himself, "Goddam. . . . Time fur inspectin' now, goddam. Won't never pass this time."

His face froze suddenly into obsequious immobility. He brought his hand up to the brim of his hat. A group of officers strode past him into the nearest building.

John Andrews, coming back from emptying the garbage pails, went in the back door of his barracks.

"Attention!" came the cry from the other end. He made his neck and arms as rigid as possible.

Through the silent barracks came the hard clank of the heels of the officers inspecting.

A sallow face with hollow eyes and heavy square jaw came close to Andrews's eyes. He stared straight before him noting the few reddish hairs on the officer's Adam's apple and the new insignia on either side of his collar.

"Sergeant, who is this man?" came a voice from the sallow face.

"Don't know, sir; a new recruit, sir. Corporal Valori, who is this man?"

"The name's Andrews, sergeant," said the Italian corporal with an ob-sequious whine in his voice.

The officer addressed Andrews directly, speaking fast and loud.

"How long have you been in the army?"

"One week, sir."

"Don't you know you have to be clean and shaved and ready for in-spection every Saturday morning at nine?"

"I was cleaning the barracks, sir."

"To teach you not to answer back when an officer addresses you. . . ." The officer spaced his words carefully, lingering on them. As he spoke he glanced out of the corner of his eye at his superior and noticed the major was frowning. His tone changed ever so slightly. "If this ever occurs again you may be sure that disciplinary action will be taken. . . . Attention there!" At the other end of the barracks a man had moved. Again, amid absolute silence, could be heard the clanking of the officers' heels as the inspection continued.

"Now, fellows, all together," cried the "Y" man who stood with his arms stretched wide in front of the movie screen. The piano started jingling and the roomful of crowded soldiers roared out:

> "Hail, Hail, the gang's all here;
> We're going to get the Kaiser,
> We're going to get the Kaiser,
> We're going to get the Kaiser
> Now!"

The rafters rang with their deep voices.

The "Y" man twisted his lean face into a facetious expression.

"Somebody tried to put one over on the 'Y' man and sing 'What the hell do we care?' But you do care, don't you, Buddy?" he shouted.

There was a little rattle of laughter.

"Now, once more," said the "Y" man again, "and lots of guts in the get and lots of kill in the Kaiser. Now all together. . . ."

The moving pictures had begun. John Andrews looked furtively about him, at the face of the Indiana boy beside him intent on the screen, at the tanned faces and the close-cropped heads that rose above the mass of khaki-covered bodies about him. Here and there a pair of eyes glinted in the white flickering light from the screen. Waves of laughter or of little exclamations passed over them. They were all so alike, they seemed at moments to be but one organism. This was what he had sought when he had enlisted, he said to himself. It was in this that he would take refuge from the horror of the world that had fallen upon him. He was sick of revolt, of thought, of carrying his individuality like a banner above the turmoil. This was much better, to let everything go, to stamp out his maddening desire for music, to humble himself into the mud of common slavery. He was still tingling with sudden anger from the officer's voice that morning: "Sergeant, who is this man?" The officer had stared in his face, as a man might stare at a piece of furniture.

"Ain't this some film?" Chrisfield turned to him with a smile that drove his anger away in a pleasant feeling of comradeship.

"The part that's comin's fine. I seen it before out in Frisco," said the man on the other side of Andrews. "Gee, it makes ye hate the Huns."

The man at the piano jingled elaborately in the intermission between the two parts of the movie.

The Indiana boy leaned in front of John Andrews, putting an arm round his shoulders, and talked to the other man.

"You from Frisco?"

"Yare."

"That's goddam funny. You're from the Coast, this feller's from New York, an' Ah'm from ole Indiana, right in the middle."

"What company you in?"

"Ah ain't yet. This feller an me's in Casuals."

"That's a hell of a place. . . . Say, my name's Fuselli."

"Mahn's Chrisfield."

"Mine's Andrews."

"How soon's it take a feller to git out o' this camp?"

"Dunno. Some guys says three weeks and some says six months. . . . Say, mebbe you'll get into our company. They transferred a lot of men out the other day, an' the corporal says they're going to give us rookies instead."

"Goddam it, though, but Ah want to git overseas."

"It's swell over there," said Fuselli, "everything's awful pretty-like. Picturesque, they call it. And the people wears peasant costumes. . . . I had an uncle who used to tell me about it. He came from near Torino."

"Where's that?"

"I dunno. He's an Eyetalian."

"Say, how long does it take to git overseas?"

"Oh, a week or two," said Andrews.

"As long as that?" But the movie had begun again, unfolding scenes of soldiers in spiked helmets marching into Belgian cities full of little milk carts drawn by dogs and old women in peasant costume. There were hisses and catcalls when a German flag was seen, and as the troops were pictured advancing, bayonetting the civilians in wide Dutch pants, the old women with starched caps, the soldiers packed into the stuffy Y.M.C.A. hut shouted oaths at them. Andrews felt blind hatred stirring like something that had a life of its own in the young men about him. He was lost in it, carried away in it, as in a stampede of wild cattle. The terror of it was like ferocious hands clutching his throat. He glanced at the faces round him. They were all intent and flushed, glinting with sweat in the heat of the room.

As he was leaving the hut, pressed in a tight stream of soldiers moving towards the door, Andrews heard a man say:

"I never raped a woman in my life, but by God, I'm going to. I'd give a lot to rape some of those goddam German women."

"I hate 'em too," came another voice, "men, women, children and un-born children. They're either jackasses or full of the lust for power like their rulers are, to let themselves be governed by a bunch of warlords like that."

"Ah'd lahk te cepture a German officer an' make him shine ma boots an' then shoot him dead," said Chris to Andrews as they walked down the long row towards their barracks.

"You would?"

"But Ah'd a damn side rather shoot somebody else Ah know," went on Chris intensely. "Don't stay far from here either. An' Ah'll do it too, if he don't let off pickin' on me."

"Who's that?"

"That big squirt Anderson they made a file closer at drill yesterday. He seems te think that just because Ah'm littler than him he can do anything he likes with me."

Andrews turned sharply and looked in his companion's face; some-thing in the gruffness of the boy's tone startled him. He was not accus-tomed to this. He had thought of himself as a passionate person, but never in his life had he wanted to kill a man.

"D'you really want to kill him?"

"Not now, but he gits the hell started in me, the way he teases me. Ah pulled ma knife on him yesterday. You wasn't there. Didn't ye notice Ah looked sort o' upsot at drill?"

"Yes . . . but how old are you, Chris!"

"Ah'm twenty. You're older than me, ain't yer?"

"I'm twenty-two."

They were leaning against the wall of their barracks, looking up at the brilliant starry night.

"Say, is the stars the same over there, overseas, as they is here?"

"I guess so," said Andrews, laughing. "Though I've never been to see."

"Ah never had much schoolin'," went on Chris. "I lef' school when I was twelve, 'cause it warn't much good, an' dad drank so the folks needed me to work on the farm."

"What do you grow in your part of the country?"

"Mostly coan. A little wheat an' tobacca. Then we raised a lot o' stock. . . . But Ah was juss going to tell ye Ah nearly did kill a guy once."

"Tell me about it."

"Ah was drunk at the time. Us boys round Tallyville was a pretty tough bunch then. We used ter work juss long enough to git some money to tear things up with. An' then we used to play craps an' drink whiskey. This happened just at coan-shuckin' time. Hell, Ah don't even know what it was about, but Ah got to quarrellin' with a feller Ah'd been right smart friends with. Then he laid off an' hit me in the jaw. Ah don't know what Ah done next, but before Ah knowed it Ah had a hold of a shuckin' knife and was slashin' at him with it. A knife like that's a turruble thing to stab a man with. It took four of 'em to hold me down an' git it away from me. They didn't keep me from givin' him a good cut across the chest, though. Ah was juss crazy drunk at the time. An' man, if Ah wasn't a mess to go home, with half ma clothes pulled off and ma shirt torn. Ah juss fell in the ditch an' slep' there till daylight an' got mud all through ma hair. . . . Ah don't scarcely tech a drop now, though."

"So you're in a hurry to get overseas, Chris, like me," said Andrews after a long pause.

"Ah'll push that guy Anderson into the sea, if we both go over on the same boat," said Chrisfield laughing; but he added after a pause: "It would have been hell if Ah'd killed that feller, though. Honest Ah wouldn't a-wanted to do that."

"That's the job that pays, a violinist," said somebody.

"No, it don't," came a melancholy drawling voice from a lanky man who sat doubled up with his long face in his hands and his elbows resting on his knees. "Just brings a living wage . . . a living wage."

Several men were grouped at the end of the barracks. From them the long row of cots, with here and there a man asleep or a man hastily undressing, stretched, lighted by occasional feeble electric-light bulbs, to the sergeant's little table beside the door.

"You're gettin' a dis-charge, aren't you?" asked a man with a brogue, and the red face of a jovial gorilla, that signified the bartender.

"Yes, Flannagan, I am," said the lanky man dolefully.

"Ain't he got hard luck?" came a voice from the crowd.

"Yes, I have got hard luck, Buddy," said the lanky man, looking at the faces about him out of sunken eyes. "I ought to be getting forty dollars a week and here I am getting seven and in the army besides."

"I meant that you were gettin' out of this goddam army."

"The army, the army, the democratic army," chanted someone under his breath.

"But, begorry, I want to go overseas and 'ave a look at the 'uns," said Flannagan, who managed with strange skill to combine a cockney whine with his Irish brogue.

"Overseas?" took up the lanky man. "If I could have gone an' studied overseas, I'd be making as much as Kubelik. I had the makings of a good player in me."

"Why don't you go?" asked Andrews, who stood on the outskirts with Fuselli and Chris.

"Look at me . . . t. b.," said the lanky man.

"Well, they can't get me over there soon enough," said Flannagan.

"Must be funny not bein' able to understand what folks say. They say 'we' over there when they mean 'yes,' a guy told me."

"Ye can make signs to them, can't ye?" said Flannagan "an' they can understand an Irishman anywhere. But ye won't 'ave to talk to the 'uns. Begorry I'll set up in business when I get there, what d'ye think of that?"

Everybody laughed.

"How'd that do? I'll start an Irish House in Berlin, I will, and there'll be O'Casey and O'Ryan and O'Reilly and O'Flarrety, and begod the King of England himself'll come an' set the goddam Kaiser up to a drink."

"The Kaiser'll be strung up on a telephone pole by that time; ye needn't worry, Flannagan."

"They ought to torture him to death, like they do niggers when they lynch 'em down south."

A bugle sounded far away outside on the parade ground. Everyone slunk away silently to his cot.

John Andrews arranged himself carefully in his blankets, promising himself a quiet time of thought before going to sleep. He needed to lie awake and think at night this way, so that he might not lose entirely the thread of his own life, of the life he would take up again some day if he lived through it. He brushed away the thought of death. It was uninteresting. He didn't care anyway. But some day he would want to play the piano again, to write music. He must not let himself sink too deeply into the helpless mentality of the soldier. He must keep his will power.

No, but that was not what he had wanted to think about. He was so bored with himself. At any cost he must forget himself. Ever since his first year at college he seemed to have done nothing but think about himself, talk about himself. At least at the bottom, in the utterest degradation of slavery, he could find forgetfulness and start rebuilding the fabric of his life, out of real things this time, out of work and comradeship and scorn. Scorn—that was the quality he needed. It was such a raw, fantastic world he had suddenly fallen into. His life before this week seemed a dream read in a novel, a picture he had seen in a shop window—it was so different. Could it have been in the same world at all? He must have died without knowing it and been born again into a new, futile hell.

When he had been a child he had lived in a dilapidated mansion that stood among old oaks and chestnuts, beside a road where buggies and oxcarts passed rarely to disturb the sandy ruts that lay in the mottled shade. He had had so many dreams; lying under the crêpe-myrtle bush at the end of the overgrown garden he had passed the long Virginia afternoons, thinking, while the dryflies whizzed sleepily in the sunlight, of the world he would live in when he grew up. He had planned so many lives for himself: a general, like Caesar, he was to conquer the world and die murdered in a great marble hall; a wandering minstrel, he would go through all countries singing and have intricate endless adventures; a great musician, he would sit at the piano playing, like Chopin in the engraving, while beautiful women wept and men with long, curly hair hid their faces in their hands. It was only slavery that he had not foreseen. His race had dominated for too many centuries for that. And yet the world was made of various slaveries.

John Andrews lay on his back on his cot while everyone about him slept and snored in the dark barracks. A certain terror held him. In a week the great structure of his romantic world, so full of many colors and harmonies, that had survived school and college and the buffeting of making a living in New York, had fallen in dust about him. He was utterly in the void. "How silly," he thought; "this is the world as it has appeared to the majority of men, this is just the lower half of the pyramid."

He thought of his friends, of Fuselli and Chrisfield and that funny little man Eisenstein. They seemed at home in this army life. They did not seem appalled by the loss of their liberty. But they had never lived in the glittering other world. Yet he could not feel the scorn of them he wanted to feel. He thought of them singing under the direction of the "Y" man:

"Hail, Hail, the gang's all here;
We're going to get the Kaiser,

             We're going to get the Kaiser,
             We're going to get the Kaiser
             Now!"

He thought of himself and Chrisfield picking up cigarette butts and the tramp, tramp, tramp of feet on the drill field. Where was the connection? Was this all futile madness? They'd come from such various worlds, all these men sleeping about him, to be united in this. And what did they think of it, all these sleepers? Had they too not had dreams when they were boys? Or had the generations prepared them only for this?

He thought of himself lying under the crêpe-myrtle bush through the hot, droning afternoon, watching the pale magenta flowers flutter down into the dry grass, and felt, again, wrapped in his warm blankets among all these sleepers, the straining of limbs burning with desire to rush untrammelled through some new keen air. Suddenly darkness overspread his mind.

He woke with a start. The bugle was blowing outside. "All right, look lively!" the sergeant was shouting. Another day.

IV

The stars were very bright when Fuselli, eyes stinging with sleep, stumbled out of the barracks. They trembled like bits of brilliant jelly in the black velvet of the sky, just as something inside him trembled with excitement.

"Anybody know where the electricity turns on?" asked the sergeant in a good-humored voice. "Here it is." The light over the door of the barracks snapped on, revealing a rotund cheerful man with a little yellow mustache and an unlit cigarette dangling out of the corner of his mouth. Grouped about him, in overcoats and caps, the men of the company rested their packs against their knees.

"All right; line up, men."

Eyes looked curiously at Fuselli as he lined up with the rest. He had been transferred into the company the night before.

"Attenshun," shouted the sergeant. Then he wrinkled up his eyes and grinned hard at the slip of paper he had in his hand, while the men of his company watched him affectionately.

"Answer 'Here' when your name is called. Allan, B. C."

"Yo!" came a shrill voice from the end of the line.

"Anspach."

"Here."

Meanwhile outside the other barracks other companies could be heard calling the roll. Somewhere from the end of the street came a cheer.

"Well, I guess I can tell you now, fellers," said the sergeant with his air of quiet omniscience, when he had called the last name. "We're going overseas."

Everybody cheered.

"Shut up, you don't want the Huns to hear us, do you?"

The company laughed, and there was a broad grin on the sergeant's round face.

"Seem to have a pretty decent top-kicker," whispered Fuselli to the man next to him.

"You bet yer, kid, he's a peach," said the other man in a voice full of devotion. "This is some company, I can tell you that."

"You bet it is," said the next man along. "The corporal's in the Red Sox outfield."

The lieutenant appeared suddenly in the area of light in front of the barracks. He was a pink-faced boy. His trench coat, a little too large, was very new and stuck out stiffly from his legs.

"Everything all right, sergeant? Everything all right?" he asked several times, shifting his weight from one foot to the other.

"All ready for entrainment, sir," said the sergeant heartily.

"Very good, I'll let you know the order of march in a minute."

Fuselli's ears pounded with strange excitement. These phrases, "entrainment," "order of march," had a businesslike sound. He suddenly started to wonder how it would feel to be under fire. Memories of movies flickered in his mind.

"Gawd, ain't I glad to git out o' this hell-hole," he said to the man next him.

"The next one may be more of a hell-hole yet, buddy," said the sergeant striding up and down with his important confident walk.

Everybody laughed.

"He's some sergeant, our sergeant is," said the man next to Fuselli. "He's got brains in his head, that boy has."

"All right, break ranks," said the sergeant, "but if anybody moves away from this barracks, I'll put him in K.P. till—till he'll be able to peel spuds in his sleep."

The company laughed again. Fuselli noticed with displeasure that the tall man with the shrill voice whose name had been called first on the roll did not laugh but spat disgustedly out of the corner of his mouth.

"Well, there are bad eggs in every good bunch," thought Fuselli.

It gradually grew grey with dawn. Fuselli's legs were tired from standing so long. Outside all the barracks, as far as he could see up the street, men stood in ragged lines waiting.

The sun rose hot on a cloudless day. A few sparrows twittered about the tin roof of the barracks.

"Hell, we're not goin' this day."

"Why?" asked somebody savagely.

"Troops always leaves at night."

"The hell they do!"

"Here comes Sarge."

Everybody craned their necks in the direction pointed out.

The sergeant strolled up with a mysterious smile on his face.

"Put away your overcoats and get out your mess kits."

Mess kits clattered and gleamed in the slanting rays of the sun. They marched to the mess hall and back again, lined up again with packs and waited some more.

Everybody began to get tired and peevish. Fuselli wondered where his old friends of the other company were. They were good kids too, Chris and that educated fellow, Andrews. Tough luck they couldn't have come along.

The sun rose higher. Men sneaked into the barracks one by one and lay down on the bare cots.

"What you want to bet we won't leave this camp for a week yet?" asked someone.

At noon they lined up for mess again, ate dismally and hurriedly. As Fuselli was leaving the mess hall tapping a tattoo on his kit with two dirty finger nails, the corporal spoke to him in a low voice.

"Be sure to wash yer kit, buddy. We may have pack inspection."

The corporal was a slim yellow-faced man with a wrinkled skin, though he was still young, and an arrow-shaped mouth that opened and shut like the paper mouths children make.

"All right, corporal," Fuselli answered cheerfully. He wanted to make a good impression. "Fellers'll be sayin' 'All right, corporal,' to me soon," he thought. An idea that he repelled came into his mind. The corporal didn't look strong. He wouldn't last long overseas. And he pictured Mabe writing Corporal Dan Fuselli, O.A.R.D.5.

At the end of the afternoon, the lieutenant appeared suddenly, his face flushed, his trench coat stiffer than ever.

"All right, sergeant; line up your men," he said in a breathless voice.

All down the camp street companies were forming. One by one they marched out in columns of fours and halted with their packs on. The day was getting amber with sunset. Retreat sounded.

Fuselli's mind had suddenly become very active. The notes of the bugle and of the band playing "The Star Spangled Banner" sifted into his consciousness through a dream of what it would be like over there. He was in a place like the Exposition ground, full of old men and women in peasant costume, like in the song, "When It's Apple Blossom Time in Normandy." Men in spiked helmets who looked like firemen kept charging through, like the Ku-Klux Klan in the movies, jumping from their horses and setting fire to buildings with strange outlandish gestures, spitting babies on their long swords. Those were the Huns. Then there were flags blowing very hard in the wind, and the sound of a band. The Yanks were coming. Everything was lost in a scene from a movie in which khaki-clad regiments marched fast, fast across the scene. The memory of the shouting that always accompanied it drowned out the picture. "The guns must make a racket, though," he added as an afterthought.

"Atten-shun!"

"Forwa-ard, march!"

The long street of the camp was full of the tramping of feet. They were off. As they passed through the gate Fuselli caught a glimpse of Chris standing with his arm about Andrews's shoulders. They both waved. Fuselli grinned and expanded his chest. They were just rookies still. He was going overseas.

The weight of the pack tugged at his shoulders and made his feet heavy as if they were charged with lead. The sweat ran down his close-clipped head under the overseas cap and streamed into his eyes and down the sides of his nose. Through the tramp of feet he heard confusedly cheering from the sidewalk. In front of him the backs of heads and the swaying packs got smaller, rank by rank up the street. Above them flags dangled from windows, flags leisurely swaying in the twilight. But the weight of the pack, as the column marched under arc lights glaring through the afterglow, inevitably forced his head to droop forward. The soles of boots and legs wrapped in puttees and the bottom strap of the pack of the man ahead of him were all he could see. The pack seemed heavy enough to push him through the asphalt pavement. And all about him was the faint jingle of equipment and the tramp of feet. Every part of him was full of sweat. He could feel vaguely the steam of sweat that rose from the ranks of struggling bodies about him. But gradually he forgot everything but the pack tugging at his shoulders, weighing down his thighs and ankles and feet, and the monotonous rhythm of his feet striking the pavement and of the other feet, in front of him, behind him, beside him, crunching, crunching.

The train smelt of new uniforms on which the sweat had dried, and of the smoke of cheap cigarettes. Fuselli awoke with a start. He had been asleep with his head on Bill Grey's shoulder. It was already broad day-

light. The train was jolting slowly over cross-tracks in some dismal sub-
urb, full of long soot-smeared warehouses and endless rows of freight
cars, beyond which lay brown marshland and slate-grey stretches of
water.

"God! that must be the Atlantic Ocean," cried Fuselli in excitement.

"Ain't yer never seen it before? That's the Perth River," said Bill Grey
scornfully.

"No, I come from the Coast."

They stuck their heads out of the window side by side so that their
cheeks touched.

"Gee, there's some skirts," said Bill Grey. The train jolted to a stop.
Two untidy red-haired girls were standing beside the track waving their
hands.

"Give us a kiss," cried Bill Grey.

"Sure," said a girl,—"anythin' fer one of our boys."

She stood on tiptoe and Grey leaned far out of the window, just man-
aging to reach the girl's forehead.

Fuselli felt a flush of desire all over him.

"Hol' onter my belt," he said. "I'll kiss her right."

He leaned far out, and, throwing his arms around the girl's pink ging-
ham shoulders, lifted her off the ground and kissed her furiously on the
lips.

"Lemme go, lemme go," cried the girl.

Men leaning out of the other windows of the car cheered and
shouted.

Fuselli kissed her again and then dropped her.

"Ye're too rough, damn ye," said the girl angrily.

A man from one of the windows yelled, "I'll go an' tell mommer";
and everybody laughed. The train moved on. Fuselli looked about him
proudly. The image of Mabe giving him the five-pound box of candy
rose a moment in his mind.

"Ain't no harm in havin' a little fun. Don't mean nothin'," he said
aloud.

"You just wait till we hit France. We'll hit it up some with the
Madimerzels, won't we, kid?" said Bill Grey, slapping Fuselli on the knee.

> "Beautiful Katy,
> Ki-Ki-Katy,
> You're the only gugugu-girl that I adore;
> And when the mo-moon shines
> Over the cowshed,
> I'll be waiting at the ki-ki-ki-kitchen door."

Everybody sang as the thumping of wheels over rails grew faster.

Fuselli looked about contentedly at the company sprawling over their packs and equipment in the smoky car.

"It's great to be a soldier," he said to Bill Grey. "Ye kin do anything ye goddam please."

"This," said the corporal, as the company filed into barracks identical to those they had left two days before, "is an embarkation camp, but I'd like to know where the hell we embark at." He twisted his face into a smile, and then shouted with lugubrious intonation: "Fall in for mess."

It was pitch dark in that part of the camp. The electric lights had a sparse reddish glow. Fuselli kept straining his eyes, expecting to see a wharf and the masts of a ship at the end of every alley. The line filed into a dim mess hall, where a thin stew was splashed into the mess kits. Behind the counter of the kitchen the non-coms, the jovial first sergeant, and the business-like sergeant who looked like a preacher, and the wrinkled-faced corporal who had been on the Red Sox outfield, could be seen eating steak. A faint odor of steak frying went through the mess hall and made the thin chilly stew utterly tasteless in comparison.

Fuselli looked enviously towards the kitchen and thought of the day when he would be a non-com too. "I got to get busy," he said to himself earnestly. Overseas, under fire, he'd have a chance to show what he was worth; and he pictured himself heroically carrying a wounded captain back to a dressing tent, pursued by fierce-whiskered men with spiked helmets like firemen's helmets.

The strumming of a guitar came strangely down the dark street of the camp.

"Some guy sure can play," said Bill Grey who, with his hands in his pockets, slouched along beside Fuselli.

They looked in the door of one of the barracks. A lot of soldiers were sitting in a ring round two tall negroes whose black faces and chests glistened like jet in the faint light. "Come on, Charley, give us another," said someone.

"Do Ah git it now, or mus' Ah hesit-ate?"

One negro began chanting while the other strummed carelessly on the guitar.

"No, give us the 'Titanic.'"

The guitar strummed in a crooning rag-time for a moment. The negro's voice broke into it suddenly, pitched high.

"Dis is de song ob de Titanic,
Sailin' on de sea."

The guitar strummed on. There had been a tension in the negro's voice that had made everyone stop talking. The soldiers looked at him curiously.

> "How de Titanic ran in dat cole iceberg,
> How de Titanic ran in dat cole iceberg
> Sailin' on de sea."

His voice was confidential and soft, and the guitar strummed to the same sobbing rag-time. Verse after verse the voice grew louder and the strumming faster.

> "De Titanic's sinkin' in de deep blue,
> Sinkin' in de deep blue, deep blue,
> Sinkin' in de sea.
> O de women an' de chilen a-floatin' in de sea,
> O de women an' de chilen a-floatin' in de sea,
> Roun' dat cole iceberg,
> Sung 'Nearer, my gawd, to Thee,'
> Sung 'Nearer, my gawd, to Thee,
> Nearer to Thee.'"

The guitar was strumming the hymn-tune. The negro was singing with every cord in his throat taut, almost sobbing.

A man next to Fuselli took careful aim and spat into the box of saw-dust in the middle of the ring of motionless soldiers.

The guitar played the rag-time again, fast, almost mockingly. The negro sang in low confidential tones.

> "O de women an' de chilen dey sank in de sea.
> O de women an' de chilen dey sank in de sea,
> Roun' dat cole iceberg."

Before he had finished a bugle blew in the distance. Everybody scattered.

Fuselli and Bill Grey went silently back to their barracks.

"It must be an awful thing to drown in the sea," said Grey as he rolled himself in his blankets. "If one of those bastard U-boats . . ."

"I don't give a damn," said Fuselli boisterously; but as he lay staring into the darkness, cold terror stiffened him suddenly. He thought for a moment of deserting, pretending he was sick, anything to keep from going on the transport.

> "O de women an' de chilen dey sank in de sea,
> Roun' dat cole iceberg."

He could feel himself going down through icy water. "It's a hell of a thing to send a guy over there to drown," he said to himself, and he thought of the hilly streets of San Francisco, and the glow of the sunset over the harbor and ships coming in through the Golden Gate. His mind went gradually blank and he went to sleep.

The column was like some curious khaki-colored carpet, hiding the road as far as you could see. In Fuselli's company the men were shifting their weight from one foot to the other, muttering, "What the hell a' they waiting for now?" Bill Grey, next to Fuselli in the ranks, stood bent double so as to take the weight of his pack off his shoulders. They were at a cross-roads on fairly high ground so that they could see the long sheds and barracks of the camp stretching away in every direction, in rows and rows, broken now and then by a grey drill field. In front of them the column stretched to the last bend in the road, where it disappeared on a hill among mustard-yellow suburban houses.

Fuselli was excited. He kept thinking of the night before, when he had helped the sergeant distribute emergency rations, and had carried about piles of boxes of hard bread, counting them carefully without a mistake. He felt full of desire to do things, to show what he was good for. "Gee," he said to himself, "this war's a lucky thing for me. I might have been in the R. C. Vicker Company's store for five years an' never got a raise. An' here in the army I got a chance to do almost anything."

Far ahead down the road the column was beginning to move. Voices shouting orders beat crisply on the morning air. Fuselli's heart was thumping. He felt proud of himself and of the company—the damn best company in the whole outfit. The company ahead was moving, it was their turn now.

"Forwa-ard, march!"

They were lost in the monotonous tramp of feet. Dust rose from the road, along which like a drab brown worm crawled the column.

A sickening unfamiliar smell choked their nostrils.

"What are they taking us down here for?"

"Damned if I know."

They were filing down ladders into the terrifying pit which the hold of the ship seemed to them. Every man had a blue card in his hand with a number on it. In a dim place like an empty warehouse they stopped. The sergeant shouted out:

"I guess this is our diggings. We'll have to make the best of it." Then he disappeared.

Fuselli looked about him. He was sitting in one of the lowest of three tiers of bunks roughly built of new pine boards. Electric lights placed here and there gave a faint reddish tone to the gloom, except at the ladders, where high-power lamps made a white glare. The place was full of tramping of feet and the sound of packs being thrown on bunks as end-less files of soldiers poured in down every ladder. Somewhere down the alley an officer with a shrill voice was shouting to his men: "Speed it up there; speed it up there." Fuselli sat on his bunk looking at the terrifying confusion all about, feeling bewildered and humiliated. For how many days would they be in that dark pit? He suddenly felt angry. They had no right to treat a feller like that. He was a man, not a bale of hay to be bundled about as anybody liked.

"An' if we're torpedoed a fat chance we'll have down here," he said aloud.

"They got sentries posted to keep us from goin' up on deck," said someone.

"God damn them. They treat you like you was a steer being taken over for meat."

"Well, you're not a damn sight more. Meat for the guns."

A little man lying in one of the upper bunks had spoken suddenly, contracting his sallow face into a curious spasm, as if the words had burst from him in spite of an effort to keep them in.

Everybody looked up at him angrily.

"That goddam kike Eisenstein," muttered someone.

"Say, tie that bull outside," shouted Bill Grey good-naturedly.

"Fools," muttered Eisenstein, turning over and burying his face in his hands.

"Gee, I wonder what it is makes it smell so funny down here," said Fuselli.

Fuselli lay flat on deck resting his head on his crossed arms. When he looked straight up he could see a lead-colored mast sweep back and forth across the sky full of clouds of light grey and silver and dark purplish-grey showing yellowish at the edges. When he tilted his head a little to one side he could see Bill Grey's heavy colorless face and the dark bris-tles of his unshaven chin and his mouth a little twisted to the left, from which a cigarette dangled unlighted. Beyond were heads and bodies huddled together in a mass of khaki overcoats and life preservers. And when the roll tipped the deck he had a view of moving green waves and of a steamer striped grey and white, and the horizon, a dark taut line, broken here and there by the tops of waves.

"O God, I feel sick," said Bill Grey, taking the cigarette out of his mouth and looking at it revengefully.

"I'd be all right if everything didn't stink so. An' that mess hall. Nearly makes a guy puke to think of it." Fuselli spoke in a whining voice, watching the top of the mast move like a pencil scrawling on paper, back and forth across the mottled clouds.

"You belly-achin' again?" A brown moon-shaped face with thick black eyebrows and hair curling crisply about a forehead with many horizontal wrinkles rose from the deck on the other side of Fuselli.

"Get the hell out of here."

"Feel sick, sonny?" came the deep voice again, and the dark eyebrows contracted in an expression of sympathy.—"Funny, I'd have my sixshooter out if I was home and you told me to get the hell out, sonny."

"Well, who wouldn't be sore when they have to go on K.P.?" said Fuselli peevishly.

"I ain't been down to mess in three days. A feller who lives on the plains like I do ought to take to the sea like a duck, but it don't seem to suit me."

"God, they're a sick lookin' bunch I have to sling the hash to," said Fuselli more cheerfully. "I don't know how they get that way. The fellers in our company ain't that way. They look like they was askeered somebody was going to hit 'em. Ever noticed that, Meadville?"

"Well, what d'ye expect of you guys who live in the city all your lives and don't know the butt from the barrel of a gun an' never straddled anything more like a horse than a broomstick. Ye're juss made to be sheep. No wonder they have to herd you round like calves." Meadville got to his feet and went unsteadily to the rail, keeping, as he threaded his way through the groups that covered the transport's after deck, a little of his cowboy's bow-legged stride.

"I know what it is that makes men's eyes blink when they go down to that putrid mess," came a nasal voice.

Fuselli turned round.

Eisenstein was sitting in the place Meadville had just left.

"You do, do you?"

"It's part of the system. You've got to turn men into beasts before ye can get 'em to act that way. Ever read Tolstoi?"

"No. Say, you want to be careful how you go talkin' around the way you do." Fuselli lowered his voice confidentially. "I heard of a feller bein' shot at Camp Merritt for talkin' around."

"I don't care. . . . I'm a desperate man," said Eisenstein.

"Don't ye feel sick? Gawd, I do. . . . Did you get rid o' any of it, Meadville?"

"Why don't they fight their ole war somewhere a man can get to on a horse? . . . Say that's my seat."

"The place was empty. . . . I sat down in it," said Eisenstein, lowering his head sullenly.

"You kin have three winks to get out o' my place," said Meadville, squaring his broad shoulders.

"You are stronger than me," said Eisenstein, moving off.

"God, it's hell not to have a gun," muttered Meadville as he settled himself on the deck again. "D'ye know, sonny, I nearly cried when I found I was going to be in this damn medical corps? I enlisted for the tanks. This is the first time in my life I haven't had a gun. I even think I had one in my cradle."

"That's funny," said Fuselli.

The sergeant appeared suddenly in the middle of the group, his face red.

"Say, fellers," he said in a low voice, "go down an' straighten out the bunks as fast as you goddam can. They're having an inspection. It's a hell of a note."

They all filed down the gang planks into the foul-smelling hold, where there was no light but the invariable reddish glow of electric bulbs. They had hardly reached their bunks when someone called, "Attention!"

Three officers stalked by, their firm important tread a little disturbed by the rolling. Their heads were stuck forward and they peered from side to side among the bunks with the cruel, searching glance of hens looking for worms.

"Fuselli," said the first sergeant, "bring up the record book to my stateroom; 213 on the lower deck."

"All right, Sarge," said Fuselli with alacrity. He admired the first sergeant and wished he could imitate his jovial, domineering manner.

It was the first time he had been in the upper part of the ship. It seemed a different world. The long corridors with red carpets, the white paint and the gilt mouldings on the partitions, the officers strolling about at their ease—it all made him think of the big liners he used to watch come in through the Golden Gate, the liners he was going to Europe on some day, when he got rich. Oh, if he could only get to be a sergeant first-class, all this comfort and magnificence would be his. He found the number and knocked on the door. Laughter and loud talking came from inside the stateroom.

"Wait a sec!" came an unfamiliar voice.

"Sergeant Olster here?"

"Oh, it's one o' my gang," came the sergeant's voice. "Let him in. He won't peach on us."

The door opened and he saw Sergeant Olster and two other young men sitting with their feet dangling over the red varnished boards that enclosed the bunks. They were talking gaily, and had glasses in their hands.

"Paris is some town, I can tell you," one was saying. "They say the girls come up an' put their arms round you right in the main street."

"Here's the records, sergeant," said Fuselli stiffly in his best military manner.

"Oh thanks. . . . There's nothing else I want," said the sergeant, his voice more jovial than ever. "Don't fall overboard like the guy in Company C."

Fuselli laughed as he closed the door, growing serious suddenly on noticing that one of the young men wore in his shirt the gold bar of a second lieutenant.

"Gee," he said to himself. "I ought to have saluted."

He waited a moment outside the closed door of the stateroom, listening to the talk and the laughter, wishing he were one of that merry group talking about women in Paris. He began thinking. Sure he'd get private first-class as soon as they got overseas. Then in a couple of months he might be corporal. If they saw much service, he'd move along all right, once he got to be a non-com.

"Oh, I mustn't get in wrong. Oh, I mustn't get in wrong," he kept saying to himself as he went down the ladder into the hold. But he forgot everything in the seasickness that came on again as he breathed in the fetid air.

The deck now slanted down in front of him, now rose so that he was walking up an incline. Dirty water slushed about from one side of the passage to the other with every lurch of the ship. When he reached the door the whistling howl of the wind through the hinges and cracks made Fuselli hesitate a long time with his hand on the knob. The moment he turned the knob the door flew open and he was in the full sweep of the wind. The deck was deserted. The wet ropes strung along it shivered dismally in the wind. Every other moment came the rattle of spray, that rose up in white fringy trees to windward and smashed against him like hail. Without closing the door he crept forward along the deck, clinging as hard as he could to the icy rope. Beyond the spray he could see huge marbled green waves rise in constant succession out of the mist. The roar of the wind in his ears confused him and terrified him. It seemed ages before he reached the door of the forward house that opened on a passage that smelt of drugs and breathed out air, where men waited in a packed line, thrown one against the other by the lurching of the boat, to get into the dispensary. The roar of the wind came to them faintly, and only now and then the hollow thump of a wave against the bow.

"You sick?" a man asked Fuselli.

"Naw, I'm not sick; but Sarge sent me to get some stuff for some guys that's too sick to move."

"An awful lot o' sickness on this boat."

"Two fellers died this mornin' in that there room," said another man solemnly, pointing over his shoulder with a jerk of the thumb. "Ain't buried 'em yet. It's too rough."

"What'd they die of?" asked Fuselli eagerly.

"Spinal somethin'. . . ."

"Menegitis," broke in a man at the end of the line.

"Say, that's awful catchin' ain't it?"

"It sure is."

"Where does it hit yer?" asked Fuselli.

"Yer neck swells up, an' then you juss go stiff all over," came the man's voice from the end of the line.

There was a silence. From the direction of the infirmary a man with a packet of medicines in his hand began making his way towards the door.

"Many guys in there?" asked Fuselli in a low voice as the man brushed past him.

"Right smart . . ." The rest of the man's words were caught away in the shriek of the wind when he opened the door.

When the door closed again the man beside Fuselli, who was tall and broad shouldered with heavy black eyebrows, burst out, as if he were saying something he'd been trying to keep from saying for a long while:

"It won't be right if that sickness gets me; indeed it won't. . . . I've got a girl waitin' for me at home. It's two years since I ain't touched a woman all on account of her. It ain't natural for a fellow to go so long as that."

"Why didn't you marry her before you left?" somebody asked mockingly.

"Said she didn't want to be no war bride, that she could wait for me better if I didn't."

Several men laughed.

"It wouldn't be right if I took sick an' died of this sickness, after keepin' myself clean on account of that girl. . . . It wouldn't be right," the man muttered again to Fuselli.

Fuselli was picturing himself lying in his bunk with a swollen neck, while his arms and legs stiffened, stiffened.

A red-faced man half way up the passage started speaking:

"When I thinks to myself how much the folks need me home, it makes me feel sort o' confident-like, I dunno why. I juss can't cash in my checks, that's all." He laughed jovially.

No one joined in the laugh.

"Is it awfully catchin'?" asked Fuselli of the man next him.

"Most catchin' thing there is," he answered solemnly.

"The worst of it is," another man was muttering in a shrill hysterical voice, "bein' thrown over to the sharks. Gee, they ain't got a right to do that, even if it is war time, they ain't got a right to treat a Christian like he was a dead dawg."

"They got a right to do anythin' they goddam please, buddy. Who's goin' to stop 'em I'd like to know," cried the red-faced man.

"If he was an awficer, they wouldn't throw him over like that," came the shrill hysterical voice again.

"Cut that," said someone else, "no use gettin' in wrong juss for the sake of talkin'."

"But ain't it dangerous, waitin' round up here so near where those fellers are with that sickness," whispered Fuselli to the man next to him.

"Reckon it is, buddy," came the other man's voice dully.

Fuselli started making his way toward the door.

"Lemme out, fellers, I've got to puke," he said. "Shoot," he was thinking, "I'll tell 'em the place was closed; they'll never come to look."

As he opened the door he thought of himself crawling back to his bunk and feeling his neck swell and his hands burn with fever and his arms and legs stiffen until everything would be effaced in the blackness of death. But the roar of the wind and the lash of the spray as he staggered back along the deck drowned all other thought.

Fuselli and another man carried the dripping garbage can up the ladder that led up from the mess hall. It smelt of rancid grease and coffee grounds and greasy juice trickled over their fingers as they struggled with it. At last they burst out on to the deck where a free wind blew out of the black night. They staggered unsteadily to the rail and emptied the pail into the darkness. The splash was lost in the sound of the waves and of churned water fleeing along the sides. Fuselli leaned over the rail and looked down at the faint phosphorescence that was the only light in the whole black gulf. He had never seen such darkness before. He clutched hold of the rail with both hands, feeling lost and terrified in the blackness, in the roaring of the wind in his ears and the sound of churned water fleeing astern. The alternative was the stench of below decks.

"I'll bring down the rosie, don't you bother," he said to the other man, kicking the can that gave out a ringing sound as he spoke.

He strained his eyes to make out something. The darkness seemed to press in upon his eyeballs, blinding him. Suddenly he noticed voices near him. Two men were talking.

"I ain't never seen the sea before this, I didn't know it was like this."

"We're in the zone, now."

"That means we may go down any minute."

"Yare."

"Christ, how black it is. . . . It'ld be awful to drown in the dark like this."

"It'ld be over soon."

"Say, Fred, have you ever been so skeered that . . . ?"

"D'you feel a-skeert?"

"Feel my hand, Fred. . . . No . . . There it is. God, it's so hellish black you can't see yer own hand."

"It's cold. Why are you shiverin' so? God, I wish I had a drink."

"I ain't never seen the sea before . . . I didn't know . . ."

Fuselli heard distinctly the man's teeth chattering in the darkness.

"God, pull yerself together, kid. You can't be skeered like this."

"O God."

There was a long pause. Fuselli heard nothing but the churned water speeding along the ship's side and the wind roaring in his ears.

"I ain't never seen the sea before this time, Fred, an' it sort o' gits my goat, all this sickness an' all. . . . They dropped three of 'em overboard yesterday."

"Hell, kid, don't think of it."

"Say, Fred, if I . . . if I . . . if you're saved, Fred, an' not me, you'll write to my folks, won't you?"

"Indeed I will. But I reckon you an' me'll both go down together."

"Don't say that. An' you won't forget to write that girl I gave you the address of?"

"You'll do the same for me."

"Oh, no, Fred, I'll never see land. . . . Oh, it's no use. An' I feel so well an' husky. . . . I don't want to die. I can't die like this."

"If it only wasn't so goddam black."

PART TWO

THE METAL COOLS

I

It was purplish dusk outside the window. The rain fell steadily making long flashing stripes on the cracked panes, beating a hard monotonous tattoo on the tin roof overhead. Fuselli had taken off his wet slicker and stood in front of the window looking out dismally at the rain. Behind him was the smoking stove into which a man was poking wood, and beyond that a few broken folding chairs on which soldiers sprawled in attitudes of utter boredom, and the counter where the "Y" man stood with a set smile doling out chocolate to a line of men that filed past.

"Gee, you have to line up for everything here, don't you?" Fuselli muttered.

"That's about all you do do in this hell-hole, buddy," said a man beside him.

The man pointed with his thumb at the window and said again:

"See that rain? Well, I been in this camp three weeks and it ain't stopped rainin' once. What d'yer think of that fer a country?"

"It certainly ain't like home," said Fuselli. "I'm going to have some chauclate."

"It's damn rotten."

"I might as well try it once."

Fuselli slouched over to the end of the line and stood waiting his turn. He was thinking of the steep streets of San Francisco and the glimpses he used to get of the harbor full of yellow lights, the color of amber in a cigarette holder, as he went home from work through the blue dusk. He had begun to think of Mabe handing him the five-pound box of candy when his attention was distracted by the talk of the men behind him. The man next to him was speaking with hurried nervous intonation. Fuselli could feel his breath on the back of his neck.

"I'll be goddamned," the man said, "was you there too? Where d'you get yours?"

"In the leg; it's about all right, though."

"I ain't. I won't never be all right. The doctor says I'm all right now, but I know I'm not, the lyin' fool."

"Some time, wasn't it?"

"I'll be damned to hell if I do it again. I can't sleep at night thinkin' of the shape of the Fritzies' helmets. Have you ever thought that there was somethin' about the shape of them goddam helmets . . . ?"

"Ain't they just or'nary shapes?" asked Fuselli, half turning round. "I seen 'em in the movies." He laughed apologetically.

"Listen to the rookie, Tub, he's seen 'em in the movies!" said the man with the nervous twitch in his voice, laughing a croaking little laugh. "How long you been in this country, buddy?"

"Two days."

"Well, we only been here two months, ain't we, Tub?"

"Four months; you're forgettin', kid."

The "Y" man turned his set smile on Fuselli while he filled his tin cup up with chocolate.

"How much?"

"A franc; one of those looks like a quarter," said the "Y" man, his well-fed voice full of amiable condescension.

"That's a hell of a lot for a cup of chauclate," said Fuselli.

"You're at the war, young man, remember that," said the "Y" man severely. "You're lucky to get it at all."

A cold chill gripped Fuselli's spine as he went back to the stove to drink the chocolate. Of course he mustn't crab. He was in the war now. If the sergeant had heard him crabbing, it might have spoiled his chances for a corporalship. He must be careful. If he just watched out and kept on his toes, he'd be sure to get it.

"And why ain't there no more chocolate, I want to know?" the nervous voice of the man who had stood in line behind Fuselli rose to a sudden shriek. Everybody looked round. The "Y" man was moving his head from side to side in a flustered way, saying in a shrill little voice:

"I've told you there's no more. Go away!"

"You ain't got no right to tell me to go away. You got to get me some chocolate. You ain't never been at the front, you goddam slacker." The man was yelling at the top of his lungs. He had hold of the counter with two hands and swayed from side to side. His friend was trying to pull him away.

"Look here, none of that, I'll report you," said the "Y" man. "Is there a non-commissioned officer in the hut?"

"Go ahead, you can't do nothin'. I can't never have nothing done worse than what's been done to me already." The man's voice had reached a sing-song fury.

"Is there a non-commissioned officer in the room?" The "Y" man kept looking from side to side. His little eyes were hard and spiteful and his lips were drawn up in a thin straight line.

"Keep quiet, I'll get him away," said the other man in a low voice. "Can't you see he's not . . . ?"

A strange terror took hold of Fuselli. He hadn't expected things to be like that. When he had sat in the grandstand in the training camp and watched the jolly soldiers in khaki marching into towns, pursuing terrified Huns across potato fields, saving Belgian milk-maids against picturesque backgrounds.

"Does many of 'em come back that way?" he asked a man beside him.

"Some do. It's this convalescent camp."

The man and his friend stood side by side near the stove talking in low voices.

"Pull yourself together, kid," the friend was saying.

"All right, Tub; I'm all right now, Tub. That slacker got my goat, that was all."

Fuselli was looking at him curiously. He had a yellow parchment face and a high, gaunt forehead going up to sparse, curly brown hair. His eyes had a glassy look about them when they met Fuselli's. He smiled amiably.

"Oh, there's the kid who's seen Fritzie's helmets in the movies. . . . Come on, buddy, come and have a beer at the English canteen."

"Can you get beer?"

"Sure, over in the English camp."

They went out into the slanting rain. It was nearly dark, but the sky had a purplish-red color that was reflected a little on the slanting sides of tents and on the roofs of the rows of sheds that disappeared into the rainy mist in every direction. A few lights gleamed, a very bright polished yellow. They followed a board-walk that splashed mud up from the puddles under the tramp of their heavy boots.

At one place they flattened themselves against the wet flap of a tent and saluted as an officer passed waving a little cane jauntily.

"How long does a fellow usually stay in these rest camps?" asked Fuselli.

"Depends on what's goin' on out there," said Tub, pointing carelessly to the sky beyond the peaks of the tents.

"You'll leave here soon enough. Don't you worry, buddy," said the man with the nervous voice. "What you in?"

"Medical Replacement Unit."

"A medic, are you? Those boys didn't last long at the Château, did they, Tub?"

"No, they didn't."

Something inside Fuselli was protesting; "I'll last out though. I'll last out though."

"Do you remember the fellers went out to get poor ole Corporal Jones, Tub? I'll be goddamned if anybody ever found a button of their pants." He laughed his creaky little laugh. "They got in the way of a torpedo."

The "wet" canteen was full of smoke and a cosy steam of beer. It was crowded with red-faced men, with shiny brass buttons on their khaki uniforms, among whom was a good sprinkling of lanky Americans.

"Tommies," said Fuselli to himself.

After standing in line a while, Fuselli's cup was handed back to him across the counter, foaming with beer.

"Hello, Fuselli," Meadville clapped him on the shoulder. "You found the liquor pretty damn quick, looks like to me."

Fuselli laughed.

"May I sit with you fellers?"

"Sure, come along," said Fuselli proudly, "these guys have been to the front."

"You have?" asked Meadville. "The Huns are pretty good scrappers, they say. Tell me, do you use your rifle much, or is it mostly big gun work?"

"Naw; after all the months I spent learnin' how to drill with my goddam rifle, I'll be a sucker if I've used it once. I'm in the grenade squad."

Someone at the end of the room had started singing:

> "O Mademerselle from Armenteers,
>   Parley voo!"

The man with the nervous voice went on talking, while the song roared about them.

"I don't spend a night without thinkin' o' them funny helmets the Fritzies wear. Have you ever thought that there was something goddam funny about the shape o' them helmets?"

"Can the helmets, kid," said his friend. "You told us all about them onct."

"I ain't told you why I can't forgit 'em, have I?"

> "A German officer crossed the Rhine;
>   Parley voo?
> A German officer crossed the Rhine;
> He loved the women and liked the wine;
>   Hanky Panky, parley voo . . ."

"Listen to this, fellers," said the man in his twitching nervous voice, staring straight into Fuselli's eyes. "We made a little attack to straighten out our trenches a bit just before I got winged. Our barrage cut off a bit of Fritzie's trench an' we ran right ahead juss about dawn an' occupied it. I'll be goddamned if it wasn't as quiet as a Sunday morning at home."

"It was!" said his friend.

"An' I had a bunch of grenades an' a feller came runnin' up to me, whisperin', 'There's a bunch of Fritzies playin' cards in a dug-out. They don't seem to know they're captured. We'd better take 'em pris'ners!'"

"'Pris'ners, hell,' says I, 'We'll go and clear the beggars out.' So we crept along to the steps and looked down. . . ."

The song had started again:

> "O Mademerselle from Armenteers,
>   Parley voo?"

"Their helmets looked so damn like toadstools I came near laughin'. An' they sat round the lamp layin' down the cards serious-like, the way I've seen Germans do in the Rathskeller at home."

> "He loved the women and liked the wine,
>   Parley voo?"

"I lay there lookin' at 'em for a hell of a time, an' then I clicked a grenade an' tossed it gently down the steps. An' all those funny helmets like toadstools popped up in the air an' somebody gave a yell an' the light went out an' the damn grenade went off. Then I let 'em have the rest of 'em an' went away 'cause one o' 'em was still moanin'-like. It was about that time they let their barrage down on us and I got mine."

> "The Yanks are havin' a hell of a time,
>   Parley voo?"

"An' the first thing I thought of when I woke up was how those god-dam helmets looked. It upsets a feller to think of a thing like that." His voice ended in a whine like the broken voice of a child that has been beaten.

"You need to pull yourself together, kid," said his friend.

"I know what I need, Tub. I need a woman."

"You know where you get one?" asked Meadville. "I'd like to get me a nice little French girl on a rainy night like this."

"It must be a hell of a ways to the town. . . . They say it's full of M.P.'s too," said Fuselli.

"I know a way," said the man with the nervous voice, "Come on; Tub."

"No, I've had enough of these goddam frog women."

They all left the canteen.

As the two men went off down the side of the building, Fuselli heard the nervous twitching voice through the metallic patter of the rain:

"I can't find no way of forgettin' how funny those helmets looked all round the lamp . . . I can't find no way . . ."

Bill Grey and Fuselli pooled their blankets and slept together. They lay on the hard floor of the tent very close to each other, listening to the rain pattering endlessly on the drenched canvas that slanted above their heads.

"Hell, Bill, I'm gettin' pneumonia," said Fuselli, clearing his nose.

"That's the only thing that scares me in the whole goddam business. I'd hate to die o' sickness . . . an' they say another kid's kicked off with that—what d'they call it?—menegitis."

"Was that what was the matter with Stein?"

"The corporal won't say."

"Ole Corp looks sort o' sick himself," said Fuselli.

"It's this rotten climate," whispered Bill Grey, in the middle of a fit of coughing.

"For cat's sake quit that coughin'. Let a feller sleep," came a voice from the other side of the tent.

"Go an' get a room in a hotel if you don't like it."

"That's it, Bill, tell him where to get off."

"If you fellers don't quit yellin', I'll put the whole blame lot of you on K. P.," came the sergeant's good-natured voice. "Don't you know that taps has blown?"

The tent was silent except for the fast patter of the rain and Bill Grey's coughing.

"That sergeant gives me a pain in the neck," muttered Bill Grey peevishly, when his coughing had stopped, wriggling about under the blankets.

After a while Fuselli said in a very low voice, so that no one but his friend should hear:

"Say, Bill, ain't it different from what we thought it was going to be?"

"Yare."

"I mean fellers don't seem to think about beatin' the Huns at all, they're so busy crabbin' on everything."

"It's the guys higher up that does the thinkin'," said Grey grandiloquently.

"Hell, but I thought it'd be excitin' like in the movies."

"I guess that was a lot o' talk."

"Maybe."

Fuselli went to sleep on the hard floor, feeling the comfortable warmth of Grey's body along the side of him, hearing the endless, monotonous patter of the rain on the drenched canvas above his head. He tried to stay awake a minute to remember what Mabe looked like, but sleep closed down on him suddenly.

The bugle wrenched them out of their blankets before it was light. It was not raining. The air was raw and full of white mist that was cold as snow against their faces still warm from sleep. The corporal called the roll, lighting matches to read the list. When he dismissed the formation the sergeant's voice was heard from the tent, where he still lay rolled in his blankets.

"Say, Corp, go an' tell Fuselli to straighten out Lieutenant Stanford's room at eight sharp in Officers' Barracks, Number Four."

"Did you hear, Fuselli?"

"All right," said Fuselli. His blood boiled up suddenly. This was the first time he'd had to do servants' work. He hadn't joined the army to be a slavey to any damned first loot. It was against army regulations anyway. He'd go and kick. He wasn't going to be a slavey. . . . He walked towards the door of the tent, thinking what he'd say to the sergeant. But he noticed the corporal coughing into his handkerchief with an expression of pain on his face. He turned and strolled away. It would get him in wrong if he started kicking like that. Much better shut his mouth and put up with it. The poor old corp couldn't last long at this rate. No, it wouldn't do to get in wrong.

At eight, Fuselli, with a broom in his hand, feeling dull fury pounding and fluttering within him, knocked on the unpainted board door.

"Who's that?"

"To clean the room, sir," said Fuselli.

"Come back in about twenty minutes," came the voice of the lieutenant.

"All right, sir."

Fuselli leaned against the back of the barracks and smoked a cigarette. The air stung his hands as if they had been scraped by a nutmeg-grater. Twenty minutes passed slowly. Despair seized hold of him. He was so far from anyone who cared about him, so lost in the vast machine. He was telling himself that he'd never get on, would never get up where he could show what he was good for. He felt as if he were in a treadmill. Day after day it would be like this,—the same routine, the same helplessness. He looked at his watch. Twenty-five minutes had passed. He picked up his broom and moved round to the lieutenant's room.

"Come in," said the lieutenant carelessly. He was in his shirt-sleeves, shaving. A pleasant smell of shaving soap filled the dark clapboard room, which had no furniture but three cots and some officers' trunks. He was a red-faced young man with flabby cheeks and dark straight eyebrows. He had taken command of the company only a day or two before.

"Looks like a decent feller," thought Fuselli.

"What's your name?" asked the lieutenant, speaking into the small nickel mirror, while he ran the safety razor obliquely across his throat. He stuttered a little. To Fuselli he seemed to speak like an Englishman.

"Fuselli."

"Italian parentage, I presume?"

"Yes," said Fuselli sullenly, dragging one of the cots away from the wall.

"Parla Italiano?"

"You mean, do I speak Eyetalian? Naw, sir," said Fuselli emphatically, "I was born in Frisco."

"Indeed? But get me some more water, will you, please?"

When Fuselli came back, he stood with his broom between his knees, blowing on his hands that were blue and stiff from carrying the heavy bucket. The lieutenant was dressed and was hooking the top hook of the uniform carefully. The collar made a red mark on his pink throat.

"All right; when you're through, report back to the Company." The lieutenant went out, drawing on a pair of khaki-colored gloves with a satisfied and important gesture.

Fuselli walked back slowly to the tents where the Company was quartered, looking about him at the long lines of barracks, gaunt and dripping in the mist, at the big tin sheds of the cook shacks where the cooks and K. P.'s in greasy blue denims were slouching about amid a steam of cooking food.

Something of the gesture with which the lieutenant drew on his gloves caught in the mind of Fuselli. He had seen peoople make gestures like that in the movies, stout dignified people in evening suits. The president of the Company that owned the optical goods store, where he had worked, at home in Frisco, had had something of that gesture about him.

And he pictured himself drawing on a pair of gloves that way, importantly, finger by finger, with a little wave of self-satisfaction when the gesture was completed. . . . He'd have to get that corporalship.

> "There's a long, long trail a-winding
> Through no man's land in France."

The company sang lustily as it splashed through the mud down a grey road between high fences covered with great tangles of barbed wire, above which peeked the ends of warehouses and the chimneys of factories.

The lieutenant and the top sergeant walked side by side chatting, now and then singing a little of the song in a deprecating way. The corporal sang, his eyes sparkling with delight. Even the sombre sergeant who rarely spoke to anyone, sang. The company strode along, its ninety-six legs splashing jauntily through the deep putty-colored puddles. The packs swayed merrily from side to side as if it were they and not the legs that were walking.

> "There's a long, long trail a-winding
> Through no man's land in France."

At last they were going somewhere. They had separated from the contingent they had come over with. They were all alone now. They were going to be put to work. The lieutenant strode along importantly. The sergeant strode along importantly. The corporal strode along importantly. The right guard strode along more importantly than anyone. A sense of importance, of something tremendous to do, animated the company like wine, made the packs and the belts seem less heavy, made their necks and shoulders less stiff from struggling with the weight of the packs, made the ninety-six legs tramp jauntily in spite of the oozy mud and the deep putty-colored puddles.

It was cold in the dark shed of the freight station where they waited. Some gas lamps flickered feebly high up among the rafters, lighting up in a ghastly way white piles of ammunition boxes and ranks and ranks of shells that disappeared in the darkness. The raw air was full of coal smoke and a smell of freshly-cut boards. The captain and the top sergeant had disappeared. The men sat about, huddled in groups, sinking as far as they could into their overcoats, stamping their numb wet feet on the mud-covered cement of the floor. The sliding doors were shut. Through them came a monotonous sound of cars shunting, of buffers bumping against buffers, and now and then the shrill whistle of an engine.

"Hell, the French railroads are rotten," said someone.

"How d'you know?" snapped Eisenstein, who sat on a box away from the rest with his lean face in his hands staring at his mud-covered boots.

"Look at this," Bill Grey made a disgusted gesture towards the ceiling. "Gas. Don't even have electric light."

"Their trains run faster than ours," said Eisenstein.

"The hell they do. Why, a fellow back in that rest camp told me that it took four or five days to get anywhere."

"He was stuffing you," said Eisenstein. "They used to run the fastest trains in the world in France."

"Not so fast as the 'Twentieth Century.' Goddam, I'm a railroad man and I know."

"I want five men to help me sort out the eats," said the top sergeant, coming suddenly out of the shadows. "Fuselli, Grey, Eisenstein, Meadville, Williams . . . all right, come along."

"Say, Sarge, this guy says that frog trains are faster than our trains. What d'ye think o' that?"

The sergeant put on his comic expression. Everybody got ready to laugh.

"Well, if he'd rather take the side-door Pullmans we're going to get aboard tonight than the 'Sunset Limited,' he's welcome. I've seen 'em. You fellers haven't."

Everybody laughed. The top sergeant turned confidentially to the five men who followed him into a small well-lighted room that looked like a freight office.

"We've got to sort out the grub, fellers. See those cases? That's three days' rations for the outfit. I want to sort it into three lots, one for each car. Understand?"

Fuselli pulled open one of the boxes. The cans of bully beef flew under his fingers. He kept looking out of the corner of his eye at Eisenstein, who seemed very skillful in a careless way. The top sergeant stood beaming at them with his legs wide apart. Once he said something in a low voice to the corporal. Fuselli thought he caught the words: "privates first-class," and his heart started thumping hard. In a few minutes the job was done, and everybody stood about lighting cigarettes.

"Well, fellers," said Sergeant Jones, the sombre man who rarely spoke, "I certainly didn't reckon when I used to be teachin' and preachin' and tendin' Sunday School and the like that I'd come to be usin' cuss words, but I think we got a damn good company."

"Oh, we'll have you sayin' worse things than 'damn' when we get you out on the front with a goddam German aëroplane droppin' bombs on you," said the top sergeant, slapping him on the back. "Now, I want you five men to look out for the grub." Fuselli's chest swelled. "The company'll be in charge of the corporal for the night. Sergeant Jones and I have got to be with the lieutenant, understand?"

They all walked back to the dingy room where the rest of the company waited huddled in their coats, trying to keep their importance from being too obvious in their step.

"I've really started now," thought Fuselli to himself. "I've really started now."

The bare freight car clattered and rumbled monotonously over the rails. A bitter cold wind blew up through the cracks in the grimy splintered boards of the floor. The men huddled in the corners of the car, curled up together like puppies in a box. It was pitch black. Fuselli lay half asleep, his head full of curious fragmentary dreams, feeling through his sleep the aching cold and the unending clattering rumble of the wheels and the bodies and arms and legs muffled in coats and blankets pressing against him. He woke up with a start. His teeth were chattering. The clanking rumble of wheels seemed to be in his head. His head was being dragged along, bumping over cold iron rails. Someone lighted a match. The freight car's black swaying walls, the packs piled in the center, the bodies heaped in the corners where, out of khaki masses here and there gleamed an occasional white face or a pair of eyes—all showed clear for a moment and then vanished again in the utter blackness. Fuselli pillowed his head in the crook of someone's arm and tried to go to sleep, but the scraping rumble of wheels over rails was too loud; he stayed with open eyes staring into the blackness, trying to draw his body away from the blast of cold air that blew up through a crack in the floor.

When the first greyness began filtering into the car, they all stood up and stamped and pounded each other and wrestled to get warm.

When it was nearly light, the train stopped and they opened the sliding doors. They were in a station, a foreign-looking station where the walls were plastered with unfamiliar advertisements. "V-E-R-S-A-I-L-L-E-S"; Fuselli spelt out the name.

"Versales," said Eisenstein. "That's where the kings of France used to live."

The train started moving again slowly. On the platform stood the top sergeant.

"How d'ye sleep," he shouted as the car passed him. "Say, Fuselli, better start some grub going."

"All right, Sarge," said Fuselli.

The sergeant ran back to the front of the car and climbed on.

With a delicious feeling of leadership, Fuselli divided up the bread and the cans of bully beef and the cheese. Then he sat on his pack eating dry bread and unsavoury beef, whistling joyfully, while the train rumbled and clattered along through a strange, misty-green countryside,—whistling joyfully because he was going to the front, where there would be glory and excitement, whistling joyfully because he felt he was getting along in the world.

It was noon. A pallid little sun like a toy balloon hung low in the reddish-grey sky. The train had stopped on a siding in the middle of a russet plain. Yellow poplars, faint as mist, rose slender against the sky along a black shining stream that swirled beside the track. In the distance a steeple and a few red roofs were etched faintly in the greyness.

The men stood about balancing first on one foot and then on the other, stamping to get warm. On the other side of the river an old man with an oxcart had stopped and was looking sadly at the train.

"Say, where's the front?" somebody shouted to him.

Everybody took up the cry: "Say, where's the front?"

The old man waved his hand, shook his head and shouted to the oxen.

The oxen took up again their quiet processional gait and the old man walked ahead of them, his eyes on the ground.

"Say, ain't the frogs dumb?"

"Say, Dan," said Bill Grey, strolling away from a group of men he had been talking to. "These guys say we are going to the Third Army."

"Say, fellers," shouted Fuselli. "They say we're going to the Third Army."

"Where's that?"

"In the Oregon forest," ventured somebody.

"That's at the front, ain't it?"

At that moment the lieutenant strode by. A long khaki muffler was thrown carelessly round his neck and hung down his back.

"Look here, men," he said severely, "the orders are to stay in the cars."

The men slunk back into the cars sullenly.

A hospital train passed, clanking slowly over the crosstracks. Fuselli looked fixedly at the dark enigmatic windows, at the red crosses, at the orderlies in white who leaned out of the doors, waving their hands. Somebody noticed that there were scars on the new green paint of the last car.

"The Huns have been shooting at it."

"D'ye hear that? The Huns tried to shoot up that hospital train."

Fuselli remembered the pamphlet "German Atrocities" he had read one night in the Y.M.C.A. His mind became suddenly filled with pictures of children with their arms cut off, of babies spitted on bayonets, of women strapped on tables and violated by soldier after soldier. He thought of Mabe. He wished he were in a combatant service; he wanted to fight, fight. He pictured himself shooting dozens of men in green uniforms, and he thought of Mabe reading about it in the papers. He'd have to try to get into a combatant service. No, he couldn't stay in the medics.

The train had started again. Misty russet fields slipped by and dark clumps of trees that gyrated slowly waving branches of yellow and brown leaves and patches of black lace-work against the reddish-grey sky. Fuselli was thinking of the good chance he had of getting to be corporal.

At night. A dim-lighted station platform. The company waited in two lines, each man sitting on his pack. On the opposite platform crowds of little men in blue with mustaches and long, soiled overcoats that reached almost to their feet were shouting and singing. Fuselli watched them with a faint disgust.

"Gee, they got funny lookin' helmets, ain't they?"

"They're the best fighters in the world," said Eisenstein, "not that that's sayin' much about a man."

"Say, that's an M.P.," said Bill Grey, catching Fuselli's arm. "Let's go ask him how near the front we are. I thought I heard guns a minute ago."

"Did you? I guess we're in for it now," said Fuselli.

"Say, buddy, how near the front are we?" they spoke together excitedly.

"The front?" said the M.P., who was a red-faced Irishman with a crushed nose. "You're 'way back in the middle of France." The M.P. spat disgustedly. "You fellers ain't never goin' to the front, don't you worry."

"Hell!" said Fuselli.

"I'll be goddamned if I don't get there somehow," said Bill Grey, squaring his jaw.

A fine rain was falling on the unprotected platform. On the other side the little men in blue were singing a song Fuselli could not understand, drinking out of their ungainly-looking canteens.

Fuselli announced the news to the company. Everybody clustered round him cursing. But the faint sense of importance it gave him did not compensate for the feeling he had of being lost in the machine, of being as helpless as a sheep in a flock.

Hours passed. They stamped about the platform in the fine rain or sat in a row on their packs, waiting for orders. A grey belt appeared behind the trees. The platform began to take on a silvery gleam. They sat in a row on their packs, waiting.

II

The company stood at attention lined up outside of their barracks, a long wooden shack covered with tar paper. In front of them was a row of dishevelled plane trees with white trunks that looked like ivory in the faint ruddy sunlight. Then there was a rutted road on which stood a long line of French motor trucks with hunched grey backs like elephants. Beyond these were more plane trees and another row of barracks covered with tar paper, outside of which other companies were lined up standing at attention.

A bugle was sounding far away.

The lieutenant stood at attention very stiffly. Fuselli's eyes followed the curves of his brilliantly-polished puttees up to the braid on his sleeves.

"Parade rest!" shouted the lieutenant in a muffled voice.

Feet and hands moved in unison.

Fuselli was thinking of the town. After retreat you could go down the irregular cobbled street from the old fair-ground where the camp was to a little square where there was a grey stone fountain and a gin-mill where

you could sit at an oak table and have beer and eggs and fried potatoes
served you by a girl with red cheeks and plump white appetizing arms.

"Attention!"

Feet and hands moved in unison again. They could hardly hear the
bugle, it was so faint.

"Men, I have some appointments to announce," said the lieutenant,
facing the company and taking on an easy conversational tone. "At rest!
. . . You've done good work in the storehouse here, men. I'm glad I have
such a willing bunch of men under me. And I certainly hope that we can
manage to make as many promotions as possible—as many as possible."

Fuselli's hands were icy, and his heart was pumping the blood so fast
to his ears that he could hardly hear.

"The following privates to private first-class, read the lieutenant in a
routine voice: "Grey, Appleton, Williams, Eisenstein, Porter . . .
Eisenstein will be company clerk. . . ." Fuselli was almost ready to cry.
His name was not on the list.

The sergeant's voice came after a long pause, smooth as velvet.

"You forget Fuselli, sir."

"Oh, so I did," the lieutenant laughed a small dry laugh.—"And
Fuselli."

"Gee, I must write Mabe tonight," Fuselli was saying to himself.
"She'll be a proud kid when she gets that letter."

"Companee dis . . . missed!" shouted the sergeant genially.

> "O Madermoiselle from Armenteers,
> Parley voo?
> O Madermoiselle from Armenteers,"

struck up the sergeant in his mellow voice.

The front room of the café was full of soldiers. Their khaki hid the
worn oak benches and the edges of the square tables and the red tiles of
the floor. They clustered round the tables, where glasses and bottles
gleamed vaguely through the tobacco smoke. They stood in front of the
bar, drinking out of bottles, laughing, scraping their feet on the floor. A
stout girl with red cheeks and plump white arms moved contentedly
among them, carrying away empty bottles, bringing back full ones, taking the money to a grim old woman with a grey face and eyes like bits
of jet, who stared carefully at each coin, fingered it with her grey hands
and dropped it reluctantly into the cash drawer. In the corner sat
Sergeant Olster with a flush on his face, and the corporal who had been
on the Red Sox outfield and another sergeant, a big man with black hair
and a black mustache. About them clustered, with approbation and re-
spect in their faces, Fuselli, Bill Grey and Meadville the cowboy, and Earl
Williams, the blue-eyed and yellow-haired drug-clerk.

> "O the Yanks are having the hell of a time,
>   Parley voo?"

They pounded their bottles on the table in time to the song.

"It's a good job," the top sergeant said, suddenly interrupting the song. "You needn't worry about that, fellers. I saw to it that we got a good job. . . . And about getting to the front, you needn't worry about that. We'll all get to the front soon enough. . . . Tell me this war is going to last ten years."

"I guess we'll all be generals by that time, eh, Sarge?" said Williams. "But, man, I wish I was back slingin' soda water."

"It's a great life if you don't weaken," murmured Fuselli automatically.

"But I'm beginnin' to weaken," said Williams. "Man, I'm homesick. I don't care who knows it. I wish I could get to the front and be done with it."

"Say, have a heart. You need a drink," said the top sergeant, banging his fist on the table. "Say, mamselle, mame shows, mame shows!"

"I didn't know you could talk French, Sarge," said Fuselli.

"French, hell!" said the top sergeant. "Williams is the boy can talk French."

"Voulay vous couchay aveck moy. . . . That's all I know."

Everybody laughed.

"Hey, mamzelle," cried the top sergeant. "Voulay vous couchay aveck moy? We, We, champagne." Everybody laughed, uproariously.

The girl slapped his head good-naturedly.

At that moment a man stamped noisily into the café, a tall broad-shouldered man in a loose English tunic, who had a swinging swagger that made the glasses ring on all the tables. He was humming under his breath and there was a grin on his broad red face. He went up to the girl and pretended to kiss her, and she laughed and talked familiarly with him in French.

"There's wild Dan Cohen," said the dark-haired sergeant. "Say, Dan, Dan."

"Here, yer honor."

"Come over and have a drink. We're going to have some fizzy."

"Never known to refuse."

They made room for him on the bench.

"Well, I'm confined to barracks," said Dan Cohen. "Look at me!" He laughed and gave his head a curious swift jerk to one side. "Compree?"

"Ain't ye scared they'll nab you?" said Fuselli.

"Nab me, hell, they can't do nothin' to me. I've had three court-martials already and they're gettin' a fourth up on me." Dan Cohen pushed his head to one side and laughed. "I got a friend. My old boss is captain, and he's goin' to fix it up. I used to alley around politics chez moy. Compree?"

The champagne came and Dan Cohen popped the cork up to the ceiling with dexterous red fingers.

"I was just wondering who was going to give me a drink," he said. "Ain't had any pay since Christ was a corporal. I've forgotten what it looks like."

The champagne fizzed into the beer-glasses.

"This is the life," said Fuselli.

"Ye're damn right, buddy, if ye're don't let them ride yer," said Dan.

"What they got yer up for now, Dan?"

"Murder."

"Murder, hell! How's that?"

"That is, if that bloke dies."

"The hell you say!"

"It all started by that goddam convoy down from Nantes . . . Bill Rees an' me. . . . They called us the shock troops.—Hy! Marie! Ancore champagne, beaucoup.—I was in the Ambulance service then. God knows what rotten service I'm in now. . . . Our section was on repo and they sent some of us fellers down to Nantes to fetch a convoy of cars back to Sandrecourt. We started out like regular racers, just the chassis, savey? Bill Rees an' me was the goddam tail of the peerade. An' the loot was a hell of a blockhead that didn't know if he was coming or going."

"Where the hell's Nantes?" asked the top sergeant, as if it had just slipped his mind.

"On the coast," answered Fuselli. "I seen it on the map."

"Nantes's way off to hell and gone anyway," said wild Dan Cohen, taking a gulp of champagne that he held in his mouth a moment, making his mouth move like a cow ruminating.

"An' as Bill Rees an' me was the tail of the peerade an' there was lots of cafés and little gin-mills, Bill Rees an' me'ld stop off every now and then to have a little drink an' say 'Bonjour' to the girls an' talk to the people, an' then we'd go like a bat out of hell to catch up. Well, I don't know if we went too fast for 'em or if they lost the road or what, but we never saw that goddam convoy from the time we went out of Nantes. Then we thought we might as well see a bit of the country, compree? . . . An' we did, goddam it. . . . We landed up in Orleans, soused to the gills and without any gas an' with an M. P; climbing up on the dashboard."

"Did they nab you, then?"

"Not a bit of it," said wild Dan Cohen, jerking his head to one side. "They gave us gas and commutation of rations an' told us to go on in the mornin'. You see we put up a good line of talk, compree? . . . Well,

we went to the swankiest restaurant. . . . You see we had on those bloody
British uniforms they gave us when the O. D. gave out, an' the M.P.'s
didn't know just what sort o' birds we were. So we went and ordered up
a regular meal an' lots o' vin rouge an' vin blank an' drank a few cognacs
an' before we knew it we were eating dinner with two captains and a
sergeant. One o' the captains was the drunkest man I ever did see. . . .
Good kid! We all had dinner and Bill Rees says, 'Let's go for a joy-ride.'
An' the captains says, 'Fine,' and the sergeant would have said, 'Fine,' but
he was so goggle-eyed drunk he couldn't. An' we started off! . . . Say,
fellers, I'm dry as hell! Let's order up another bottle."

"Sure," said everyone.

> "Ban swar, ma cherie,
>   Comment allez vous?"

"Encore champagne, Marie, gentille!"

"Well," he went on, "we went like a bat out of hell along a good state
road, and it was all fine until one of the captains thought we ought to
have a race. We did. . . . Compree? The flivvers flivved all right, but the
hell of it was we got so excited about the race we forgot about the
sergeant an' he fell off an' nobody missed him. An' at last we all pull up
before a gin-mill an' one captain says, 'Where's the sergeant?' an' the
other captain says there hadn't been no sergeant. An' we all had a drink
on that. An' one captain kept sayin', 'It's all imagination. Never was a
sergeant. I wouldn't associate with a sergeant, would I, lootenant?' He
kept on calling me lootenant. . . . Well that was how they got this new
charge against me. Somebody picked up the sergeant an' he got concussion o' the brain an' there's hell to pay, an' if the poor buggar croaks. . . .
I'm it. . . . Compree? About that time the captains start wantin' to go to
Paris, an' we said we'd take 'em, an' so we put all the gas in my car an'
the four of us climbed on that goddam chassis an' off we went like a bat
out of hell! It'ld all have been fine if I wasn't lookin' cross-eyed. . . . We
piled up in about two minutes on one of those nice little stone piles an'
there we were. We all got up an' one o' the captains had his arm broke,
an' there was hell to pay, worse than losing the sergeant. So we walked
on down the road. I don't know how it got to be daylight. But we got
to some hell of a town or other an' there was two M.P.'s all ready to meet
us, . . . Compree? . . . Well, we didn't mess around with them captains.
We just lit off down a side street an' got into a little café an' went in back
an' had a hell of a lot o' café o' lay. That made us feel sort o' good an' I
says to Bill, 'Bill, we've got to get to headquarters an' tell 'em that we accidentally smashed up our car, before the M.P.'s get busy.' An' he says,
'You're goddamned right,' an' at that minute I sees an M.P. through a
crack in the door comin' into the café. We lit out into the garden and

made for the wall. We got over that, although we left a good piece of my pants in the broken glass. But the hell of it was the M.P.'s got over too an' they had their pop-guns out. An' the last I saw of Bill Rees was— there was a big fat woman in a pink dress washing clothes in a big tub, an' poor ole Bill Rees runs head on into her an' over they both goes into the washtub. The M.P.'s got him all right. That's how I got away. An' the last I saw of Bill Rees he was squirming about on top of the washtub like he was swimmin', an' the fat woman was sittin' on the ground shaking her fist at him. Bill Rees was the best buddy I ever had."

He paused and poured the rest of the champagne in his glass and wiped the sweat off his face with his big red hand.

"You ain't stringin' us, are you?" asked Fuselli.

"You just ask Lieutenant Whitehead, who's defending me in the court-martial, if I'm stringin' yer. I been in the ring, kid, and you can bet your bottom dollar that a man's been in the ring'll tell the truth."

"Go on, Dan," said the sergeant.

"An' I never heard a word about Bill Rees since. I guess they got him into the trenches and made short work of him."

Dan Cohen paused to light a cigarette.

"Well, one o' the M.P.'s follows after me and starts shootin'. An' don't you believe I ran. Gee, I was scared! But I was in luck 'cause a Frenchman had just started his camion an' I jumped in and said the gendarmes were after me. He was white, that frog was. He shot the juice into her an' went off like a bat out of hell an' there was a hell of a lot of traffic on the road because there was some damn-fool attack or other goin' on. So I got up to Paris. . . . An' then it'ld all have been fine if I hadn't met up with a Jane I knew. I still had five hundred francs on me, an' so we raised hell until one day we was havin' dinner in the café de Paris, both of us sort of jagged up, an' we didn't have enough money to pay the bill an' Janey made a run for it, but an M.P. got me an' then there was hell to pay. . . . Compree? They put me in the Bastille, great place. . . . Then they shipped me off to some damn camp or other an' gave me a gun an' made me drill for a week an' then they packed a whole gang of us, all A. W. O. L.'s, into a train for the front. That was nearly the end of little Daniel again. But when we was in Vitry-le-François, I chucked my rifle out of one window and jumped out of the other an' got on a train back to Paris an' went an' reported to headquarters how I'd smashed the car an' been in the Bastille an' all, an' they were sore as hell at the M.P.'s an' sent me out to a section an' all went fine until I got ordered back an' had to alley down to this goddam camp. Ah' now I don't know what they're goin' to do to me."

"Gee whiz!"

"It's a great war, I tell you, Sarge. It's a great war. I wouldn't have missed it."

Across the room someone was singing.

"Let's drown 'em out," said the top sergeant boisterously.

> "O Madermoiselle from Armenteers,
>   Parley voo?"

"Well, I've got to get the hell out of here," said wild Dan Cohen, after a minute. "I've got a Jane waitin' for me. I'm all fixed up, . . . Compree?"

He swaggered out singing:

> "Bon soir, ma cherie,
>   Comment alley vous?
>   Si vous voulez
>   Couche avec moi. . . ."

The door slammed behind him, leaving the café quiet.

Many men had left. Madame had taken up her knitting and Marie of the plump white arms sat beside her, leaning her head back among the bottles that rose in tiers behind the bars.

Fuselli was staring at a door on one side of the bar. Men kept opening it and looking in and closing it again with a peculiar expression on their faces. Now and then someone would open it with a smile and go into the next room, shuffling his feet and closing the door carefully behind him.

"Say, I wonder what they've got there," said the top sergeant, who had been staring at the door. "Mush be looked into, mush be looked into," he added, laughing drunkenly.

"I dunno," said Fuselli. The champagne was humming in his head like a fly against a window pane. He felt very bold and important.

The top sergeant got to his feet unsteadily.

"Corporal, take charge of the colors," he said, and walked to the door. He opened it a little, peeked in; winked elaborately to his friends and skipped into the other room, closing the door carefully behind him.

The corporal went over next. He said, "Well, I'll be damned," and walked straight in, leaving the door ajar. In a moment it was closed from the inside.

"Come on, Bill, let's see what the hell they got in there," said Fuselli.

"All right, old kid," said Bill Grey.

They went together over to the door. Fuselli opened it and looked in. He let out a breath through his teeth with a faint whistling sound.

"Gee, come in, Bill," he said, giggling.

The room was small, nearly filled up by a dining table with a red cloth. On the mantel above the empty fireplace were candlesticks with dangling crystals that glittered red and yellow and purple in the lamplight, in front of a cracked mirror that seemed a window into another dingier room. The paper was peeling off the damp walls, giving a mortuary smell of mildewed plaster that not even the reek of beer and tobacco had done away with.

"Look at her, Bill, ain't she got style?" whispered Fuselli.

Bill Grey grunted.

"Say, d'ye think the Jane that feller was tellin' us he raised hell with in Paris was like that?"

At the end of the table, leaning on her elbows, was a woman with black frizzy hair cut short, that stuck out from her head in all directions. Her eyes were dark and her lips red with a faint swollen look. She looked with a certain defiance at the men who stood about the walls and sat at the table.

The men stared at her silently. A big man with red hair and a heavy jaw who sat next her kept edging up nearer. Someone knocked against the table making the bottles and liqueur glasses clustered in the center jingle.

"She ain't clean; she's got bobbed hair," said the man next to Fuselli.

The woman said something in French.

Only one man understood it. His laugh rang hollowly in the silent room and stopped suddenly.

The woman looked attentively at the faces round her for a moment, shrugged her shoulders, and began straightening the ribbon on the hat she held on her lap.

"How the hell did she get here? I thought the M.P.'s ran them out of town the minute they got here," said one man.

The woman continued plucking at her hat.

"You venay Paris?" said a boy with a soft voice who sat near her. He had blue eyes and a milky complexion, faintly tanned, that went strangely with the rough red and brown faces in the room.

"Oui, de Paris," she said after a pause, glancing suddenly in the boy's face.

"She's a liar, I can tell you that," said the red-haired man, who by this time had moved his chair very close to the woman's.

"You told him you came from Marseilles, and him you came from Lyon," said the boy with the milky complexion, smiling genially. "Vraiment de où venay vous?"

"I come from everywhere," she said, and tossed the hair back from her face.

"Travelled a lot?" asked the boy again.

"A feller told me," said Fuselli to Bill Grey, "that he'd talked to a girl like that who'd been to Turkey an' Egypt. . . . I bet that girl's seen some life."

The woman jumped to her feet suddenly screaming with rage. The man with the red hair moved away sheepishly. Then he lifted his large dirty hands in the air.

"Kamarad," he said.

Nobody laughed. The room was silent except for feet scraping occasionally on the floor.

She put her hat on and took a little box from the chain bag in her lap and began powdering her face, making faces into the mirror she held in the palm of her hand.

The men stared at her.

"Guess she thinks she's the Queen of the May," said one man, getting to his feet. He leaned across the table and spat into the fireplace. "I'm going back to barracks." He turned to the woman and shouted in a voice full of hatred, "Bon swar."

The woman was putting the powder puff away in her jet bag. She did not look up; the door closed sharply.

"Come along," said the woman, suddenly, tossing her head back. "Come along; who go with me?"

Nobody spoke. The men stared at her silently. There was no sound except that of feet scraping occasionally on the floor.

III

The oatmeal flopped heavily into the mess-kit. Fuselli's eyes were still glued together with sleep. He sat at the dark greasy bench and took a gulp of the scalding coffee that smelt vaguely of dish rags. That woke him up a little. There was little talk in the mess shack. The men, that the bugle had wrenched out of their blankets but fifteen minutes before, sat in rows, eating sullenly or blinking at each other through the misty darkness. You could hear feet scraping in the ashes of the floor and mess kits clattering against the tables and here and there a man coughing. Near the counter where the food was served out one of the cooks swore interminably in a whiny sing-sing voice.

"Gee, Bill, I've got a head," said Fuselli.

"Ye're ought to have," growled Bill Grey. "I had to carry you up into the barracks. You said you were goin' back and love up that goddam girl."

"Did I?" said Fuselli, giggling.

"I had a hell of a time getting you past the guard."

"Some cognac! . . . I got a hangover now," said Fuselli.

"I'm goddamned if I can go this much longer."

"What?"

They were washing their mess-kits in the tub of warm water thick with grease from the hundred mess-kits that had gone before, in front of the shack. An electric light illumined faintly the wet trunk of a plane tree and the surface of the water where bits of oatmeal floated and coffee grounds,—and the garbage pails with their painted signs: WET GARBAGE, DRY GARBAGE; and the line of men who stood waiting to reach the tub.

"This hell of a life!" said Bill Grey, savagely.

"What d'ye mean?"

"Doin' nothin' but pack bandages in packin' cases and take bandages out of packin' cases. I'll go crazy. I've tried gettin' drunk; it don't do no good."

"Gee; I've got a head," said Fuselli.

Bill Grey put his heavy muscular hand round Fuselli's shoulder as they strolled towards the barracks.

"Say, Dan, I'm goin' A.W.O.L."

"Don't ye do it, Bill. Hell, look at the chance we've got to get ahead. We can both of us get promoted if we don't get in wrong."

"I don't give a hoot in hell for all that. . . . What d'ye think I got in this goddamned army for? Because I thought I'd look nice in the uniform?"

Bill Grey thrust his hands into his pockets and spat dismally in front of him.

"But, Bill, you don't want to stay a buck private, do you?"

"I want to get to the front. . . . I don't want to stay here till I get in the jug for being spiffed or get a court-martial. . . . Say, Dan, will you come with me?"

"Hell, Bill, you ain't goin'. You're just kiddin', ain't yer? They'll send us there soon enough. I want to get to be a corporal,"—he puffed out his chest a little—"before I go to the front, so's to be able to show what I'm good for. See, Bill?"

A bugle blew.

"There's fatigue, an' I ain't done my bunk."

"Me neither. . . . They won't do nothin', Dan. . . . Don't let them ride yer, Dan."

They lined up in the dark road feeling the mud slopping under their feet. The ruts were full of black water, in which gleamed a reflection of distant electric lights.

"All you fellows work in Storehouse A today," said the sergeant, who had been a preacher, in his sad, drawling voice. "Lieutenant says that's all got to be finished by noon. They're sending it to the front today."

Somebody let his breath out in a whistle of surprise.

"Who did that?"

Nobody answered.

"Dismissed!" snapped the sergeant disgustedly.

They straggled off into the darkness towards one of the lights, their feet splashing confusedly in the puddles.

Fuselli strolled up to the sentry at the camp gate. He was picking his teeth meditatively with the splinter of a pine board.

"Say, Phil, you couldn't lend me a half a dollar, could you?" Fuselli stopped, put his hands in his pockets and looked at the sentry with the splinter sticking out of a corner of his mouth.

"Sorry, Dan," said the other man; "I'm cleaned out. Ain't had a cent since New Year's."

"Why the hell don't they pay us?"

"You guys signed the pay roll yet?"

"Sure. So long!"

Fuselli strolled on down the dark road, where the mud was frozen into deep ruts, towards the town. It was still strange to him, this town of little houses faced with cracked stucco, where the damp made grey stains and green stains, of confused red-tiled roofs, and of narrow cobbled streets that zigzagged in and out among high walls overhung with balconies. At night, when it was dark except for where a lamp in a window spilt gold reflections out on the wet street or the light streamed out from a store or a café, it was almost frighteningly unreal. He walked down into the main square, where he could hear the fountain gurgling. In the middle he stopped indecisively, his coat unbuttoned, his hands pushed to the bottom of his trousers pockets, where they encountered nothing but the cloth. He listened a long time to the gurgling of the fountain and to the shunting of trains far away in the freight yards. "An' this is the war," he thought. "Ain't it queer? It's quieter than it was at home nights." Down the street at the end of the square a band of white light appeared, the searchlight of a staff car. The two eyes of the car stared straight into his eyes, dazzling him, then veered off to one side and whizzed past, leaving a faint smell of petrol and a sound of voices. Fuselli watched the fronts of houses light up as the car made its way to the main road. Then the town was dark and silent again.

He strolled across the square towards the Cheval Blanc, the large café where the officers went.

"Button yer coat," came a gruff voice. He saw a stiff tall figure at the edge of the curve. He made out the shape of the pistol holster that hung like a thin ham at the man's thigh. An M.P. He buttoned his coat hurriedly and walked off with rapid steps.

He stopped outside a café that had "Ham and Eggs" written in white paint on the window and looked in wistfully. Someone from behind him put two big hands over his eyes. He wriggled his head free.

"Hello, Dan," he said. "How did you get out of the jug?"

"I'm a trusty, kid," said Dan Cohen. "Got any dough?"

"Not a damn cent!"

"Me neither. . . . Come on in anyway," said Cohen. "I'll fix it up with Marie." Fuselli followed doubtfully. He was a little afraid of Dan Cohen; he remembered how a man had been court-martialed last week for trying to bolt out of a café without paying for his drinks.

He sat down at a table near the door. Dan had disappeared into the back room. Fuselli felt homesick. He was thinking how long it was since he had had a letter from Mabe. "I bet she's got another feller," he told himself savagely. He tried to remember how she looked, but he had to take out his watch and peep in the back before he could make out if her nose were straight or snub. He looked up, clicking the watch in his pocket. Marie of the white arms was coming laughing out of the inner room. Her large firm breasts, neatly held in by the close-fitting blouse, shook a little when she laughed. Her cheeks were very red and a strand of chestnut hair hung down along her neck. She picked it up hurriedly and caught it up with a hairpin, walking slowly into the middle of the room as she did so with her hands behind her head. Dan Cohen followed her into the room, a broad grin on his face.

"All right, kid," he said. "I told her you'd pay when Uncle Sam came across. Ever had any Kümmel?"

"What the hell's that?"

"You'll see."

They sat down before a dish of fried eggs at the table in the corner, the favoured table, where Marie herself often sat and chatted, when wizened Madame did not have her eye upon her.

Several men drew up their chairs. Wild Dan Cohen always had an audience.

"Looks like there was going to be another offensive at Verdun," said Dan Cohen. Someone answered vaguely.

"Funny how little we know about what's going on out there," said one man. "I knew more about the war when I was home in Minneapolis than I do here."

"I guess we're lightin' into 'em all right," said Fuselli in a patriotic voice.

"Hell! Nothin' doin' this time o' year anyway," said Cohen. A grin spread across his red face. "Last time I was at the front the Boche had just made a coup de main and captured a whole trenchful."

"Of who?"

"Of Americans—of us!"

"The hell you say!"

"That's a goddam lie," shouted a black-haired man with an ill-shaven

jaw, who had just come in. "There ain't never been an American captured, an' there never will be, by God!"

"How long were you at the front, buddy," asked Cohen coolly. "I
guess you been to Berlin already, ain't yer?"

"I say that any man who says an American'ld let himself be captured
by a stinkin' Hun, is a goddam liar," said the man with the ill-shaven jaw,
sitting down sullenly.

"Well, you'd better not say it to me," said Cohen laughing, looking
meditatively at one of his big red fists.

There had been a look of apprehension on Marie's face. She looked
at Cohen's fist and shrugged her shoulders and laughed.

Another crowd had just slouched into the café.

"Well if that isn't wild Dan! Hello, old kid, how are you?"

"Hello, Dook!"

A small man in a coat that looked almost like an officer's coat, it was
so well cut, was shaking hands effusively with Cohen. He wore a corporal's stripes and a British aviator's fatigue cap. Cohen made room for him
on the bench.

"What are you doing in this hole, Dook?"

The man twisted his mouth so that his neat black mustache was a slant.

"G. O. 42," he said.

"Battle of Paris?" said Cohen in a sympathetic voice.

"Battle of Nice! I'm going back to my section soon. I'd never have got
a court-martial if I'd been with my outfit. I was in the Base Hospital 15
with pneumonia."

"Tough luck!"

"It was a hell of a note."

"Say, Dook, your outfit was working with ours at Chamfort that time,
wasn't it?"

"You mean when we evacuated the nut hospital?"

"Yes, wasn't that hell?" Dan Cohen gulped down half a glass of red
wine, smacked his thick lips, and began in his story-telling voice:

"Our section had just come out of Verdun where we'd been getting
hell for three weeks on the Bras road. There was one little hill where
we'd have to get out and shove every damn time, the mud was so deep,
and God, it stank there with the shells turning up the ground all full of
mackabbies as the poilu call them. . . . Say, Dook, have you got any
money?"

"I've got some," said Dook, without enthusiasm.

"Well, the champagne's damn good here. I'm part of the outfit in this
gin mill; they'll give it to you at a reduction."

"All right!"

Dan Cohen turned round and whispered something to Marie. She laughed and dived down behind the curtain.

"But that Chamfort was worse yet. Everybody was sort o' nervous because the Germans had dropped a message sayin' they'd give 'em three days to clear the hospital out, and that then they'd shell hell out of the place."

"The Germans done that! Quit yer kiddin'," said Fuselli.

"They did it at Souilly, too," said Dook.

"Hell, yes. . . . A funny thing happened there. The hospital was in a big rambling house, looked like an Atlantic City hotel. . . . We used to run our car in back and sleep in it. It was where we took the shell-shock cases, fellows who were roarin' mad, and tremblin' all over, and some of 'em paralysed like. . . . There was a man in the wing opposite where we slept who kept laughin'. Bill Rees was on the car with me, and we laid in our blankets in the bottom of the car and every now and then one of us'ld turn over and whisper: 'Ain't this hell, kid?' 'cause that feller kept laughin' like a man who had just heard a joke that was so funny he couldn't stop laughin'. It wasn't like a crazy man's laugh usually is. When I first heard it I thought it was a man really laughin', and I guess I laughed too. But it didn't stop. . . . Bill Rees an' me laid in our car shiverin', listenin' to the barrage in the distance with now and then the big noise of an aeroplane bomb, an' that feller laughin', laughin', like he'd just heard a joke, like something had struck him funny." Cohen took a gulp of champagne and jerked his head to one side. "An that damn laughin' kept up until about noon the next day when the orderlies strangled the feller. . . . Got their goat, I guess."

Fuselli was looking towards the other side of the room, where a faint murmur of righteous indignation was rising from the dark man with the unshaven jaw and his companions. Fuselli was thinking that it wasn't good to be seen round too much with a fellow like Cohen, who talked about the Germans notifying hospitals before they bombarded them, and who was waiting for a court-martial. Might get him in wrong. He slipped out of the café into the dark. A dank wind blew down the irregular street, ruffling the reflected light in the puddles, making a shutter bang interminably somewhere. Fuselli went to the main square again, casting an envious glance in the window of the Cheval Blanc, where he saw officers playing billiards in a well-lighted room painted white and gold, and a blond girl in a raspberry-colored shirtwaist enthroned haughtily behind the bar. He remembered the M.P. and automatically hastened his steps. In a narrow street the other side of the square he stopped before the window of a small grocery shop and peered inside, keeping carefully out of the oblong of light that showed faintly the grass-grown cobbles and the green and grey walls opposite.

A girl sat knitting beside the small counter with her two little black feet placed demurely side by side on the edge of a box full of red beets. She was very small and slender. The lamplight gleamed on her black hair, done close to her head. Her face was in the shadow. Several soldiers lounged awkwardly against the counter and the jambs of the door, following her movements with their eyes as dogs watch a plate of meat being moved about in a kitchen.

After a little the girl rolled up her knitting and jumped to her feet, showing her face,—an oval white face with large dark lashes and an impertinent mouth. She stood looking at the soldiers who stood about her in a circle, then twisted up her mouth in a grimace and disappeared into the inner room.

Fuselli walked to the end of the street where there was a bridge over a small stream. He leaned on the cold stone rail and looked into the water that was barely visible gurgling beneath between rims of ice.

"O this is a hell of a life," he muttered.

He shivered in the cold wind but remained leaning over the water. In the distance trains rumbled interminably, giving him a sense of vast desolate distances. The village clock struck eight. The bell had a soft note like the bass string of a guitar. In the darkness Fuselli could almost see the girl's face grimacing with its broad impertinent lips. He thought of the sombre barracks and men sitting about on the end of their cots. Hell, he couldn't go back yet. His whole body was taut with desire for warmth and softness and quiet. He slouched back along the narrow street cursing in a dismal monotone. Before the grocery store he stopped. The men had gone. He went in jauntily pushing his cap a little to one side so that some of his thick curly hair came out over his forehead. The little bell in the door clanged.

The girl came out of the inner room. She gave him her hand indifferently.

"Comment ça va! Yvonne? Bon?"

His pidgin-French made her show her little pearly teeth in a smile.

"Good," she said in English.

They laughed childishly.

"Say, will you be my girl, Yvonne?"

She looked in his eyes and laughed.

"Non compris," she said.

"We, we; voulez vous et' ma fille?"

She shrieked with laughter and slapped him hard on the cheek.

"Venez," she said, still laughing. He followed her. In the inner room was a large oak table with chairs round it. At the end Eisenstein and a French soldier were talking excitedly, so absorbed in what they were saying that they did not notice the other two. Yvonne took the Frenchman

by the hair and pulled his head back and told him, still laughing, what
Fuselli had said. He laughed.

"No, you must not say that," he said in English, turning to Fuselli.

Fuselli was angry and sat down sullenly at the end of the table, keeping his eyes on Yvonne. She drew the knitting out of the pocket of her
apron and holding it up comically between two fingers, glanced towards
the dark corner of the room where an old woman with a lace cap on her
head sat asleep, and then let herself fall into a chair.

"Boom!" she said.

Fuselli laughed until the tears filled his eyes. She laughed too. They sat
a long while looking at each other and giggling, while Eisenstein and the
Frenchman talked. Suddenly Fuselli caught a phrase that startled him.

"What would you Americans do if revolution broke out in France?"

"We'd do what we were ordered to," said Eisenstein bitterly. "We're
a bunch of slaves." Fuselli noticed that Eisenstein's puffy sallow face
was flushed and that there was a flash in his eyes he had never seen
before.

"How do you mean, revolution?" asked Fuselli in a puzzled voice.

The Frenchman turned black eyes searchingly upon him.

"I mean, stop the butchery,—overthrow the capitalist government.—
The social revolution."

"But you're a republic already, ain't yer?"

"As much as you are."

"You talk like a socialist," said Fuselli. "They tell me they shoot guys
in America for talkin' like that."

"You see!" said Eisenstein to the Frenchman.

"Are they all like that?"

"Except a very few. It's hopeless," said Eisenstein, burying his face in
his hands. "I often think of shooting myself."

"Better shoot someone else," said the Frenchman. "It will be more
useful."

Fuselli stirred uneasily in his chair.

"Where'd you fellers get that stuff anyway?" he asked. In his mind he
was saying: "A kike and a frog, that's a good combination."

His eye caught Yvonne's and they both laughed. Yvonne threw her
knitting ball at him. It rolled down under the table and they both scram-
bled about under the chairs looking for it.

"Twice I have thought it was going to happen," said the Frenchman.

"When was that?"

"A little while ago a division started marching on Paris. . . . And when
I was in Verdun. . . . O there will be a revolution. . . . France is the country of revolutions."

"We'll always be here to shoot you down," said Eisenstein.

"Wait till you've been in the war a little while. A winter in the trenches will make any army ready for revolution."

"But we have no way of learning the truth. And in the tyranny of the army a man becomes a brute, a piece of machinery. Remember you are freer than we are. We are worse than the Russians!"

"It is curious! . . . O but you must have some feeling of civilization. I have always heard that Americans were free and independent. Will they let themselves be driven to the slaughter always?"

"O I don't know." Eisenstein got to his feet. "We'd better be getting to barracks. Coming, Fuselli?" he said.

"Guess so," said Fuselli indifferently, without getting up.

Eisenstein and the Frenchman went out into the shop.

"Bon swar," said Fuselli, softly, leaning across the table. "Hey, girlie?"

He threw himself on his belly on the wide table and put his arms round her neck and kissed her, feeling everything go blank in a flame of desire.

She pushed him away calmly with strong little arms.

"Stop!" she said, and jerked her head in the direction of the old woman in the chair in the dark corner of the room. They stood side by side listening to her faint wheezy snoring.

He put his arms round her and kissed her long on the mouth.

"Demain," he said.

She nodded her head.

Fuselli walked fast up the dark street towards the camp. The blood pounded happily through his veins. He caught up with Eisenstein.

"Say, Eisenstein," he said in a comradely voice, "I don't think you ought to go talking round like that. You'll get yourself in too deep one of these days."

"I don't care!"

"But, hell, man, you don't want to get in the wrong that bad. They shoot fellers for less than you said."

"Let them."

"Christ, man, you don't want to be a damn fool," expostulated Fuselli.

"How old are you, Fuselli?"

"I'm twenty now."

"I'm thirty. I've lived more, kid. I know what's good and what's bad. This butchery makes me unhappy."

"God, I know. It's a hell of a note. But who brought it on? If somebody had shot that Kaiser."

Eisenstein laughed bitterly. At the entrance of camp Fuselli lingered a moment watching the small form of Eisenstein disappear with its curious waddly walk into the darkness.

"I'm going to be damn careful who I'm seen goin' into barracks with," he said to himself. "That damn kike may be a German spy or a secret-service officer." A cold chill of terror went over him, shattering his mood of joyous self-satisfaction. His feet slopped in the puddles, breaking through the thin ice, as he walked up the road towards the barracks. He felt as if people were watching him from everywhere out of the darkness, as if some gigantic figure were driving him forward through the darkness, holding a fist over his head, ready to crush him.

When he was rolled up in his blankets in the bunk next to Bill Grey, he whispered to his friend:

"Say, Bill, I think I've got a skirt all fixed up in town."

"Who?"

"Yvonne—don't tell anybody."

Bill Grey whistled softly.

"You're some highflyer, Dan."

Fuselli chuckled.

"Hell, man, the best ain't good enough for me."

"Well, I'm going to leave you," said Bill Grey.

"When?"

"Damn soon. I can't go this life. I don't see how you can."

Fuselli did not answer. He snuggled warmly into his blankets, thinking of Yvonne and the corporalship.

In the light of the one flickering lamp that made an unsteady circle of reddish glow on the station platform Fuselli looked at his pass. From Reveille on February fourth to Reveille on February fifth he was a free man. His eyes smarted with sleep as he walked up and down the cold station platform. For twenty-four hours he wouldn't have to obey anybody's orders. Despite the loneliness of going away on a train in a night like this in a strange country Fuselli was happy. He clinked the money in his pocket.

Down the track a red eye appeared and grew nearer. He could hear the hard puffing of the engine up the grade. Huge curves gleamed as the engine roared slowly past him. A man with bare arms black with coal dust was leaning out of the cab, lit up from behind by a yellowish red glare. Now the cars were going by, flat cars with guns, tilted up like the muzzles of hunting dogs, freight cars out of which here and there peered a man's head. The train almost came to a stop. The cars clanged one against the other all down the train. Fuselli was looking into a pair of eyes that shone in the lamplight; a hand was held out to him.

"So long, kid," said a boyish voice. "I don't know who the hell you are, but so long; good luck."

"So long," stammered Fuselli. "Going to the front?"

"Yer goddam right," answered another voice.

The train took up speed again; the clanging of car against car ceased and in a moment they were moving fast before Fuselli's eyes. Then the station was dark and empty again, and he was watching the red light grow smaller and paler while the train rumbled on into the darkness.

A confusion of gold and green and crimson silks and intricate designs of naked pink-fleshed cupids filled Fuselli's mind, when, full of wonder, he walked down the steps of the palace out into the faint ruddy sunlight of the afternoon. A few names, Napoleon, Josephine, the Empire, that had never had significance in his mind before, flared with a lurid gorgeous light in his imagination like a tableau of living statues at a vaudeville theatre.

"They must have had a heap of money, them guys," said the man who was with him, a private in Aviation. "Let's go have a drink."

Fuselli was silent and absorbed in his thoughts. Here was something that supplemented his visions of wealth and glory that he used to tell Al about, when they'd sit and watch the big liners come in, all glittering with lights, through the Golden Gate.

"They didn't mind having naked women about, did they?" said the private in Aviation, a morose foul-mouthed little man who had been in the woolen business.

"D'ye blame them?"

"No, I can't say's I do. . . . I bet they was immoral, them guys," he continued vaguely.

They wandered about the streets of Fontainebleau listlessly, looking into shop windows, staring at women, lolling on benches in the parks where the faint sunlight came through a lacework of twigs purple and crimson and yellow, that cast intricate lavender-grey shadows on the asphalt.

"Let's go have another drink," said the private in Aviation.

Fuselli looked at his watch; they had hours before train time.

A girl in a loose dirty blouse wiped off the table.

"Vin blank," said the other man.

"Mame shows," said Fuselli.

His head was full of gold and green mouldings and silk and crimson velvet and intricate designs in which naked pink-fleshed cupids writhed indecently. Some day, he was saying to himself, he'd make a hell of a lot of money and live in a house like that with Mabe; no, with Yvonne, or with some other girl.

"Must have been immoral, them guys," said the private in Aviation, leering at the girl in the dirty blouse.

Fuselli remembered a revel he'd seen in a moving picture of "Quo Vadis," people in bath robes dancing around with large cups in their hands and tables full of dishes being upset.

"Cognac, beaucoup," said the private in Aviation.

"Mame shows," said Fuselli.

The café was full of gold and green silks, and great brocaded beds with heavy carvings above them, beds in which writhed, pink-fleshed and indecent, intricate patterns of cupids.

Somebody said, "Hello, Fuselli."

He was on the train; his ears hummed and his head had an iron band round it. It was dark except for the little light that flickered in the ceiling. For a minute he thought it was a goldfish in a bowl, but it was a light that flickered in the ceiling.

"Hello, Fuselli," said Eisenstein. "Feel all right?"

"Sure," said Fuselli with a thick voice. "Why shouldn't I?"

"How did you find that house?" said Eisenstein seriously.

"Hell, I don't know," muttered Fuselli. "I'm goin' to sleep."

His mind was a jumble. He remembered vast halls full of green and gold silks, and great beds with crowns over them where Napoleon and Josephine used to sleep. Who were they? O yes, the Empire,—or was it the Abdication? Then there were patterns of flowers and fruits and cupids, all gilded, and a dark passage and stairs that smelt musty, where he and the man in Aviation fell down. He remembered how it felt to rub his nose hard on the gritty red plush carpet of the stairs. Then there were women in open-work skirts standing about, or were those the pictures on the walls? And there was a bed with mirrors round it. He opened his eyes. Eisenstein was talking to him. He must have been talking to him for some time.

"I look at it this way," he was saying. "A feller needs a little of that to keep healthy. Now, if he's abstemious and careful . . ."

Fuselli went to sleep. He woke up again thinking suddenly: he must borrow that little blue book of army regulations. It would be useful to know that in case something came up. The corporal who had been in the Red Sox outfield had been transferred to a Base Hospital. It was t. b. so Sergeant Osler said. Anyway they were going to appoint an acting corporal. He stared at the flickering little light in the ceiling.

"How did you get a pass?" Eisenstein was asking.

"Oh, the sergeant fixed me up with one," answered Fuselli mysteriously.

"You're in pretty good with the sergeant, ain't yer?" said Eisenstein.

Fuselli smiled deprecatingly.

"Say, d'ye know that little kid Stockton?"

"The white-faced little kid who's clerk in that outfit that has the other end of the barracks?"

"That's him," said Eisenstein. "I wish I could do something to help that kid. He just can't stand the discipline. . . . You ought to see him wince when the red-haired sergeant over there yells at him. . . . The kid looks sicker every day."

"Well, he's got a good soft job: clerk," said Fuselli.

"Ye think it's soft? I worked twelve hours day before yesterday getting out reports," said Eisenstein, indignantly. "But the kid's lost it and they keep ridin' him for some reason or other. It hurts a feller to see that. He ought to be at home at school."

"He's got to take his medicine," said Fuselli.

"You wait till we get butchered in the trenches. We'll see how you like your medicine," said Eisenstein.

"Damn fool," muttered Fuselli, composing himself to sleep again.

The bugle wrenched Fuselli out of his blankets, half dead with sleep.

"Say, Bill, I got a head again," he muttered.

There was no answer. It was only then that he noticed that the cot next to his was empty. The blankets were folded neatly at the foot. Sudden panic seized him. He couldn't get along without Bill Grey, he said to himself, he wouldn't have anyone to go round with. He looked fixedly at the empty cot.

"Attention!"

The company was lined up in the dark with their feet in the mud puddles of the road. The lieutenant strode up and down in front of them with the tail of his trench coat sticking out behind. He had a pocket flashlight that he kept flashing at the gaunt trunks of trees, in the faces of the company, at his feet, in the puddles of the road.

"If any man knows anything about the whereabouts of Private 1st-class William Grey, report at once, as otherwise we shall have to put him down A.W.O.L. You know what that means?" The lieutenant spoke in short shrill periods, chopping off the ends of his words as if with a hatchet.

No one said anything.

"I guess he's S.O.L."; this from someone behind Fuselli.

"And I have one more announcement to make, men," said the lieutenant in his natural voice. "I'm going to appoint Fuselli, 1st-class private, acting corporal."

Fuselli's knees were weak under him. He felt like shouting and dancing with joy. He was glad it was dark so that no one could see how excited he was.

"Sergeant, dismiss the company," said the lieutenant bringing his voice back to its military tone.

"Companee dis-missed!" said out the sergeant jovially.

In groups, talking with crisp voices, cheered by the occurrence of events, the company straggled across the great stretch of mud puddles towards the mess shack.

IV

Yvonne tossed the omelette in the air. It landed sizzling in the pan again, and she came forward into the light, holding the frying pan before her. Behind her was the dark stove and above it a row of copper kettles that gleamed through the bluish obscurity. She flicked the omelette out of the pan into the white dish that stood in the middle of the table, full in the yellow lamplight.

"Tiens," she said, brushing a few stray hairs off her forehead with the back of her hand.

"You're some cook," said Fuselli getting to his feet. He had been sprawling on a chair in the other end of the kitchen, watching Yvonne's slender body in tight black dress and blue apron move in and out of the area of light as she got dinner ready. A smell of burnt butter with a faint tang of pepper in it, filled the kitchen, making his mouth water.

"This is the real stuff," he was saying to himself,—"like home."

He stood with his hands deep in his pockets and his head thrown back, watching her cut the bread, holding the big loaf to her chest and pulling the knife towards her. She brushed some crumbs off her dress with a thin white hand.

"You're my girl, Yvonne; ain't yer?" Fuselli put his arms round her.

"Sale bête," she said, laughing and pushing him away.

There was a brisk step outside and another girl came into the kitchen, a thin yellow-faced girl with a sharp nose and long teeth.

"Ma cousine. . . . Mon 'tit americain." They both laughed. Fuselli blushed as he shook the girl's hand.

"Il est beau, hein?" said Yvonne gruffly.

"Mais, ma petite, il est charmant, vot' americain!" They laughed again. Fuselli who did not understand laughed too, thinking to himself, "They'll let the dinner get cold if they don't sit down soon."

"Get maman, Dan," said Yvonne.

Fuselli went into the shop through the room with the long oak table. In the dim light that came from the kitchen he saw the old woman's white bonnet. Her face was in shadow but there was a faint gleam of light in her small beady eyes.

"Supper, ma'am," he shouted.

Grumbling in her creaky little voice, the old woman followed him back into the kitchen.

Steam, gilded by the lamplight, rose in pillars to the ceiling from the big tureen of soup.

There was a white cloth on the table and a big loaf of bread at the end. The plates, with borders of little roses on them, seemed, after the army mess, the most beautiful things Fuselli had ever seen. The wine bottle was black beside the soup tureen and the wine in the glasses cast a dark purple stain on the cloth.

Fuselli ate his soup silently understanding very little of the French that the two girls rattled at each other. The old woman rarely spoke and when she did one of the girls would throw her a hasty remark that hardly interrupted their chatter.

Fuselli was thinking of the other men lining up outside the dark mess shack and the sound the food made when it flopped into the mess kits. An idea came to him. He'd have to bring Sarge to see Yvonne. They could set him up to a feed. "It would help me to stay in good with him," He had a minute's worry about his corporalship. He was acting corporal right enough, but he wanted them to send in his appointment.

The omelette melted in his mouth.

"Damn bon," he said to Yvonne with his mouth full.

She looked at him fixedly.

"Bon, bon," he said again.

"You. . . . Dan, bon," she said and laughed. The cousin was looking from one to the other enviously, her upper lip lifted away from her teeth in a smile.

The old woman munched her bread in a silent preoccupied fashion.

"There's somebody in the store," said Fuselli after a long pause. "Je irey." He put his napkin down and went out wiping his mouth on the back of his hand. Eisenstein and a chalky-faced boy were in the shop.

"Hullo! are you keepin' house here?" asked Eisenstein.

"Sure," said Fuselli conceitedly.

"Have you got any chawclit?" asked the chalky-faced boy in a thin bloodless voice.

Fuselli looked round the shelves and threw a cake of chocolate down on the counter.

"Anything else?"

"Nothing, thank you, corporal. How much is it?"

Whistling "There's a long, long trail a-winding," Fuselli strode back into the inner room.

"Combien chocolate?" he asked.

When he had received the money, he sat down at his place at table again, smiling importantly. He must write Al about all this, he was thinking, and he was wondering vaguely whether Al had been drafted yet.

After dinner the women sat a long time chatting over their coffee, while Fuselli squirmed uneasily on his chair, looking now and then at his watch. His pass was till twelve only; it was already getting on to ten. He tried to catch Yvonne's eye, but she was moving about the kitchen putting things in order for the night, and hardly seemed to notice him. At last the old woman shuffled into the shop and there was the sound of a key clicking hard in the outside door. When she came back, Fuselli said good-night to everyone and left by the back door into the court. There he leaned sulkily against the wall and waited in the dark, listening to the sounds that came from the house. He could see shadows passing across the orange square of light the window threw on the cobbles of the court. A light went on in an upper window, sending a faint glow over the disorderly tiles of the roof of the shed opposite. The door opened and Yvonne and her cousin stood on the broad stone doorstep chattering. Fuselli had pushed himself in behind a big hogshead that had a pleasant tang of old wood damp with sour wine. At last the heads of the shadows on the cobbles came together for a moment and the cousin clattered across the court and out into the empty streets. Her rapid footsteps died away. Yvonne's shadow was still in the door:

"Dan," she said softly.

Fuselli came out from behind the hogshead, his whole body flushing with delight. Yvonne pointed to his shoes. He took them off, and left them beside the door. He looked at his watch. It was a quarter to eleven.

"Viens," she said.

He followed her, his knees trembling a little from excitement, up the steep stairs.

The deep broken strokes of the town clock had just begun to strike midnight when Fuselli hurried in the camp gate. He gave up his pass jauntily to the guard and strolled towards his barracks. The long shed was pitch black, full of a sound of deep breathing and of occasional snoring. There was a thick smell of uniform wool on which the sweat had dried. Fuselli undressed without haste, stretching his arms luxuriously. He wriggled into his blankets feeling cool and tired, and went to sleep with a smile of self-satisfaction on his lips.

The companies were lined up for retreat, standing stiff as toy soldiers outside their barracks. The evening was almost warm. A little playful wind, oozing with springtime, played with the swollen buds on the plane trees. The sky was a drowsy violet color, and the blood pumped hot and stinging through the stiffened arms and legs of the soldiers who stood at attention. The voices of the non-coms were particularly harsh and metallic this evening. It was rumoured that a general was about. Orders were shouted with fury.

Standing behind the line of his company, Fuselli's chest was stuck out until the buttons of his tunic were in danger of snapping off. His shoes were well-shined, and he wore a new pair of puttees, wound so tightly that his legs ached.

At last the bugle sounded across the silent camp.

"Parade rest!" shouted the lieutenant.

Fuselli's mind was full of the army regulations which he had been studying assiduously for the last week. He was thinking of an imaginary examination for the corporalship, which he would pass, of course.

When the company was dismissed, he went up familiarly to the top sergeant:

"Say, Sarge, doin' anything this evenin'?"

"What the hell can a man do when he's broke?" said the top sergeant.

"Well, you come down town with me. I want to introduce you to somebody."

"Great!"

"Say, Sarge, have they sent that appointment in yet?"

"No, they haven't, Fuselli," said the top sergeant. "It's all made out," he added encouragingly.

They walked towards the town silently. The evening was silvery-violet. The few windows in the old grey-green houses that were lighted shone orange.

"Well, I'm goin' to get it, ain't I?"

A staff car shot by, splashing them with mud, leaving them a glimpse of officers leaning back in the deep cushions.

"You sure are," said the top sergeant in his good-natured voice.

They had reached the square. They saluted stiffly as two officers brushed past them.

"What's the regulations about a feller marryin' a French girl?" broke out Fuselli suddenly.

"Thinking of getting hitched up, are you?"

"Hell, no." Fuselli was crimson. "I just sort o' wanted to know."

"Permission of C. O., that's all I know of."

They had stopped in front of the grocery shop. Fuselli peered in through the window. The shop was full of soldiers lounging against the counter and the walls. In the midst of them, demurely knitting, sat Yvonne.

"Let's go and have a drink an' then come back," said Fuselli.

They went to the café where Marie of the white arms presided. Fuselli paid for two hot rum punches.

"You see it's this way, Sarge," he said confidentially, "I wrote all my folks at home I'd been made corporal, an' it'ld be a hell of a note to be let down now."

The top sergeant was drinking his hot drink in little sips. He smiled broadly and put his hand paternal-fashion on Fuselli's knee.

"Sure; you needn't worry, kid. I've got you fixed up all right," he said; then he added jovially, "Well, let's go see that girl of yours."

They went out into the dark streets, where the wind, despite the smell of burnt gasoline and army camps, had a faint suavity, something like the smell of mushrooms; the smell of spring.

Yvonne sat under the lamp in the shop, her feet up on a box of canned peas, yawning dismally. Behind her on the counter was the glass case full of yellow and greenish-white cheeses. Above that shelves rose to the ceiling in the brownish obscurity of the shop where gleamed faintly large jars and small jars, cans neatly placed in rows, glass jars and vegetables. In the corner, near the glass curtained door that led to the inner room, hung clusters of sausages large and small, red, yellow, and speckled. Yvonne jumped up when Fuselli and the sergeant opened the door.

"You are good," she said. "Je mourrais de cafard." They laughed.

"You know what that mean—cafard?"

"Sure."

"It is only since the war. Avant la guerre on ne savais pas ce que c'etait le cafard. The war is no good."

"Funny, ain't it?" said Fuselli to the top sergeant, "a feller can't juss figure out what the war is like."

"Don't you worry. We'll all get there," said the top sergeant knowingly.

"This is the sargon, Yvonne," said Fuselli.

"Oui, oui, je sais," said Yvonne, smiling at the top sergeant.

They sat in the little room behind the shop and drank white wine, and talked as best they could to Yvonne, who, very trim in her black dress and blue apron, perched on the edge of her chair with her feet in tiny pumps pressed tightly together, and glanced now and then at the elaborate stripes on the top sergeant's arm.

Fuselli strode familiarly into the grocery shop, whistling, and threw open the door to the inner room. His whistling stopped in the middle of a bar.

"Hello," he said in an annoyed voice.

"Hello, corporal," said Eisenstein. Eisenstein, his French soldier friend, a lanky man with a scraggly black heard and burning black eyes, and Stockton, the chalky-faced boy, were sitting at the table that filled up the room, chatting intimately and gaily with Yvonne, who leaned against the yellow wall beside the Frenchman and showed all her little pearly teeth in a laugh. In the middle of the dark oak table was a pot of hyacinths and some glasses that had had wine in them. The odor of the hyacinths hung in the air with a faint warm smell from the kitchen.

After a second's hesitation, Fuselli sat down to wait until the others should leave. It was long after pay-day and his pockets were empty, so he had nowhere else to go.

"How are they treatin' you down in your outfit now?" asked Eisenstein of Stockton, after a silence.

"Same as ever," said Stockton in his thin voice, stuttering a little. . . . "Sometimes I wish I was dead."

"Hum," said Eisenstein, a curious expression of understanding on his flabby face. "We'll be civilians some day."

"I won't" said Stockton.

"Hell," said Eisenstein. "You've got to keep your upper lip stiff. I thought I was goin' to die in that troopship coming over here. An' when I was little an' came over with the emigrants from Poland, I thought I was goin' to die. A man can stand more than he thinks for. . . . I never thought I could stand being in the army, bein' a slave like an' all that, an' I'm still here. No, you'll live long and be successful yet." He put his hand on Stockton's shoulder. The boy winced and drew his chair away.

"What for you do that? I ain't goin' to hurt you," said Eisenstein.

Fuselli looked at them both with a disgusted interest.

"I'll tell you what you'd better do, kid," he said condescendingly. "You get transferred to our company. It's an A1 bunch, ain't it, Eisenstein? We've got a good loot an' a good top-kicker, an' a damn good bunch o' fellers."

"Our top-kicker was in here a few minutes ago," said Eisenstein.

"He was?" asked Fuselli. "Where'd he go?"

"Damned if I know."

Yvonne and the French soldier were talking in low voices, laughing a little now and then. Fuselli leaned back in his chair looking at them, feeling out of things, wishing despondently that he knew enough French to understand what they were saying. He scraped his feet angrily back and forth on the floor. His eyes lit on the white hyacinths. They made him think of florists' windows at home at Eastertime and the noise and bustle of San Francisco's streets. "God, I hate this rotten hole," he muttered to himself. He thought of Mabe. He made a noise with his lips. Hell, she was married by this time. Anyway Yvonne was the girl for him. If he could only have Yvonne to himself; far away somewhere, away from the other men and that damn frog and her old mother. He thought of himself going to the theatre with Yvonne. When he was a sergeant he would be able to afford that sort of thing. He counted up the months. It was March. Here he'd been in Europe five months and he was still only a corporal, and not that yet. He clenched his fists with impatience. But once he got to be a non-com it would go faster, he told himself reassuringly.

He leaned over and sniffed loudly at the hyacinths.

"They smell good," he said. "Que disay vous, Yvonne?"

Yvonne looked at him as if she had forgotten that he was in the room. Her eyes looked straight into his, and she burst out laughing. Her glance had made him feel warm all over, and he leaned back in his chair again, looking at her slender body so neatly cased in its black dress and at her little head with its tightly-done hair, with a comfortable feeling of possession.

"Yvonne, come over here," he said, beckoning with his head.

She looked from him to the Frenchman provocatively. Then she came over and stood behind him.

"Que voulez vous?"

Fuselli glanced at Eisenstein. He and Stockton were deep in excited conversation with the Frenchman again. Fuselli heard that uncomfortable word that always made him angry, he did not know why, "Revolution."

"Yvonne," he said so that only she could hear, "what you say you and me get married?"

"Marriés . . . moi et toi?" asked Yvonne in a puzzled voice.

"We we."

She looked him in the eyes a moment, and then threw back her head in a paroxysm of hysterical laughter.

Fuselli flushed scarlet, got to his feet and strode out, slamming the door behind him so that the glass rang. He walked hurriedly back to camp, splashed with mud by the long lines of grey motor trucks that were throbbing their way slowly through the main street, each with a yellow eye that lit up faintly the tailboards of the truck ahead. The barracks were dark and nearly empty. He sat down at the sergeant's desk and began moodily turning over the pages of the little blue book of Army Regulations.

The moonlight glittered in the fountain at the end of the main square of the town. It was a warm dark night of faint clouds through which the moon shone palely as through a thin silk canopy. Fuselli stood by the fountain smoking a cigarette, looking at the yellow windows of the Cheval Blanc at the other end of the square, from which came a sound of voices and of billiard balls clinking. He stood quiet letting the acrid cigarette smoke drift out through his nose, his ears full of the silvery tinkle of the water in the fountain beside him. There were little drifts of warm and chilly air in the breeze that blew fitfully from the west. Fuselli was waiting. He took out his watch now and then and strained his eyes to see the time, but there was not light enough. At last the deep broken note of the bell in the church spire struck once. It must be half past ten.

He started walking slowly towards the street where Yvonne's grocery shop was. The faint glow of the moon lit up the grey houses with the shuttered windows and tumultuous red roofs full of little dormers and skylights. Fuselli felt deliciously at ease with the world. He could almost feel Yvonne's body in his arms and he smiled as he remembered the little faces she used to make at him. He slunk past the shuttered windows of the shop and dove into the darkness under the arch that led to the court. He walked cautiously, on tiptoe, keeping close to the moss-covered wall, for he heard voices in the court. He peeped round the edge of the building and saw that there were several people in the kitchen door talking. He drew his head back into the shadow. But he had caught a glimpse of the dark round form of the hogshead beside the kitchen door. If he only could get behind that as he usually did, he would be hidden until the people went away.

Keeping well in the shadow round the edge of the court, he slipped to the other side, and was just about to pop himself in behind the hogshead when he noticed that someone was there before him.

He caught his breath and stood still, his heart thumping. The figure turned and in the dark he recognised the top sergeant's round face.

"Keep quiet, can't you?" whispered the top sergeant peevishly.

Fuselli stood still with his fists clenched. The blood flamed through his head, making his scalp tingle.

Still the top sergeant was the top sergeant, came the thought. It would never do to get in wrong with him. Fuselli's legs moved him automatically back into a corner of the court, where he leaned against the damp wall; glaring with smarting eyes at the two women who stood talking outside the kitchen door, and at the dark shadow behind the hogshead. At last, after several smacking kisses, the women went away and the kitchen door closed. The bell in the church spire struck eleven slowly and mournfully. When it had ceased striking, Fuselli heard a discreet tapping and saw the shadow of the top sergeant against the door. As he slipped in, Fuselli heard the top sergeant's good-natured voice in a large stage whisper, followed by a choked laugh from Yvonne. The door closed and the light was extinguished, leaving the court in darkness except for a faint marbled glow in the sky.

Fuselli strode out, making as much noise as he could with his heels on the cobble stones. The streets of the town were silent under the pale moon. In the square the fountain sounded loud and metallic. He gave up his pass to the guard and strode glumly towards the barracks. At the door he met a man with a pack on his back.

"Hullo, Fuselli," said a voice he knew. "Is my old bunk still there?"

"Damned if I know," said Fuselli; "I thought they'd shipped you home."

The corporal who had been on the Red Sox outfield broke into a fit of coughing.

"Hell, no," he said. "They kep' me at that goddam hospital till they saw I wasn't goin' to die right away, an' then they told me to come back to my outfit. So here I am!"

"Did they bust you?" said Fuselli with sudden eagerness.

"Hell, no. Why should they? They ain't gone and got a new corporal, have they?"

"No, not exactly," said Fuselli.

V

Meadville stood near the camp gate watching the motor trucks go by on the main road. Grey, lumbering, and mud-covered, they throbbed by sloughing in and out of the mud holes in the worn road in an endless train stretching as far as he could see into the town and as far as he could see up the road.

He stood with his legs far apart and spat into the center of the road; then he turned to the corporal who had been in the Red Sox outfield and said:

"I'll be goddamned if there ain't somethin' doin'!"

"A hell of a lot doin'," said the corporal, shaking his head. "Seen that guy Daniels who's been to the front?"

"No."

"Well, he says hell's broke loose. Hell's broke loose!"

"What's happened? . . . Be gorry, we may see some active service," said Meadville, grinning. "By God, I'd give the best colt on my ranch to see some action."

"Got a ranch?" asked the corporal.

The motor trucks kept on grinding past monotonously; their drivers were so splashed with mud it was hard to see what uniform they wore.

"What d'ye think?" asked Meadville. "Think I keep store?"

Fuselli walked past them towards the town.

"Say, Fuselli," shouted Meadville. "Corporal says hell's broke loose out there. We may smell gunpowder yet."

Fuselli stopped and joined them.

"I guess poor old Bill Grey's smelt plenty of gunpowder by this time," he said.

"I wish I had gone with him," said Meadville. "I'll try that little trick myself now the good weather's come on if we don't get a move on soon."

"Too damn risky!"

"Listen to the kid. It'll be too damn risky in the trenches. . . . Or do you think you're goin' to get a cushy job in camp here?"

"Hell, no! I want to go to the front. I don't want to stay in this hole."

"Well?"

"But ain't no good throwin' yerself in where it don't do no good. . . . A guy wants to get on in this army if he can."

"What's the good o' gettin' on?" said the corporal. "Won't get home a bit sooner."

"Hell! but you're a non-com."

Another train of motor trucks went by, drowning their talk.

Fuselli was packing medical supplies in a box in a great brownish warehouse full of packing cases where a little sun filtered in through the dusty air at the corrugated sliding tin doors. As he worked, he listened to Daniels talking to Meadville who worked beside him.

"An' the gas is the goddamndest stuff I ever heard of," he was saying. "I've seen fellers with their arms swelled up to twice the size like blisters from it. Mustard gas, they call it."

"What did you get to go to the hospital?" said Meadville.

"Only pneumonia," said Daniels, "but I had a buddy who was split right in half by a piece of a shell. He was standin' as near me as you are an' was whistlin' 'Tipperary' under his breath when all at once there was a big spurt o' blood an' there he was with his chest split in half an' his head hangin' by a thread like."

Meadville moved his quid of tobacco from one cheek to the other and spat on to the sawdust of the floor. The men within earshot stopped working and looked admiringly at Daniels.

"Well; what d'ye reckon's goin' on at the front now?" said Meadville.

"Damned if I know. The goddam hospital at Orleans was so full up there was guys in stretchers waiting all day on the pavement outside. I know that. . . . Fellers there said hell'd broke loose for fair. Looks to me like the Fritzies was advancin'."

Meadville looked at him incredulously.

"Those skunks?" said Fuselli. "Why they can't advance. They're starvin' to death."

"The hell they are," said Daniels. "I guess you believe everything you see in the papers."

Eyes looked at Daniels indignantly. They all went on working in silence.

Suddenly the lieutenant, looking strangely flustered, strode into the warehouse, leaving the tin door open behind him.

"Can anyone tell me where Sergeant Osler is?"

"He was here a few minutes ago," spoke up Fuselli.

"Well, where is he now?" snapped the lieutenant angrily.

"I don't know, sir," mumbled Fuselli, flushing.

"Go and see if you can find him."

Fuselli went off to the other end of the warehouse. Outside the door he stopped and bit off a cigarette in a leisurely fashion. His blood boiled sullenly. How the hell should he know where the top sergeant was? They didn't expect him to be a mind-reader, did they? And all the flood of bitterness that had been collecting in his spirit seethed to the surface. They had not treated him right. He felt full of hopeless anger against this vast treadmill to which he was bound. The endless succession of the days, all alike, all subject to orders, to the interminable monotony of drills and line-ups, passed before his mind. He felt he couldn't go on, yet he knew that he must and would go on, that there was no stopping, that his feet would go on beating in time to the steps of the treadmill.

He caught sight of the sergeant coming towards the warehouse, across the new green grass, scarred by the marks of truck wheels.

"Sarge," he called. Then he went up to him mysteriously. "The loot wants to see you at once in Warehouse B."

He slouched back to his work, arriving just in time to hear the lieutenant say in a severe voice to the sergeant:

"Sergeant, do you know how to draw up court-martial papers?"

"Yes, sir," said the sergeant, a look of surprise on his face. He followed the precise steps of the lieutenant out of the door.

Fuselli had a moment of panic terror, during which he went on working methodically, although his hands trembled. He was searching his memory for some infringement of a regulation that might be charged against him. The terror passed as fast as it had come. Of course he had no reason to fear. He laughed softly to himself. What a fool he'd been to get scared like that, and a summary court-martial couldn't do much to you anyway. He went on working as fast and as carefully as he could, through the long monotonous afternoon.

That night nearly the whole company gathered in a group at the end of the barracks. Both sergeants were away. The corporal said he knew nothing, and got sulkily into bed, where he lay, rolled in his blankets, shaken by fit after fit of coughing.

At last someone said:

"I bet that kike Eisenstein's turned out to be a spy."

"I bet he has too."

"He's foreign born, ain't he? Born in Poland or some goddam place."

"He always did talk queer."

"I always thought," said Fuselli, "he'd get into trouble talking the way he did."

"How'd he talk?" asked Daniels.

"Oh, he said that war was wrong and all that goddamned pro-German stuff."

"D'ye know what they did out at the front?" said Daniels. "In the second division they made two fellers dig their own graves and then shot 'em for sayin' the war was wrong."

"Hell, they did?"

"You're goddam right, they did. I tell you, fellers, it don't do to monkey with the buzz-saw in this army."

"For God's sake shut up. Taps has blown. Meadville, turn the lights out!" said the corporal angrily. The barracks was dark, full of a sound of men undressing in their bunks, and of whispered talk.

The company was lined up for morning mess. The sun that had just risen was shining in rosily through the soft clouds of the sky. The sparrows kept up a great clattering in the avenue of plane trees. Their riotous chirping could be heard above the sound of motors starting that came from a shed opposite the mess shack.

The sergeant appeared suddenly; walking past with his shoulders stiff, so that everyone knew at once that something important was going on.

"Attention, men, a minute," he said.

Mess kits clattered as the men turned round.

"After mess I want you to go immediately to barracks and roll your packs. After that every man must stand by his pack until orders come." The company cheered and mess kits clattered together like cymbals.

"As you were," shouted the top sergeant jovially.

Gluey oatmeal and greasy bacon were hurriedly bolted down, and every man in the company, his heart pounding, ran to the barracks to do up his pack, feeling proud under the envious eyes of the company at the other end of the shack that had received no orders.

When the packs were done up, they sat on the empty hunks and drummed their feet against the wooden partitions, waiting.

"I don't suppose we'll leave here till hell freezes over," said Meadville, who was doing up the last strap on his pack.

"It's always like this. . . . You break your neck to obey orders an'. . ."

"Outside!" shouted the sergeant, poking his head in the door. "Fall in! Atten-shun!"

The lieutenant in his trench coat and in a new pair of roll puttees stood facing the company, looking solemn.

"Men," he said, biting off his words as a man bites through a piece of hard stick candy; "one of your number is up for court-martial for possibly disloyal statements found in a letter addressed to friends at home. I have been extremely grieved to find anything of this sort in any company of mine; I don't believe there is another man in the company . . . . low enough to hold . . . entertain such ideas. . . ."

Every man in the company stuck out his chest, vowing inwardly to entertain no ideas at all rather than run the risk of calling forth such disapproval from the lieutenant. The lieutenant paused:

"All I can say is if there is any such man in the company, he had better keep his mouth shut and be pretty damn careful what he writes home. . . . Dismissed!"

He shouted the order grimly, as if it were the order for the execution of the offender.

"That goddam skunk Eisenstein," said someone.

The lieutenant heard it as he walked away.

"Oh, sergeant," he said familiarly; "I think the others have got the right stuff in them."

The company went into the barracks and waited.

The sergeant-major's office was full of a clicking of typewriters, and was overheated by a black stove that stood in the middle of the floor, letting out occasional little puffs of smoke from a crack in the stove pipe. The sergeant-major was a small man with a fresh boyish face and a drawling voice who lolled behind a large typewriter reading a magazine that lay on his lap.

Fuselli slipped in behind the typewriter and stood with his cap in his hand beside the sergeant-major's chair.

"Well what do you want?" asked the sergeant-major gruffly.

"A feller told me, Sergeant-Major, that you was lookin' for a man with optical experience;" Fuselli's voice was velvety.

"Well?"

"I worked three years in an optical-goods store at home in Frisco."

"What's your name, rank, company?"

"Daniel Fuselli, Private 1st-class, Company C, medical supply warehouse."

"All right, I'll attend to it."

"But, sergeant."

"All right; out with what you've got to say, quick." The sergeant-major fingered the leaves of his magazine impatiently.

"My company's all packed up to go. The transfer'll have to be today, sergeant."

"Why the hell didn't you come in earlier? . . . Stevens, make out a transfer to headquarters company and get the major to sign it when he goes through. . . . That's the way it always is," he cried, leaning back tragically in his swivel chair. "Everybody always puts everything off on me at the last minute."

"Thank you, sir," said Fuselli, smiling.

The sergeant-major ran his hand through his hair and took up his magazine again peevishly.

Fuselli hurried back to barracks where he found the company still waiting. Several men were crouched in a circle playing craps. The rest lounged in their bare bunks or fiddled with their packs. Outside it had begun to rain softly, and a smell of wet sprouting earth came in through the open door. Fuselli sat on the floor beside his bunk throwing his knife down so that it stuck in the boards between his knees. He was whistling softly to himself. The day dragged on. Several times he heard the town clock strike in the distance.

At last the top sergeant came in, shaking the water off his slicker, a serious, important expression on his face.

"Inspection of medical belts," he shouted. "Everybody open up their belt and lay it on the foot of their bunk and stand at attention on the left side."

The lieutenant and a major appeared suddenly at one end of the barracks and came through slowly, pulling the little packets out of the belts. The men looked at them out of the corners of their eyes. As they examined the belts, they chatted easily, as if they had been alone.

"Yes," said the major. "We're in for it this time. . . . That damned offensive."

"Well, we'll be able to show 'em what we're good for," said the lieutenant, laughing. "We haven't had a chance yet."

"Hum! Better mark that belt, lieutenant, and have it changed. Been to the front yet?"

"No, sir."

"Hum, well. . . . You'll look at things differently when you have," said the major.

The lieutenant frowned.

"Well, on the whole, lieutenant, your outfit is in very good shape. . . . At ease, men!" The lieutenant and the major stood at the door a moment raising the collars of their coats; then they dove out into the rain.

A few minutes later the sergeant came in.

"All right, get your slickers on and line up."

They stood lined up in the rain for a long while. It was a leaden afternoon. The even clouds had a faint coppery tinge. The rain beat in their faces, making them tingle. Fuselli was looking anxiously at the sergeant. At last the lieutenant appeared.

"Attention!" cried the sergeant.

The roll was called and a new man fell in at the end of the line, a tall man with large protruding eyes like a calf's.

"Private 1st-class Daniel Fuselli, fall out and report to headquarters company!"

Fuselli saw a look of surprise come over men's faces. He smiled wanly at Meadville.

"Sergeant, take the men down to the station."

"Squads, right," cried the sergeant. "March!"

The company tramped off into the streaming rain.

Fuselli went back to the barracks, took off his pack and slicker and wiped the water off his face.

The rails gleamed gold in the early morning sunshine above the deep purple cinders of the track. Fuselli's eyes followed the track until it curved into a cutting where the wet clay was a bright orange in the clear light. The station platform, where puddles from the night's rain glittered as the wind ruffled them, was empty. Fuselli started walking up and down with his hands in his pockets. He had been sent down to unload some supplies that were coming on that morning's train. He felt free and successful since he joined the headquarters company. At last, he told himself, he had a job where he could show what he was good for. He walked up and down whistling shrilly.

A train pulled slowly into the station. The engine stopped to take water and the couplings clanked all down the line of cars. The platform was suddenly full of men in khaki, stamping their feet, running up and down shouting.

"Where you guys goin'?" asked Fuselli.

"We're bound for Palm Beach. Don't we look like it?" someone snarled in reply.

But Fuselli had seen a familiar face. He was shaking hands with two browned men whose faces were grimy with days of travelling in freight cars.

"Hullo, Chrisfield. Hullo, Andrews!" he cried. "When did you fellows get over here?"

"Oh, 'bout four months ago," said Chrisfield, whose black eyes looked at Fuselli searchingly. "Oh! Ah 'member you. You're Fuselli. We was at trainin' camp together. 'Member him, Andy?"

"Sure," said Andrews.

"How are you makin' out?"

"Fine," said Fuselli. "I'm in the optical department here."

"Where the hell's that?"

"Right here." Fuselli pointed vaguely behind the station.

"We've been training about four months near Bordeaux," said Andrews; "and now we're going to see what it's like."

The whistle blew and the engine started puffing hard. Clouds of white steam filled the station platform, where the soldiers scampered for their cars.

"Good luck!" said Fuselli; but Andrews and Chrisfield had already gone. He saw them again as the train pulled out, two brown and dirt-grimed faces among many other brown and dirt-grimed faces. The steam floated up tinged with yellow in the bright early morning air as the last car of the train disappeared round the curve into the cutting.

The dust rose thickly about the worn broom. As it was a dark morning, very little light filtered into the room full of great white packing cases, where Fuselli was sweeping. He stopped now and then and leaned on his broom. Far away he heard a sound of trains shunting and shouts and the sound of feet tramping in unison from the drill ground. The building where he was was silent. He went on sweeping, thinking of his company tramping off through the streaming rain, and of those fellows he had known in training camp in America, Andrews and Chrisfield, jolting in box cars towards the front, where Daniel's buddy had had his chest split in half by a piece of shell. And he'd written home he'd been made a corporal. What was he going to do when letters came for him, addressed Corporal Dan Fuselli? Putting the broom away, he dusted the yellow chair and the table covered with order slips that stood in the middle of the piles of packing boxes. The door slammed somewhere below and there was a step on the stairs that led to the upper part of the warehouse. A little man with a monkey-like greyish-brown face and spectacles appeared and slipped out of his overcoat, like a very small bean popping out of a very large pod.

The sergeant's stripes looked unusually wide and conspicuous on his thin arm.

He grunted at Fuselli, sat down at the desk, and began at once peering among the order slips.

"Anything in our mailbox this morning?" he asked Fuselli in a hoarse voice.

"It's all there, sergeant," said Fuselli.

The sergeant peered about the desk some more.

"Ye'll have to wash that window today," he said after a pause. "Major's likely to come round here any time. . . . Ought to have been done yesterday."

"All right," said Fuselli dully.

He slouched over to the corner of the room, got the worn broom and began sweeping down the stairs. The dust rose about him, making him cough. He stopped and leaned on the broom. He thought of all the days that had gone by since he'd last seen those fellows, Andrews and Chrisfield, at training camp in America; and of all the days that would go by. He started sweeping again, sweeping the dust down from stair to stair.

Fuselli sat on the end of his bunk. He had just shaved. It was a Sunday morning and he looked forward to having the afternoon off. He rubbed his face on his towel and got to his feet. Outside, the rain fell in great silvery sheets, so that the noise on the tar-paper roof of the barracks was almost deafening.

Fuselli noticed, at the other end of the row of bunks, a group of men who all seemed to be looking at the same thing. Rolling down his sleeves, with his tunic hitched over one arm, he walked down to see what was the matter. Through the patter of the rain, he heard a thin voice say:

"It ain't no use, sergeant, I'm sick. I ain't a' goin' to get up."

"The kid's crazy," someone beside Fuselli said, turning away.

"You get up this minute," roared the sergeant. He was a big man with black hair who looked like a lumberman. He stood over the bunk. In the bunk at the end of a bundle of blankets was the chalk-white face of Stockton. The boy's teeth were clenched, and his eyes were round and protruding, it seemed from terror.

"You get out o' bed this minute," roared the sergeant again.

The boy was silent; his white cheeks quivered.

"What the hell's the matter with him?"

"Why don't you yank him out yourself, Sarge?"

"You get out of bed this minute," shouted the sergeant again, paying no attention.

The men gathered about walked away. Fuselli watched fascinated from a little distance.

"All right, then, I'll get the lieutenant. This is a court-martial offence. Here, Morton and Morrison, you're guards over this man."

The boy lay still in his blankets. He closed his eyes. By the way the blanket rose and fell over his chest, they could see that he was breathing heavily.

"Say, Stockton, why don't you get up, you fool?" said Fuselli. "You can't buck the whole army."

The boy didn't answer.

Fuselli walked away.

"He's crazy," he muttered.

The lieutenant was a stoutish red-faced man who came in puffing followed by the tall sergeant. He stopped and shook the water off his campaign hat. The rain kept up its deafening patter on the roof.

"Look here, are you sick? If you are, report sick call at once," said the lieutenant in an elaborately kind voice.

The boy looked at him dully and did not answer.

"You should get up and stand at attention when an officer speaks to you."

"I ain't goin' to get up," came the thin voice.

The officer's red face became crimson.

"Sergeant, what's the matter with the man?" he asked in a furious tone.

"I can't do anything with him, lieutenant. I think he's gone crazy."

"Rubbish. . . . Mere insubordination. . . . You're under arrest, d'ye hear?" he shouted towards the bed.

There was no answer. The rain pattered hard on the roof.

"Have him brought down to the guardhouse, by force if necessary," snapped the lieutenant. He strode towards the door. "And sergeant, start drawing up court-martial papers at once." The door slammed behind him.

"Now you've got to get him up," said the sergeant to the two guards.

Fuselli walked away.

"Ain't some people damn fools?" he said to a man at the other end of the barracks. He stood looking out of the window at the bright sheets of the rain.

"Well, get him up," shouted the sergeant.

The boy lay with his eyes closed, his chalk-white face half-hidden by the blankets; he was very still.

"Well, will you get up and go to the guardhouse, or have we to carry you there?" shouted the sergeant.

The guards laid hold of him gingerly and pulled him up to a sitting posture.

"All right, yank him out of bed."

The frail form in khaki shirt and whitish drawers was held up for a moment between the two men. Then it fell a limp heap on the floor.

"Say, Sarge, he's fainted."

"The hell he has. . . . Say, Morrison, ask one of the orderlies to come up from the Infirmary."

"He ain't fainted. . . . The kid's dead," said the other man. "Give me a hand."

The sergeant helped lift the body on the bed again.

"Well, I'll be goddamned," said the sergeant.

The eyes had opened. They covered the head with a blanket.

PART THREE

MACHINES

I

The fields and the misty blue-green woods slipped by slowly as the box car rumbled and jolted over the rails, now stopping for hours on sidings amid meadows, where it was quiet and where above the babel of voices of the regiment you could hear the skylarks, now clattering fast over bridges and along the banks of jade-green rivers where the slim poplars were just coming into leaf and where now and then a fish jumped. The men crowded in the door, grimy and tired, leaning on each other's shoulders and watching the plowed lands slip by and the meadows where the golden-green grass was dappled with buttercups, and the villages of huddled red roofs lost among pale budding trees and masses of peach blossom. Through the smells of steam and coal smoke and of unwashed bodies in uniforms came smells of moist fields and of manure from fresh-sowed patches and of cows and pasture lands just coming into flower.

"Must be right smart o' craps in this country. . . . Ain't like that damn Polignac, Andy?" said Chrisfield.

"Well they made us drill so hard there wasn't any time for the grass to grow."

"You're damn right there warn't."

"Ah'd lak te live in this country a while," said Chrisfield.

"We might ask 'em to let us off right here."

"Can't be that the front's like this," said Judkins, poking his head out between Andrews's and Chrisfield's heads so that the bristles of his unshaven chin rubbed against Chrisfield's cheek. It was a large square head with closely cropped light hair and porcelain-blue eyes under lids that showed white in the red sunburned face, and a square jaw made a little grey by the sprouting beard.

"Say, Andy, how the hell long have we all been in this goddam train? . . . Ah've done lost track o' the time. . . ."

"What's the matter; are you gettin' old, Chris?" asked Judkins laughing.

Chrisfield had slipped out of the place he held and began poking himself in between Andrews and Judkins.

"We've been on this train four days and five nights, an' we've got half a day's rations left, so we must be getting somewhere," said Andrews.

"It can't be like this at the front."

"It must be spring there as well as here," said Andrews.

It was a day of fluffy mauve-tinted clouds that moved across the sky, sometimes darkening to deep blue where a small rainstorm trailed across the hills, sometimes brightening to moments of clear sunlight that gave blue shadows to the poplars and shone yellow on the smoke of the engine that puffed on painfully at the head of the long train.

"Funny, ain't it? How li'l everythin' is," said Chrisfield. "Out Indiana way we wouldn't look at a cornfield that size. But it sort o' reminds me the way it used to be out home in the spring o' the year."

"I'd like to see Indiana in the springtime," said Andrews.

"Well you'll come out when the wa's over and us guys is all home . . . won't you, Andy?"

"You bet I will."

They were going into the suburbs of a town. Rows and clusters of little brick and stucco houses were appearing along the roads. It began to rain from a sky full of lights of amber and lilac color. The slate roofs and the pinkish-grey streets of the town shone cheerfully in the rain. The little patches of garden were all vivid emerald-green. Then they were looking at rows and rows of red chimney pots over wet slate roofs that reflected the bright sky. In the distance rose the purple-grey spire of a church and the irregular forms of old buildings. They passed through a station.

"Dijon," read Andrews. On the platform were French soldiers in their blue coats and a good sprinkling of civilians.

"Gee, those are about the first real civies I've seen since I came overseas," said Judkins. "Those goddam country people down at Polignac didn't look like real civilians. There's folks dressed like it was New York."

They had left the station and were rumbling slowly past interminable freight trains. At last the train came to a dead stop.

A whistle sounded.

"Don't nobody get out," shouted the sergeant from the car ahead.

"Hell! They keep you in this goddam car like you was a convict," muttered Chrisfield.

"I'd like to get out and walk around Dijon."

"O boy!"

"I swear I'd make a bee line for a dairy lunch," said Judkins.

"Hell of a fine dairy lunch you'll find among those goddam frogs. No, vin blank is all you'ld get in that goddam town."

"Ah'm goin' to sleep," said Chrisfield. He stretched himself out on the pile of equipment at the end of the car. Andrews sat down near him and stared at his mud-caked boots, running one of his long hands, as brown as Chrisfield's now, through his light short-cut hair.

Chrisfield lay looking at the gaunt outline of Andrews's face against the light through half-closed eyes. And he felt a warm sort of a smile inside him as he said to himself: "He's a damn good kid." Then he thought of the spring in the hills of southern Indiana and the mocking-bird singing in the moonlight among the flowering locust trees behind the house. He could almost smell the heavy sweetness of the locust blooms, as he used to smell them sitting on the steps after supper, tired from a day's heavy plowing, while the clatter of his mother's housework came from the kitchen. He didn't wish he was back there, but it was pleasant to think of it now and then, and how the yellow farmhouse looked and the red barn where his father never had been able to find time to paint the door, and the tumble-down cowshed where the shingles were always coming off. He wondered dully what it would be like out there at the front. It couldn't be green and pleasant, the way the country was here. Fellows always said it was hell out there. Well, he didn't give a damn. He went to sleep.

He woke up gradually, the warm comfort of sleep giving place slowly to the stiffness of his uncomfortable position with the hobnails of a boot from the back of a pack sticking into his shoulder. Andrews was sitting in the same position, lost in thought. The rest of the men sat at the open doors or sprawled over the equipment.

Chrisfield got up, stretched himself, yawned, and went to the door to look out. There was a heavy important step on the gravel outside. A large man with black eyebrows that met over his nose and a very black stubbly beard passed the car. There were a sergeant's stripes on his arm.

"Say, Andy," cried Chrisfield, "that bastard is a sergeant."

"Who's that?" asked Andrews getting up with a smile, his blue eyes looking mildly into Chrisfield's black ones.

"You know who Ah mean."

Under their heavy tan Chrisfield's rounded cheeks were flushed. His eyes snapped under their long black lashes. His fists were clutched.

"Oh, I know, Chris. I didn't know he was in this regiment."

"God damn him!" muttered Chrisfield in a low voice, throwing himself down on his packs again.

"Hold your horses, Chris," said Andrews. "We may all cash in our checks before long . . . no use letting things worry us."

"I don't give a damn if we do."

"Nor do I, now." Andrews sat down beside Chrisfield again.

After a while the train got jerkily into motion. The wheels rumbled and clattered over the rails and the clots of mud bounced up and down on the splintered boards of the floor. Chrisfield pillowed his head on his arm and went to sleep again, still smarting from the flush of his anger.

Andrews looked out through his fingers at the swaying black box car, at the men sprawled about on the floor, their heads nodding with each jolt, and at the mauve-grey clouds and bits of sparkling blue sky that he could see behind the silhouettes of the heads and shoulders of the men who stood in the doors. The wheels ground on endlessly.

The car stopped with a jerk that woke up all the sleepers and threw one man off his feet. A whistle blew shrilly outside.

"All right, out of the cars! Snap it up; snap it up!" yelled the sergeant.

The men piled out stiffly, handing the equipment out from hand to hand till it formed a confused heap of packs and rifles outside. All down the train at each door there was a confused pile of equipment and struggling men.

"Snap it up. . . . Full equipment. . . . Line up!" the sergeant yelled.

The men fell into line slowly, with their packs and rifles. Lieutenants hovered about the edges of the forming lines, tightly belted into their stiff trench coats, scrambling up and down the coal piles of the siding. The men were given "at ease" and stood leaning on their rifles staring at a green water-tank on three wooden legs, over the top of which had been thrown a huge piece of torn grey cheese-cloth. When the confused sound of tramping feet subsided, they could hear a noise in the distance, like someone lazily shaking a piece of heavy sheet-iron. The sky was full of little dabs of red, purple and yellow and the purplish sunset light was over everything.

The order came to march. They marched down a rutted road where the puddles were so deep they had continually to break ranks to avoid them. In a little pine-wood on one side were rows of heavy motor trucks and ammunition caissons; supper was cooking in a field kitchen about which clustered the truck drivers in their wide visored caps. Beyond the wood the column turned off into a field behind a little group of stone and stucco houses that had lost their roofs. In the field they halted. The grass was brilliant emerald and the wood and the distant hills were shades of clear deep blue. Wisps of pale-blue mist lay across the field. In the turf here and there were small clean bites, that might have been made by some strange animal. The men looked at them curiously.

"No lights, remember we're in sight of the enemy. A match might annihilate the detachment," announced the lieutenant dramatically after having given the orders for the pup tents to be set up.

When the tents were ready, the men stood about in the chilly white mist that kept growing denser, eating their cold rations. Everywhere were grumbling snorting voices.

"God, let's turn in, Chris, before our bones are frozen," said Andrews.

Guards had been posted and walked up and down with a business-like stride, peering now and then suspiciously into the little wood where the truck-drivers were.

Chrisfield and Andrews crawled into their little tent and rolled up together in their blankets, getting as close to each other as they could. At first it was very cold and hard, and they squirmed about restlessly, but gradually the warmth from their bodies filled their thin blankets and their muscles began to relax. Andrews went to sleep first and Chrisfield lay listening to his deep breathing. There was a frown on his face. He was thinking of the man who had walked past the train at Dijon. The last time he had seen that man Anderson was at training camp. He had only been a corporal then. He remembered the day the man had been made corporal. It had not been long before that that Chrisfield had drawn his knife on him, one night in the barracks. A fellow had caught his hand just in time. Anderson had looked a bit pale that time and had walked away. But he'd never spoken a word to Chrisfield since. As he lay with his eyes closed, pressed close against Andrews's limp sleeping body, Chrisfield could see the man's face, the eyebrows that joined across the nose and the jaw, always blackish from the heavy beard, that looked blue when he had just shaved. At last the tenseness of his mind slackened; he thought of women for a moment, of a fair-haired girl he'd seen from the train, and then suddenly crushing sleepiness closed down on him and everything went softly warmly black, as he drifted off to sleep with no sense but the coldness of one side and the warmth of his bunkie's body on the other.

In the middle of the night he awoke and crawled out of the tent. Andrews followed him. Their teeth chattered a little, and they stretched their legs stiffly. It was cold, but the mist had vanished. The stars shone brilliantly. They walked out a little way into the field away from the bunch of tents.

A faint rustling and breathing noise, as of animals. herded together, came from the sleeping regiment. Somewhere a brook made a shrill gurgling. They strained their ears, but they could hear no guns. They stood side by side looking up at the multitudes of stars.

"That's Orion," said Andrews.

"What?"

"That bunch of stars there is called Orion. D'you see 'em. It's supposed to look like a man with a bow, but he always looks to me like a fellow striding across the sky."

"Some stars tonight, ain't there? Gee, what's that?"

Behind the dark hills a glow rose and fell like the glow in a forge.

"The front must be that way," said Andrews, shivering.

"I guess we'll know tomorrow."

"Yes; tomorrow night we'll know more about it," said Andrews.

They stood silent a moment listening to the noise the brook made.

"God, it's quiet, ain't it? This can't be the front. Smell that?"

"What is it?"

"Smells like an apple tree in bloom somewhere. . . . Hell, let's git in, before our blankets git cold."

Andrews was still staring at the group of stars he had said was Orion.

Chrisfield pulled him by the arm. They crawled into their tent again, rolled up together and immediately were crushed under an exhausted sleep.

As far ahead of him as Chrisfield could see were packs and heads with caps at a variety of angles, all bobbing up and down with the swing of the brisk marching time. A fine warm rain was falling, mingling with the sweat that ran down his face. The column had been marching a long time along a straight road that was worn and scarred with heavy traffic. Fields and hedges where clusters of yellow flowers were in bloom had given place to an avenue of poplars. The light wet trunks and the stiff branches hazy with green filed by, interminable, as interminable as the confused tramp of feet and jingle of equipment that sounded in his ears.

"Say, are we goin' towards the front?"

"Goddamned if I know."

"Ain't no front within miles."

Men's sentences came shortly through their heavy breathing.

The column shifted over to the side of the road to avoid a train of motor trucks going the other way. Chrisfield felt the heavy mud spurt up over him as truck after truck rumbled by. With the wet back of one hand he tried to wipe it off his face, but the grit, when he rubbed it, hurt his skin, made tender by the rain. He swore long and whiningly, half aloud. His rifle felt as heavy as an iron girder.

They entered a village of plaster-and-timber houses. Through open doors they could see into comfortable kitchens where copper pots gleamed and where the floors were of clean red tiles. In front of some of the houses were little gardens full of crocuses and hyacinths where box-bushes shone a very dark green in the rain. They marched through the square with its pavement of little yellow rounded cobbles, its grey church with a pointed arch in the door, its cafés with names painted over them. Men and women looked out of doors and windows. The column perceptibly slackened its speed, but kept on, and as the houses dwindled and became farther apart along the road the men's hope of stopping vanished. Ears were deafened by the confused tramp of feet on the macadam road. Men's feet seemed as lead, as if all the weight of the pack hung on them. Shoulders, worn callous, began to grow tender and sore under the constant sweating. Heads drooped. Each man's eyes were on the heels of the man ahead of him that rose and fell, rose and fell endlessly. Marching became for each man a personal struggle with his pack, that seemed to have come alive, that seemed something malicious and overpowering, wrestling to throw him.

The rain stopped and the sky brightened a little, taking on pale yellowish lights as if the clouds that hid the sun were growing thin.

The column halted at the edge of a group of farms and barns that scattered along the road. The men sprawled in all directions along the roadside hiding the bright green grass with the mud-color of their uniforms.

Chrisfield lay in the field beside the road, pressing his hot face into the wet sprouting clover. The blood throbbed through his ears. His arms and legs seemed to cleave to the ground, as if he would never be able to move them again. He closed his eyes. Gradually a cold chill began stealing through his body. He sat up and slipped his arms out of the harness of his pack. Someone was handing him a cigarette, and he sniffed a little acrid sweet smoke.

Andrews was lying beside him, his head propped against his pack, smoking, and poking a cigarette towards his friend with a muddy hand. His blue eyes looked strangely from out the flaming red of his mud-splotched face.

Chrisfield took the cigarette, and fumbled in his pocket for a match.

"That nearly did it for me," said Andrews.

Chrisfield grunted. He pulled greedily on the cigarette.

A whistle blew.

Slowly the men dragged themselves off the ground and fell into line, drooping under the weight of their equipment.

The companies marched off separately.

Chrisfield overheard the lieutenant saying to a sergeant:

"Damn fool business that. Why the hell couldn't they have sent us here in the first place?"

"So we ain't goin' to the front after all?" said the sergeant.

"Front, hell!" said the lieutenant. The lieutenant was a small man who looked like a jockey with a coarse red face, which, now that he was angry, was almost purple.

"I guess they're going to quarter us here," said somebody.

Immediately everybody began saying: "We're going to be quartered here."

They stood waiting in formation a long while, the packs cutting into their backs and shoulders.

At last the sergeant shouted out:

"All right, take yer stuff upstairs." Stumbling on each others' heels they climbed up into a dark loft, where the air was heavy with the smell of hay and with an acridity of cow manure from the stables below. There was a little straw in the corners, on which those who got there first spread their blankets.

Chrisfield and Andrews tucked themselves in a corner from which through a hole where the tiles had fallen off the roof, they could see down into the barnyard, where white and speckled chickens pecked about with jerky movements. A middle-aged woman stood in the doorway of the house looking suspiciously at the files of khaki-clad soldiers that shuffled slowly into the barns by every door.

An officer went up to her, a little red book in his hand. A conversation about some matter proceeded painfully. The officer grew very red. Andrews threw back his head and laughed, luxuriously rolling from side to side in the straw. Chrisfield laughed too, he hardly knew why. Over their heads they could hear the feet of pigeons on the roof, and a constant drowsy rou-cou-cou-cou.

Through the barnyard smells began to drift the greasiness of food cooking in the field kitchen.

"Ah hope they give us somethin' good to eat," said Chrisfield. "Ah'm hongry as a thrasher."

"So am I," said Andrews.

"Say, Andy, you kin talk their language a li'l', can't ye?"

Andrews nodded his head vaguely.

"Well, maybe we kin git some aigs or somethin' out of the lady down there. Will ye try after mess?"

"All right."

They both lay back in the straw and closed their eyes. Their cheeks still burned from the rain. Everything seemed very peaceful; the men sprawled about talking in low drowsy voices. Outside, another shower had come up and beat softly on the tiles of the roof. Chrisfield thought he had never been so comfortable in his life, although his soaked shoes pinched his cold feet and his knees were wet and cold. But in the drowsiness of the rain and of voices talking quietly about him, he fell asleep.

He dreamed he was home in Indiana, but instead of his mother cooking at the stove in the kitchen, there was the Frenchwoman who had stood in the farmhouse door, and near her stood a lieutenant with a little red book in his hand. He was eating cornbread and syrup off a broken plate. It was fine cornbread with a great deal of crust on it, crisp and hot, on which the butter was cold and sweet to his tongue. Suddenly he stopped eating and started swearing, shouting at the top of his lungs: "You goddam . . ." he started, but he couldn't seem to think of anything more to say. "You goddam . . ." he started again. The lieutenant looked towards him, wrinkling his black eyebrows that met across his nose. He was Sergeant Anderson. Chris drew his knife and ran at him, but it was Andy his bunkie he had run his knife into. He threw his arms round Andy's body, crying hot tears. . . . He woke up. Mess kits were clinking all about the dark crowded loft. The men had already started piling down the stairs.

The larks filled the wine-tinged air with a constant chiming of little bells. Chrisfield and Andrews were strolling across a field of white clover that covered the brow of a hill. Below in the valley they could see a cluster of red roofs of farms and the white ribbon of the road where long trains of motor trucks crawled like beetles. The sun had just set behind the blue hills the other side of the shallow valley. The air was full of the smell of clover and of hawthorn from the hedgerows. They took deep breaths as they crossed the field.

"It's great to get away from that crowd," Andrews was saying.

Chrisfield walked on silently, dragging his feet through the matted clover. A leaden dullness weighed like some sort of warm choking coverlet on his limbs, so that it seemed an effort to walk, an effort to speak. Yet under it his muscles were taut and trembling as he had known them to be before when he was about to get into a fight or to make love to a girl.

"Why the hell don't they let us git into it?" he said suddenly.

"Yes, anything'ld be better than this . . . wait, wait, wait."

They walked on, hearing the constant chirrup of the larks, the brush of their feet through the clover, the faint jingle of some coins in Chrisfield's pocket, and in the distance the irregular snoring of an aëroplane motor. As they walked Andrews leaned over from time to time and picked a couple of the white clover flowers.

The aëroplane came suddenly nearer and swooped in a wide curve above the field, drowning every sound in the roar of its exhaust. They made out the figures of the pilot and the observer before the plane rose again and vanished against the ragged purple clouds of the sky. The observer had waved a hand at them as he passed. They stood still in the darkening field, staring up at the sky, where a few larks still hung chirruping.

"Ah'd lahk to be one o' them guys," said Chrisfield.

"You would?"

"God damn it, Ah'd do anything to git out o' this hellish infantry. This ain't no sort o' life for a man to be treated lahk he was a nigger."

"No, it's no sort of life for a man."

"If they'd let us git to the front an' do some fightin' an' be done with it. . . . But all we do is drill and have grenade practice an' drill again and then have bayonet practice an' drill again. 'Nough to drive a feller crazy."

"What the hell's the use of talking about it, Chris? We can't be any lower than we are, can we?" Andrews laughed.

"There's that plane again."

"Where?"

"There, just goin' down behind the piece o' woods."

"That's where their field is."

"Ah bet them guys has a good time. Ah put in an application back in trainin' camp for Aviation. Ain't never heard nothing from it though. If Ah had, Ah wouldn't be lower than dirt in this hawg-pen."

"It's wonderful up here on the hill this evening," said Andrews, looking dreamily at the pale orange band of light where the sun had set. "Let's go down and get a bottle of wine."

"Now yo're talkin'. Ah wonder if that girl's down there tonight."

"Antoinette?"

"Um-hum. . . . Boy, Ah'd lahk to have her all by maself some night."

Their steps grew brisker as they strode along a grass-grown road that led through high hedgerows to a village under the brow of the hill. It was almost dark under the shadow of the bushes on either side. Overhead the purple clouds were washed over by a pale yellow light that gradually faded to grey. Birds chirped and rustled among the young leaves.

Andrews put his hand on Chrisfield's shoulder.

"Let's walk slow," he said, "we don't want to get out of here too soon." He grabbed carelessly at little cluster of hawthorn flowers as he passed them, and seemed reluctant to untangle the thorny branches that caught in his coat and on his loosely wound puttees.

"Hell, man," said Chrisfield, "we won't have time to get a bellyful. It must be gettin' late already."

They hastened their steps again and came in a moment to the first tightly shuttered houses of the village.

In the middle of the road was an M.P., who stood with his legs wide apart, waving his "billy" languidly. He had a red face, his eyes were fixed on the shuttered upper window of a house, through the chinks of which came a few streaks of yellow light. His lips were puckered up as if to whistle, but no sound came. He swayed back and forth indecisively. An officer came suddenly out of the little green door of the house in front of the M.P., who brought his heels together with a jump and saluted, holding his hand a long while to his cap. The officer flicked a hand up hastily to his hat, snatching his cigar out of his mouth for an instant. As the officer's steps grew fainter down the road, the M.P. gradually returned to his former position.

Chrisfield and Andrews had slipped by on the other side and gone in at the door of a small ramshackle house of which the windows were closed by heavy wooden shutters.

"I bet there ain't many of them bastards at the front," said Chris.

"Not many of either kind of bastards," said Andrews laughing, as he closed the door behind them. They were in a room that had once been the parlor of a farmhouse. The chandelier with its bits of crystal and the orange-blossoms on a piece of dusty red velvet under a bell glass on the mantelpiece denoted that. The furniture had been taken out, and four square oak tables crowded in. At one of the tables sat three Americans and at another a very young olive-skinned French soldier, who sat hunched over his table looking moodily down into his glass of wine.

A girl in a faded frock of some purplish material that showed the strong curves of her shoulders and breasts slouched into the room, her hands in the pocket of a dark blue apron against which her rounded forearms showed golden brown. Her face had the same golden tan under a mass of dark blonde hair. She smiled when she saw the two soldiers, drawing her thin lips away from her ugly yellow teeth.

"Ça va bien, Antoinette?" asked Andrews.

"Oui," she said, looking beyond their heads at the French soldier who sat at the other side of the little room.

"A bottle of vin rouge, vite," said Chrisfield.

"Ye needn't be so damn vite about it tonight, Chris," said one of the men at the other table.

"Why?"

"Ain't a-goin' to be no roll call. Corporal tole me hisself. Sarge's gone out to git stewed, an' the Loot's away."

"Sure," said another man, "we kin stay out as late's we goddam please tonight."

"There's a new M.P. in town," said Chrisfield. . . . "Ah saw him maself. . . . You did, too, didn't you, Andy?"

Andrews nodded. He was looking at the Frenchman, who sat with his face in shadow and his black lashes covering his eyes. A purplish flash had suffused the olive skin at his cheekbones.

"Oh, boy," said Chrisfield. "That ole wine sure do go down fast. . . . Say, Antoinette, got any cognac?"

"I'm going to have some more wine," said Andrews.

"Go ahead, Andy; have all ye want. Ah want somethin' to warm ma guts."

Antoinette brought a bottle of cognac and two small glasses and sat down in an empty chair with her red hands crossed on her apron. Her eyes moved from Chrisfield to the Frenchman and back again.

Chrisfield turned a little round in his chair and looked at the Frenchman, feeling in his eyes for a moment a glance of the man's yellowish-brown eyes.

Andrews leaned back against the wall sipping his dark-colored wine, his eyes contracted dreamily, fixed on the shadow of the chandelier, which the cheap oil-lamp with its tin reflector cast on the peeling plaster of the wall opposite.

Chrisfield punched him.

"Wake up, Andy, are you asleep?"

"No," said Andy smiling.

"Have a li'l mo' cognac."

Chrisfield poured out two more glasses unsteadily. His eyes were on Antoinette again. The faded purple frock was hooked at the neck. The first three hooks were undone revealing a V-shape of golden brown skin and a bit of whitish underwear.

"Say, Andy," he said, putting his arm round his friend's neck and talking into his ear, "talk up to her for me, will yer, Andy? . . . Ah won't let that goddam frog get her, no, I won't, by Gawd. Talk up to her for me, Andy."

Andrews laughed.

"I'll try," he said. "But there's always the Queen of Sheba, Chris."

"Antoinette, J'ai un ami," started Andrews, making a gesture with a long dirty hand towards Chris.

Antoinette showed her bad teeth in a smile.

"Joli garçon," said Andrews.

Antoinette's face became impassive and beautiful again. Chrisfield leaned back in his chair with an empty glass in his hand and watched his friend admiringly.

"Antoinette, mon ami vous . . . vous admire," said Andrews in a courtly voice.

A woman put her head in the door. It was the same face and hair as Antoinette's, ten years older, only the skin, instead of being golden brown, was sallow and wrinkled.

"Viens," said the woman in a shrill voice.

Antoinette got up, brushed heavily against Chrisfield's leg as she passed him and disappeared. The Frenchman walked across the room from his corner, saluted gravely and went out.

Chrisfield jumped to his feet. The room was like a white box reeling about him.

"That frog's gone after her," he shouted.

"No, he ain't, Chris," cried someone from the next table. "Sit tight, ole boy. We're bettin' on yer."

"Yes, sit down and have a drink, Chris," said Andy. "I've got to have somethin' more to drink. I haven't had a thing to drink all the evening." He pulled him back into his chair. Chrisfield tried to get up again. Andrews hung on him so that the chair upset. Then both sprawled on the red tiles of the floor.

"The house is pinched!" said a voice.

Chrisfield saw Judkins standing over him, a grin on his large red face. He got to his feet and sat sulkily in his chair again. Andrews was already sitting opposite him, looking impassive as ever.

The tables were full now. Someone was singing in a droning voice.

> "O the oak and the ash and the weeping willow tree,
>   O green grows the grass in God's countree!"

"Ole Indiana," shouted Chris. "That's the only God's country I know." He suddenly felt that he could tell Andy all about his home and the wide corn-fields shimmering and rustling under the July sun, and the creek with red clay banks where he used to go in swimming. He seemed to see it all before him, to smell the winey smell of the silo, to see the cattle, with their chewing mouths always stained a little with green, waiting to get through the gate to the water trough, and the yellow dust and roar of wheat-thrashing, and the quiet evening breeze cooling his throat and neck when he lay out on a shack of hay that he had been tossing all day long under the tingling sun. But all he managed to say was:

"Indiana's God's country, ain't it, Andy?"

"Oh, he has so many," muttered Andrews.

"Ah've seen a hailstone measured nine inches around out home, honest to Gawd, Ah have."

"Must be as good as a barrage."

"Ah'd like to see any goddam barrage do the damage one of our thunder an' lightnin' storms'll do," shouted Chris.

"I guess all the barrage we're going to see's grenade practice."

"Don't you worry, buddy," said somebody across the room. "You'll see enough of it. This war's going to last damn long . . ."

"Ah'd lake to get in some licks at those Huns tonight; honest to Gawd Ah would, Andy," muttered Chris in a low voice. He felt his muscles contract with a furious irritation. He looked through half-closed eyes at the men in the room, seeing them in distorted white lights and reddish shadows. He thought of himself throwing a grenade among a crowd of men. Then he saw the face of Anderson, a ponderous white face with eyebrows that met across his nose and a bluish, shaved chin.

"Where does he stay at, Andy? I'm going to git him."

Andrews guessed what he meant.

"Sit down and have a drink, Chris," he said, "Remember you're going to sleep with the Queen of Sheba tonight."

"Not if I can't git them goddam . . ." his voice trailed off into an inaudible muttering of oaths.

> "O the oak and the ash and the weeping willow tree,
>   O green grows the grass in God's countree,"

somebody sang again.

Chrisfield saw a woman standing beside the table with her back to him, collecting the bottles. Andy was paying her.

"Antoinette," he said. He got to his feet and put his arms round her shoulders. With a quick movement of the elbows she pushed him back into his chair. She turned round. He saw the sallow face and thin breasts of the older sister. She looked in his eyes with surprise. He was grinning drunkenly. As she left the room she made a sign to him with her head to follow her. He got up and staggered out the door, pulling Andrews after him.

In the inner room was a big bed with curtains where the women slept, and the fireplace where they did their cooking. It was dark except for the corner where he and Andrews stood blinking in the glare of a candle on the table. Beyond they could only see ruddy shadows and the huge curtained bed with its red coverlet.

The Frenchman, somewhere in the dark of the room, said something several times.

"Avions boches . . . ss-t!"

They were quiet.

Above them they heard the snoring of aëroplane motors, rising and falling like the buzzing of a fly against a window pane.

They all looked at each other curiously. Antoinette was leaning against the bed, her face expressionless. Her heavy hair had come undone and fell in smoky gold waves about her shoulders. The older woman was giggling.

"Come on, let's see what's doing, Chris," said Andrews.

They went out into the dark village street.

"To hell with women, Chris, this is the war!" cried Andrews in a loud drunken voice as they reeled arm in arm up the street.

"You bet it's the war. . . . Ah'm a-goin' to beat up . . ." Chrisfield felt his friend's hand clapped over his mouth. He let himself go limply, feeling himself pushed to the side of the road.

Somewhere in the dark he heard an officer's voice say:

"Bring those men to me."

"Yes, sir," came another voice.

Slow heavy footsteps came up the road in their direction. Andrews kept pushing him back along the side of a house, until suddenly they both fell sprawling in a manure pit.

"Lie still for God's sake," muttered Andrews, throwing an arm over Chrisfield's chest. A thick odor of dry manure filled their nostrils.

They heard the steps come nearer, wander about irresolutely and then go off in the direction from which they had come. Meanwhile the throb of motors overhead grew louder and louder.

"Well?" came the officer's voice.

"Couldn't find them, sir," mumbled the other voice.

"Nonsense. Those men were drunk," came the officer's voice.

"Yes, sir," came the other voice humbly.

Chrisfield started to giggle. He felt he must yell aloud with laughter.

The nearest motor stopped its singsong roar, making the night seem deathly silent.

Andrews jumped to his feet.

The air was split by a shriek followed by a racking snorting explosion. They saw the wall above their pit light up with a red momentary glare.

Chrisfield got to his feet, expecting to see flaming ruins. The village street was the same as ever. There was a little light from the glow the moon, still under the horizon, gave to the sky. A window in the house opposite showed yellow. In it was a blue silhouette of an officer's cap and uniform.

A little group stood in the street below.

"What was that?" the form in the window was shouting in a peremptory voice.

"German aëroplane just dropped a bomb, Major," came a breathless voice in reply.

"Why the devil don't he close that window?" a voice was muttering all the while. "Juss a target for 'em to aim at . . . a target to aim at."

"Any damage done?" asked the major.

Through the silence the snoring of the motors singsonged ominously overhead, like giant mosquitoes.

"I seem to hear more," said the major, in his drawling voice.

"O yes sir, yes sir, lots," answered an eager voice.

"For God's sake tell him to close the window, Lieutenant," muttered another voice.

"How the hell can I tell him? You tell him."

"We'll all be killed, that's all there is about it."

"There are no shelters or dugouts," drawled the major from the window. "That's Headquarters' fault."

"There's the cellar!" cried the eager voice, again.

"Oh," said the major.

Three snorting explosions in quick succession drowned everything in a red glare. The street was suddenly filled with a scuttle of villagers running to shelter.

"Say, Andy, they may have a roll call," said Chrisfield.

"We'd better cut for home across country," said Andrews.

They climbed cautiously out of their manure pit. Chrisfield was surprised to find that he was trembling. His hands were cold. It was with difficulty he kept his teeth from chattering.

"God, we'll stink for a week."

"Let's git out," muttered Chrisfield, "o' this goddam village."

They ran out through an orchard, broke through a hedge and climbed up the hill across the open fields.

Down the main road an anti-aircraft gun had started barking and the sky sparkled with exploding shrapnel. The "put, put, put" of a machine gun had begun somewhere.

Chrisfield strode up the hill in step with his friend. Behind them bomb followed bomb, and above them the air seemed full of exploding shrapnel and droning planes. The cognac still throbbed a little in their blood. They stumbled against each other now and then as they walked. From the top of the hill they turned and looked back. Chrisfield felt a tremendous elation thumping stronger than the cognac through his veins. Unconsciously he put his arm round his friend's shoulders. They seemed the only live things in a reeling world.

Below in the valley a house was burning brightly. From all directions came the yelp of anti-aircraft guns, and overhead unperturbed continued the leisurely singsong of the motors.

Suddenly Chrisfield burst out laughing.

"By God, Ah always have fun when Ah'm out with you, Andy," he said.

They turned and hurried down the other slope of the hill towards the farms where they were quartered.

II

As far as he could see in every direction were the grey trunks of beeches bright green with moss on one side. The ground was thick with last year's leaves that rustled maddeningly with every step. In front of him his eyes followed other patches of olive-drab moving among the tree trunks. Overhead, through the mottled light and dark green of the leaves he could see now and then a patch of heavy grey sky, greyer than the silvery trunks that moved about him in every direction as he walked. He strained his eyes down each alley until they were dazzled by the reiteration of mottled grey and green. Now and then the rustling stopped ahead of him, and the olive-drab patches were still. Then, above the clamour of the blood in his ears, he could hear batteries "pong, pong, pong" in the distance, and the woods ringing with a sound like hail as a heavy shell hurtled above the tree tops to end in a dull rumble miles away.

Chrisfield was soaked with sweat, but he could not feel his arms or legs. Every sense was concentrated in eyes and ears, and in the consciousness of his gun. Time and again he pictured himself taking sight at something grey that moved, and firing. His forefinger itched to press the trigger. He would take aim very carefully, he told himself; he pictured a dab of grey starting up from behind a grey tree trunk, and the sharp detonation of his rifle, and the dab of grey rolling among the last year's leaves.

A branch carried his helmet off his head so that it rolled at his feet and bounced with a faint metallic sound against the root of a tree.

He was blinded by the sudden terror that seized him. His heart seemed to roll from side to side in his chest. He stood stiff, as if paralyzed for a moment before he could stoop and pick the helmet up. There was a curious taste of blood in his mouth.

"Ah'll pay 'em fer that," he muttered between clenched teeth.

His fingers were still trembling when he stooped to pick up the helmet, which he put on again very carefully, fastening it with the strap under his chin.

Furious anger had taken hold of him.

The olive-drab patches ahead had moved forward again. He followed, looking eagerly to the right and the left, praying he might see something. In every direction were the silvery trunk of the beeches, each with a vivid green streak on one side. With every step the last year's russet leaves rustled underfoot, maddeningly loud.

Almost out of sight among the moving tree trunks was a log. It was not a log; it was a bunch of grey-green cloth. Without thinking Chrisfield strode towards it. The silver trunks of the beeches circled about him, waving jagged arms. It was a German lying full length among the leaves.

Chrisfield was furiously happy in the angry pumping of blood through his veins.

He could see the buttons on the back of the long coat of the German, and the red band on his cap.

He kicked the German. He could feel the ribs against his toes through the leather of his boot. He kicked again and again with all his might. The German rolled over heavily. He had no face. Chrisfield felt the hatred suddenly ebb out of him. Where the face had been was a spongy mass of purple and yellow and red, half of which stuck to the russet leaves when the body rolled over. Large flies with bright shiny green bodies circled about it. In a brown clay-grimed hand was a revolver.

Chrisfield felt his spine go cold; the German had shot himself.

He ran off suddenly, breathlessly, to join the rest of the reconnoitering squad. The silent beeches whirled about him, waving gnarled boughs above his head. The German had shot himself. That was why he had no face.

Chrisfield fell into line behind the other men. The corporal waited for him.

"See anything?" he asked.

"Not a goddam thing," muttered Chrisfield almost inaudibly. The corporal went off to the head of the line.

Chrisfield was alone again. The leaves rustled maddeningly loud underfoot.

III

Chrisfield's eyes were fixed on the leaves at the tops of the walnut trees, etched like metal against the bright colorless sky, edged with flicks and fringes of gold where the sunlight struck them. He stood stiff and motionless at attention, although there was a sharp pain in his left ankle that seemed swollen enough to burst the worn boot. He could feel the presence of men on both sides of him, and of men again beyond them. It seemed as if the stiff line of men in olive-drab, standing at attention, waiting endlessly for someone to release them from their erect paralysis, must stretch unbroken round the world. He let his glance fall to the trampled grass of the field where the regiment was drawn up. Somewhere behind him he could hear the clinking of spurs at some officer's heels. Then there was the sound of a motor on the road suddenly shut off, and there were steps coming down the line of men, and a group of officers passed hurriedly, with a business-like stride, as if they did nothing else all their lives. Chrisfield made out eagles on tight khaki shoulders, then a single star and a double star, above which was a red ear and some grey hair; the general passed too soon for him to make out his face. Chrisfield swore to himself a little because his ankle hurt so. His eyes travelled back to the fringe of the trees against the bright sky. So this was what he got for those weeks in dugouts, for all the times he had thrown himself on his belly in the mud, for the bullets he had shot into the unknown at grey specks that moved among the grey mud. Something was crawling up the middle of his back. He wasn't sure if it were a louse or if he were imagining it. An order had been shouted. Automatically he had changed his position to parade rest. Somewhere far away a little man was walking towards the long drab lines. A wind had come up, rustling the stiff leaves of the grove of walnut trees. The voice squeaked above it, but Chrisfield could not make out what it said. The wind in the trees made a vast rhythmic sound like the churning of water astern of the transport he had come over on. Gold flicks and olive shadows danced among the indented clusters of leaves as they swayed, as if sweeping something away, against the bright sky. An idea came into Chrisfield's head. Suppose the leaves should sweep in broader and broader curves until they should reach the ground and sweep and sweep until all this was swept away, all these pains and lice and uniforms and officers with maple leaves or eagles or single stars or double stars or triple stars on their shoulders. He had a sudden picture of himself in his old comfortable overalls, with his shirt open so that the wind caressed his neck like a girl blowing down it playfully, lying on a shuck of hay under the hot Indiana sun. Funny he'd thought all that, he said to himself. Before he'd known Andy he'd never have thought of that. What had come over him these days?

The regiment was marching away in columns of fours. Chrisfield's ankle gave him sharp hot pain with every step. His tunic was too tight and the sweat tingled on his back. All about him were sweating irritated faces; the woollen tunics with their high collars were like straight-jackets that hot afternoon. Chrisfield marched with his fists clenched; he wanted to fight somebody, to run his bayonet into a man as he ran it into the dummy in that everlasting bayonet drill, he wanted to strip himself naked, to squeeze the wrists of a girl until she screamed.

His company was marching past another company that was lined up to be dismissed in front of a ruined barn which had a roof that sagged in the middle like an old cow's back. The sergeant stood in front of them with his arms crossed, looking critically at the company that marched past. He had a white heavy face and black eyebrows that met over his nose. Chrisfield stared hard at him as he passed, but Sergeant Anderson did not seem to recognize him. It gave him a dull angry feeling as if he'd been cut by a friend.

The company melted suddenly into a group of men unbuttoning their shirts and tunics in front of the little board shanty where they were quartered, which had been put up by the French at the time of the Marne, years before, so a man had told Andy.

"What are you dreamin' about, Indiana?" said Judkins punching Chrisfield jovially in the ribs.

Chrisfield doubled his fists and gave him a smashing blow in the jaw that Judkins warded off just in time.

Judkins's face flamed red. He swung with a long bent arm.

"What the hell d'you think this is?" shouted somebody.

"What's he want to hit me for?" spluttered Judkins, breathless.

Men had edged in between them.

"Lemme git at him."

"Shut up, you fool," said Andy, drawing Chrisfield away. The company scattered sullenly. Some of the men lay down in the long uncut grass in the shade of the ruins of the house, one of the walls of which made a wall of the shanty where they lived.

Andrews and Chrisfield strolled in silence down the road, kicking their feet into the deep dust. Chrisfield was limping. On both sides of the road were fields of ripe wheat, golden under the sun. In the distance were low green hills fading to blue, pale yellow in patches with the ripe grain. Here and there a thick clump of trees or a screen of poplars broke the flatness of the long smooth hills. In the hedge-rows were blue corn-flowers and poppies in all colors from carmine to orange that danced in the wind on their wiry stalks. At the turn in the road they lost the noise of the division and could hear the bees droning in the big dull purple cloverheads and in the gold hearts of the daisies.

"You're a wild man, Chris. What the hell came over you to try an' smash poor old Judkie's jaw? He could lick you anyway. He's twice as heavy as you are."

Chrisfield walked on in silence.

"God, I should think you'ld have had enough of that sort of thing. . . . I should think you'ld be sick of wanting to hurt people. You don't like pain yourself, do you?" Andrews spoke in spurts, bitterly, his eyes on the ground.

"Ah think Ah sprained ma goddam ankle when Ah tumbled off the back o' the truck yesterday."

"Better go on sick call. . . . Say, Chris, I'm sick of this business. . . . Almost like you'd rather shoot yourself than keep on."

"Ah guess you're gettin' the dolefuls, Andy. Look . . . let's go in swim-min'. There's a lake down the road."

"I've got my soap in my pocket. We can wash a few cooties off."

"Don't walk so goddam fast . . . Andy, you got more learnin' than I have. You ought to be able to tell what it is makes a feller go crazy like that. . . . Ah guess Ah got a bit o' the devil in me."

Andrews was brushing the soft silk of a poppy petal against his face.

"I wonder if it'ld have any effect if I ate some of these," he said.

"Why?"

"They say you go to sleep if you lie down in a poppy-field. Wouldn't you like to do that, Chris, an' not wake up till the war was over and you could be a human being again."

Andrews bit into the green seed capsule he held in his hand. A milky juice came out.

"It's bitter . . . I guess it's the opium," he said.

"What's that?"

"A stuff that makes you go to sleep and have wonderful dreams. In China . . ."

"Dreams," interrupted Chrisfield. "Ah had one of them last night. Dreamed Ah saw a feller that had shot hisself that I saw one time recon-noitrin' out in the Bringy Wood."

"What was that?"

"Nawthin', juss a Fritzie had shot hisself."

"Better than opium," said Andrews, his voice trembling with sudden excitement.

"Ah dreamed the flies buzzin' round him was aëroplanes. . . . Remember the last rest village?"

"And the major who wouldn't close the window? You bet I do!"

They lay down on the grassy bank that sloped from the road to the pond. The road was hidden from them by the tall reeds through which the wind lisped softly. Overhead huge white cumulus clouds, piled tier on tier like fantastic galleons in full sail, floated, changing slowly in a greenish sky. The reflection of clouds in the silvery glisten of the pond's surface was broken by clumps of grasses and bits of floating weeds. They lay on their backs for some time before they started taking their clothes off, looking up at the sky, that seemed vast and free, like the ocean, vaster and freer than the ocean.

"Sarge says a delousin' machine's comin' through this way soon."

"We need it, Chris."

Andrews pulled his clothes off slowly.

"It's great to feel the sun and the wind on your body, isn't it, Chris?"

Andrews walked towards the pond and lay flat on his belly on the fine soft grass near the edge.

"It's great to have your body all there, isn't it?" he said in a dreamy voice. "Your skin's so soft and supple, and nothing in the world has the feel a muscle has. . . . Gee, I don't know what I'd do without my body."

Chrisfield laughed.

"Look how ma ole ankle's raised. . . . Found any cooties yet?" he said.

"I'll try and drown 'em," said Andrews. "Chris, come away from those stinking uniforms and you'll feel like a human being with the sun on your flesh instead of like a lousy soldier."

"Hello, boys," came a high-pitched voice unexpectedly. A "Y" man with sharp nose and chin had come up behind them.

"Hello," said Chrisfield sullenly, limping towards the water.

"Want the soap?" said Andrews.

"Going to take a swim, boys?" asked the "Y" man. Then he added in a tone of conviction, "That's great."

"Better come in, too," said Andrews.

"Thanks, thanks. . . . Say, if you don't mind my suggestion, why don't you fellers get under the water. . . . You see there's two French girls looking at you from the road." The "Y" man giggled faintly.

"They don't mind," said Andrews soaping himself vigorously.

"Ah reckon they lahk it," said Chrisfield.

"I know they haven't any morals. . . . But still."

"And why should they not look at us? Maybe there won't be many people who get a chance."

"What do you mean?"

"Have you ever seen what a little splinter of a shell does to a feller's body?" asked Andrews savagely. He splashed into the shallow water and swam towards the middle of the pond.

"Ye might ask 'em to come down and help us pick the cooties off," said Chrisfield and followed in Andrews's wake. In the middle he lay on a sand bank in the warm shallow water and looked back at the "Y" man, who still stood on the bank. Behind him were other men undressing, and soon the grassy slope was filled with naked men and yellowish grey underclothes, and many dark heads and gleaming backs were bobbing up and down in the water. When he came out, he found Andrews sitting cross-legged near his clothes. He reached for his shirt and drew it on him.

"God, I can't make up my mind to put the damn thing on again," said Andrews in a low voice, almost as if he were talking to himself; "I feel so clean and free. It's like voluntarily taking up filth and slavery again. . . . I think I'll just walk off naked across the fields."

"D'you call serving your country slavery, my friend?" The "Y" man, who had been roaming among the bathers, his neat uniform and well-polished boots and puttees contrasting strangely with the mud-clotted, sweat-soaked clothing of the men about him, sat down on the grass beside Andrews.

"You're goddam right I do."

"You'll get into trouble, my boy, if you talk that way," said the "Y" man in a cautious voice.

"Well, what is your definition of slavery?"

"You must remember that you are a voluntary worker in the cause of democracy. . . . You're doing this so that your children will be able to live peaceful. . . ."

"Ever shot a man?"

"No. . . . No, of course not, but I'd have enlisted, really I would. Only my eyes are weak."

"I guess so," said Andrews under his breath.

"Remember that your women folks, your sisters and sweethearts and mothers, are praying for you at this instant."

"I wish somebody'd pray me into a clean shirt," said Andrews, starting to get into his clothes. "How long have you been over here?"

"Just three months." The man's sallow face, with its pinched nose and chin lit up. "But, boys, those three months have been worth all the other years of my min—" he caught himself—"life. . . . I've heard the great heart of America beat. O boys, never forget that you are in a great Christian undertaking."

"Come on, Chris, let's beat it." They left the "Y" man wandering among the men along the bank of the pond, to which the reflection of the greenish silvery sky and the great piled white clouds gave all the free immensity of space. From the road they could still hear his high pitched voice.

"And that's what'll survive you and me," said Andrews.

"Say, Andy, you sure can talk to them guys," said Chris admiringly.

"What's the use of talking? God, there's a bit of honeysuckle still in bloom. Doesn't that smell like home to you, Chris?"

"Say, how much do they pay those 'Y' men, Andy?"

"Damned if I know."

They were just in time to fall into line for mess. In the line everyone was talking and laughing, enlivened by the smell of food and the tinkle of mess-kits. Near the field kitchen Chrisfield saw Sergeant Anderson talking with Higgins, his own sergeant. They were laughing together, and he heard Anderson's big voice saying jovially, "We've pulled through this time, Higgins. . . . I guess we will again." The two sergeants looked at each other and cast a paternal, condescending glance over their men and laughed aloud.

Chrisfield felt powerless as an ox under the yoke. All he could do was work and strain and stand at attention, while that white-faced Anderson could lounge about as if he owned the earth and laugh importantly like that. He held out his plate. The K.P. splashed the meat and gravy into it. He leaned against the tar-papered wall of the shack, eating his food and looking sullenly over at the two sergeants, who laughed and talked with an air of leisure while the men of their two companies ate hurriedly as dogs all round them.

Chrisfield glanced suddenly at Anderson, who sat in the grass at the back of the house, looking out over the wheat fields, while the smoke of a cigarette rose in spirals about his face and his fair hair. He looked peaceful, almost happy. Chrisfield clenched his fists and felt the hatred of that other man rising stingingly within him.

"Guess Ah got a bit of the devil in me," he thought.

The windows were so near the grass that the faint light had a greenish color in the shack where the company was quartered. It gave men's faces, tanned as they were, the sickly look of people who work in offices, when they lay on their blankets in the bunks made of chicken wire, stretched across mouldy scantlings. Swallows had made their nests in the peak of the roof, and their droppings made white dobs and blotches on the floor-boards in the alley between the bunks, where a few patches of yellow grass had not yet been completely crushed away by footsteps. Now that the shack was empty, Chrisfield could hear plainly the peep-peep of the little swallows in their mud nests. He sat quiet on the end of one of the

bunks, looking out of the open door at the blue shadows that were beginning to lengthen on the grass of the meadow behind. His hands, that
had got to be the color of terra cotta, hung idly between his legs. He was
whistling faintly. His eyes, in their long black eyelashes, were fixed on the
distance, though he was not thinking. He felt a comfortable unexpressed
well-being all over him. It was pleasant to be alone in the barracks like
this, when the other men were out at grenade practice. There was no
chance of anyone shouting orders at him.

A warm drowsiness came over him. From the field kitchen alongside
came the voice of a man singing:

> "O my girl's a lulu, every inch a lulu,
>   Is Lulu, that pretty lil' girl o' mi-ine."

In their mud nests the young swallows twittered faintly overhead. Now
and then there was a beat of wings and a big swallow skimmed into the
shack. Chrisfield's cheeks began to feel very softly flushed. His head
drooped over on his chest. Outside the cook was singing over and over
again in a low voice, amid a faint clatter of pans:

> "O my girl's a lulu, every inch a lulu,
>   Is Lulu, that pretty lil' girl o' mi-ine."

Chrisfield fell asleep.

He woke up with a start. The shack was almost dark. A tall man stood
out black against the bright oblong of the door.

"What are you doing here?" said a deep snarling voice.

Chrisfield's eyes blinked. Automatically he got to his feet; it might be
an officer. His eyes focussed suddenly. It was Anderson's face that was between him and the light. In the greenish obscurity the skin looked
chalk-white in contrast to the heavy eyebrows that met over the nose and
the dark stubble on the chin.

"How is it you ain't out with the company?"

"Ah'm barracks guard," muttered Chrisfield. He could feel the blood
beating in his wrists and temples, stinging his eyes like fire. He was staring at the floor in front of Anderson's feet.

"Orders was all the companies was to go out an' not leave any guard."

"Ah!'

"We'll see about that when Sergeant Higgins comes in. Is this place tidy?"

"You say Ah'm a goddamned liar, do ye?" Chrisfield felt suddenly cool
and joyous. He felt anger taking possession of him. He seemed to be
standing somewhere away from himself watching himself get angry.

"This place has got to be cleaned up. . . . That damn General may
come back to look over quarters," went on Anderson coolly.

"You call me a goddam liar," said Chrisfield again, putting as much insolence as he could summon into his voice. "Ah guess you doan' re-member me."

"Yes, I know, you're the guy tried to run a knife into me once," said Anderson coolly, squaring his shoulders. "I guess you've learned a little discipline by this time. Anyhow you've got to clean this place up. God, they haven't even brushed the birds' nests down! Must be some com-pany!" said Anderson with a half laugh.

"Ah ain't agoin' to neither, fur you."

"Look here, you do it or it'll be the worse for you," shouted the sergeant in his deep rasping voice.

"If ever Ah gits out o' the army Ah'm goin' to shoot you. You've picked on me enough." Chrisfield spoke slowly, as coolly as Anderson.

"Well, we'll see what a court-martial has to say to that."

"Ah doan give a hoot in hell what ye do."

Sergeant Anderson turned on his heel and went out, twisting the cor-ner button of his tunic in his big fingers. Already the sound of tramping feet was heard and the shouted order, "Dis-missed." Then men crowded into the shack, laughing and talking. Chrisfield sat still on the end of the bunk, looking at the bright oblong of the door. Outside he saw Anderson talking to Sergeant Higgins. They shook hands, and Anderson disappeared. Chrisfield heard Sergeant Higgins call after him:

"I guess the next time I see you I'll have to put my heels together an' salute."

Anderson's booming laugh faded as he walked away.

Sergeant Higgins came into the shack and walked straight up to Chrisfield, saying in a hard official voice:

"You're under arrest. . . . Small, guard this man; get your gun and car-tridge belt. I'll relieve you so you can get mess."

He went out. Everyone's eyes were turned curiously on Chrisfield. Small, a red-faced man with a long nose that hung down over his upper lip, shuffled sheepishly over to his place beside Chrisfield's cot and let the butt of his rifle come down with a bang on the floor. Somebody laughed. Andrews walked up to them, a look of trouble in his blue eyes and in the lines of his lean tanned cheeks.

"What's the matter, Chris?" he asked in a low voice.

"Tol' that bastard Ah didn't give a hoot in hell what he did," said Chrisfield in a broken voice.

"Say, Andy, I don't think I ought ter let anybody talk to him," said Small in an apologetic tone. "I don't see why Sarge always gives me all his dirty work."

Andrews walked off without replying.

"Never mind, Chris; they won't do nothin' to ye," said Jenkins, grin-ning at him good-naturedly from the door.

"Ah doan give a hoot in hell what they do," said Chrisfield again.

He lay back in his bunk and looked at the ceiling. The barracks was full of a bustle of cleaning up. Judkins was sweeping the floor with a broom made of dry sticks. Another man was knocking down the swallows' nests with a bayonet. The mud nests crumbled and fell on the floor and the bunks, filling the air with a flutter of feathers and a smell of birdlime. The little naked bodies, with their orange bills too big for them, gave a soft plump when they hit the boards of the floor, where they lay giving faint gasping squeaks. Meanwhile, with shrill little cries, the big swallows flew back and forth in the shanty, now and then striking the low roof.

"Say, pick 'em up, can't yer?" said Small. Judkins was sweeping the little gasping bodies out among the dust and dirt.

A stoutish man stooped and picked the little birds up one by one, puckering his lips into an expression of tenderness. He made his two hands into a nest-shaped hollow, out of which stretched the long necks and the gaping orange mouths. Andrews ran into him at the door.

"Hello, Dad," he said. "What the hell?"

"I just picked these up."

"So they couldn't let the poor little devils stay there? God! it looks to me as if they went out of their way to give pain to everything, bird, beast or man."

"War ain't no picnic," said Judkins.

"Well, God damn it, isn't that a reason for not going out of your way to raise more hell with people's feelings than you have to?"

A face with peaked chin and nose on which was stretched a parchment-colored skin appeared in the door.

"Hello, boys," said the "Y" man. "I just thought I'd tell you I'm going to open the canteen tomorrow, in the last shack on the Beaucourt road. There'll be chocolate, ciggies, soap, and everything."

Everybody cheered. The "Y" man beamed.

His eye lit on the little birds in Dad's hands.

"How could you?" he said. "An American soldier being deliberately cruel. I would never have believed it."

"Ye've got somethin' to learn," muttered Dad, waddling out into the twilight on his bandy legs.

Chrisfield had been watching the scene at the door with unseeing eyes. A terrified nervousness that he tried to beat off had come over him. It was useless to repeat to himself again and again that he didn't give a damn; the prospect of being brought up alone before all those officers, of being cross-questioned by those curt voices, frightened him. He would rather have been lashed. Whatever was he to say, he kept asking himself; he would get mixed up or say things he didn't mean to, or else he wouldn't be able to get a word out at all. If only Andy could go up with him, Andy was educated, like the officers were; he had more learning than the whole shooting-match put together. He'd be able to defend himself, and defend his friends, too, if only they'd let him.

"I felt just like those little birds that time they got the bead on our trench at Boticourt," said Jenkins, laughing.

Chrisfield listened to the talk about him as if from another world. Already he was cut off from his outfit. He'd disappear and they'd never know or care what became of him.

The mess-call blew and the men filed out. He could hear their talk outside, and the sound of their mess-kits as they opened them. He lay on his bunk staring up into the dark. A faint blue light still came from outside, giving a curious purple color to Small's red face and long drooping nose at the end of which hung a glistening drop of moisture.

Chrisfield found Andrews washing a shirt in the brook that flowed through the ruins of the village the other side of the road from the buildings where the division was quartered. The blue sky flicked with pinkish-white clouds gave a shimmer of blue and lavender and white to the bright water. At the bottom could be seen battered helmets and bits of equipment and tin cans that had once held meat. Andrews turned his head; he had a smudge of mud down his nose and soapsuds on his chin.

"Hello, Chris," he said, looking him in the eyes with his sparkling blue eyes, "how's things?" There was a faint anxious frown on his forehead.

"Two-thirds of one month's pay an' confined to quarters," said Chrisfield cheerfully.

"Gee, they were easy."

"Um-hum, said Ah was a good shot an' all that, so they'd let me off this time."

Andrews started scrubbing at his shirt again.

"I've got this shirt so full of mud I don't think I ever will get it clean," he said.

"Move ye ole hide away, Andy. Ah'll wash it. You ain't no good for nothin'."

"Hell no, I'll do it."

"Move ye hide out of there."

"Thanks awfully."

Andrews got to his feet and wiped the mud off his nose with his bare forearm.

"Ah'm goin' to shoot that bastard," said Chrisfield, scrubbing at the shirt.

"Don't be an ass, Chris."

"Ah swear to God Ah am."

"What's the use of getting all wrought up. The thing's over. You'll probably never see him again."

"Ah ain't all het up. . . . Ah'm goin' to do it though." He wrung the shirt out carefully and flipped Andrews in the face with it. "There ye are," he said.

"You're a good fellow, Chris, even if you are an ass."

"Tell me we're going into the line in a day or two."

"There's been a devil of a lot of artillery going up the road; French, British, every old kind."

"Tell me they's raisin' hell in the Oregon forest."

They walked slowly across the road. A motorcycle despatch-rider whizzed past them.

"It's them guys has the fun," said Chrisfield.

"I don't believe anybody has much."

"What about the officers?"

"They're too busy feeling important to have a real hell of a time."

The hard cold rain beat like a lash in his face. There was no light anywhere and no sound but the hiss of the rain in the grass. His eyes strained to see through the dark until red and yellow blotches danced before them. He walked very slowly and carefully, holding something very gently in his hand under his raincoat. He felt himself full of a strange subdued fury; he seemed to be walking behind himself spying on his own actions, and what he saw made him feel joyously happy, made him want to sing.

He turned so that the rain beat against his cheek. Under his helmet he felt his hair full of sweat that ran with the rain down his glowing face. His fingers clutched very carefully the smooth stick he had in his hand.

He stopped and shut his eyes for a moment; through the hiss of the rain he had heard a sound of men talking in one of the shanties. When he shut his eyes he saw the white face of Anderson before him, with its unshaven chin and the eyebrows that met across the nose.

Suddenly he felt the wall of a house in front of him. He put out his hand. His hand jerked back from the rough wet feel of the tar paper, as if it had touched something dead. He groped along the wall, stepping very cautiously. He felt as he had felt reconnoitering in the Bringy Wood. Phrases came to his mind as they had then. Without thinking what they meant, the words *Make the world safe for Democracy* formed themselves in his head. They were very comforting. They occupied his thoughts. He said them to himself again and again. Meanwhile his free hand was fumbling very carefully with the fastening that held the wooden shutter over a window. The shutter opened a very little, creaking loudly, louder than the patter of rain on the roof of the shack. A stream of water from the roof was pouring into his face.

Suddenly a beam of light transformed everything, cutting the darkness in two. The rain glittered like a bead curtain. Chrisfield was looking into a little room where a lamp was burning. At a table covered with printed blanks of different size sat a corporal; behind him was a bunk and a pile of equipment. The corporal was reading a magazine. Chrisfield looked at him a long time; his fingers were tight about the smooth stick. There was no one else in the room.

A sort of panic seized Chrisfield; he strode away noisily from the window and pushed open the door of the shack.

"Where's Sergeant Anderson?" he asked in a breathless voice of the first man he saw.

"Corp's there if it's anything important," said the man. "Anderson's gone to an O.T.C. Left day before yesterday."

Chrisfield was out in the rain again. It was beating straight in his face, so that his eyes were full of water. He was trembling. He had suddenly become terrified. The smooth stick he held seemed to burn him. He was straining his ears for an explosion. Walking straight before him down the road, he went faster and faster as if trying to escape from it. He stumbled on a pile of stones. Automatically he pulled the string out of the grenade and threw it far from him.

There was a minute's pause.

Red flame spurted in the middle of the wheatfield. He felt the sharp crash in his eardrums.

He walked fast through the rain. Behind him, at the door of the shack, he could hear excited voices. He walked recklessly on, the rain blinding him. When he finally stepped into the light he was so dazzled he could not see who was in the wine shop.

"Well, I'll be damned, Chris," said Andrews's voice. Chrisfield blinked the rain out of his lashes. Andrews sat writing with a pile of papers before him and a bottle of champagne. It seemed to Chrisfield to soothe his nerves to hear Andy's voice. He wished he would go on talking a long time without a pause.

"If you aren't the crowning idiot of the ages," Andrews went on in a low voice. He took Chrisfield by the arm and led him into the little back room, where was a high bed with a brown coverlet and a big kitchen table on which were the remnants of a meal.

"What's the matter? Your arm's trembling like the devil. But why. . . . O pardon, Crimpette. C'est un ami. . . . You know Crimpette, don't you?" He pointed to a youngish woman who had just appeared from behind the bed. She had a flabby rosy face and violet circles under her eyes, dark as if they'd been made by blows, and untidy hair. A dirty grey muslin dress with half the hooks off held in badly her large breasts and flabby figure. Chrisfield looked at her greedily, feeling his furious irritation flame into one desire.

"What's the matter with you, Chris? You're crazy to break out of quarters this way?"

"Say, Andy, git out o' here. Ah ain't your sort anyway. . . . Git out o' here."

"You're a wild man. I'll grant you that. . . . But I'd just as soon be your sort as anyone else's. . . . Have a drink."

"Not now."

Andrews sat down with his bottle and his papers, pushing away the broken plates full of stale food to make a place on the greasy table. He took a gulp out of the bottle, that made him cough, then put the end of his pencil in his mouth and stared gravely at the paper.

"No, I'm your sort, Chris," he said over his shoulder, "only they've tamed me. O God, how tame I am."

Chrisfield did not listen to what he was saying. He stood in front of the woman, staring in her face. She looked at him in a stupid frightened way. He felt in his pockets for some money. As he had just been paid he had a fifty-franc note. He spread it out carefully before her. Her eyes glistened. The pupils seemed to grow smaller as they fastened on the bit of daintily colored paper. He crumpled it up suddenly in his fist and shoved it down between her breasts.

Some time later Chrisfield sat down in front of Andrews. He still had his wet slicker on.

"Ah guess you think Ah'm a swine," he said in his normal voice. "Ah guess you're about right."

"No, I don't," said Andrews. Something made him put his hand on Chrisfield's hand that lay on the table. It had a feeling of cool health.

"Say, why were you trembling so when you came in here? You seem all right now."

"Oh, Ah dunno'," said Chrisfield in a soft resonant voice.

They were silent for a long while. They could hear the woman's footsteps going and coming behind them.

"Let's go home," said Chrisfield.

"All right. . . . Bonsoir, Crimpette."

Outside the rain had stopped. A stormy wind had torn the clouds to rags. Here and there clusters of stars showed through.

They splashed merrily through the puddles. But here and there reflected a patch of stars when the wind was not ruffling them.

"Christ, Ah wish Ah was like you, Andy," said Chrisfield.

"You don't want to be like me, Chris. I'm no sort of a person at all. I'm tame. O you don't know how damn tame I am."

"Learnin' sure do help a feller to git along in the world."

"Yes, but what's the use of getting along if you haven't any world to get along in? Chris, I belong to a crowd that just fakes learning. I guess the best thing that can happen to us is to get killed in this butchery. We're a tame generation. . . . It's you that it matters to kill."

"Ah ain't no good for anythin'. . . . Ah doan give a damn. . . . Lawsee, Ah feel sleepy."

As they slipped in the door of their quarters, the sergeant looked at Chrisfield searchingly. Andrews spoke up at once.

"There's some rumors going on at the latrine, Sarge. The fellows from the Thirty-second say we're going to march into hell's half-acre about Thursday."

"A lot they know about it."

"That's the latest edition of the latrine news."

"The hell it is! Well, d'you want to know something, Andrews. . . . It'll be before Thursday, or I'm a Dutchman." Sergeant Higgins put on a great air of mystery.

Chrisfield went to his bunk, undressed quietly and climbed into his blankets. He stretched his arms languidly a couple of times, and while Andrews was still talking to the sergeant, fell asleep.

IV

The moon lay among clouds on the horizon, like a big red pumpkin among its leaves.

Chrisfield squinted at it through the boughs of the apple trees laden with apples that gave a winey fragrance to the crisp air. He was sitting on the ground, his legs stretched limply before him, leaning against the rough trunk of an apple tree. Opposite him, leaning against another tree, was the square form, surmounted by a large long-jawed face, of Judkins. Between them lay two empty cognac bottles. All about them was the rustling orchard, with its crooked twigs that made a crackling sound rubbing together in the gusts of the autumn wind, that came heavy with a smell of damp woods and of rotting fruits and of all the ferment of the over-ripe fields. Chrisfield felt it stirring the moist hair on his forehead and through the buzzing haze of the cognac heard the plunk, plunk, plunk of apples dropping that followed each gust, and the twanging of night insects, and, far in the distance, the endless rumble of guns, like tomtoms beaten for a dance.

"Ye heard what the Colonel said, didn't ye?" said Judkins in a voice hoarse from too much drink.

Chrisfield belched and nodded his head vaguely. He remembered

Andrews's white fury after the men had been dismissed,—how he had sat down on the end of a log by the field kitchen, staring at the patch of earth he beat into mud with the toe of his boot.

"Then," went on Judkins, trying to imitate the Colonel's solemn efficient voice, "'On the subject of prisoners'"—he hiccoughed and made a limp gesture with his hand—"'On the subject of prisoners, well, I'll leave that to you, but juss remember . . . juss remember what the Huns did to Belgium, an' I might add that we have barely enough emergency rations as it is, and the more prisoners you have the less you fellers'll git to eat.'"

"That's what he said, Judkie; that's what he said."

"'An the more prisoners ye have, the less youse'll git to eat,'" chanted Judkins, making a triumphal flourish with his hand.

Chrisfield groped for the cognac bottle; it was empty; he waved it in the air a minute and then threw it into the tree opposite him. A shower of little apples fell about Judkins's head. He got unsteadily to his feet.

"I tell you, fellers," he said, "war ain't no picnic."

Chrisfield stood up and grabbed at an apple. His teeth crunched into it.

"Sweet," he said.

"Sweet, nauthin'," mumbled Judkins, "war ain't no picnic. . . . I tell you, buddy, if you take any prisoners"—he hiccoughed—"after what the Colonel said, I'll lick the spots out of you, by God I will. . . . Rip up their guts that's all, like they was dummies. Rip up their guts." His voice suddenly changed to one of childish dismay. "Gee, Chris, I'm going to be sick," he whispered.

"Look out," said Chrisfield, pushing him away. Judkins leaned against a tree and vomited.

The full moon had risen above the clouds and filled the apple orchard with chilly golden light that cast a fantastic shadow pattern of interlaced twigs and branches upon the bare ground littered with apples. The sound of the guns had grown nearer. There were loud eager rumbles as of bowls being rolled very hard on a bowling alley, combined with a continuous roar like sheets of iron being shaken.

"Ah bet it's hell out there," said Chrisfield.

"I feel better," said Judkins. "Let's go get some more cognac."

"Ah'm hungry," said Chrisfield. "Let's go an' get that ole woman to cook us some aigs."

"Too damn late," growled Judkins.

"How the hell late is it?"

"Dunno, I sold my watch."

They were walking at random through the orchard. They came to a field full of big pumpkins that gleamed in the moonlight and cast shadows black as holes. In the distance they could see wooded hills.

Chrisfield picked up a medium-sized pumpkin and threw it as hard as he could into the air. It split into three when it landed with a thud on the ground, and the moist yellow seeds spilled out.

"Some strong man, you are," said Judkins, tossing up a bigger one.

"Say, there's a farmhouse, maybe we could get some aigs from the hen-roost."

"Hell of a lot of hens. . . ."

At that moment the crowing of a rooster came across the silent fields. They ran towards the dark farm buildings.

"Look out, there may be officers quartered there."

They walked cautiously round the square, silent group of buildings. There were no lights. The big wooden door of the court pushed open easily, without creaking. On the roof of the barn the pigeon-cot was etched dark against the disc of the moon. A warm smell of stables blew in their faces as the two men tiptoed into the manure-littered farmyard. Under one of the sheds they found a table on which a great many pears were set to ripen. Chrisfield put his teeth into one. The rich sweet juice ran down his chin. He ate the pear quickly and greedily, and then bit into another.

"Fill yer pockets with 'em," whispered Judkins.

"They might ketch us."

"Ketch us, hell. We'll be goin' into the offensive in a day or two."

"Ah sure would like to git some aigs."

Chrisfield pushed open the door of one of the barns. A smell of creamy milk and cheeses filled his nostrils.

"Come here," he whispered. "Want some cheese?"

A lot of cheeses ranged on a board shone silver in the moonlight that came in through the open door.

"Hell, no, ain't fit te eat," said Judkins, pushing his heavy fist into one of the new soft cheeses.

"Doan do that."

"Well, ain't we saved 'em from the Huns?"

"But, hell."

"War ain't no picnic, that's all," said Judkins.

In the next door they found chickens roosting in a small room with straw on the floor. The chickens ruffled their feathers and made a muffled squeaking as they slept.

Suddenly there was a loud squawking and all the chickens were cackling with terror.

"Beat it," muttered Judkins, running for the gate of the farmyard.

There were shrill cries of women in the house. A voice shrieking, "C'est les Boches, C'est les Boches," rose above the cackling of chickens and the clamor of guinea-hens. As they ran, they heard the rasping cries of a woman in hysterics, rending the rustling autumn night.

"God damn," said Judkins breathless, "they ain't got no right, those frogs ain't, to carry on like that."

They ducked into the orchard again. Above the squawking of the chicken Judkins still held, swinging it by its legs, Chrisfield could hear the woman's voice shrieking. Judkins dexterously wrung the chicken's neck. Crushing the apples underfoot they strode fast through the orchard. The voice faded into the distance until it could not be heard above the sound of the guns.

"Gee, Ah'm kind o' cut up 'bout that lady," said Chrisfield.

"Well, ain't we saved her from the Huns?"

"Andy don't think so."

"Well, if you want to know what I think about that guy Andy. . . . I don't think much of him. I think he's yaller, that's all," said Judkins.

"No, he ain't."

"I heard the lootenant say so. He's a goddam yeller dawg."

Chrisfield swore sullenly.

"Well, you juss wait 'n see. I tell you, buddy, war ain't no picnic."

"What the hell are we goin' to do with that chicken?" said Judkins.

"You remember what happened to Eddie White?"

"Hell, we'd better leave it here."

Judkins swung the chicken by its neck round his head and threw it as hard as he could into the bushes.

They were walking along the road between chestnut trees that led to their village. It was dark except for irregular patches of bright moonlight in the centre that lay white as milk among the indentated shadows of the leaves. All about them rose a cool scent of woods, of ripe fruits and of decaying leaves, of the ferment of the autumn countryside.

The lieutenant sat at a table in the sun, in the village street outside the company office. In front of him sparkled piles of money and daintily tinted banknotes. Beside him stood Sergeant Higgins with an air of solemnity and the second sergeant and the corporal. The men stood in line and as each came before the table he saluted with deference, received his money and walked away with a self-conscious air. A few villagers looked on from the small windows with grey frames of their rambling whitewashed houses. In the ruddy sunshine the line of men cast an irregular blue-violet shadow, like a gigantic centipede, on the yellow gravel road.

From the table by the window of the café of "Nos Braves Poilus" where Small and Judkins and Chrisfield had established themselves with their pay crisp in their pockets, they could see the little front garden of the house across the road, where, behind a hedge of orange marigolds, Andrews sat on the doorstep talking to an old woman hunched on a low chair in the sun just inside the door, who leant her small white head over towards his yellow one.

"There ye are," said Judkins in a solemn tone. "He don't even go after his pay. That guy thinks he's the whole show, he does."

Chrisfield flushed, but said nothing.

"He don't do nothing all day long but talk to that ole lady," said Small with a grin. "Guess she reminds him of his mother, or somethin'."

"He always does go round with the frogs all he can. Looks to me like he'd rather have a drink with a frog than with an American."

"Reckon he wants to learn their language," said Small.

"He won't never come to much in this army, that's what I'm telling yer," said Judkins.

The little houses across the way had flushed red with the sunset. Andrews got to his feet slowly and languidly and held out his hand to the old woman. She stood up, a small tottering figure in a black silk shawl. He leaned over towards her and she kissed both his cheeks vigorously several times. He walked down the road towards the billets, with his fatigue cap in his hand, looking at the ground.

"He's got a flower behind his ear, like a cigarette," said Judkins, with a disgusted snort.

"Well, I guess we'd better go," said Small. "We got to be in quarters at six."

They were silent a moment. In the distance the guns kept up a continual tomtom sound.

"Guess we'll be in that soon," said Small.

Chrisfield felt a chill go down his spine. He moistened his lips with his tongue.

"Guess it's hell out there," said Judkins. "War ain't no picnic."

"Ah doan give a hoot in hell," said Chrisfield.

The men were lined up in the village street with their packs on, waiting for the order to move. Thin wreaths of white mist still lingered in the trees and over the little garden plots. The sun had not yet risen, but ranks of clouds in the pale blue sky overhead were brilliant with crimson and gold. The men stood in an irregular line, bent over a little by the weight of their equipment, moving back and forth, stamping their feet and beating their arms together, their noses and ears red from the chill of the morning. The haze of their breath rose above their heads.

Down the misty road a drab-colored limousine appeared, running slowly. It stopped in front of the line of men. The lieutenant came hurriedly out of the house opposite, drawing on a pair of gloves. The men standing in line looked curiously at the limousine. They could see that two of the tires were flat and that the glass was broken. There were scratches on the drab paint and in the door three long jagged holes that obliterated the number. A little murmur went down the line of men. The door opened with difficulty, and a major in a light buff-colored coat stumbled out. One arm, wrapped in bloody bandages, was held in a sling made of a handkerchief. His face was white and drawn into a stiff mask with pain. The lieutenant saluted.

"For God's sake where's a repair station?" he asked in a loud shaky voice.

"There's none in this village, Major."

"Where the hell is there one?"

"I don't know," said the lieutenant in a humble tone.

"Why the hell don't you know? This organization's rotten, no good. . . . Major Stanley's just been killed. What the hell's the name of this village?"

"Thiocourt."

"Where the hell's that?"

The chauffeur had leaned out. He had no cap and his hair was full of dust.

"You see, Lootenant, we wants to get to Châlons——"

"Yes, that's it. Châlons sur . . . Châlons-sur-Marne," said the Major.

"The billeting officer has a map," said the lieutenant, "last house to the left."

"O let's go there quick," said the major. He fumbled with the fastening of the door.

The lieutenant opened it for him.

As he opened the door, the men nearest had a glimpse of the interior of the car. On the far side was a long object huddled in blankets, propped up on the seat.

Before he got in the major leaned over and pulled a woollen rug out, holding it away from him with his one good arm. The car moved off slowly, and all down the village street the men, lined up waiting for orders, stared curiously at the three jagged holes in the door.

The lieutenant looked at the rug that lay in the middle of the road. He touched it with his foot. It was soaked with blood that in places had dried into clots.

The lieutenant and the men of his company looked at it in silence. The sun had risen and shone on the roofs of the little whitewashed houses behind them. Far down the road a regiment had begun to move.

V

At the brow of the hill they rested. Chrisfield sat on the red clay bank and looked about him, his rifle between his knees. In front of him on the side of the road was a French burying ground, where the little wooden crosses, tilting in every direction, stood up against the sky, and the bead wreaths glistened in the warm sunlight. All down the road as far as he could see was a long drab worm, broken in places by strings of motor trucks, a drab worm that wriggled down the slope, through the roofless shell of the village and up into the shattered woods on the crest of the next hills. Chrisfield strained his eyes to see the hills beyond. They lay blue and very peaceful in the moon mist. The river glittered about the piers of the wrecked stone bridge, and disappeared between rows of yellow poplars. Somewhere in the valley a big gun fired. The shell shrieked into the distance, towards the blue, peaceful hills.

Chrisfield's regiment was moving again. The men, their feet slipping in the clayey mud, went downhill with long strides, the straps of their packs tugging at their shoulders.

"Isn't this great country?" said Andrews, who marched beside him.

"Ah'd liever be at an O.T.C. like that bastard Anderson."

"Oh, to hell with that," said Andrews. He still had a big faded orange marigold in one of the buttonholes of his soiled tunic. He walked with his nose in the air and his nostrils dilated, enjoying the tang of the autumnal sunlight.

Chrisfield took the cigarette, that had gone out half-smoked, from his mouth and spat savagely at the heels of the man in front of him.

"This ain't no life for a white man," he said.

"I'd rather be this than . . . than that," said Andrews bitterly. He tossed his head in the direction of a staff car full of officers that was stalled at the side of the road. They were drinking something out of a thermos bottle that they passed round with the air of Sunday excursionists. They waved, with a conscious relaxation of discipline, at the men as they passed. One, a little lieutenant with a black mustache with pointed ends, kept crying: "They're running like rabbits, fellers; they're running like rabbits." A wavering half-cheer would come from the column now and then where it was passing the staff car.

The big gun fired again. Chrisfield was near it this time and felt the concussion like a blow in the head.

"Some baby," said the man behind him.

Someone was singing:

> "Good morning, mister Zip Zip Zip,
>   With your hair cut just as short as,
>   With your hair cut just as short as,
>   With your hair cut just as short as mi–ine."

Everybody took it up. Their steps rang in rhythm in the paved street that zigzagged among the smashed houses of the village. Ambulances passed them, big trucks full of huddled men with grey faces, from which came a smell of sweat and blood and carbolic.

Somebody went on:

> "O ashes to ashes
>   An' dust to dust . . ."

"Can that," cried Judkins, "it ain't lucky."

But everybody had taken up the song. Chrisfield noticed that Andrews's eyes were sparkling. "If he ain't the damnedest," he thought to himself. But he shouted at the top of his lungs with the rest:

> "O ashes to ashes
>   An' dust to dust;
>   If the gasbombs don't get yer
>   The eighty-eights must."

They were climbing the hill again. The road was worn into deep ruts and there were many shell holes, full of muddy water, into which their feet slipped. The woods began, a shattered skeleton of woods, full of old artillery emplacements and dugouts, where torn camouflage fluttered from splintered trees. The ground and the road were littered with tin cans and brass shell-cases. Along both sides of the road the trees were festooned, as with creepers, with strand upon strand of telephone wire.

When next they stopped Chrisfield was on the crest of the hill beside a battery of French seventy-fives. He looked curiously at the Frenchmen, who sat about on logs in their pink and blue shirt-sleeves playing cards and smoking. Their gestures irritated him.

"Say, tell 'em we're advancin'," he said to Andrews.

"Are we?" said Andrews. "All right. . . . Dites-donc, les Boches courent-ils comme des lapins?" he shouted.

One of the men turned his head and laughed.

"He says they've been running that way for four years," said Andrews. He slipped his pack off, sat down on it, and fished for a cigarette. Chrisfield took off his helmet and rubbed a muddy hand through his hair. He took a bite of chewing tobacco and sat with his hands clasped over his knees.

"How the hell long are we going to wait this time?" he muttered. The shadows of the tangled and splintered trees crept slowly across the road. The French artillerymen were eating their supper. A long train of motor trucks growled past, splashing mud over the men crowded along the sides of the road. The sun set, and a lot of batteries down in the valley began firing, making it impossible to talk. The air was full of a shrieking and droning of shells overhead. The Frenchmen stretched and yawned and went down into their dugout. Chrisfield watched them enviously. The stars were beginning to come out in the green sky behind the tall lacerated trees. Chrisfield's legs ached with cold. He began to get crazily anxious for something to happen, for something to happen, but the column waited, without moving, through the gathering darkness. Chrisfield chewed steadily, trying to think of nothing but the taste of the tobacco in his mouth.

The column was moving again; as they reached the brow of another hill Chrisfield felt a curious sweetish smell that made his nostrils smart. "Gas," he thought, full of panic, and put his hand to the mask that hung round his neck. But he did not want to be the first to put it on. No order came. He marched on, cursing the sergeant and the lieutenant. But maybe they'd been killed by it. He had a vision of the whole regiment sinking down in the road suddenly, overcome by the gas.

"Smell anythin', Andy?" he whispered cautiously.

"I can smell a combination of dead horses and tuberoses and banana oil and the ice cream we used to have at college and dead rats in the garret, but what the hell do we care now?" said Andrews, giggling. "This is the damnedest fool business ever. . . ."

"He's crazy," muttered Chrisfield to himself. He looked at the stars in the black sky that seemed to be going along with the column on its march. Or was it that they and the stars were standing still while the trees moved away from them, waving their skinny shattered arms? He could hardly hear the tramp of feet on the road, so loud was the pandemonium of the guns ahead and behind. Every now and then a rocket would burst in front of them and its red and green lights would mingle for a moment with the stars. But it was only overhead he could see the stars. Everywhere else white and red glows rose and fell as if the horizon were on fire.

As they started down the slope, the trees suddenly broke away and they saw the valley between them full of the glare of guns and the white light of star shells. It was like looking into a stove full of glowing embers. The hillside that sloped away from them was full of crashing detonations and yellow tongues of flame. In a battery near the road, that seemed to crush their skulls each time a gun fired, they could see the dark forms of the artillerymen silhouetted in fantastic attitudes against the intermittent red glare. Stunned and blinded, they kept on marching down the road. It seemed to Chrisfield that they were going to step any minute into the flaring muzzle of a gun.

At the foot of the hill, beside a little grove of uninjured trees, they stopped again. A new train of trucks was crawling past them, huge blots in the darkness. There were no batteries near, so they could hear the grinding roar of the gears as the trucks went along the uneven road, plunging in and out of shellholes.

Chrisfield lay down in the dry ditch, full of bracken, and dozed with his head on his pack. All about him were stretched other men. Someone was resting his head on Chrisfield's thigh. The noise had subsided a little. Through his doze he could hear men's voices talking in low crushed tones, as if they were afraid of speaking aloud. On the road the truck-drivers kept calling out to each other shrilly, raspingly. The motors stopped running one after another, making almost a silence, during which Chrisfield fell asleep.

Something woke him. He was stiff with cold and terrified. For a moment he thought he had been left alone, that the company had gone on, for there was no one touching him.

Overhead was a droning as of gigantic mosquitoes, growing fast to a loud throbbing. He heard the lieutenant's voice calling shrilly:

"Sergeant Higgins, Sergeant Higgins!"

The lieutenant stood out suddenly black against a sheet of flame. Chrisfield could see his fatigue cap a little on one side and his trench coat, drawn in tight at the waist and sticking out stiffly at the knees. He was shaken by the explosion. Everything was black again. Chrisfield got to his feet, his ears ringing. The column was moving on. He heard moaning near him in the darkness. The tramp of feet and jingle of equipment drowned all other sound. He could feel his shoulders becoming raw under the tugging of the pack. Now and then the flare from aëroplane bombs behind him showed up wrecked trucks on the side of the road. Somewhere a machine gun spluttered. But the column tramped on, weighed down by the packs, by the deadening exhaustion.

The turbulent flaring darkness was calming to the grey of dawn when Chrisfield stopped marching. His eyelids stung as if his eyeballs were flaming hot. He could not feel his feet and legs. The guns continued incessantly like a hammer beating on his head. He was walking very slowly in a single file, now and then stumbling against the man ahead of him. There was earth on both sides of him, clay walls that dripped moisture. All at once he stumbled down some steps into a dugout, where it was pitch-black. An unfamiliar smell struck him, made him uneasy; but his thoughts seemed to reach him from out of a great distance. He groped to the wall. His knees struck against a bunk with blankets in it. In another second he was sunk fathoms deep in sleep.

When he woke up his mind was very clear. The roof of the dugout was of logs. A bright spot far away was the door. He hoped desperately that he wasn't on duty. He wondered where Andy was; then he remembered that Andy was crazy,—"a yaller dawg," Judkins had called him. Sitting up with difficulty he undid his shoes and puttees, wrapped himself in his blanket. All round him were snores and the deep breathing of exhausted sleep. He closed his eyes.

He was being court-martialled. He stood with his hands at his sides before three officers at a table. All three had the same white faces with heavy blue jaws and eyebrows that met above the nose. They were reading things out of papers aloud, but, although he strained his ears, he couldn't make out what they were saying. All he could hear was a faint moaning. Something had a curious unfamiliar smell that troubled him. He could not stand still at attention, although the angry eyes of officers stared at him from all round. "Anderson, Sergeant Anderson, what's that smell?" he kept asking in a small whining voice. "Please tell a feller what that smell is." But the three officers at the table kept reading from their papers, and the moaning grew louder and louder in his ears until he shrieked aloud. There was a grenade in his hand. He pulled the string out and threw it, and he saw the lieutenant's trench coat stand out against a sheet of flame. Someone sprang at him. He was wrestling for his life with Anderson, who turned into a woman with huge flabby breasts. He crushed her to him and turned to defend himself against three officers who came at him, their trench coats drawn in tightly at the waist until they looked like wasps. Everything faded, he woke up.

His nostrils were still full of the strange troubling smell. He sat on the edge of the bunk, wriggling in his clothes, for his body crawled with lice.

"Gee, it's funny to be in where the Fritzies were not long ago," he heard a voice say.

"Kiddo! we're advancin'," came another voice.

"But, hell, this ain't no kind of an advance. I ain't seen a German yet."

"Ah kin smell 'em though," said Chrisfield, getting suddenly to his feet.

Sergeant Higgins' head appeared in the door. "Fall in," he shouted. Then he added in his normal voice, "It's up and at 'em, fellers."

Chrisfield caught his puttee on a clump of briars at the edge of the clearing and stood kicking his leg back and forth to get it free. At last he broke away, the torn puttee dragging behind him. Out in the sunlight in the middle of the clearing he saw a man in olive-drab kneeling beside something on the ground. A German lay face down with a red hole in his back. The man was going through his pockets. He looked up into Chrisfield's face.

"Souvenirs," he said.

"What outfit are you in, buddy?"

"143rd," said the man, getting to his feet slowly.

"Where the hell are we?"

"Damned if I know."

The clearing was empty, except for the two Americans and the German with the hole in his back. In the distance they heard a sound of

artillery and nearer the "put, put, put" of isolated machine guns. The
leaves of the trees about them, all shades of brown and crimson and yellow, danced in the sunlight.

"Say, that damn money ain't no good, is it?" asked Chrisfield.

"German money? Hell, no. . . . I got a watch that's a peach though."
The man held out a gold watch, looking suspiciously at Chrisfield all the
while through half-closed eyes.

"Ah saw a feller had a gold-handled sword," said Chrisfield.

"Where's that?"

"Back there in the wood"; he waved his hand vaguely. "Ah've got to
find ma outfit; comin' along?" Chrisfield started towards the other edge
of the clearing.

"Looks to me all right here," said the other man, lying down on the
grass in the sun.

The leaves rustled underfoot as Chrisfield strode through the wood.
He was frightened by being alone. He walked ahead as fast as he could,
his puttee still dragging behind him. He came to a barbed-wire entanglement half embedded in fallen beech leaves. It had been partly cut in
one place, but in crossing he tore his thigh on a barb. Taking off the torn
puttee, he wrapped it round the outside of his trousers and kept on walking, feeling a little blood trickle down his leg.

Later he came to a lane that cut straight through the wood where
there were many ruts through the putty-coloured mud puddles. Down
the lane in a patch of sunlight he saw a figure, towards which he hurried.
It was a young man with red hair and a pink-and-white face. By a gold
bar on the collar of his shirt Chrisfield saw that he was a lieutenant. He
had no coat or hat and there was greenish slime all over the front of his
clothes as if he had lain on his belly in a mud puddle.

"Where you going?"

"Dunno, sir."

"All right, come along." The lieutenant started walking as fast as he
could up the lane, swinging his arms wildly.

"Seen any machine-gun nests?"

"Not a one."

"Hum."

He followed the lieutenant, who walked so fast he had difficulty keeping up, splashing recklessly through the puddles.

"Where's the artillery? That's what I want to know," cried the lieutenant, suddenly stopping in his tracks and running a hand through his
red hair. "Where the hell's the artillery?" He looked at Chrisfield savagely out of green eyes. "No use advancing without artillery." He started
walking faster than ever.

All at once they saw sunlight ahead of them and olive-drab uniforms.

Machine guns started firing all around them in a sudden gust. Chrisfield found himself running forward across a field full of stubble and sprouting clover among a group of men he did not know. The whip-like sound of rifles had chimed in with the stuttering of the machine guns. Little white clouds sailed above him in a blue sky, and in front of him was a group of houses that had the same color, white with lavender-grey shadows, as the clouds.

He was in a house, with a grenade like a tin pineapple in each hand. The sudden loneliness frightened him again. Outside the house was a sound of machine-gun firing, broken by the occasional bursting of a shell. He looked at the red-tiled floor and at a chromo of a woman nursing a child that hung on the whitewashed wall opposite him. He was in a small kitchen. There was a fire in the hearth where something boiled in a black pot. Chrisfield tiptoed over and looked in. At the bottom of the bubbling water he saw five potatoes. At the other end of the kitchen, beyond two broken chairs, was a door. Chrisfield crept over to it, the tiles seeming to sway under foot. He put his finger to the latch and took it off again suddenly. Holding in his breath he stood a long time looking at the door. Then he pulled it open recklessly. A young man with fair hair was sitting at a table, his head resting on his hands. Chrisfield felt a spurt of joy when he saw that the man's uniform was green. Very coolly he pressed the spring, held the grenade a second and then threw it, throwing himself backwards into the middle of the kitchen. The light-haired man had not moved; his blue eyes still stared straight before him.

In the street Chrisfield ran into a tall man who was running. The man clutched him by the arm and said:

"The barrage is moving up."

"What barrage?"

"Our barrage; we've got to run, we're ahead of it." His voice came in wheezy pants. There were red splotches on his face. They ran together down the empty village street. As they ran they passed the little red-haired lieutenant, who leaned against a whitewashed wall, his legs a mass of blood and torn cloth. He was shouting in a shrill delirious voice that followed them out along the open road.

"Where's the artillery? That's what I want to know; where's the artillery?"

The woods were grey and dripping with dawn. Chrisfield got stiffly to his feet from the pile of leaves where he had slept. He felt numb with cold and hunger, lonely and lost away from his outfit. All about him were men of another division. A captain with a sandy mustache was striding up and down with a blanket about him, on the road just behind a clump of beech trees. Chrisfield had watched him passing back and forth, back and forth, behind the wet clustered trunks of the trees, ever since it had been light. Stamping his feet among the damp leaves, Chrisfield strolled away from the group of men. No one seemed to notice him. The trees closed about him. He could see nothing but moist trees, grey-green and black, and the yellow leaves of saplings that cut off the view in every direction. He was wondering dully why he was walking off that way. Somewhere in the back of his mind there was a vague idea of finding his outfit. Sergeant Higgins and Andy and Judkins and Small—he wondered what had become of them. He thought of the company lined up for mess, and the smell of greasy food that came from the field-kitchen. He was desperately hungry. He stopped and leaned against the moss-covered trunk of a tree. The deep scratch in his leg was throbbing as if all the blood in his body beat through it. Now that his rustling footsteps had ceased, the woods were absolutely silent, except for the dripping of dew from the leaves and branches. He strained his ears to hear some other sound. Then he noticed that he was staring at a tree full of small red crab apples. He picked a handful greedily, but they were hard and sour and seemed to make him hungrier. The sour flavour in his mouth made him furiously angry. He kicked at the thin trunk of the tree while tears smarted in his eyes. Swearing aloud in a whining singsong voice, he strode off through the woods with his eyes on the ground. Twigs snapped viciously in his face, crooked branches caught at him, but he plunged on. All at once he stumbled against something hard that bounced among the leaves.

He stopped still, looking about him, terrified. Two grenades lay just under his foot, a little further on a man was propped against a tree with his mouth open. Chrisfield thought at first he was asleep, as his eyes were closed. He looked at the grenades carefully. The fuses had not been sprung. He put one in each pocket, gave a glance at the man who seemed to be asleep, and strode off again, striking another alley in the woods, at the end of which he could see sunlight. The sky overhead was full of heavy purple clouds, tinged here and there with yellow. As he walked towards the patch of sunlight, the thought came to him that he ought to have looked in the pockets of the man he had just passed to see if he had any hard bread. He stood still a moment in hesitation, but started walking again doggedly towards the patch of sunlight.

Something glittered in the irregular fringe of sun and shadow. A man was sitting hunched up on the ground with his fatigue cap pulled over his eyes so that the little gold bar just caught the horizontal sunlight. Chrisfield's first thought was that he might have food on him.

"Say, Lootenant," he shouted, "d'you know where a fellow can get somethin' to eat."

The man lifted his head slowly. Chrisfield turned cold all over when he saw the white heavy face of Anderson; an unshaven beard was very black on his square chin; there was a long scratch clotted with dried blood from the heavy eyebrow across the left cheek to the corner of the mouth.

"Give me some water, buddy," said Anderson in a weak voice.

Chrisfield handed him his canteen roughly in silence. He noticed that Anderson's arm was in a sling, and that he drank greedily, spilling the water over his chin and his wounded arm.

"Where's Colonel Evans?" asked Anderson in a thin petulant voice.

Chrisfield did not reply but stared at him sullenly. The canteen had dropped from his hand and lay on the ground in front of him. The water gleamed in the sunlight as it ran out among the russet leaves. A wind had come up, making the woods resound. A shower of yellow leaves dropped about them.

"First you was a corporal, then you was a sergeant, and now you're a lootenant," said Chrisfield slowly.

"You'ld better tell me where Colonel Evans is. . . . You must know. . . . He's up that road somewhere," said Anderson, struggling to get to his feet.

Chrisfield walked away without answering. A cold hand was round the grenade in his pocket. He walked away slowly, looking at his feet.

Suddenly he found he had pressed the spring of the grenade. He struggled to pull it out of his pocket. It stuck in the narrow pocket. His arm and his cold fingers that clutched the grenade seemed paralyzed. Then a warm joy went through him. He had thrown it.

Anderson was standing up, swaying backwards and forwards. The explosion made the woods quake. A thick rain of yellow leaves came down. Anderson was flat on the ground. He was so flat he seemed to have sunk into the ground.

Chrisfield pressed the spring of the other grenade and threw it with his eyes closed. It burst among the thick new-fallen leaves.

A few drops of rain were falling. Chrisfield kept on along the lane, walking fast, feeling full of warmth and strength. The rain beat hard and cold against his back.

He walked with his eyes to the ground. A voice in a strange language stopped him. A ragged man in green with a beard that was clotted with mud stood in front of him with his hands up. Chrisfield burst out laughing.

"Come along," he said, "quick!"

The man shambled in front of him; he was trembling so hard he nearly fell with each step.

Chrisfield kicked him.

The man shambled on without turning round. Chrisfield kicked him again, feeling the point of the man's spine and the soft flesh of his thighs against his toes with each kick, laughing so hard all the while that he could hardly see where he was going.

"Halt!" came a voice.

"Ah've got a prisoner," shouted Chrisfield still laughing.

"He ain't much of a prisoner," said the man, pointing his bayonet at the German. "He's gone crazy, I guess. I'll take keer o' him . . . ain't no use sendin' him back."

"All right," said Chrisfield still laughing. "Say, buddy, where can Ah' git something to eat? Ah ain't had nothin' fur a day an a half."

"There's a reconnoitrin' squad up the line; they'll give you somethin'. . . . How's things goin' up that way?" The man pointed up the road.

"Gawd, Ah doan know. Ah ain't had nothin' to eat fur a day and a half."

The warm smell of a stew rose to his nostrils from the mess-kit. Chrisfield stood, feeling warm and important, filling his mouth with soft greasy potatoes and gravy, while men about him asked him questions. Gradually he began to feel full and content, and a desire to sleep came over him. But he was given a gun, and had to start advancing again with the reconnoitering squad. The squad went cautiously up the same lane through the woods.

"Here's an officer done for," said the captain, who walked ahead. He made a little clucking noise of distress with his tongue. "Two of you fellows go back and git a blanket and take him back to the cross-roads. Poor fellow." The captain walked on again, still making little clucking noises with his tongue.

Chrisfield looked straight ahead of him. He did not feel lonely any more now that he was marching in ranks again. His feet beat the ground in time with the other feet. He would not have to think whether to go to the right or to the left. He would do as the others did.

PART FOUR

RUST

I

There were tiny green frogs in one of the putty-colored puddles by the roadside. John Andrews fell out of the slowly advancing column a moment to look at them. The frogs' triangular heads stuck out of the water in the middle of the puddle. He leaned over, his hands on his knees, easing the weight of the equipment on his back. That way he could see their tiny jewelled eyes, topaz-colored. His eyes felt as if tears were coming to them with tenderness towards the minute lithe bodies of the frogs. Something was telling him that he must run forward and fall into line again, that he must shamble on through the mud, but he remained staring at the puddle, watching the frogs. Then he noticed his reflection in the puddle. He looked at it curiously. He could barely see the outlines of a stained grimacing mask, and the silhouette of the gun barrel slanting behind it. So this was what they had made of him. He fixed his eyes again on the frogs that swam with elastic, leisurely leg strokes in the putty-colored water.

Absently, as if he had no connection with all that went on about him, he heard the twang of bursting shrapnel down the road. He had straightened himself wearily and taken a step forward, when he found himself sinking into the puddle. A feeling of relief came over him. His legs sunk in the puddle; he lay without moving against the muddy bank. The frogs had gone, but from somewhere a little stream of red was creeping out slowly into the putty-colored water. He watched the irregular files of men in olive-drab shambling by. Their footsteps drummed in his ears. He felt triumphantly separated from them, as if he were in a window somewhere watching soldiers pass, or in a box of a theater watching some dreary monotonous play. He drew farther and farther away from them until they had become very small, like toy soldiers forgotten among the dust in a garret. The light was so dim he couldn't see, he could only hear their feet tramping interminably through the mud.

131

John Andrews was on a ladder that shook horribly. A gritty sponge in his hand, he was washing the windows of a barracks. He began in the left hand corner and soaped the small oblong panes one after the other. His arms were like lead and he felt that he would fall from the shaking ladder, but each time he turned to look towards the ground before climbing down he saw the top of the general's cap and the general's chin protruding from under the visor, and a voice snarled: "Attention," terrifying him so that the ladder shook more than ever; and he went on smearing soap over the oblong panes with the gritty sponge through interminable hours, though every joint in his body was racked by the shaking of the ladder. Bright light flared from inside the windows which he soaped, pane after pane, methodically. The windows were mirrors. In each pane he saw his thin face, in shadow, with the shadow of a gun barrel slanting beside it. The jolting stopped suddenly. He sank into a deep pit of blackness.

A shrill broken voice was singing in his ear:

> "There's a girl in the heart of Maryland
> With a heart that belo–ongs to mee."

John Andrews opened his eyes. It was pitch black, except for a series of bright yellow oblongs that seemed to go up into the sky, where he could see the stars. His mind became suddenly acutely conscious. He began taking account of himself in a hurried frightened way. He craned his neck a little. In the darkness he could make out the form of a man stretched out flat beside him who kept moving his head strangely from side to side, singing at the top of his lungs in a shrill broken voice. At that moment Andrews noticed that the smell of carbolic was overpoweringly strong, that it dominated all the familiar smells of blood and sweaty clothes. He wriggled his shoulders so that he could feel the two poles of the stretcher. Then he fixed his eyes again in the three bright yellow oblongs, one above the other, that rose into the darkness. Of course, they were windows; he was near a house.

He moved his arms a little. They felt like lead, but unhurt. Then he realized that his legs were on fire. He tried to move them; everything went black again in a sudden agony of pain. The voice was still shrieking in his ears:

> "There's a girl in the heart of Maryland
> With a heart that belongs to mee."

But another voice could be heard, softer, talking endlessly in tender clear tones:

"An' he said they were goin' to take me way down south where there was a little house on the beach, all so warm an' quiet. . . ."

The song of the man beside him rose to a tuneless shriek, like a phonograph running down:

> "An' Mary-land was fairy-land
> When she said that mine she'd be . . ."

Another voice broke in suddenly in short spurts of whining groans that formed themselves into fragments of drawn-out intricate swearing. And all the while the soft voice went on. Andrews strained his ears to hear it. It soothed his pain as if some cool fragrant oil were being poured over his body.

"An' there'll be a garden full of flowers, roses an' hollyhocks, way down there in the south, an' it'll be so warm an' quiet, an' the sun'll shine all day, and the sky'll be so blue . . ."

Andrews felt his lips repeating the words like lips following a prayer.

"—An' it'll be so warm an' quiet, without any noise at all. An' the gar-den'll be full of roses an'. . ."

But the other voices kept breaking in, drowning out the soft voice with groans, and strings of whining oaths.

"An' he said I could sit on the porch, an' the sun'll be so warm an' quiet, an' the garden'll smell so good, an' the beach'll be all white, an' the sea . . ."

Andrews felt his head suddenly rise in the air and then his feet. He swung out of the darkness into a brilliant white corridor. His legs throbbed with flaming agony. The face of a man with a cigarette in his mouth peered close to his. A hand fumbled at his throat, where the tag was, and someone read:

"Andrews, I.432.286."

But he was listening to the voice out in the dark, behind him, that shrieked in rasping tones of delirium:

> "There's a girl in the heart of Mary-land
> With a heart that belongs to mee."

Then he discovered that he was groaning. His mind became entirely taken up in the curious rhythm of his groans. The only parts of his body that existed were his legs and something in his throat that groaned and groaned. It was absorbing. White figures hovered about him, he saw the hairy forearms of a man in shirt sleeves, lights glared and went out, strange smells entered at his nose and circulated through his whole body, but nothing could distract his attention from the singsong of his groans.

Rain fell in his face. He moved his head from side to side, suddenly feeling conscious of himself. His mouth was dry, like leather; he put out his tongue to try to catch raindrops in it. He was swung roughly about in the stretcher. He lifted his head cautiously, feeling a great throb of delight that he still could lift his head.

"Keep yer head down, can't yer?" snarled a voice beside him.

He had seen the back of a man in a gleaming wet slicker at the end of the stretcher.

"Be careful of my leg, can't yer?" he found himself whining over and over again. Then suddenly there was a lurch that rapped his head against the crosspiece of the stretcher, and he found himself looking up at a wooden ceiling from which the white paint had peeled in places. He smelt gasoline and could hear the throb of an engine. He began to think back; how long was it since he had looked at the little frogs in the puddle? A vivid picture came to his mind of the puddle with its putty-colored water and the little triangular heads of the frogs. But it seemed as long ago as a memory of childhood; all of his life before that was not so long as the time that had gone by since the car had started. And he was jolting and swinging about in the stretcher, clutching hard with his hands at the poles of the stretcher. The pain in his legs grew worse; the rest of his body seemed to shrivel under it. From below him came a rasping voice that cried out at every lurch of the ambulance. He fought against the desire to groan, but at last he gave in and lay lost in the monotonous singsong of his groans.

The rain was in his face again for a moment, then his body was tilted. A row of houses and russet trees and chimney pots against a leaden sky swung suddenly up into sight and were instantly replaced by a ceiling and the coffred vault of a staircase. Andrews was still groaning softly, but his eyes fastened with sudden interest on the sculptured rosettes of the coffres and the coats of arms that made the center of each section of ceiling. Then he found himself staring in the face of the man who was carrying the lower end of the stretcher. It was a white face with pimples round the mouth and good-natured, watery blue eyes. Andrews looked at the eyes and tried to smile, but the man carrying the stretcher was not looking at him.

Then after more endless hours of tossing about on the stretcher, lost in a groaning agony of pain, hands laid hold of him roughly and pulled his clothes off and lifted him on a cot where he lay gasping, breathing in the cool smell of disinfectant that hung about the bedclothes. He heard voices over his head.

"Isn't bad at all, this leg wound. . . . I thought you said we'd have to amputate?"

"Well, what's the matter with him, then?"

"Maybe shell-shock. . . ."

A cold sweat of terror took hold of Andrews. He lay perfectly still with his eyes closed. Spasm after spasm of revolt went through him. No, they hadn't broken him yet; he still had hold of his nerves, he kept saying to himself. Still, he felt that his hands, clasped across his belly, were trembling. The pain in his legs disappeared in the fright in which he lay, trying desperately to concentrate his mind on something outside himself. He tried to think of a tune to hum to himself, but he only heard again shrieking in his ears the voice which, it seemed to him months and years ago, had sung:

> "There's a girl in the heart of Maryland
> With a heart that belo-ongs to mee."

The voice shrieking the blurred tune and the pain in his legs mingled themselves strangely, until they seemed one and the pain seemed merely a throbbing of the maddening tune.

He opened his eyes. Darkness fading into a faint yellow glow. Hastily he took stock of himself, moved his head and his arms. He felt cool and very weak and quiet; he must have slept a long time. He passed his rough dirty hand over his face. The skin felt soft and cool. He pressed his cheek on the pillow and felt himself smiling contentedly, he did not know why.

The Queen of Sheba carried a parasol with little vermillion bells all round it that gave out a cool tinkle as she walked towards him. She wore her hair in a high headdress thickly powdered with blue iris powder, and on her long train, that a monkey held up at the end, were embroidered in gaudy colors the signs of the zodiac. She was not the Queen of Sheba, she was a nurse whose face he could not see in the obscurity, and, sticking an arm behind his head in a deft professional manner, she gave him something to drink from a glass without looking at him. He said "Thank you," in his natural voice, which surprised him in the silence; but she went off without replying and he saw that it was a trayful of glasses that had tinkled as she had come towards him.

Dark as it was he noticed the self-conscious tilt of the nurse's body as she walked silently to the next cot, holding the tray of glasses in front of her. He twisted his head round on the pillow to watch how gingerly she put her arm under the next man's head to give him a drink.

"A virgin," he said to himself, "very much a virgin," and he found himself giggling softly, notwithstanding the twinges of pain from his legs. He felt suddenly as if his spirit had awakened from a long torpor. The spell of dejection that had deadened him for months had slipped off. He was free. The thought came to him gleefully, that as long as he stayed in that cot in the hospital no one would shout orders at him. No one would tell him to clean his rifle. There would be no one to salute. He would not have to worry about making himself pleasant to the sergeant. He would lie there all day long, thinking his own thoughts.

Perhaps he was badly enough wounded to be discharged from the army. The thought set his heart beating like mad. That meant that he, who had given himself up for lost, who had let himself be trampled down unresistingly into the mud of slavery, who had looked for no escape from the treadmill but death, would live. He, John Andrews, would live.

And it seemed inconceivable that he had ever given himself up, that he had ever let the grinding discipline have its way with him. He saw himself vividly once more as he had seen himself before his life had suddenly blotted itself out, before he had become a slave among slaves. He remembered the garden where, in his boyhood, he had sat dreaming through the droning summer afternoons under the crêpe myrtle bushes, while the cornfields beyond rustled and shimmered in the heat. He remembered the day he had stood naked in the middle of a base room while the recruiting sergeant prodded him and measured him. He wondered suddenly what the date was. Could it be that it was only a year ago? Yet in that year all the other years of his life had been blotted out. But now he would begin living again. He would give up this cowardly cringing before external things. He would be recklessly himself.

The pain in his legs was gradually localizing itself into the wounds. For a while he struggled against it to go on thinking, but its constant throb kept impinging in his mind until, although he wanted desperately to comb through his pale memories to remember, if ever so faintly, all that had been vivid and lusty in his life, to build himself a new foundation of resistance against the world from which he could start afresh to live, he became again the querulous piece of hurt flesh, the slave broken on the treadmill; he began to groan.

Cold steel-gray light filtered into the ward, drowning the yellow glow which first turned ruddy and then disappeared. Andrews began to make out the row of cots opposite him, and the dark beams of the ceiling above his head. "This house must be very old," he said to himself, and the thought vaguely excited him. Funny that the Queen of Sheba had come to his head, it was ages since he'd thought of all that. *From the girl at the cross-roads singing under her street-lamp to the patrician pulling roses to pieces from the height of her litter, all the aspects half-guessed, all the imaginings of your desire . . .* that was the Queen of Sheba. He whispered the words aloud, "la reine de Saba, la reine de Saba"; and, with a tremor of anticipation of the sort he used to feel when he was a small boy the night before Christmas, with a sense of new things in store for him, he pillowed his head on his arm and went quietly to sleep.

"Ain't it juss like them frawgs te make a place like this into a hauspital?" said the orderly, standing with his feet wide apart and his hands on his hips, facing a row of cots and talking to anyone who felt well enough to listen. "Honest, I doan see why you fellers doan all cash in yer checks

in this hole. . . . There warn't even electric light till we put it in. . . .
What d'you think o' that? That shows how much the goddam frawgs
care. . . ." The orderly was a short man with a sallow, lined face and large
yellow teeth. When he smiled the horizontal lines in his forehead and the
lines that ran from the sides of his nose to the ends of his mouth deep-
ened so that his face looked as if it were made up to play a comic part in
the movies.

"It's kind of artistic, though, ain't it?" said Applebaum, whose cot was
next Andrews's,—a skinny man with large, frightened eyes and an inordinately red face that looked as if the skin had been peeled off. "Look at
the work there is on that ceiling. Must have cost some dough when it
was noo."

"Wouldn't be bad as a dance hall with a little fixin' up, but a hauspital; hell!"

Andrews lay, comfortable in his cot, looking into the ward out of another world. He felt no connection with the talk about him, with the
men who lay silent or tossed about groaning in the rows of narrow cots
that filled the Renaissance hall. In the yellow glow of the electric
lights, looking beyond the orderly's twisted face and narrow head, he
could see very faintly, where the beams of the ceiling sprung from the
wall, a row of half-obliterated shields supported by figures carved out
of the grey stone of the wall, handed satyrs with horns and goats'
beards and deep-set eyes, little squat figures of warriors and townsmen
in square hats with swords between their bent knees, naked limbs
twined in scrolls of spiked acanthus leaves, all seen very faintly, so that
when the electric lights swung back and forth in the wind made by the
orderly's hurried passing, they all seemed to wink and wriggle in shadowy mockery of the rows of prostrate bodies in the room beneath
them. Yet they were familiar, friendly to Andrews. He kept feeling a
half-formulated desire to be up there too, crowded under a beam, grimacing through heavy wreaths of pomegranates and acanthus leaves,
the incarnation of old rich lusts, of clear fires that had sunk to dust ages
since. He felt at home in that spacious hall, built for wide gestures and
stately steps, in which all the little routine of the army seemed unreal,
and the wounded men discarded automatons, broken toys laid away in
rows.

Andrews was snatched out of his thoughts. Applebaum was speaking
to him; he turned his head.

"How d'you loike it bein' wounded, buddy?"

"Fine."

"Foine, I should think it was. . . . Better than doin' squads right all
day."

"Where did you get yours?"

"Ain't got only one arm now. . . . I don't give a damn. . . . I've driven my last fare, that's all."

"How d'you mean?"

"I used to drive a taxi."

"That's a pretty good job, isn't it?"

"You bet, big money in it, if yer in right."

"So you used to be a taxi-driver, did you?" broke in the orderly. "That's a fine job. . . . When I was in the Providence Hospital half the fractures was caused by taxis. We had a little girl of six in the children's ward had her feet cut clean off at the ankles by a taxi. Pretty yellow hair she had, too. Gangrene. . . . Only lasted a day. . . . Well, I'm going off. I guess you guys wish you was going to be where I'm goin' to be tonight. . . . That's one thing you guys are lucky in, don't have to worry about propho." The orderly wrinkled his face up and winked elaborately.

"Say, will you do something for me?" asked Andrews.

"Sure, if it ain't no trouble."

"Will you buy me a book?"

"Ain't ye got enough with all the books at the 'Y'?"

"No. . . . This is a special book," said Andrews smiling, "a French book."

"A French book, is it? Well, I'll see what I can do. What's it called?"

"By Flaubert. . . . Look, if you've got a piece of paper and a pencil, I'll write it down."

Andrews scrawled the title on the back of an order slip.

"There."

"What the hell? Who's Antoine? Gee whiz, I bet that's hot stuff. I wish I could read French. We'll have you breakin' loose out o' here an' going down to number four, roo Villiay, if you read that kind o' book."

"Has it got pictures?" asked Applebaum.

"One feller did break out o' here a month ago. . . . Couldn't stand it any longer, I guess. Well, his wound opened an' he had a hemorrhage, an' now he's planted out in the back lot. . . . But I'm goin'. Goodnight." The orderly bustled to the end of the ward and disappeared.

The lights went out, except for the bulb over the nurse's desk at the end, beside the ornate doorway, with its wreathed pinnacles carved out of the grey stone, which could be seen above the white canvas screen that hid the door.

"What's that book about, buddy?" asked Applebaum, twisting his head at the end of his lean neck so as to look Andrews full in the face.

"Oh, it's about a man who wants everything so badly that he decides there's nothing worth wanting."

"I guess youse had a college edication," said Applebaum sarcastically.

Andrews laughed.

"Well, I was goin' to tell youse about when I used to drive a taxi. I was makin' big money when I enlisted. Was you drafted?"

"Yes."

"Well, so was I. I doan think nauthin o' them guys that are so stuck up 'cause they enlisted, d'you?"

"Not a hell of a lot."

"Don't yer?" came a voice from the other side of Andrews,—a thin voice that stuttered. "W-w-well, all I can say is, it'ld have sss-spoiled my business if I hadn't enlisted. No, sir, nobody can say I didn't enlist."

"Well, that's your look-out," said Applebaum.

"You're goddam right, it was."

"Well, ain't your business spoiled anyway?"

"No, sir. I can pick it right up where I left off. I've got an established reputation."

"What at?"

"I'm an undertaker by profession; my dad was before me."

"Gee, you were right at home!" said Andrews.

"You haven't any right to say that, young feller," said the undertaker angrily. "I'm a humane man. I won't never be at home in this dirty butchery."

The nurse was walking by their cots.

"How can you say such dreadful things?" she said. "But lights are out. You boys have got to keep quiet. . . . And you," she plucked at the undertaker's bedclothes, "just remember what the Huns did in Belgium. . . . Poor Miss Cavell, a nurse just like I am."

Andrews closed his eyes. The ward was quiet except for the rasping sound of the snores and heavy breathing of the shattered men all about him. "And I thought she was the Queen of Sheba," he said to himself, making a grimace in the dark. Then he began to think of the music he had intended to write about the Queen of Sheba before he had stripped his life off in the bare room where they had measured him and made a soldier of him. Standing in the dark in the desert of his despair, he would hear the sound of a caravan in the distance, tinkle of bridles, rasping of horns, braying of donkeys, and the throaty voices of men singing the songs of desolate roads. He would look up, and before him he would see, astride their foaming wild asses, the three green horsemen motionless, pointing at him with their long forefingers. Then the music would burst in a sudden hot whirlwind about him, full of flutes and kettledrums and braying horns and whining bagpipes, and torches would flare red and yellow, making a tent of light about him, on the edges of which would crowd the sumpter mules and the brown mule drivers, and the gaudily caparisoned camels, and the elephants glistening with jewelled harness. Naked slaves would bend their gleaming backs before him as they laid

out a carpet at his feet; and, through the flare of torch-light, the Queen
of Sheba would advance towards him, covered with emeralds and dull-
gold ornaments, with a monkey hopping behind holding up the end of
her long train. She would put her hand with its slim fantastic nails on his
shoulder; and, looking into her eyes, he would suddenly feel within reach
all the fiery imaginings of his desire.

Oh, if he could only be free to work. All the months he had wasted
in his life seemed to be marching like a procession of ghosts before his
eyes. And he lay in his cot, staring with wide open eyes at the ceiling,
hoping desperately that his wounds would be long in healing.

Applebaum sat on the edge of his cot, dressed in a clean new uniform,
of which the left sleeve hung empty, still showing the creases in which it
had been folded.

"So you really are going," said Andrews, rolling his head over on his
pillow to look at him.

"You bet your pants I am, Andy. . . . An' so could you, poifectly well,
if you'ld talk it up to 'em a little."

"Oh, I wish to God I could. Not that I want to go home, now, but
. . . if I could get out of uniform."

"I don't blame ye a bit, Kid; well, next time, we'll know better. . . .
Local Board Chairman's going to be my job."

Andrews laughed.

"If I wasn't a sucker . . ."

"You weren't the only wewe-one," came the undertaker's stuttering
voice from behind Andrews.

"Hell, I thought you enlisted, undertaker."

"Well, I did, by God. But I didn't think it was going to be like
this. . . ."

"What did ye think it was going to be, a picnic?"

"Hell, I doan care about that, or gettin' gassed, and smashed up, or
anythin', but I thought we was goin' to put things to rights by comin'
over here. . . . Look here, I had a lively business in the undertaking way,
like my father had had before me. . . . We did all the swellest work in
Tilletsville. . . ."

"Where?" interrupted Applebaum, laughing.

"Tilletsville; don't you know any geography?"

"Go ahead, tell us about Tilletsville," said Andrews soothingly.

"Why, when Senator Wallace d-d-deceased there, who d'you think
had charge of embalming the body and taking it to the station an' seeing everything was done fitting? We did. . . . And I was going to be married to a dandy girl, and I knowed I had enough pull to get fixed up,
somehow, or to get a commission even, but there I went like a sucker an'

enlisted in the infantry, too. . . . But, hell, everybody was saying that we was going to fight to make the world safe for democracy, and that, if a feller didn't go, no one'ld trade with him any more."

He started coughing suddenly and seemed unable to stop. At last he said weakly, in a thin little voice between coughs:

"Well, here I am. There ain't nothing to do about it."

"Democracy. . . . That's democracy, ain't it: we eat stinkin' goolash an' that there fat 'Y' woman goes out with Colonels eatin' chawklate souf-flay. . . . Poifect democracy! . . . But I tell you what: it don't do to be the goat."

"But there's so damn many more goats than anything else," said Andrews.

"There's a sucker born every minute, as Barnum said. You learn that drivin' a taxicab, if ye don't larn nothin' else. . . . No, sir, I'm goin' into politics. I've got good connections up Hundred and Twenty-fif' street way. . . . You see, I've got an aunt, Mrs. Sallie Schultz, owns a hotel on a Hundred and Tirty-tird street. Heard of Jim O'Ryan, ain't yer? Well, he's a good friend o' hers; see? Bein' as they're both Catholics . . . But I'm goin' out this afternoon, see what the town's like . . . an ole Ford says the skirts are just peaches an' cream."

"He juss s-s-says that to torment a feller," stuttered the undertaker.

"I wish I were going with you," said Andrews.

"You'll get well plenty soon enough, Andy, and get yourself marked Class A, and get given a gun, an—'Over the top, boys!'. . . to see if the Fritzies won't make a better shot next time. . . . Talk about suckers! You're the most poifect sucker I ever met. . . . What did you want to tell the loot your legs didn't hurt bad for? They'll have you out o' here before you know it. . . . Well, I'm goin' out to see what the mamzelles look like."

Applebaum, the uniform hanging in folds about his skinny body, swaggered to the door, followed by the envious glances of the whole ward.

"Gee, guess he thinks he's goin' to get to be president," said the undertaker bitterly.

"He probably will," said Andrews.

He settled himself in his bed again, sinking back into the dull contemplation of the teasing, smarting pain where the torn ligaments of his thighs were slowly knitting themselves together. He tried desperately to forget the pain; there was so much he wanted to think out. If he could only lie perfectly quiet, and piece together the frayed ends of thoughts that kept flickering to the surface of his mind. He counted up the days he had been in the hospital; fifteen! Could it be that long? And he had not thought of anything yet. Soon, as Applebaum said, they'd be putting him in Class A and sending him back to the treadmill, and he would not have reconquered his courage, his dominion over himself. What a coward he had been anyway, to submit. The man beside him kept coughing. Andrews stared for a moment at the silhouette of the yellow face on the pillow, with its pointed nose and small greedy eyes. He thought of the swell undertaking establishment, of the black gloves and long faces and soft tactful voices. That man and his father before him lived by pretending things they didn't feel, by swathing reality with all manner of crêpe and trumpery. For those people, no one ever died, they passed away, they deceased. Still, there had to be undertakers. There was no more stain about that than about any other trade. And it was so as not to spoil his trade that the undertaker had enlisted, and to make the world safe for democracy, too. The phrase came to Andrews's mind amid·an avalanche of popular tunes, of visions of patriotic numbers on the vaudeville stage. He remembered the great flags waving triumphantly over Fifth Avenue, and the crowds dutifully cheering. But those were valid reasons for the undertaker; but for him, John Andrews, were they valid reasons? No. He had no trade, he had not been driven into the army by the force of public opinion, he had not been carried away by any wave of blind confidence in the phrases of bought propagandists. He had not had the strength to live. The thought came to him of all those who, down the long tragedy of history, had given themselves smilingly for the integrity of their thoughts. He had not had the courage to move a muscle for his freedom, but he had been fairly cheerful about risking his life as a soldier, in a cause he believed useless. What right had a man to exist who was too cowardly to stand up for what he thought and felt, for his whole makeup, for everything that made him an individual apart from his fellows, and not a slave to stand cap in hand waiting for someone of stronger will to tell him to act?

Like a sudden nausea, disgust surged up in him. His mind ceased formulating phrases and thoughts. He gave himself over to disgust as a man who has drunk a great deal, holding on tight to the reins of his will, suddenly gives himself over pellmell to drunkenness.

He lay very still, with his eyes closed, listening to the stir of the ward, the voices of men talking and the fits of coughing that shook the man next him. The smarting pain throbbed monotonously. He felt hungry and wondered vaguely if it were supper time. How little they gave you to eat in the hospital!

He called over to the man in the opposite cot:

"Hay, Stalky, what time is it?"

"It's after messtime now. Got a good appetite for the steak and onions and French fried potatoes?"

"Shut up."

A rattling of tin dishes at the other end of the ward made Andrews wriggle up further on his pillow. Verses from the "Shropshire Lad" jingled mockingly through his head:

> "The world, it was the old world yet,
> I was I, my things were wet,
> And nothing now remained to do
> But begin the game anew."

After he had eaten, he picked up the "Tentation de Saint Antoine," that lay on the cot beside his immovable legs, and buried himself in it, reading the gorgeously modulated sentences voraciously, as if the book were a drug in which he could drink deep forgetfulness of himself.

He put the book down and closed his eyes. His mind was full of intangible floating glow, like the ocean on a warm night, when every wave breaks into pale flame, and mysterious milky lights keep rising to the surface out of the dark waters and gleaming and vanishing. He became absorbed in the strange fluid harmonies that permeated his whole body, as a grey sky at nightfall suddenly becomes filled with endlessly changing patterns of light and color and shadow.

When he tried to seize hold of his thoughts, to give them definite musical expression in his mind, he found himself suddenly empty, the way a sandy inlet on the beach that has been full of shoals of silver fishes, becomes suddenly empty when a shadow crosses the water, and the man who is watching sees wanly his own reflection instead of the flickering of thousands of tiny silver bodies.

John Andrews awoke to feel a cold hand on his head.

"Feeling all right?" said a voice in his ear.

He found himself looking in a puffy, middle-aged face, with a lean nose and grey eyes, with dark rings under them. Andrews felt the eyes looking him over inquisitively. He saw the red triangle on the man's khaki sleeve.

"Yes," he said.

"If you don't mind, I'd like to talk to you a little while, buddy."

"Not a bit; have you got a chair?" said Andrews smiling.

"I don't suppose it was just right of me to wake you up, but you see it was this way. . . . You were the next in line, an' I was afraid I'd forget you, if I skipped you."

"I understand," said Andrews, with a sudden determination to take the initiative away from the "Y" man. "How long have you been in France? D'you like the war?" he asked hurriedly.

The "Y" man smiled sadly.

"You seem pretty spry," he said. "I guess you're in a hurry to get back at the front and get some more Huns." He smiled again, with an air of indulgence.

Andrews did not answer.

"No, sonny, I don't like it here," the "Y" man said, after a pause. "I wish I was home—but it's great to feel you're doing your duty."

"It must be," said Andrews.

"Have you heard about the great air raids our boys have pulled off? They've bombarded Frankfort; now if they could only wipe Berlin off the map."

"Say, d'you hate 'em awful hard?" said Andrews in a low voice. "Because, if you do, I can tell you something will tickle you most to death. . . . Lean over."

The "Y" man leant over curiously.

"Some German prisoners come to this hospital at six every night to get the garbage; now all you need to do if you really hate 'em so bad is borrow a revolver from one of your officer friends, and just shoot up the convoy. . . ."

"Say . . . where were you raised, boy?" The "Y" man sat up suddenly with a look of alarm on his face. "Don't you know that prisoners are sacred?"

"D'you know what our colonel told us before going into the Argonne offensive? The more prisoners we took, the less grub there'ld be; and do you know what happened to the prisoners that were taken? Why do you hate the Huns?"

"Because they are barbarians, enemies of civilization. You must have enough education to know that," said the "Y" man, raising his voice angrily. "What church do you belong to?"

"None."

"But you must have been connected with some church, boy. You can't have been raised a heathen in America. Every Christian belongs or has belonged to some church or other from baptism."

"I make no pretensions to Christianity."

Andrews closed his eyes and turned his head away. He could feel the "Y" man hovering over him irresolutely. After a while he opened his eyes. The "Y" man was leaning over the next bed.

Through the window at the opposite side of the ward he could see a bit of blue sky among white scroll-like clouds, with mauve shadows. He stared at it until the clouds, beginning to grow golden into evening, covered it. Furious, hopeless irritation consumed him. How these people enjoyed hating! At that rate it was better to be at the front. Men were more humane when they were killing each other than when they were talking about it. So was civilization nothing but a vast edifice of sham, and the war, instead of its crumbling, was its fullest and most ultimate expression.

Oh, but there must be something more in the world than greed and hatred and cruelty. Were they all shams, too, these gigantic phrases that floated like gaudy kites high above mankind? Kites, that was it, contraptions of tissue paper held at the end of a string, ornaments not to be taken seriously. He thought of all the long procession of men who had been touched by the unutterable futility of the lives of men, who had tried by phrases to make things otherwise, who had taught unworldliness. Dim enigmatic figures they were—Democritus, Socrates, Epicurus, Christ; so many of them, and so vague in the silvery mist of history that he hardly knew that they were not his own imagining; Lucretius, St. Francis, Voltaire, Rousseau, and how many others, known and unknown, through the tragic centuries; they had wept, some of them, and some of them had laughed, and their phrases had risen glittering, soap bubbles to dazzle men for a moment, and had shattered. And he felt a crazy desire to join the forlorn ones, to throw himself into inevitable defeat, to live his life as he saw it in spite of everything, to proclaim once more the falseness of the gospels under the cover of which greed and fear filled with more and yet more pain the already unbearable agony of human life.

As soon as he got out of the hospital he would desert; the determination formed suddenly in his mind, making the excited blood surge gloriously through his body. There was nothing else to do; he would desert. He pictured himself hobbling away in the dark on his lame legs, stripping his uniform off, losing himself in some out of the way corner of France, or slipping by the sentries to Spain and freedom. He was ready to endure anything, to face any sort of death, for the sake of a few months of liberty in which to forget the degradation of this last year. This was his last run with the pack.

An enormous exhilaration took hold of him. It seemed the first time in his life he had ever determined to act. All the rest had been aimless drifting. The blood sang in his ears. He fixed his eyes on the half-obliterated figures that supported the shields under the beams in the wall opposite. They seemed to be wriggling out of their contorted positions and smiling encouragement to him. He imagined them, warriors out of old tales, on their way to slay dragons in enchanted woods, clever-fingered guildsmen and artisans, cupids and satyrs and fauns, jumping from their niches and carrying him off with them in a headlong rout, to a sound of flutes, on a last forlorn assault on the citadels of pain.

The lights went out, and an orderly came round with chocolate that poured with a pleasant soothing sound into the tin cups. With a greasiness of chocolate in his mouth and the warmth of it in his stomach, John Andrews went to sleep.

There was a stir in the ward when he woke up. Reddish sunlight filtered in through the window opposite, and from outside came a confused noise, a sound of bells ringing and whistles blowing.

Andrews looked past his feet towards Stalky's cot opposite. Stalky was sitting bolt upright in bed, with his eyes round as quarters.

"Fellers, the war's over!"

"Put him out."

"Cut that."

"Pull the chain."

"Tie that bull outside," came from every side of the ward.

"Fellers," shouted Stalky louder than ever, "it's straight dope, the war's over. I just dreamt the Kaiser came up to me on Fourteenth Street and bummed a nickel for a glass of beer. The war's over. Don't you hear the whistles?"

"All right; let's go home."

"Shut up, can't you let a feller sleep?"

The ward quieted down again, but all eyes were wide open, men lay strangely still in their cots, waiting, wondering.

"All I can say," shouted Stalky again, "is that she was some war while she lasted. . . . What did I tell yer?"

As he spoke the canvas screen in front of the door collapsed and the major appeared with his cap askew over his red face and a brass bell in his hand, which he rang frantically as he advanced into the ward.

"Men," he shouted in the deep roar of one announcing baseball scores, "the war ended at 4:03 A.M. this morning. . . . The Armistice is signed. To hell with the Kaiser!" Then he rang the dinner bell madly and danced along the aisle between the rows of cots, holding the head nurse by one hand, who held a little yellow-headed lieutenant by the other hand, who, in turn, held another nurse, and so on. The line advanced jerkily into the ward; the front part was singing "The Star Spangled Banner," and the rear the "Yanks are Coming," and through it all the major rang his brass bell. The men who were well enough sat up in bed and yelled. The others rolled restlessly about, sickened by the din.

They made the circuit of the ward and filed out, leaving confusion behind them. The dinner bell could be heard faintly in the other parts of the building.

"Well, what d'you think of it, undertaker?" said Andrews.

"Nothing."

"Why?"

The undertaker turned his small black eyes on Andrews and looked him straight in the face.

"You know what's the matter with me, don't yer, outside o' this wound?"

"No."

"Coughing like I am, I'd think you'd be more observant. I got t.b., young feller."

"How do you know that?"

"They're going to move me out o' here to a t.b. ward tomorrow."

"The hell they are!" Andrews's words were lost in the paroxysm of coughing that seized the man next to him.

"Home, boys, home; it's home we want to be."

Those well enough were singing, Stalky conducting, standing on the end of his cot in his pink Red Cross pajamas, that were too short and showed a long expanse of skinny leg, fuzzy with red hairs. He banged together two bed pans to beat time.

"Home. . . . I won't never go home," said the undertaker when the noise had subsided a little. "D'you know what I wish? I wish the war'd gone on and on until everyone of them bastards had been killed in it."

"Which bastards?"

"The men who got us fellers over here." He began coughing again weakly.

"But they'll be safe if every other human being . . ." began Andrews. He was interrupted by a thundering voice from the end of the ward.

"Attention!"

"Home, boys, home, it's home we want to be,"

went on the song. Stalky glanced towards the end of the ward, and seeing it was the major, dropped the bed pans that smashed at the foot of his cot, and got as far as possible under his blankets.

"Attention!" thundered the major again. A sudden uncomfortable silence fell upon the ward, broken only by the coughing of the man next to Andrews.

"If I hear any more noise from this ward, I'll chuck everyone of you men out of this hospital; if you can't walk you'll have to crawl. . . . The war may be over, but you men are in the Army, and don't you forget it."

The major glared up and down the lines of cots. He turned on his heel and went out of the door, glancing angrily as he went at the overturned screen. The ward was still. Outside whistles blew and churchbells rang madly, and now and then there was a sound of singing.

II

The snow beat against the windows and pattered on the tin roof of the lean-to, built against the side of the hospital, that went by the name of sun parlor. It was a dingy place, decorated by strings of dusty little paper flags that one of the "Y" men had festooned about the slanting beams of the ceiling to celebrate Christmas. There were tables with torn magazines piled on them, and a counter where cracked white cups were ranged waiting for one of the rare occasions when cocoa could be bought. In the middle of the room, against the wall of the main building, a stove was burning, about which sat several men in hospital denims talking in drowsy voices. Andrews watched them from his seat by the window, looking at their broad backs bent over towards the stove and at the hands that hung over their knees, limp from boredom. The air was heavy with a smell of coal gas mixed with carbolic from men's clothes, and stale cigarette smoke. Behind the cups at the counter a "Y" man, a short, red-haired man with freckles, read the Paris edition of the *New York Herald*. Andrews, in his seat by the window, felt permeated by the stagnation about him: He had a sheaf of pencilled music-papers on his knees, that he rolled and unrolled nervously, staring at the stove and the motionless backs of the men about it. The stove roared a little, the "Y" man's paper rustled, men's voices came now and then in a drowsy whisper, and outside the snow beat evenly and monotonously against the window panes. Andrews pictured himself vaguely walking fast through the streets, with the snow stinging his face and the life of a city swirling about him, faces flushed by the cold, bright eyes under hatbrims, looking for a second into his and passing on; slim forms of women bundled in shawls that showed vaguely the outline of their breasts and hips. He wondered if he would ever be free again to walk at random through city streets. He stretched his legs out across the floor in front of him; strange, stiff, tremulous legs they were, but it was not the wounds that gave them their leaden weight. It was the stagnation of the life about him that he felt sinking into every crevice of his spirit, so that he could never shake it off, the stagnation of dusty ruined automatons that had lost all life of their own, whose limbs had practised the drill manual so long that they had no movements of their own left, who sat limply, sunk in boredom, waiting for orders.

Andrews was roused suddenly from his thoughts; he had been watching the snowflakes in their glittering dance just outside the window pane, when the sound of someone rubbing his hands very close to him made him look up. A little man with chubby cheeks and steel-grey hair very neatly flattened against his skull, stood at the window rubbing his fat little white hands together and making a faint unctuous puffing with each breath. Andrews noticed that a white clerical collar enclosed the little man's pink neck, that starched cuffs peeped from under the well-tailored sleeves of his officer's uniform. Sam Brown belt and puttees, too, were highly polished. On his shoulder was a demure little silver cross.

Andrews's glance had reached the pink cheeks again, when he suddenly found a pair of steely eyes looking sharply into his.

"You look quite restored, my friend," said a chanting clerical voice.

"I suppose I am."

"Splendid, splendid. . . . But do you mind moving into the end of the room? That's it." He followed Andrews, saying in a deprecatory tone: "We're going to have just a little bit of a prayer and then I have some interesting things to tell you boys."

The red-headed "Y" man had left his seat and stood in the center of the room, his paper still dangling from his hand, saying in a bored voice: "Please fellows, move down to the end. . . . Quiet, please. . . . Quiet, please."

The soldiers shambled meekly to the folding chairs at the end of the room and after some chattering were quiet. A couple of men left, and several tiptoed in and sat in the front row. Andrews sank into a chair with a despairing sort of resignation, and burying his face in his hands stared at the floor between his feet.

"Fellers," went on the bored voice of the "Y" man, "let me introduce the Reverend Dr. Skinner, who—" the "Y" man's voice suddenly took on deep patriotic emotion—"who has just come back from the Army of Occupation in Germany."

At the words "Army of Occupation," as if a spring had been touched, everybody clapped and cheered.

The Reverend Dr. Skinner looked about his audience with smiling confidence and raised his hands for silence, so that the men could see the chubby pink palms.

"First, boys, my dear friends, let us indulge in a few moments of silent prayer to our Great Creator," his voice rose and fell in the suave chant of one accustomed to going through the episcopal liturgy for the edification of well-dressed and well-fed congregations. "Inasmuch as He has vouchsafed us safety and a mitigation of our afflictions, and let us pray that in His good time He may see fit to return us whole in limb and pure in heart to our families, to the wives, mothers, and to those whom we will some day honor with the name of wife, who eagerly await our return; and that we may spend the remainder of our lives in useful service of the great country for whose safety and glory we have offered up our youth a willing sacrifice. . . . Let us pray!"

Silence fell dully on the room. Andrews could hear the self-conscious breathing of the men about him, and the rustling of the snow against the tin roof. A few feet scraped. The voice began again after a long pause, chanting:

"Our Father which art in Heaven . . ."

At the "Amen" everyone lifted his head cheerfully. Throats were cleared, chairs scraped. Men settled themselves to listen.

"Now, my friends, I am going to give you in a few brief words a little glimpse into Germany, so that you may be able to picture to yourselves the way your comrades of the Army of Occupation manage to make themselves comfortable among the Huns. . . . I ate my Christmas dinner in Coblenz. What do you think of that? Never had I thought that a Christmas would find me away from my home and loved ones. But what unexpected things happen to us in this world! Christmas in Coblenz under the American flag!"

He paused a moment to allow a little scattered clapping to subside.

"The turkey was fine, too, I can tell you. . . . Yes, our boys in Germany are very, very comfortable, and just waiting for the word, if necessary, to continue their glorious advance to Berlin. For I am sorry to say, boys, that the Germans have not undergone the change of heart for which we had hoped. They have, indeed, changed the name of their institutions, but their spirit they have not changed. . . . How grave a disappointment it must be to our great President, who has exerted himself so to bring the German people to reason, to make them understand the horror that they alone have brought deliberately upon the world! Alas! Far from it. Indeed, they have attempted with insidious propaganda to undermine the morale of our troops. . . ." A little storm of muttered epithets went through the room. The Reverend Dr. Skinner elevated his chubby pink palms and smiled benignantly . . . "to undermine the morale of our troops; so that the most stringent regulations have had to be made by the commanding general to prevent it. Indeed, my friends, I very much fear that we stopped too soon in our victorious advance; that Germany should have been utterly crushed. But all we can do is watch and wait, and abide by the decision of those great men who in a short time will be gathered together at the Conference at Paris. . . . Let me, boys, my dear friends, express the hope that you may speedily be cured of your wounds, ready again to do willing service in the ranks of the glorious army that must be vigilant for some time yet, I fear, to defend, as Americans and Christians, the civilization you have so nobly saved from a ruthless foe. . . . Let us all join together in singing the hymn, 'Stand up, stand up for Jesus,' which I am sure you all know."

The men got to their feet, except for a few who had lost their legs, and sang the first verse of the hymn unsteadily. The second verse petered out altogether, leaving only the "Y" man and the Reverend Dr. Skinner singing away at the top of their lungs.

The Reverend Dr. Skinner pulled out his gold watch and looked at it frowning.

"Oh, my, I shall miss the train," he muttered. The "Y" man helped him into his voluminous trench coat and they both hurried out of the door.

"Those are some puttees he had on, I'll tell you," said the legless man who was propped in a chair near the stove.

Andrews sat down beside him, laughing. He was a man with high cheekbones and powerful jaws to whose face the pale brown eyes and delicately pencilled lips gave a look of great gentleness. Andrews did not look at his body.

"Somebody said he was a Red Cross man giving out cigarettes. . . . Fooled us that time," said Andrews.

"Have a butt? I've got one," said the legless man. With a large shrunken hand that was the transparent color of alabaster he held out a box of cigarettes.

"Thanks." When Andrews struck a match he had to lean over the legless man to light his cigarette for him. He could not help glancing down the man's tunic at the drab trousers that hung limply from the chair. A cold shudder went through him; he was thinking of the zigzag scars on his own thighs.

"Did you get it in the legs, too, Buddy?" asked the legless man, quietly.

"Yes, but I had luck. . . . How long have you been here?"

"Since Christ was a corporal. Oh, I doan know. I've been here since two weeks after my outfit first went into the lines. . . . That was on November 16th, 1917. . . . Didn't see much of the war, did I? . . . Still, I guess I didn't miss much."

"No. . . . But you've seen enough of the army."

"That's true. . . . I guess I wouldn't mind the war if it wasn't for the army."

"They'll be sending you home soon, won't they?"

"Guess so. . . . Where are you from?"

"New York," said Andrews.

"I'm from Cranston, Wisconsin. D'you know that country? It's a great country for lakes. You can canoe for days an' days without a portage. We have a camp on Big Loon Lake. We used to have some wonderful times there . . . lived like wild men. I went for a trip for three weeks once without seeing a house. Ever done much canoeing?"

"Not so much as I'd like to."

"That's the thing to make you feel fit. First thing you do when you shake out of your blankets is jump in an' have a swim. Gee, it's great to swim when the morning mist is still on the water an' the sun just strikes the tops of the birch trees. Ever smelt bacon cooking? I mean out in the woods, in a frying pan over some sticks of pine and beech wood. . . . Some great old smell, isn't it? . . . And after you've paddled all day, an'

feel tired and sunburned right to the palms of your feet, to sit around the
fire with some trout roastin' in the ashes and hear the sizzlin' the bacon
makes in the pan. . . . O boy!" He stretched his arms wide.

"God, I'd like to have wrung that damn little parson's neck," said
Andrews suddenly.

"Would you?" The legless man turned brown eyes on Andrews with a
smile. "I guess he's about as much to blame as anybody is . . . guys like
him. . . . I guess they have that kind in Germany, too."

"You don't think we've made the world quite as safe for Democracy
as it might be?" said Andrews in a low voice.

"Hell, how should I know? I bet you never drove an ice wagon. . . .
I did, all one summer down home. . . . It was some life. Get up at three
o'clock in the morning an' carry a hundred or two hundred pounds of
ice into everybody's ice box. That was the life to make a feller feel fit. I
was goin' around with a big Norwegian named Olaf, who was the
strongest man I ever knew. An' drink! He was the boy could drink. I
once saw him put away twenty-five dry Martini cocktails an' swim across
the lake on top of it. . . . I used to weigh a hundred and eighty pounds,
and he could pick me up with one hand and put me across his shoulder.
. . . That was the life to make a feller feel fit. Why, after bein' out late
the night before, we'd jump up out of bed at three o'clock feeling
springy as a cat."

"What's he doing now?" asked Andrews.

"He died on the transport coming 'cross here. Died o' the flu. . . . I
met a feller came over in his regiment. They dropped him overboard
when they were in sight of the Azores. . . . Well, I didn't die of the flu.
Have another butt?"

"No, thanks," said Andrews.

They were silent. The fire roared in the stove. No one was talking.
The men lolled in chairs somnolently. Now and then someone spat.
Outside of the window Andrews could see the soft white dancing of the
snowflakes. His limbs felt very heavy; his mind was permeated with dusty
stagnation like the stagnation of old garrets and lumber rooms, where,
among superannuated bits of machinery and cracked grimy crockery, lie
heaps of broken toys.

John Andrews sat on a bench in a square full of linden trees, with the pale
winter sunshine full on his face and hands. He had been looking up
through his eyelashes at the sun, that was the color of honey, and he let
his dazzled glance sink slowly through the black lacework of twigs, down
the green trunks of the trees to the bench opposite where sat two nursemaids and, between them, a tiny girl with a face daintily colored and life-
less like a doll's face, and a frilled dress under which showed small ivory

knees and legs encased in white socks and yellow sandals. Above the yellow halo of her hair floated, with the sun shining through it, as through a glass of claret, a bright carmine balloon which the child held by a string. Andrews looked at her for a long time, enraptured by the absurd daintiness of the figure between the big bundles of flesh of the nursemaids. The thought came to him suddenly that months had gone by,—was it only months?—since his hands had touched anything soft, since he had seen any flowers. The last was a flower an old woman had given him in a village in the Argonne, an orange marigold, and he remembered how soft the old woman's withered lips had been against his cheek when she had leaned over and kissed him. His mind suddenly lit up, as with a strain of music, with a sense of the sweetness of quiet lives worn away monotonously in the fields, in the grey streets of little provincial towns, in old kitchens full of fragrance of herbs and tang of smoke from the hearth, where there are pots on the window-sill full of basil in flower.

Something made him go up to the little girl and take her hand. The child, looking up suddenly and seeing a lanky soldier with pale lean face and light, straw-colored hair escaping from under a cap too small for him, shrieked and let go the string of the balloon, which soared slowly into the air trembling a little in the faint cool wind that blew. The child wailed dismally, and Andrews, quailing under the furious glances of the nursemaids, stood before her, flushed crimson, stammering apologies, not knowing what to do. The white caps of the nursemaids bent over and ribbons fluttered about the child's head as they tried to console her. Andrews walked away dejectedly, now and then looking up at the balloon, which soared, a black speck against the grey and topaz-colored clouds.

"Sale Américain," he heard one nursemaid exclaim to the other.

But this was the first hour in months he had had free, the first moment of solitude; he must live; soon he would be sent back to his division. A wave of desire for furious fleshly enjoyments went through him, making him want steaming dishes of food drenched in rich, spice-flavored sauces; making him want to get drunk on strong wine; to roll on thick carpets in the arms of naked, libidinous women. He was walking down the quiet grey street of the provincial town, with its low houses with red chimney pots, and blue slate roofs and its irregular yellowish cobbles. A clock somewhere was striking four with deep booming strokes, Andrews laughed. He had to be in hospital at six.

Already he was tired; his legs ached.

The window of a pastry shop appeared invitingly before him, denuded as it was by wartime. A sign in English said: "Tea." Walking in, he sat down in a fussy little parlor where the tables had red cloths, and a print, in pinkish and greenish colors, hung in the middle of the imitation brocade paper of each wall. Under a print of a poster bed with curtains in front of which eighteen to twenty people bowed, with the title of "Secret d'Amour," sat three young officers, who cast cold, irritated glances at this private with a hospital badge on who invaded their tea shop. Andrews stared back at them, flaming with dull anger.

Sipping the hot, fragrant tea, he sat with a blank sheet of music paper before him, listening in spite of himself to what the officers were saying. They were talking about Ronsard. It was with irritated surprise that Andrews heard the name. What right had they to be talking about Ronsard? He knew more about Ronsard than they did. Furious, conceited phrases kept surging up in his mind. He was as sensitive, as humane, as intelligent, as well-read as they were; what right had they to the cold suspicious glance with which they had put him in his place when he had come into the room? Yet that had probably been as unconscious, as unavoidable as was his own biting envy. The thought that if one of those men should come over to him, he would have to stand up and salute and answer humbly, not from civility, but from the fear of being punished, was bitter as wormwood, filled him with a childish desire to prove his worth to them, as when older boys had ill-treated him at school and he had prayed to have the house burn down so that he might heroically save them all. There was a piano in an inner room, where in the dark the chairs, upside down, perched dismally on the table tops. He almost obeyed an impulse to go in there and start playing, by the brilliance of his playing to force these men, who thought of him as a coarse automaton, something between a man and a dog, to recognize him as an equal, a superior.

"But the war's over. I want to start living. *Red wine, the nightingale cries to the rose,*" said one of the officers.

"What do you say we go A.W.O.L. to Paris?"

"Dangerous."

"Well, what can they do? We are not enlisted men; they can only send us home. That's just what I want."

"I'll tell you what; we'll go to the Cochon Bleu and have a cocktail and think about it."

"*The lion and the lizard keep their courts where . . .* what the devil was his name? Anyway, we'll glory and drink deep, while Major Peabody keeps his court in Dijon to his heart's content."

Spurs jingled as the three officers went out. A fierce disgust took possession of John Andrews. He was ashamed of his spiteful irritation. If, when he had been playing the piano to a roomful of friends in New York, a man dressed as a laborer had shambled in, wouldn't he have felt a moment of involuntary scorn? It was inevitable that the fortunate should hate the unfortunate because they feared them. But he was so tired of all those thoughts. Drinking down the last of his tea at a gulp, he went into the shop to ask the old woman, with little black whiskers over her bloodless lips, who sat behind the white desk at the end of the counter, if she minded his playing the piano.

In the deserted tea room, among the dismal upturned chairs, his crassened fingers moved stiffly over the keys. He forgot everything else. Locked doors in his mind were swinging wide, revealing forgotten sumptuous halls of his imagination. The Queen of Sheba, grotesque as a satyr, white and flaming with worlds of desire, as the great implacable Aphrodite, stood with her hand on his shoulder sending shivers of warm sweetness rippling through his body, while her voice intoned in his ears all the inexhaustible voluptuousness of life.

An asthmatic clock struck somewhere in the obscurity of the room. "Seven!" John Andrews paid, said good-bye to the old woman with the mustache, and hurried out into the street. "Like Cinderella at the ball," he thought. As he went towards the hospital, down faintly lighted streets, his steps got slower and slower. "Why go back?" a voice kept saying inside him. "Anything is better than that." Better throw himself in the river, even, than go back. He could see the olive-drab clothes in a heap among the dry bullrushes on the river bank. . . . He thought of himself crashing naked through the film of ice into water black as Chinese lacquer. And when he climbed out numb and panting on the other side, wouldn't he be able to take up life again as if he had just been born? How strong he would be if he could begin life a second time! How madly, how joyously he would live now that there was no more war. . . . He had reached the door of the hospital. Furious shudders of disgust went through him.

He was standing dumbly humble while a sergeant bawled him out for being late.

Andrews stared for a long while at the line of shields that supported the dark ceiling beams on the wall opposite his cot. The emblems had been erased and the grey stone figures that crowded under the shields,—the satyr with his shaggy goat's legs, the townsman with his square hat, the warrior with the sword between his legs,—had been clipped and scratched long ago in other wars. In the strong afternoon light they were so dilapidated he could hardly make them out. He wondered how they had seemed so vivid to him when he had lain in his cot, comforted by their comradeship, while his healing wounds itched and tingled. Still he glanced tenderly at the grey stone figures as he left the ward.

Downstairs in the office where the atmosphere was stuffy with a smell of varnish and dusty papers and cigarette smoke, he waited a long time, shifting his weight restlessly from one foot to the other.

"What do you want?" said a red-haired sergeant, without looking up from the pile of papers on his desk.

"Waiting for travel orders."

"Aren't you the guy I told to come back at three?"

"It is three."

"H'm!" The sergeant kept his eyes fixed on the papers, which rustled as he moved them from one pile to another. In the end of the room a typewriter clicked slowly and jerkily. Andrews could see the dark back of a head between bored shoulders in a woolen shirt leaning over the machine. Beside the cylindrical black stove against the wall a man with large mustaches and the complicated stripes of a hospital sergeant was reading a novel in a red cover. After a long silence the red-headed sergeant looked up from his papers and said suddenly:

"Ted."

The man at the typewriter turned slowly round, showing a large red face and blue eyes.

"We-ell," he drawled.

"Go in an' see if the loot has signed them papers yet."

The man got up, stretched himself deliberately, and slouched out through a door beside the stove. The red-haired sergeant leaned back in his swivel chair and lit a cigarette.

"Hell," he said, yawning.

The man with the mustache beside the stove let the book slip from his knees to the floor, and yawned too.

"This goddam armistice sure does take the ambition out of a feller," he said.

"Hell of a note," said the red-haired sergeant. "D'you know that they had my name in for an O.T.C.? Hell of a note goin' home without a Sam Brown."

The other man came back and sank down into his chair in front of the typewriter again. The slow, jerky clicking recommenced.

Andrews made a scraping noise with his foot on the ground.

"Well, what about that travel order?" said the red-haired sergeant.

"Loot's out," said the other man, still typewriting.

"Well, didn't he leave it on his desk?" shouted the red-haired sergeant angrily.

"Couldn't find it."

"I suppose I've got to go look for it. . . . God!" The red-haired sergeant stamped out of the room. A moment later he came back with a bunch of papers in his hand.

"Your name Jones?" he snapped to Andrews.

"No."

"Snivisky?"

"No. . . . Andrews, John."

"Why the hell couldn't you say so?"

The man with the mustaches beside the stove got to his feet suddenly. An alert, smiling expression came over his face.

"Good afternoon, Captain Higginsworth," he said cheerfully.

An oval man with a cigar slanting out of his broad mouth came into the room. When he talked the cigar wobbled in his mouth. He wore greenish kid gloves, very tight for his large hands, and his puttees shone with a dark lustre like mahogany.

The red-haired sergeant turned round and half-saluted.

"Goin' to another swell party, Captain?" he asked.

The Captain grinned.

"Say, have you boys got any Red Cross cigarettes? I ain't only got cigars, an' you can't hand a cigar to a lady, can you?" The Captain grinned again. An appreciative giggle went round.

"Will a couple of packages do you? Because I've got some here," said the red-haired sergeant reaching in the drawer of his desk.

"Fine." The captain slipped them into his pocket and swaggered out doing up the buttons of his buff-colored coat.

The sergeant settled himself at his desk again with an important smile.

"Did you find the travel order?" asked Andrews timidly. "I'm supposed to take the train at four-two."

"Can't make it. . . . Did you say your name was Anderson?"

"Andrews. . . . John Andrews."

"Here it is. . . . Why didn't you come earlier?"

The sharp air of the ruddy winter evening, sparkling in John Andrews's nostrils, vastly refreshing after the stale odors of the hospital, gave him a sense of liberation. Walking with rapid steps through the grey streets of the town, where in windows lamps already glowed orange, he kept telling himself that another epoch was closed. It was with relief that he felt that he would never see the hospital again or any of the people in it. He thought of Chrisfield. It was weeks and weeks since Chrisfield had come to his mind at all. Now it was with a sudden clench of affection that the Indiana boy's face rose up before him. An oval, heavily-tanned face with a little of childish roundness about it yet, with black eyebrows and long black eyelashes. But he did not even know if Chrisfield were still alive. Furious joy took possession of him. He, John Andrews, was alive; what did it matter if everyone he knew died? There were jollier companions than ever he had known, to be found in the world, cleverer people to talk to, more vigorous people to learn from. The cold air circulated through his nose and lungs; his arms felt strong and supple; he could feel the muscles of his legs stretch and contract as he walked, while his feet beat jauntily on the irregular cobble stones of the street. The waiting room at the station was cold and stuffy, full of a smell of breathed air and unclean uniforms. French soldiers wrapped in their long blue coats, slept on the benches or stood about in groups, eating bread and drinking from their canteens. A gas lamp in the center gave dingy light. Andrews settled himself in a corner with despairing resignation. He had five hours to wait for a train, and already his legs ached and he had a side feeling of exhaustion. The exhilaration of leaving the hospital and walking free through wine-tinted streets in the sparkling evening air gave way gradually to despair. His life would continue to be this slavery of unclean bodies packed together in places where the air had been breathed over and over, cogs in the great slow-moving Juggernaut of armies. What did it matter if the fighting had stopped? The armies would go on grinding out lives with lives, crushing flesh with flesh. Would he ever again stand free and solitary to live out joyous hours which would make up for all the boredom of the treadmill? He had no hope. His life would continue like this dingy, ill-smelling waiting room where men in uniform slept in the fetid air until they should be ordered out to march or to stand in motionless rows, endlessly, futilely, like toy soldiers a child has forgotten in an attic.

Andrews got up suddenly and went out on the empty platform. A cold wind blew. Somewhere out in the freight yards an engine puffed loudly, and clouds of white steam drifted through the faintly lighted station. He was walking up and down with his chin sunk into his coat and his hands in his pockets, when somebody ran into him.

"Damn," said a voice, and the figure darted through a grimy glass door that bore the sign: "Buvette." Andrews followed absent-mindedly.

"I'm sorry I ran into you. . . . I thought you were an M.P., that's why I beat it." When he spoke, the man, an American private, turned and looked searchingly in Andrews's face. He had very red cheeks and an impudent little brown mustache. He spoke slowly with a faint Bostonian drawl.

"That's nothing," said Andrews.

"Let's have a drink," said the other man. "I'm A.W.O.L. Where are you going?"

"To some place near Bar-le-Duc, back to my Division. Been in hospital."

"Long?"

"Since October."

"Gee. . . . Have some Curaçao. It'll do you good. You look pale. . . . My name's Henslowe. Ambulance with the French Army."

They sat down at an unwashed marble table where the soot from the trains made a pattern sticking to the rings left by wine and liqueur glasses.

"I'm going to Paris," said Henslowe. "My leave expired three days ago. I'm going to Paris and get taken ill with peritonitis or double pneumonia, or maybe I'll have a cardiac lesion. . . . The army's a bore."

"Hospital isn't any better," said Andrews with a sigh. "Though I shall never forget the delight with which I realized I was wounded and out of it. I thought I was bad enough to be sent home."

"Why, I wouldn't have missed a minute of the war. . . . But now that it's over . . . Hell! Travel is the password now. I've just had two weeks in the Pyrénées. Nimes, Arles, Les Baux, Carcassonne, Perpignan, Lourdes, Gavarnie, Toulouse! What do you think of that for a trip? . . . What were you in?"

"Infantry."

"Must have been hell."

"Been! It is."

"Why don't you come to Paris with me?"

"I don't want to be picked up," stammered Andrews.

"Not a chance. . . . I know the ropes. . . . All you have to do is keep away from the Olympia and the railway stations, walk fast and keep your shoes shined . . . and you've got wits, haven't you?"

"Not many. . . . Let's drink a bottle of wine. Isn't there anything to eat to be got here?"

"Not a damn thing, and I daren't go out of the station on account of the M.P. at the gate. . . . There'll be a diner on the Marseilles express."

"But I can't go to Paris."

"Sure. . . . Look, how do you call yourself?"

"John Andrews."

"Well, John Andrews, all I can say is that you've let 'em get your goat. Don't give in. Have a good time, in spite of 'em. To hell with 'em." He brought the bottle down so hard on the table that it broke and the purple wine flowed over the dirty marble and dripped gleaming on the floor.

Some French soldiers who stood in a group round the bar turned round.

"V'là un gars qui gaspille le bon vin," said a tall red-faced man, with long sloping whiskers.

"Pour vingt sous j'mangerai la bouteille," cried a little man lurching forward and leaning drunkenly over the table.

"Done," said Henslowe. "Say, Andrews, he says he'll eat the bottle for a franc."

He placed a shining silver franc on the table beside the remnants of the broken bottle. The man seized the neck of the bottle in a black, claw-like hand and gave it a preparatory flourish. He was a cadaverous little man, incredibly dirty, with mustaches and beard of a moth-eaten tow-color, and a purple flush on his cheeks. His uniform was clotted with mud. When the others crowded round him and tried to dissuade him, he said: "M'en fous, c'est mon métier," and rolled his eyes so that the whites flashed in the dim light like the eyes of dead codfish.

"Why, he's really going to do it," cried Henslowe.

The man's teeth flashed and crunched down on the jagged edge of the glass. There was a terrific crackling noise. He flourished the bottle-end again.

"My God, he's eating it," cried Henslowe, roaring with laughter, "and you're afraid to go to Paris."

An engine rumbled into the station, with a great hiss of escaping steam.

"Gee, that's the Paris train! Tiens!" He pressed the franc into the man's dirt-crusted hand.

"Come along, Andrews."

As they left the buvette they heard again the crunching crackling noise as the man bit another piece off the bottle.

Andrews followed Henslowe across the steam-filled platform to the door of a first-class carriage. They climbed in. Henslowe immediately pulled down the black cloth over the half globe of the light. The compartment was empty. He threw himself down with a sigh of comfort on the soft buff-colored cushions of the seat.

"But what on earth?" stammered Andrews.

"M'en fous, c'est mon métier," interrupted Henslowe.

The train pulled out of the station.

III

Henslowe poured wine from a brown earthen crock into the glasses, where it shimmered a bright thin red, the color of currants. Andrews leaned back in his chair and looked through half-closed eyes at the table with its white cloth and little burnt umber loaves of bread, and out of the window at the square dimly lit by lemon-yellow gas lamps and at the dark gables of the little houses that huddled round it.

At a table against the wall opposite a lame boy, with white beardless face and gentle violet-colored eyes, sat very close to the bareheaded girl who was with him and who never took her eyes off his face, leaning on his crutch all the while. A stove hummed faintly in the middle of the room, and from the half-open kitchen door came ruddy light and the sound of something frying. On the wall, in brownish colors that seemed to have taken warmth from all the rich scents of food they had absorbed since the day of their painting, were scenes of the Butte as it was fancied to have once been, with windmills and wide fields.

"I want to travel," Henslowe was saying, dragging out his words drowsily. "Abyssinia, Patagonia, Turkestan, the Caucasus, anywhere and everywhere. What do you say you and I go out to New Zealand and raise sheep?"

"But why not stay here? There can't be anywhere as wonderful as this."

"Then I'll put off starting for New Guinea for a week. But hell, I'd go crazy staying anywhere after this. It's got into my blood . . . all this murder. It's made a wanderer of me, that's what it's done. I'm an adventurer."

"God, I wish it had made me into anything so interesting."

"Tie a rock on to your scruples and throw 'em off the Pont Neuf and set out. . . . O boy, this is the golden age for living by your wits."

"You're not out of the army yet."

"I should worry. . . . I'll join the Red Cross."

"How?"

"I've got a tip about it."

A girl with oval face and faint black down on her upper lip brought them soup, a thick greenish colored soup, that steamed richly into their faces.

"If you tell me how I can get out of the army you'll probably save my life," said Andrews seriously.

"There are two ways . . . Oh, but let me tell you later. Let's talk about something worth while . . . So you write music do you?"

Andrews nodded.

An omelet lay between them, pale golden-yellow with flecks of green; a few amber bubbles of burnt butter still clustered round the edges.

"Talk about tone-poems," said Henslowe.

"But, if you are an adventurer and have no scruples, how is it you are still a private?"

Henslowe took a gulp of wine and laughed uproariously.

"That's the joke."

They ate in silence for a little while. They could hear the couple opposite them talking in low soft voices. The stove purred, and from the kitchen came a sound of something being beaten in a bowl. Andrews leaned back in his chair.

"This is so wonderfully quiet and mellow," he said. . . . "It is so easy to forget that there's any joy at all in life."

"Rot . . . It's a circus parade."

"Have you ever seen anything drearier than a circus parade? One of those jokes that aren't funny."

"Justine, encore du vin," called Henslowe.

"So you know her name?"

"I live here. . . . The Butte is the boss on the middle of the shield. It's the axle of the wheel. That's why it's so quiet, like the centre of a cyclone, of a vast whirling rotary circus parade!"

Justine, with her red hands that had washed so many dishes off which other people had dined well, put down between them a scarlet langouste, of which claws and feelers sprawled over the table-cloth that already had a few purplish stains of wine. The sauce was yellow and fluffy like the breast of a canary bird.

"D'you know," said Andrews suddenly talking fast and excitedly while he brushed the straggling yellow hair off his forehead, "I'd almost be willing to be shot at the end of a year if I could live up here all that time with a piano and a million sheets of music paper . . . It would be worth it."

"But this is a place to come back to. Imagine coming back here after the highlands of Thibet, where you'ld nearly got drowned and scalped and had made love to the daughter of an Afghan chief . . . who had red lips smeared with loukoumi so that the sweet taste stayed in your mouth." Henslowe stroked softly his little brown mustache.

"But what's the use of just seeing and feeling things if you can't express them?"

"What's the use of living at all? For the fun of it, man; damn ends."

"But the only profound fun I ever have is that . . ." Andrews's voice broke. "O God, I would give up every joy in the world if I could turn out one page that I felt was adequate. . . . D'you know it's years since I've talked to anybody?"

They both stared silently out of the window at the fog that was packed tightly against it like cotton wool, only softer, and a greenish-gold color.

"The M.P.'s sure won't get us tonight," said Henslowe, banging his fist jauntily on the table. "I've a great mind to go to Rue St. Anne and leave my card on the Provost Marshal. . . . God damn! D'you remember that man who took the bite out of our wine-bottle . . . He didn't give a hoot in hell, did he? Talk about expression. Why don't you express that? I think that's the turning point of your career. That's what made you come to Paris; you can't deny it."

They both laughed loudly rolling about on their chairs. Andrews caught glints of contagion in the pale violet eyes of the lame boy and in the dark eyes of the girl.

"Let's tell them about it," he said still laughing, with his face, bloodless after the months in hospital, suddenly flushed.

"Salut," said Henslowe turning round and elevating his glass. "Nous rions parceque nous sommes gris de vin gris." Then he told them about the man who ate glass. He got to his feet and recounted slowly in his drawling voice, with gestures. Justine stood by with a dish full of stuffed tomatoes of which the red skins showed vaguely through a mantle of dark brown sauce. When she smiled her cheeks puffed out and gave her face a little of the look of a white cat's.

"And you live here?" asked Andrews after they had all laughed.

"Always. It is not often that I go down to town. . . . It's so difficult. . . . I have a withered leg." He smiled brilliantly like a child telling about a new toy.

"And you?"

"How could I be anywhere else?" answered the girl. "It's a misfortune, but there it is." She tapped with the crutch on the floor, making a sound like someone walking with it. The boy laughed and tightened his arm round her shoulder.

"I should like to live here," said Andrews simply.

"Why don't you?"

"But don't you see he's a soldier," whispered the girl hurriedly.

A frown wrinkled the boy's forehead.

"Well, it wasn't by choice, I suppose," he said.

Andrews was silent. Unaccountable shame took possession of him before these people who had never been soldiers, who would never be soldiers.

"The Greeks used to say," he said bitterly, using a phrase that had been a long time on his mind, "that when a man became a slave, on the first day he lost one-half of his virtue."

"When a man becomes a slave," repeated the lame boy softly, "on the first day he loses one-half of his virtue."

"What's the use of virtue? It is love you need," said the girl.

"I've eaten your tomato, friend Andrews," said Henslowe. "Justine will get us some more." He poured out the last of the wine that half filled each of the glasses with its thin sparkle, the color of red currants.

Outside the fog had blotted everything out in even darkness which grew vaguely yellow and red near the sparsely scattered street lamps. Andrews and Henslowe felt their way blindly down the long gleaming flights of steps that led from the quiet darkness of the Butte towards the confused lights and noises of more crowded streets. The fog caught in their throats and tingled in their noses and brushed against their cheeks like moist hands.

"Why did we go away from that restaurant? I'd like to have talked to those people some more," said Andrews.

"We haven't had any coffee either. . . . But, man, we're in Paris. We're not going to be here long. We can't afford to stay all the time in one place. . . . It's nearly closing time already. . . ."

"The boy was a painter. He said he lived by making toys; he whittles out wooden elephants and camels for Noah's Arks. . . . Did you hear that?"

They were walking fast down a straight, sloping street. Below them already appeared the golden glare of a boulevard.

Andrews went on talking, almost to himself.

"What a wonderful life that would be to live up here in a small room that would overlook the great rosy grey expanse of the city, to have some absurd work like that to live on, and to spend all your spare time working and going to concerts. . . . A quiet mellow existence. . . . Think of my life beside it. Slaving in that iron, metallic, brazen New York to write ineptitudes about music in the Sunday paper. God! And this."

They were sitting down at a table in a noisy café, full of yellow light flashing in eyes and on glasses and bottles, of red lips crushed against the thin hard rims of glasses.

"Wouldn't you like to just rip it off?" Andrews jerked at his tunic with both hands where it bulged out over his chest. "Oh, I'd like to make the buttons fly all over the café, smashing the liqueur glasses, snapping in the faces of all those dandified French officers who look so proud of themselves that they survived long enough to be victorious."

"The coffee's famous here," said Henslowe. "The only place I ever had it better was at a bistro in Nice on this last permission."

"Somewhere else again!"

"That's it. . . . For ever and ever, somewhere else! Let's have some prunelle. Before the war prunelle."

The waiter was a solemn man, with a beard cut like a prime minister's. He came with the bottle held out before him, religiously lifted. His lips pursed with an air of intense application, while he poured the white glinting liquid into the glasses. When he had finished he held the bottle upside down with a tragic gesture; not a drop came out.

"It is the end of the good old times," he said.

"Damnation to the good old times," said Henslowe. "Here's to the good old new roughhousy circus parades."

"I wonder how many people they are good for, those circus parades of yours," said Andrews.

"Where are you going to spend the night?" said Henslowe.

"I don't know. . . . I suppose I can find a hotel or something."

"Why don't you come with me and see Berthe; she probably has friends."

"I want to wander about alone, not that I scorn Berthe's friends," said Andrews. . . . "But I am so greedy for solitude."

John Andrews was walking alone down streets full of drifting fog. Now and then a taxi dashed past him and clattered off into the obscurity. Scattered groups of people, their footsteps hollow in the muffling fog, floated about him. He did not care which way he walked, but went on and on, crossing large crowded avenues where the lights embroidered patterns of gold and orange on the fog, rolling in wide deserted squares, diving into narrow streets where other steps sounded sharply for a second now and then and faded leaving nothing in his ears when he stopped still to listen but the city's distant muffled breathing. At last he came out along the river, where the fog was densest and coldest and where he could hear faintly the sound of water gurgling past the piers of bridges. The glow of the lights glared and dimmed, glared and dimmed, as he walked along, and sometimes he could make out the bare branches of trees blurred across the halos of the lamps. The fog caressed him soothingly and shadows kept flicking past him, giving him glimpses of smooth curves of cheeks and glints of eyes bright from the mist and darkness. Friendly, familiar people seemed to fill the fog just out of his sight. The muffled murmur of the city stirred him like the sound of the voices of friends.

From the girl at the cross-roads singing under her street-lamp to the patrician pulling roses to pieces from the height of her litter . . . all the imagining of your desire. . . .

The murmur of life about him kept forming itself into long modulated sentences in his ears,—sentences that gave him by their form a sense of quiet well-being as if he were looking at a low relief of people dancing, carved out of Parian in some workshop in Attica.

Once he stopped and leaned for a long while against the moisture-beaded stem of a street-lamp. Two shadows defined, as they strolled towards him, into the forms of a pale boy and a bareheaded girl, walking tightly laced in each other's arms. The boy limped a little and his violet eyes were contracted to wistfulness. John Andrews was suddenly filled with throbbing expectation, as if those two would come up to him and put their hands on his arms and make some revelation of vast import to his life. But when they reached the full glow of the lamp, Andrews saw that he was mistaken. They were not the boy and girl he had talked to on the Butte.

He walked off hurriedly and plunged again into tortuous streets, where he strode over the cobblestone pavements, stopping now and then to peer through the window of a shop at the light in the rear where a group of people sat quietly about a table under a light, or into a bar where a tired little boy with heavy eyelids and sleeves rolled up from thin grey arms was washing glasses, or an old woman, a shapeless bundle of black clothes, was swabbing the floor. From doorways he heard talking and soft laughs. Upper windows sent yellow rays of light across the fog.

In one doorway the vague light from a lamp bracketed in the wall showed two figures, pressed into one by their close embrace. As Andrews walked past, his heavy army boots clattering loud on the wet pavement, they lifted their heads slowly. The boy had violet eyes and pale beardless cheeks; the girl was bareheaded and kept her brown eyes fixed on the boy's face. Andrews's heart thumped within him. At last he had found them. He made a step towards them, and then strode on losing himself fast in the cool effacing fog. Again he had been mistaken. The fog swirled about him, hiding wistful friendly faces, hands ready to meet his hands, eyes ready to take fire with his glance, lips cold with the mist, to be crushed under his lips. *From the girl at the cross-roads singing under her street-lamp* . . .

And he walked on alone through the drifting fog.

IV

Andrews left the station reluctantly, shivering in the raw grey mist under which the houses of the village street and the rows of motor trucks and the few figures of French soldiers swathed in long formless coats, showed as vague dark blurs in the confused dawnlight. His body felt flushed and sticky from a night spent huddled in the warm fetid air of an over-crowded compartment. He yawned and stretched himself and stood irresolutely in the middle of the street with his pack biting into his shoulders. Out of sight, behind the dark mass, in which a few ruddy lights glowed, of the station buildings, the engine whistled and the train clanked off into the distance. Andrews listened to its faint reverberation through the mist with a sick feeling of despair. It was the train that had brought him from Paris back to his division.

As he stood shivering in the grey mist he remembered the curious de-spairing reluctance he used to suffer when he went back to boarding school after a holiday. How he used to go from the station to the school by the longest road possible, taking frantic account of every moment of liberty left him. Today his feet had the same leaden reluctance as when they used to all but refuse to take him up the long sandy hill to the school.

He wandered aimlessly for a while about the silent village hoping to find a café where he could sit for a few minutes to take a last look at him-self before plunging again into the grovelling promiscuity of the army. Not a light showed. All the shutters of the shabby little brick and plaster houses were closed. With dull springless steps he walked down the road they had pointed out to him from the R. T. O.

Overhead the sky was brightening giving the mist that clung to the earth in every direction ruddy billowing outlines. The frozen road gave out a faint hard resonance under his footsteps. Occasionally the silhou-ette of a tree by the roadside loomed up in the mist ahead, its uppermost branches clear and ruddy with sunlight.

Andrews was telling himself that the war was over, and that in a few months he would be free in any case. What did a few months more or less matter? But the sane thoughts were swept recklessly away in the blind panic that was like a stampede of wild steers within him. There was no arguing. His spirit was contorted with revolt so that his flesh twitched and dark splotches danced before his eyes. He wondered vaguely whether he had gone mad. Enormous plans kept rising up out of the tumult of his mind and dissolving suddenly like smoke in a high wind. He would run away and if they caught him, kill himself. He would start a mutiny in his company, he would lash all these men to frenzy by his words, so that they too should refuse to form into Guns, so that they should laugh when the officers got red in the face shouting orders at them, so that the whole division should march off over the frosty hills, without arms, without flags, calling all the men of all the armies to join them, to march on singing, to laugh the nightmare out of their blood. Would not some lightning flash of vision sear people's consciousness into life again? What was the good of stopping the war if the armies continued?

But that was just rhetoric. His mind was flooding itself with rhetoric that it might keep its sanity. His mind was squeezing out rhetoric like a sponge that he might not see dry madness face to face.

And all the while his hard footsteps along the frozen road beat in his ears bringing him nearer to the village where the division was quartered. He was climbing a long hill. The mist thinned about him and became brilliant with sunlight. Then he was walking in the full sun over the crest of a hill with pale blue sky above his head. Behind him and before him were mist-filled valleys and beyond other ranges of long hills, with reddish-violet patches of woodland, glowing faintly in the sunlight. In the valley at his feet he could see, in the shadow of the hill he stood on, a church tower and a few roofs rising out of the mist, as out of water.

Among the houses bugles were blowing mess-call.

The jauntiness of the brassy notes ringing up through the silence was agony to him. How long the day would be. He looked at his watch. It was seven thirty. How did they come to be having mess so late?

The mist seemed doubly cold and dark when he was buried in it again after his moment of sunlight. The sweat was chilled on his face and streaks of cold went through his clothes, soaked from the effort of carrying the pack. In the village street Andrews met a man he did not know and asked him where the office was. The man, who was chewing something, pointed silently to a house with green shutters on the opposite side of the street.

At a desk sat Chrisfield smoking a cigarette. When he jumped up Andrews noticed that he had a corporal's two stripes on his arm.

"Hello, Andy."

They shook hands warmly.

"A' you all right now, ole boy?"

"Sure, I'm fine," said Andrews. A sudden constraint fell upon them.

"That's good," said Chrisfield.

"You're a corporal now. Congratulations."

"Um hum. Made me more'n a month ago."

They were silent. Chrisfield sat down in his chair again.

"What sort of a town is this?"

"It's a hell-hole, this dump is, a hell-hole."

"That's nice."

"Goin' to move soon, tell me. . . . Army o' Occupation. But Ah hadn't ought to have told you that. . . . Don't tell any of the fellers."

"Where's the outfit quartered?"

"Ye won't know it; we've got fifteen new men. No account all of 'em. Second draft men."

"Civilians in the town?"

"You bet. . . . Come with me, Andy, an Ah'll tell 'em to give you some grub at the cookshack. No . . . wait a minute an' you'll miss the hike. . . . Hikes every day since the goddam armistice. They sent out a general order telling 'em to double up on the drill."

They heard a voice shouting orders outside and the narrow street filled up suddenly with a sound of boots beating the ground in unison. Andrews kept his back to the window. Something in his legs seemed to be tramping in time with the other legs.

"There they go," said Chrisfield. "Loot's with 'em today. . . . Want some grub? If it ain't been punk since the armistice."

The "Y" hut was empty and dark; through the grimy windowpanes could be seen fields and a leaden sky full of heavy ocherous light, in which the leafless trees and the fields full of stubble were different shades of dead, greyish brown. Andrews sat at the piano without playing. He was thinking how once he had thought to express all the cramped boredom of this life; the thwarted limbs regimented together, lashed into straight lines, the monotony of servitude. Unconsciously as he thought of it, the fingers of one hand sought a chord, which jangled in the badly tuned piano. "God, how silly!" he muttered aloud, pulling his hands away. Suddenly he began to play snatches of things he knew, distorting them, willfully mutilating the rhythms, mixing into them snatches of ragtime. The piano jangled under his hands, filling the empty hut with clamor. He stopped suddenly, letting his fingers slide from bass to treble, and began to play in earnest.

There was a cough behind him that had an artificial, discreet ring to it. He went on playing without turning round. Then a voice said:

"Beautiful, beautiful."

Andrews turned to find himself staring into a face of vaguely triangular shape with a wide forehead and prominent eyelids over protruding brown eyes. The man wore a Y.M.C.A. uniform which was very tight for him, so that there were creases running from each button across the front of his tunic.

"Oh, do go on playing. It's years since I heard any Debussy."

"It wasn't Debussy."

"Oh, wasn't it? Anyway it was just lovely. Do go on. I'll just stand here and listen."

Andrews went on playing for a moment, made a mistake, started over, made the same mistake, banged on the keys with his fist and turned round again.

"I can't play," he said peevishly.

"Oh, you can, my boy, you can. . . . Where did you learn? I would give a million dollars to play like that, if I had it."

Andrews glared at him silently.

"You are one of the men just back from hospital, I presume."

"Yes, worse luck."

"Oh, I don't blame you. These French towns are the dullest places; though I just love France, don't you?" The "Y" man had a faintly whining voice.

"Anywhere's dull in the army."

"Look, we must get to know each other real well. My name's Spencer Sheffield . . . Spencer B. Sheffield. . . . And between you and me there's not a soul in the division you can talk to. It's dreadful not to have intellectual people about one. I suppose you're from New York."

Andrews nodded.

"Um hum, so am I. You're probably read some of my things in *Vain Endeavor*. . . . What, you've never read *Vain Endeavor*? I guess you didn't go round with the intellectual set. . . . Musical people often don't. . . . Of course I don't mean the Village. All anarchists and society women there. . . ."

"I've never gone round with any set, and I never . . ."

"Never mind, we'll fix that when we all get back to New York. And now you just sit down at that piano and play me Debussy's 'Arabesque.'. . . I know you love it just as much as I do. But first what's your name?"

"Andrews."

"Folks come from Virginia?"

"Yes." Andrews got to his feet.

"Then you're related to the Penneltons."

"I may be related to the Kaiser for all I know."

"The Penneltons . . . that's it. You see my mother was a Miss Spencer from Spencer Falls, Virginia, and her mother was a Miss Pennelton, so you and I are cousins. Now isn't that a coincidence?"

"Distant cousins. But I must go back to the barracks."

"Come in and see me any time," Spencer B. Sheffield shouted after him. "You know where; back of the shack. And knock twice so I'll know it's you."

Outside the house where he was quartered Andrews met the new top sergeant, a lean man with spectacles and a little mustache of the color and texture of a scrubbing brush.

"Here's a letter for you," the top sergeant said. "Better look at the new K.P. list I've just posted."

The letter was from Henslowe. Andrews read it with a smile of pleasure in the faint afternoon light, remembering Henslowe's constant drawling talk about distant places he had never been to, and the man who had eaten glass, and the day and a half in Paris.

"Andy," the letter began, "I've got the dope at last. Courses begin in Paris February fifteenth. Apply at once to your C. O. to study somethin' at University of Paris. Any amount of lies will go. Apply all pull possible via sergeants, lieutenants and their mistresses and laundresses. Yours, Henslowe."

His heart thumping, Andrews ran after the sergeant, passing, in his excitement, a lieutenant without saluting him.

"Look here," snarled the lieutenant.

Andrews saluted, and stood stiffly at attention.

"Why didn't you salute me?"

"I was in a hurry, sir, and didn't see you. I was going on very urgent company business, sir."

"Remember that just because the armistice is signed you needn't think you're out of the army; at ease."

Andrews saluted. The lieutenant saluted, turned swiftly on his heel and walked away.

Andrews caught up to the sergeant.

"Sergeant Coffin. Can I speak to you a minute?"

"I'm in a hell of a hurry."

"Have you heard anything about this army students' corps to send men to universities here in France? Something the Y.M.C.A.'s getting up."

"Can't be for enlisted men. No I ain't heard a word about it. D'you want to go to school again?"

"If I get a chance. To finish my course."

"College man, are ye? So am I. Well, I'll let you know if I get any general order about it. Can't do anything without getting a general order about it. Looks to me like it's all bushwa."

"I guess you're right."

The street was grey dark. Stung by a sense of impotence, surging with despairing rebelliousness, Andrews hurried back towards the buildings where the company was quartered. He would be late for mess. The grey street was deserted. From a window here and there ruddy light streamed out to make a glowing oblong on the wall of a house opposite.

"Goddam it, if ye don't believe me, you go ask the lootenant. . . . Look here, Toby, didn't our outfit see hotter work than any goddam engineers'?"

Toby had just stepped into the café, a tall man with a brown bulldog face and a scar on his left cheek. He spoke rarely and solemnly with a Maine coast Yankee twang.

"I reckon so," was all he said. He sat down on the bench beside the other man who went on bitterly:

"I guess you would reckon so. . . . Hell, man, you ditch diggers ain't in it."

"Ditch diggers!" The engineer banged his fist down on the table. His lean pickled face was a furious red. "I guess we don't dig half so many ditches as the infantry does . . . an' when we've dug 'em we don't crawl into 'em an' stay there like goddam cottontailed jackrabbits."

"You guys don't git near enough to the front. . . ."

"Like goddam cottontailed jackrabbits," shouted the pickle-faced engineer again, roaring with laughter. "Ain't that so?" He looked round the room for approval. The benches at the two long tables were filled with infantry men who looked at him angrily. Noticing suddenly that he had no support, he moderated his voice.

"The infantry's damn necessary, I'll admit that; but where'd you fellers be without us guys to string the barbed wire for you?"

"There warn't no barbed wire strung in the Oregon forest where we was, boy. What d'ye want barbed wire when you're advancin' for?"

"Look here . . . I'll bet you a bottle of cognac my company had more losses than yourn did."

"Tek him up, Joe," said Toby, suddenly showing an interest in the conversation.

"All right, it's a go."

"We had fifteen killed and twenty wounded," announced the engineer triumphantly.

"How badly wounded?"

"What's that to you? Hand over the cognac?"

"Like hell. We had fifteen killed and twenty wounded too, didn't we, Toby?"

"I reckon you're right," said Toby.

"Ain't I right?" asked the other man, addressing the company generally.

"Sure, goddam right," muttered voices.

"Well, I guess it's all off, then," said the engineer.

"No, it ain't," said Toby, "reckon up yer wounded. The feller who's got the worst wounded gets the cognac. Ain't that fair?"

"Sure."

"We've had seven fellers sent home already," said the engineer.

"We've had eight. Ain't we?"

"Sure," growled everybody in the room.

"How bad was they?"

"Two of 'em was blind," said Toby.

"Hell," said the engineer, jumping to his feet as if taking a trick at poker. "We had a guy who was sent home without arms nor legs, and three fellers got t.b. from bein' gassed."

John Andrews had been sitting in a corner of the room. He got up. Something had made him think of the man he had known in the hospital who had said that was the life to make a feller feel fit. Getting up at three o'clock in the morning, you jumped out of bed just like a cat. . . . He remembered how the olive-drab trousers had dangled, empty, from the man's chair.

"That's nothing; one of our sergeants had to have a new nose grafted on. . . ."

The village street was dark and deeply rutted with mud. Andrews wandered up and down aimlessly. There was only one other café. That would be just like this one. He couldn't go back to the desolate barn where he slept. It would be too early to go to sleep. A cold wind blew down the street and the sky was full of vague movement of dark clouds. The partly-frozen mud clotted about his feet as he walked along; he could feel the water penetrating his shoes. Opposite the Y.M.C.A. hut at the end of the street he stopped. After a moment's indecision he gave a little laugh, and walked round to the back where the door of the "Y" man's room was.

He knocked twice, half hoping there would be no reply. Sheffield's whining high-pitched voice said: "Who is it?"

"Andrews."

"Come right in. . . . You're just the man I wanted to see." Andrews stood with his hand on the knob.

"Do sit down and make yourself right at home."

Spencer Sheffield was sitting at a little desk in a room with walls of unplaned boards and one small window. Behind the desk were piles of cracker boxes and cardboard cases of cigarettes and in the midst of them a little opening, like that of a railway ticket office, in the wall through which the "Y" man sold his commodities to the long lines of men who would stand for hours waiting meekly in the room beyond.

Andrews was looking round for a chair.

"Oh, I just forgot. I'm sitting in the only chair," said Spencer Sheffield, laughing, twisting his small mouth into a shape like a camel's mouth and rolling about his large protruding eyes.

"Oh, that's all right. What I wanted to ask you was: do you know anything about . . . ?"

"Look, do come with me to my room," interrupted Sheffield. "I've got such a nice sitting-room with an open fire, just next to Lieutenant Bleezer. . . . An' there we'll talk . . . about everything. I'm just dying to talk to somebody about the things of the spirit."

"Do you know anything about a scheme for sending enlisted men to French universities? Men who have not finished their courses."

"Oh, wouldn't that be just fine. I tell you, boy, there's nothing like the U.S. government to think of things like that."

"But have you heard anything about it?"

"No; but I surely shall. . . . D'you mind switching the light off? . . . That's it. Now just follow me. Oh, I do need a rest. I've been working dreadfully hard since that Knights of Columbus man came down here. Isn't it hateful the way they try to run down the 'Y'? . . . Now we can have a nice long talk. You must tell me all about yourself."

"But don't you really know anything about that university scheme? They say it begins February fifteenth," Andrews said in a low voice.

"I'll ask Lieutenant Bleezer if he knows anything about it," said Sheffield soothingly, throwing an arm around Andrews's shoulder and pushing him in the door ahead of him.

They went through a dark hall to a little room where a fire burned brilliantly in the hearth, lighting up with tongues of red and yellow a square black walnut table and two heavy armchairs with leather backs and bottoms that shone like lacquer.

"This is wonderful," said Andrews involuntarily.

"Romantic I call it. Makes you think of Dickens, doesn't it, and Locksley Hall."

"Yes," said Andrews vaguely.

"Have you been in France long?" asked Andrews settling himself in one of the chairs and looking into the dancing flames of the log fire. "Will you smoke?" He handed Sheffield a crumpled cigarette.

"No, thanks, I only smoke special kinds. I have a weak heart. That's why I was rejected from the army. . . . Oh, but I think it was superb of you to join as a private. It was my dream to do that, to be one of the nameless marching throng."

"I think it was damn foolish, not to say criminal," said Andrews sullenly, still staring into the fire.

"You can't mean that. Or do you mean that you think you had abilities which would have been worth more to your country in another position? . . . I have many friends who felt that."

"No. . . . I don't think it's right of a man to go back on himself. . . . I don't think butchering people ever does any good . . . I have acted as if I did think it did good . . . out of carelessness or cowardice, one or the other; that I think bad."

"You mustn't talk that way" said Sheffield hurriedly. "So you are a musician, are you?" He asked the question with a jaunty confidential air.

"I used to play the piano a little, if that's what you mean," said Andrews.

"Music has never been the art I had most interest in. But many things have moved me intensely. . . . Debussy and those beautiful little things of Nevin's. You must know them. . . . Poetry has been more my field. When I was young, younger than you are, quite a lad . . . Oh, if we could only stay young; I am thirty-two."

"I don't see that youth by itself is worth much. It's the most superb medium there is, though, for other things," said Andrews. "Well, I must go," he said. "If you do hear anything about that university scheme, you will let me know, won't you?"

"Indeed I shall, dear boy, indeed I shall."

They shook hands in jerky dramatic fashion and Andrews stumbled down the dark hall to the door. When he stood out in the raw night air again he drew a deep breath. By the light that streamed out from a window he looked at his watch. There was time to go to the regimental sergeant-major's office before tattoo.

At the opposite end of the village street from the Y.M.C.A. hut was a cube-shaped house set a little apart from the rest in the middle of a broad lawn which the constant crossing and recrossing of a staff of cars and trains of motor trucks had turned into a muddy morass in which the wheel tracks crisscrossed in every direction. A narrow board walk led from the main road to the door. In the middle of this walk Andrews met a captain and automatically got off into the mud and saluted.

The regimental office was a large room that had once been decorated by wan and ill-drawn mural paintings in the manner of Puvis de Chavannes, but the walls had been so chipped and soiled by five years of military occupation that they were barely recognisable. Only a few bits of bare flesh and floating drapery showed here and there above the maps and notices that were tacked on the walls. At the end of the room a group of nymphs in Nile green and pastel blue could be seen emerging from under a French War Loan poster. The ceiling was adorned with an oval of flowers and little plaster cupids in low relief which had also suffered and in places showed the laths. The office was nearly empty. The littered desks and silent typewriters gave a strange air of desolation to the gutted drawing-room. Andrews walked boldly to the furthest desk, where a little red card leaning against the typewriter said "Regimental Sergeant-Major."

Behind the desk, crouched over a heap of typewritten reports, sat a little man with scanty sandy hair, who screwed up his eyes and smiled when Andrews approached the desk.

"Well, did you fix it up for me?" he asked.

"Fix what?" said Andrews.

"Oh, I thought you were someone else." The smile left the regimental sergeant-major's thin lips. "What do you want?"

"Why, Regimental Sergeant-Major, can you tell me anything about a scheme to send enlisted men to colleges over here? Can you tell me who to apply to?"

"According to what general orders? And who told you to come and see me about it, anyway?"

"Have you heard anything about it?"

"No, nothing definite. I'm busy now anyway. Ask one of your own non-coms to find out about it." He crouched once more over the papers.

Andrews was walking towards the door, flushing with annoyance, when he saw that the man at the desk by the window was jerking his head in a peculiar manner, just in the direction of the regimental sergeant-major and then towards the door. Andrews smiled at him and nodded. Outside the door, where an orderly sat on a short bench reading a torn *Saturday Evening Post,* Andrews waited. The hall was part of what must have been a ballroom, for it had a much-scarred hardwood floor and big spaces of bare plaster framed by gilt- and lavender-colored mouldings, which had probably held tapestries. The partition of unplaned boards that formed other offices cut off the major part of a highly decorated ceiling where cupids with crimson-daubed bottoms swam in all attitudes in a sea of pink- and blue- and lavender-colored clouds, wreathing themselves coyly in heavy garlands of waxy hothouse flowers, while cornucopias spilling out squashy fruits gave Andrews a feeling of distinct insecurity as he looked up from below.

"Say are you a Kappa Mu?"

Andrews looked down suddenly and saw in front of him the man who had signalled to him in the regimental sergeant-major's office.

"Are you a Kappa Mu?" he asked again.

"No, not that I know of," stammered Andrews puzzled.

"What school did you go to?"

"Harvard."

"Harvard. . . . Guess we haven't got a chapter there. . . . I'm from North Western. Anyway you want to go to school in France here if you can. So do I."

"Don't you want to come and have a drink?"

The man frowned, pulled his overseas cap down over his forehead, where the hair grew very low, and looked about him mysteriously.

"Yes," he said.

They splashed together down the muddy village street.

"We've got thirteen minutes before tattoo. . . . My name's Walters, what's yours?" He spoke in a low voice in short staccato phrases.

"Andrews."

"Andrews, you've got to keep this dark. If everybody finds out about it we're through. It's a shame you're not a Kappa Mu, but college men have got to stick together, that's the way I look at it."

"Oh, I'll keep it dark enough," said Andrews.

"It's too good to be true. The general order isn't out yet, but I've seen a preliminary circular. What school d'you want to go to?"

"Sorbonne, Paris."

"That's the stuff. D'you know the back room at Baboon's?"

Walters turned suddenly to the left up an alley, and broke through a hole in a hawthorn hedge.

"A guy's got to keep his eyes and ears open if he wants to get any-where in this army," he said.

As they ducked in the back door of a cottage, Andrews caught a glimpse of the billowy line of a tile roof against the lighter darkness of the sky. They sat down on a bench built into a chimney where a few sticks made a splutter of flames.

"Monsieur désire?" A red-faced girl with a baby in her arms came up to them.

"That's Babette; Baboon I call her," said Walters with a laugh.

"Chocolat," said Walters.

"That'll suit me all right. It's my treat, remember."

"I'm not forgetting it. Now let's get to business. What you do is this. You write an application. I'll make that out for you on the type-writer tomorrow and you meet me here at eight tomorrow night and I'll give it to you. . . . You sign it at once and hand it in to your sergeant. See?"

"This'll just be a preliminary application; when the order's out you'll have to make another."

The woman, this time without the baby, appeared out of the darkness of the room with a candle and two cracked bowls from which steam rose, faint primrose-color in the candle light.

Walters drank his bowl down at a gulp, grunted and went on talking.

"Give me a cigarette, will you? . . . You'll have to make it out darn soon too, because once the order's out every son of a gun in the division'll be making out to be a college man. How did you get your tip?"

"From a fellow in Paris."

"You've been to Paris, have you?" said Walters admiringly. "Is it the way they say it is? Gee, these French are immoral. Look at this woman here. She'll sleep with a feller soon as not. Got a baby too!"

"But who do the applications go in to?"

"To the colonel, or whoever he appoints to handle it. You a Catholic?"

"No."

"Neither am I. That's the hell of it. The regimental sergeant-major is."

"Well?"

"I guess you haven't noticed the way things run up at divisional headquarters. It's a regular cathedral. Isn't a mason in it. . . . But I must beat it. . . . Better pretend you don't know me if you meet me on the street; see?"

"All right."

Walters hurried out of the door. Andrews sat alone looking at the flutter of little flames about the pile of sticks on the hearth, while he sipped chocolate from the warm bowl held between the palms of both hands.

He remembered a speech out of some very bad romantic play he had heard when he was very small.

"About your head I fling . . . the Cross of Ro-me."

He started to laugh, sliding back and forth on the smooth bench which had been polished by the breeches of generations warming their feet at the fire. The red-faced woman stood with her hands on her hips looking at him in astonishment, while he laughed and laughed.

"Mais quelle gaieté, quelle gaieté," she kept saying.

The straw under him rustled faintly with every sleepy movement Andrews made in his blankets. In a minute the bugle was going to blow and he was going to jump out of his blankets, throw on his clothes and fall into line for roll call in the black mud of the village street. It couldn't be that only a month had gone by since he had got back from hospital. No, he had spent a lifetime in this village being dragged out of his warm blankets every morning by the bugle, shivering as he stood in line for roll call, shuffling in a line that moved slowly past the cookshack, shuffling along in another line to throw what was left of his food into garbage cans, to wash his mess kit in the greasy water a hundred other men had washed their mess kits in; lining up to drill, to march on along muddy roads, splattered by the endless trains of motor trucks; lining up twice more for mess, and at last being forced by another bugle into his blankets again to sleep heavily while a smell hung in his nostrils of sweating woolen clothing and breathed-out air and dusty blankets. In a minute the bugle was going to blow, to snatch him out of even these miserable thoughts, and throw him into an automaton under other men's orders. Childish spiteful desires surged into his mind. If the bugler would only die. He could picture him, a little man with a broad face and putty-colored cheeks, a small rusty mustache and bow-legs lying like a calf on a marble slab in a butcher's shop on top of his blankets. What nonsense! There were other buglers. He wondered how many buglers there were in the army. He could picture them all, in dirty little villages, in stone barracks, in towns, in great camps that served the country for miles with rows of black warehouses and narrow barrack buildings standing with their feet a little apart; giving their little brass bugles a preliminary tap before putting out their cheeks and blowing in them and stealing a million and a half (or was it two million or three million) lives, and throwing the warm sentient bodies into coarse automatons who must be kept busy, lest they grow restive, till killing time began again.

The bugle blew. With the last jaunty notes, a stir went through the barn.

Corporal Chrisfield stood on the ladder that led up from the yard, his head on a level with the floor shouting:

"Shake it up, fellers! If a guy's late to roll call, it's K.P. for a week."

As Andrews, while buttoning his tunic, passed him on the ladder, he whispered:

"Tell me we're going to see service again, Andy . . . Army o' Occupation."

While he stood stiffly at attention waiting to answer when the sergeant called his name, Andrews's mind was whirling in crazy circles of anxiety. What if they should leave before the General Order came on the University plan? The application would certainly be lost in the confusion of moving the Division, and he would be condemned to keep up this life for more dreary weeks and months. Would any years of work and happiness in some future existence make up for the humiliating agony of this servitude?

"Dismissed!"

He ran up the ladder to fetch his mess kit and in a few minutes was in line again in the rutted village street where the grey houses were just forming outlines as light crept slowly into the leaden sky, while a faint odor of bacon and coffee came to him, making him eager for food, eager to drown his thoughts in the heaviness of swiftly-eaten greasy food and in the warmth of watery coffee gulped down out of a tin-curved cup. He was telling himself desperately that he must do something—that he must make an effort to save himself, that he must fight against the deadening routine that numbed him.

Later, while he was sweeping the rough board floor of the company's quarters, the theme came to him which had come to him long ago, in a former incarnation it seemed, when he was smearing windows with soap from a gritty sponge along the endless side of the barracks in the training camp. Time and time again in the past year he had thought of it, and dreamed of weaving it into a fabric of sound which would express the trudging monotony of days bowed under the yoke. "Under the Yoke"; that would be a title for it. He imagined the sharp tap of the conductor's baton, the silence of a crowded hall, the first notes rasping bitterly upon the tense ears of men and women. But as he tried to concentrate his mind on the music, other things intruded upon it, blurred it. He kept feeling the rhythm of the Queen of Sheba slipping from the shoulders of her gaudily caparisoned elephant, advancing towards him through the torchlight, putting her hand, fantastic with rings and long gilded fingernails, upon his shoulders so that ripples of delight, at all the voluptuous images of his desire, went through his whole body, making it quiver like a flame with yearning for unimaginable things. It all muddled into fantastic gibberish—into sounds of horns and trombones and double basses blown off key while a piccolo shrilled the first bars of "The Star Spangled Banner."

He had stopped sweeping and looked about him dazedly. He was alone. Outside, he heard a sharp voice call "Attenshun!" He ran down the ladder and fell in at the end of the line under the angry glare of the lieutenant's small eyes, which were placed very close together on either side of a lean nose, black and hard, like the eyes of a crab.

The company marched off through the mud to the drill field.

After retreat Andrews knocked at the door at the back of the Y.M.C.A., but as there was no reply, he strode off with a long, determined stride to Sheffield's room.

In the moment that elapsed between his knock and an answer, he could feel his heart thumping. A little sweat broke out on his temples.

"Why, what's the matter, boy? You look all wrought up," said Sheffield, holding the door half open, and blocking, with his lean form, entrance to the room.

"May I come in? I want to talk to you," said Andrews.

"Oh, I suppose it'll be all right. . . . You see I have an officer with me . . ." then there was a flutter in Sheffield's voice. "Oh, do come in"; he went on, with sudden enthusiasm. "Lieutenant Bleezer is fond of music too. . . . Lieutenant, this is the boy I was telling you about. We must get him to play for us. If he had the opportunities, I am sure he'd be a famous musician."

Lieutenant Bleezer was a dark youth with a hooked nose and pince-nez. His tunic was unbuttoned and he held a cigar in his hand. He smiled in an evident attempt to put this enlisted man at his ease.

"Yes, I am very fond of music, modern music," he said, leaning against the mantelpiece. "Are you a musician by profession?"

"Not exactly . . . nearly." Andrews thrust his hands into the bottoms of his trouser pockets and looked from one to the other with a certain defiance.

"I suppose you've played in some orchestra? How is it you are not in the regimental band?"

"No, except the Pierian."

"The Pierian? Were you at Harvard?"

Andrews nodded.

"So was I."

"Isn't that a coincidence?" said Sheffield. "I'm so glad I just insisted on your coming in."

"What year were you?" asked Lieutenant Bleezer, with a faint change of tone, drawing a finger along his scant black moustache.

"Fifteen."

"I haven't graduated yet," said the lieutenant with a laugh.

"What I wanted to ask you, Mr. Sheffield. . . ."

"Oh, my boy; my boy, you know you've known me long enough to call me Spence," broke in Sheffield.

"I want to know," went on Andrews speaking slowly, "can you help me to get put on the list to be sent to the University of Paris? . . . I know that a list has been made out, although the General Order has not come yet. I am disliked by most of the non-coms and I don't see how I can get on without somebody's help . . . I simply can't go this life any longer." Andrews closed his lips firmly and looked at the ground, his face flushing.

"Well, a man of your attainments certainly ought to go," said Lieutenant Bleezer, with a faint tremor of hesitation in his voice. "I'm going to Oxford myself."

"Trust me, my boy," said Sheffield. "I'll fix it up for you, I promise. Let's shake hands on it." He seized Andrews's hand and pressed it warmly in a moist palm. "If it's within human power, within human power," he added.

"Well, I must go," said Lieutenant Bleezer, suddenly striding to the door. "I promised the Marquise I'd drop in. Good-bye. . . . Take a cigar, won't you?" He held out three cigars in the direction of Andrews.

"No, thank you."

"Oh, don't you think the old aristocracy of France is just too won-derful? Lieutenant Bleezer goes almost every evening to call on the Marquise de Rompemouville. He says she is just too spirituelle for words. . . . He often meets the Commanding Officer there."

Andrews had dropped into a chair and sat with his face buried in his hands, looking through his fingers at the fire, where a few white fingers of flame were clutching intermittently at a grey beech log. His mind was searching desperately for expedients.

He got to his feet and shouted shrilly:

"I can't go this life any more, do you hear that? No possible future is worth all this. If I can get to Paris, all right. If not, I'll desert and damn the consequences."

"But I've already promised I'll do all I can. . . ."

"Well, do it now," interrupted Andrews brutally.

"All right, I'll go and see the colonel and tell him what a great musi-cian you are."

"Let's go together, now."

"But that'ld look queer, dear boy."

"I don't give a damn, come along. . . . You can talk to him. You seem to be thick with all the officers."

"You must wait till I tidy up," said Sheffield.

"All right."

Andrews strode up and down in the mud in front of the house, snap-ping his fingers with impatience, until Sheffield came out, then they walked off in silence.

"Now wait outside a minute," whispered Sheffield when they came to the white house with bare grapevines over the front, where the colonel lived.

After a wait, Andrews found himself at the door of a brilliantly-lighted drawing room. There was a dense smell of cigar smoke. The colonel, an elderly man with a benevolent beard, stood before him with a coffee cup in his hand. Andrews saluted punctiliously.

"They tell me you are quite a pianist. . . . Sorry I didn't know it be-fore," said the colonel in a kindly tone. "You want to go to Paris to study under this new scheme?"

"Yes, sir."

"What a shame I didn't know before. The list of the men going is all made out. . . . Of course perhaps at the last minute . . . if somebody else doesn't go . . . your name can go in."

The colonel smiled graciously and turned back into the room.

"Thank you, Colonel," said Andrews, saluting.

Without a word to Sheffield, he strode off down the dark village street towards his quarters.

Andrews stood on the broad village street, where the mud was nearly dry, and a wind streaked with warmth ruffled the few puddles; he was looking into the window of the café to see if there was anyone he knew inside from whom he could borrow money for a drink. It was two months since he had had any pay, and his pockets were empty. The sun had just set on a premature spring afternoon, flooding the sky and the grey houses and the tumultuous tiled roofs with warm violet light. The faint premonition of the stirring of life in the cold earth, that came to Andrews with every breath he drew of the sparkling wind, stung his dull boredom to fury. It was the first of March, he was telling himself over and over again. The fifteenth of February, he had expected to be in Paris, free, or half-free; at least able to work. It was the first of March and here he was still helpless, still tied to the monotonous wheel of routine, incapable of any real effort, spending his spare time wandering like a lost dog up and down this muddy street, from the Y.M.C.A. hut at one end of the village to the church and the fountain in the middle, and to the Divisional Headquarters at the other end, then back again, looking listlessly into windows, staring in people's faces without seeing them. He had given up all hope of being sent to Paris. He had given up thinking about it or about anything; the same dull irritation of despair droned constantly in his head, grinding round and round like a broken phonograph record.

After looking a long while in the window of the café of the Braves Alliés, he walked a little down the street and stood in the same position staring into the Repos du Poilu, where a large sign "American spoken" blocked up half the window. Two officers passed. His hand snapped up to the salute automatically, like a mechanical signal. It was nearly dark. After a while he began to feel serious coolness in the wind, shivered and started to wander aimlessly down the street.

He recognised Walters coming towards him and was going to pass him without speaking when Walters bumped into him, muttered in his ear "Come to Baboon's," and hurried off with his swift business-like stride. Andrews stood irresolutely for a while with his head bent, then went with unresilient steps up the alley, through the hole in the hedge and into Babette's kitchen. There was no fire. He stared morosely at the grey ashes until he heard Walters's voice beside him:

"I've got you all fixed up."

"What do you mean?"

"Mean . . . are you asleep, Andrews? They've cut a name off the school list, that's all. Now if you shake a leg and somebody doesn't get in ahead of you, you'll be in Paris before you know it."

"That's damn decent of you to come and tell me."

"Here's your application," said Walters, drawing a paper out of his pocket. "Take it to the colonel; get him to O.K. it and then rush it up to the sergeant-major's office yourself. They are making out travel orders now. So long."

Walters had vanished. Andrews was alone again, staring at the grey ashes. Suddenly he jumped to his feet and hurried off towards headquarters. In the anteroom to the colonel's office he waited a long while, looking at his boots that were thickly coated with mud. "Those boots will make a bad impression; those boots will make a bad impression," a voice was saying over and over again inside of him. A lieutenant was also waiting to see the colonel, a young man with pink cheeks and a milky-white forehead, who held his hat in one hand with a pair of khaki-colored kid gloves, and kept passing a hand over his light well-brushed hair. Andrews felt dirty and ill-smelling in his badly-fitting uniform. The sight of this perfect young man in his whipcord breeches, with his manicured nails and immaculately polished puttees exasperated him. He would have liked to fight him, to prove that he was the better man, to outwit him, to make him forget his rank and his important air. . . . The lieutenant had gone in to see the colonel. Andrews found himself reading a chart of some sort tacked up on the wall. There were names and dates and figures, but he could not make out what it was about.

"All right! Go ahead," whispered the orderly to him; and he was standing with his cap in his hand before the colonel who was looking at him severely, fingering the papers he had on the desk with a heavily veined hand.

Andrews saluted. The colonel made an impatient gesture.

"May I speak to you, Colonel, about the school scheme?"

"I suppose you've got permission from somebody to come to me."

"No, sir." Andrews's mind was struggling to find something to say.

"Well, you'd better go and get it."

"But, Colonel, there isn't time; the travel orders are being made out at this minute. I've heard that there's been a name crossed out on the list."

"Too late."

"But, Colonel, you don't know how important it is. I am a musician by trade; if I can't get into practice again before being demobilized, I shan't be able to get a job. . . . I have a mother and an old aunt dependent on me. My family has seen better days, you see, sir. It's only by being high up in my profession that I can earn enough to give them what they are accustomed to. And a man in your position in the world, Colonel, must know what even a few months of study in Paris mean to a pianist."

The colonel smiled.

"Let's see your application," he said.

Andrews handed it to him with a trembling hand. The colonel made a few marks on one corner with a pencil.

"Now if you can get that to the sergeant-major in time to have your name included in the orders, well and good."

Andrews saluted, and hurried out. A sudden feeling of nausea had come over him. He was hardly able to control a mad desire to tear the paper up. "The sons of bitches . . . the sons of bitches," he muttered to himself. Still he ran all the way to the square, isolated building where the regimental office was.

He stopped panting in front of the desk that bore the little red card, Regimental Sergeant-Major. The regimental sergeant-major looked up at him enquiringly.

"Here's an application for School at the Sorbonne, Sergeant. Colonel Wilkins told me to run up to you with it, said he was very anxious to have it go in at once."

"Too late," said the regimental sergeant-major.

"But the colonel said it had to go in."

"Can't help it. . . . Too late," said the regimental sergeant-major.

Andrews felt the room and the men in their olive-drab shirt sleeves at the typewriters and the three nymphs creeping from behind the French War Loan poster whirl round his head. Suddenly he heard a voice behind him:

"Is the name Andrews, John, Sarge?"

"How the hell should I know?" said the regimental sergeant-major.

"Because I've got it in the orders already. . . . I don't know how it got in." The voice was Walters's voice, staccatto and business-like.

"Well, then, why d'you want to bother me about it? Give me that paper." The regimental sergeant-major jerked the paper out of Andrews's hand and looked at it savagely.

"All right, you leave tomorrow. A copy of the orders'll go to your company in the morning," growled the regimental sergeant-major.

Andrews looked hard at Walters as he went out, but got no glance in return. When he stood in the air again, disgust surged up within him, bitterer than before. The fury of his humiliation made tears start in his eyes. He walked away from the village down the main road, splashing carelessly through the puddles, slipping in the wet clay of the ditches. Something within him, like the voice of a wounded man swearing, was whining in his head long strings of filthy names. After walking a long while he stopped suddenly with his fists clenched. It was completely dark, the sky was faintly marbled by a moon behind the clouds. On both sides of the road rose the tall grey skeletons of poplars. When the sound of his footsteps stopped, he heard a faint lisp of running water. Standing still in the middle of the road, he felt his feelings gradually relax. He said aloud in a low voice several times: "You are a damn fool, John Andrews," and started walking slowly and thoughtfully back to the village.

V

Andrews felt an arm put round his shoulder.

"Ah've been to hell an' gone lookin' for you, Andy," said Chrisfield's voice in his ear, jerking him out of the reverie he walked in. He could feel in his face Chrisfield's breath, heavy with cognac.

"I'm going to Paris tomorrow, Chris," said Andrews.

"Ah know it, boy. Ah know it. That's why I was that right smart to talk to you. . . . You doan want to go to Paris. . . . Why doan ye come up to Germany with us? Tell me they live like kings up there."

"All right," said Andrews, "let's go to the back room at Babette's."

Chrisfield hung on his shoulder, walking unsteadily beside him. At the hole in the hedge Chrisfield stumbled and nearly pulled them both down. They laughed, and still laughing staggered into the dark kitchen, where they found the red-faced woman with her baby sitting beside the fire with no other light than the flicker of the rare flames that shot up from a little mass of wood embers. The baby started crying shrilly when the two soldiers stamped in. The woman got up and, talking automatically to the baby all the while, went off to get a light and wine.

Andrews looked at Chrisfield's face by the firelight. His cheeks had lost the faint childish roundness they had had when Andrews had first talked to him, sweeping up cigarette butts off the walk in front of the barracks at the training camp.

"Ah tell you, boy, you ought to come with us to Germany . . . nauthin' but whores in Paris."

"The trouble is, Chris, that I don't want to live like a king, or a sergeant or a major-general. . . . I want to live like John Andrews."

"What yer goin' to do in Paris, Andy?"

"Study music."

"Ah guess some day Ah'll go into a movie show an' when they turn on the lights, who'll Ah see but ma ole frien' Andy raggin' the scales on the pyaner."

"Something like that. . . . How d'you like being a corporal, Chris?"

"O, Ah doan know." Chrisfield spat on the floor between his feet. "It's funny, ain't it? You an' me was right smart friends onct. . . . Guess it's bein' a non-com."

Andrews did not answer.

Chrisfield sat silent with his eyes on the fire.

"Well, Ah got him. . . . Gawd, it was easy," he said suddenly.

"What do you mean?"

"Ah got him, that's all."

"You mean . . . ?"

Chrisfield nodded.

"Um-hum, in the Oregon forest," he said.

Andrews said nothing. He felt suddenly very tired. He thought of men he had seen in attitudes of death.

"Ah wouldn't ha' thought it had been so easy," said Chrisfield.

The woman came through the door at the end of the kitchen with a candle in her hand. Chrisfield stopped speaking suddenly.

"Tomorrow I'm going to Paris," cried Andrews boisterously. "It's the end of soldiering for me."

"Ah bet it'll be some sport in Germany, Andy. . . . Sarge says we'll be goin' up to Coab . . . what's its name?"

"Coblenz."

Chrisfield poured a glass of wine out and drank it off, smacking his lips after it and wiping his mouth on the back of his hand.

"D'ye remember, Andy, we was both of us brushin' cigarette butts at that bloody trainin' camp when we first met up with each other?"

"Considerable water has run under the bridge since then."

"Ah reckon we won't meet up again, mos' likely."

"Hell, why not?"

They were silent again, staring at the fading embers of the fire. In the dim edge of the candlelight the woman stood with her hands on her hips, looking at them fixedly.

"Reckon a feller wouldn't know what to do with himself if he did get out of the army, . . . now, would he, Andy?"

"So long, Chris. I'm beating it," said Andrews in a harsh voice, jumping to his feet.

"So long, Andy, ole man. . . . Ah'll pay for the drinks." Chrisfield was beckoning with his hand to the red-faced woman, who advanced slowly through the candlelight.

"Thanks, Chris."

Andrews strode away from the door. A cold, needle-like rain was falling. He pulled up his coat collar and ran down the muddy village street towards his quarters.

VI

In the opposite corner of the compartment Andrews could see Walters hunched up in an attitude of sleep, with his cap pulled down far over his eyes. His mouth was open, and his head wagged with the jolting of the train. The shade over the light plunged the compartment in dark-blue obscurity, which made the night sky outside the window and the shapes of trees and houses, evolving and pirouetting as they glided by, seem very near. Andrews felt no desire to sleep; he had sat a long time leaning his head against the frame of the window, looking out at the fleeing shadows and the occasional little red-green lights that darted by and the glow of the stations that flared for a moment and were lost in dark silhouettes of unlighted houses and skeleton trees and black hillsides. He was thinking how all the epochs in his life seemed to have been marked out by railway rides at night. The jolting rumble of the wheels made the blood go faster through his veins; made him feel acutely the clattering of the train along the gleaming rails, spurning fields and trees and houses, piling up miles and miles between the past and future. The gusts of cold night air when he opened the window and the faint whiffs of steam and coal gas that tingled in his nostrils excited him like a smile on a strange face seen for a moment in a crowded street. He did not think of what he had left behind. He was straining his eyes eagerly through the darkness towards the vivid life he was going to live. Boredom and abasement were over. He was free to work and hear music and make friends. He drew deep breaths; warm waves of vigor seemed flowing constantly from his lungs and throat to his finger tips and down through his body and the muscles of his legs. He looked at his watch: "One." In six hours he would be in Paris. For six hours he would sit there looking out at the fleeting shadows of the countryside, feeling in his blood the eager throb of the train, rejoicing in every mile the train carried him away from things past.

Walters still slept, half slipping off the seat, with his mouth open and his overcoat bundled round his head. Andrews looked out of the window, feeling in his nostrils the tingle of steam and coal gas. A phrase out of some translation of the Iliad came to his head: "Ambrosial night, Night ambrosial unending." But better than sitting round a camp fire drinking wine and water and listening to the boastful yarns of long-haired Achæans, was this hustling through the countryside away from the monotonous whine of past unhappiness, towards joyousness and life.

Andrews began to think of the men he had left behind. They were asleep at this time of night, in barns and barracks, or else standing on guard with cold damp feet, and cold hands which the icy rifle barrel burned when they tended it. He might go far away out of sound of the tramp of marching, away from the smell of overcrowded barracks where men slept in rows like cattle, but he would still be one of them. He would not see an officer pass him without an unconscious movement of servility, he would not hear a bugle without feeling sick with hatred. If he could only express these thwarted lives, the miserable dullness of industrialized slaughter, it might have been almost worth while—for him; for the others, it would never be worth while. "But you're talking as if you were out of the woods; you're a soldier still, John Andrews." The words formed themselves in his mind as vividly as if he had spoken them.

He smiled bitterly and settled himself again to watch silhouettes of trees and hedges and houses and hillsides fleeing against the dark sky.

When he awoke the sky was grey. The train was moving slowly, clattering loudly over switches, through a town of wet slate roofs that rose in fantastic patterns of shadow above the blue mist. Walters was smoking a cigarette.

"God! These French trains are rotten," he said when he noticed that Andrews was awake. "The most inefficient country I ever was in anyway."

"Inefficiency be damned," broke in Andrews, jumping up and stretching himself. He opened the window. "The heating's too damned efficient. . . . I think we're near Paris."

The cold air, with a flavor of mist in it, poured into the stuffy compartment. Every breath was joy. Andrews felt a crazy buoyancy bubbling up in him. The rumbling clatter of the train wheels sang in his ears. He threw himself on his back on the dusty blue seat and kicked his heels in the air like a colt.

"Liven up, for God's sake, man," he shouted. "We're getting near Paris."

"We are lucky bastards," said Walters, grinning, with the cigarette hanging out of the corner of his mouth. "I'm going to see if I can find the rest of the gang."

Andrews, alone in the compartment, found himself singing at the top of his lungs.

As the day brightened the mist lifted off the flat linden-green fields intersected by rows of leafless poplars. Salmon-colored houses with blue roofs wore already a faintly citified air. They passed brick-kilns and clay-quarries, with reddish puddles of water in the bottom of them; crossed a jade-green river where a long file of canal boats with bright paint on their prows moved slowly. The engine whistled shrilly. They clattered through a small freight yard, and rows of suburban houses began to form, at first chaotically in broad patches of garden-land, and then in orderly ranks with streets between and shops at the corners. A dark-grey dripping wall rose up suddenly and blotted out the view. The train slowed down and went through several stations crowded with people on their way to work,—ordinary people in varied clothes with only here and there a blue or khaki uniform. Then there was more dark-grey wall, and the obscurity of wide bridges under which dusty oil lamps burned orange and red, making a gleam on the wet wall above them, and where the wheels clanged loudly. More freight yards and the train pulled slowly past other trains full of faces and silhouettes of people, to stop with a jerk in a station. And Andrews was standing on the grey cement platform, sniffing smells of lumber and merchandise and steam. His ungainly pack and blanket-roll he carried on his shoulder like a cross. He had left his rifle and cartridge belt carefully tucked out of sight under the seat.

Walters and five other men straggled along the platform towards him, carrying or dragging their packs.

There was a look of apprehension on Walters's face.

"Well, what do we do now?" he said.

"Do!" cried Andrews, and he burst out laughing.

Prostrate bodies in olive drab hid the patch of tender green grass by the roadside. The company was resting. Chrisfield sat on a stump morosely whittling at a stick with a pocket knife. Judkins was stretched out beside him.

"What the hell do they make us do this damn hikin' for, Corp?"

"Guess they're askeered we'll forgit how to walk."

"Well, ain't it better than loafin' around yer billets all day, thinkin' an' cursin' an' wishin' ye was home?" spoke up the man who sat the other side, pounding down the tobacco in his pipe with a thick forefinger.

"It makes me sick, trampin' round this way in ranks all day with the goddam frawgs starin' at us an'. . ."

"They're laughin' at us, I bet," broke in another voice.

"We'll be movin' soon to the Army o' Occupation," said Chrisfield cheerfully. "In Germany it'll be a reglar picnic."

"An' d'you know what that means?" burst out Judkins, sitting bolt up-right. "D'you know how long the troops is goin' to stay in Germany? Fifteen years."

"Gawd, they couldn't keep us there that long, man."

"They can do anythin' they goddam please with us. We're the guys as is gettin' the raw end of this deal. It ain't the same with an' edicated guy like Andrews or Sergeant Coffin or them. They can suck around after 'Y' men, an' officers an' get on the inside track, an' all we can do is stand up an' salute an' say 'Yes, lootenant' an' 'No, lootenant' an' let 'em ride us all they goddam please. Ain't that gospel truth, corporal?"

"Ah guess you're right, Judkie; we gits the raw end of the stick."

"That damn yellar dawg Andrews goes to Paris an' gets schoolin' free an' all that."

"Hell, Andy waren't yellar, Judkins."

"Well, why did he go bellyachin' around all the time like he knew more'n the lootenant did?"

"Ah reckon he did," said Chrisfield.

"Anyway, you can't say that those guys who went to Paris did a god-dam thing more'n any the rest of us did. . . . Gawd, I ain't even had a leave yet."

"Well, it ain't no use crabbin'."

"No, onct we git home an' folks know the way we've been treated, there'll be a great ole investigation. I can tell you that," said one of the new men.

"It makes you mad, though, to have something like that put over on ye. . . . Think of them guys in Paris, havin' a hell of a time with wine an' women, an' we stay out here an' clean our guns an' drill. . . . God, I'd like to get even with some of them guys."

The whistle blew. The patch of grass became unbroken green again as the men lined up along the side of the road.

"Fall in!" called the Sergeant.

"Atten-shun!"

"Right dress!"

"Front! God, you guys haven't got no snap in yer. . . . Stick yer belly in, you. You know better than to stand like that."

"Squads, right! March! Hep, hep, hep!"

The Company tramped off along the muddy road. Their steps were all the same length. Their arms swung in the same rhythm. Their faces were cowed into the same expression, their thoughts were the same. The tramp, tramp of their steps died away along the road.

Birds were singing among the budding trees. The young grass by the roadside kept the marks of the soldiers' bodies.

PART FIVE

THE WORLD OUTSIDE

I

Andrews, and six other men from his division, sat at a table outside the café opposite the Gare de l'Est. He leaned back in his chair with a cup of coffee lifted, looking across it at the stone houses with many balconies. Steam, scented of milk and coffee, rose from the cup as he sipped from it. His ears were full of a rumble of traffic and a clacking of heels as people walked briskly by along the damp pavements. For a while he did not hear what the men he was sitting with were saying. They talked and laughed, but he looked beyond their khaki uniforms and their boat-shaped caps unconsciously. He was taken up with the smell of the coffee and of the mist. A little rusty sunshine shone on the table of the café and on the thin varnish of wet mud that covered the asphalt pavement. Looking down the Avenue, away from the station, the houses, dark grey tending to greenish in the shadow and to violet in the sun, faded into a soft haze of distance. Dull gilt lettering glittered along black balconies. In the foreground were men and women walking briskly, their cheeks whipped a little into color by the rawness of the morning. The sky was a faintly roseate grey.

Walters was speaking:

"The first thing I want to see is the Eiffel Tower."

"Why d'you want to see that?" said the small sergeant with a black mustache and rings round his eyes like a monkey.

"Why, man, don't you know that everything begins from the Eiffel Tower? If it weren't for the Eiffel Tower, there wouldn't be any sky-scrapers. . . ."

"How about the Flatiron Building and Brooklyn Bridge? They were built before the Eiffel Tower, weren't they?" interrupted the man from New York.

"The Eiffel Tower's the first piece of complete girder construction in the whole world," reiterated Walters dogmatically.

"First thing I'm going to do's go to the Folies Berdjairs; me for the w.w.'s."

"Better lay off the wild women, Bill," said Walters.

"I ain't goin' to look at a woman," said the sergeant with the black mustache. "I guess I seen enough women in my time, anyway. . . . The war's over, anyway."

"You just wait, kid, till you fasten your lamps on a real Parizianne," said a burly, unshaven man with a corporal's stripes on his arm, roaring with laughter.

Andrews lost track of the talk again, staring dreamily through half-closed eyes down the long straight street, where greens and violets and browns merged into a bluish grey monochrome at a little distance. He wanted to be alone, to wander at random through the city, to stare dreamily at people and things, to talk by chance to men and women, to sink his life into the misty sparkling life of the streets. The smell of the mist brought a memory to his mind. For a long while he groped for it, until suddenly he remembered his dinner with Henslowe and the faces of the boy and girl he had talked to on the Butte. He must find Henslowe at once. A second's fierce resentment went through him against all these people about him. Christ! He must get away from them all; his freedom had been hard enough won; he must enjoy it to the uttermost.

"Say, I'm going to stick to you, Andy." Walters's voice broke into his reverie. "I'm going to appoint you the corps of interpreters."

Andrews laughed.

"D'you know the way to the School Headquarters?"

"The R.T.O. said take the subway."

"I'm going to walk," said Andrews.

"You'll get lost, won't you?"

"No danger, worse luck," said Andrews, getting to his feet. "I'll see you fellows at the School Headquarters, whatever those are. . . . So long."

"Say, Andy, I'll wait for you there," Walters called after him.

Andrews darted down a side street. He could hardly keep from shouting aloud when he found himself alone, free, with days and days ahead of him to work and think, gradually to rid his limbs of the stiff attitudes of the automaton. The smell of the streets, and the mist, indefinably poignant, rose like incense smoke in fantastic spirals through his brain, making him hungry and dazzled, making his arms and legs feel lithe and as ready for delight as a crouching cat for a spring. His heavy shoes beat out a dance as they clattered on the wet pavements under his springy steps. He was walking very fast, stopping suddenly now and then to look at the greens and oranges and crimsons of vegetables in a push cart, to catch a vista down intricate streets, to look into the rich brown obscurity of a small wine shop where workmen stood at the counter sipping white wine. Oval, delicate faces, bearded faces of men, slightly gaunt faces of young women, red cheeks of boys, wrinkled faces of old women, whose ugliness seemed to have hidden in it, stirringly, all the beauty of youth and the tragedy of lives that had been lived; the faces of the people he passed moved him like rhythms of an orchestra. After much walking, turning always down the street which looked pleasantest, he came to an oval with a statue of a pompous personage on a ramping horse. "Place des Victoires," he read the name, which gave him a faint tinge of amusement. He looked quizzically at the heroic features of the sun king and walked off laughing. "I suppose they did it better in those days, the grand manner," he muttered. And his delight redoubled in rubbing shoulders with the people whose effigies would never appear astride ramping-eared horses in squares built to commemorate victories. He came out on a broad straight avenue, where there were many American officers he had to salute, and M.P.'s and shops with wide plate-glass windows, full of objects that had a shiny, expensive look. "Another case of victories," he thought, as he went off into a side street, taking with him a glimpse of the bluish-grey pile of the Opera, with its pompous windows and its naked bronze ladies holding lamps.

He was in a narrow street full of hotels and fashionable barber shops, from which came an odor of cosmopolitan perfumery, of casinos and ballrooms and diplomatic receptions, when he noticed an American officer coming towards him, reeling a little,—a tall, elderly man with a red face and a bottle nose. He saluted.

The officer stopped still, swaying from side to side, and said in a whining voice:

"Shonny, d'you know where Henry'sh Bar is?"

"No, I don't, Major," said Andrews, who felt himself enveloped in an odor of cocktails.

"You'll help me to find it, shonny, won't you? . . . It's dreadful not to be able to find it. . . . I've got to meet Lootenant Trevors in Henry'sh Bar." The major steadied himself by putting a hand on Andrews's shoulder. A civilian passed them.

"Dee-donc," shouted the major after him, "Dee-donc, Monshier, ou ay Henry'sh Bar?"

The man walked on without answering.

"Now isn't that like a frog, not to understand his own language?" said the major.

"But there's Henry's Bar, right across the street," said Andrews suddenly.

"Bon, bon," said the major.

They crossed the street and went in. At the bar the major, still clinging to Andrews's shoulder, whispered in his ear: "I'm A.W.O.L. shee? . . . Shee? . . . Whole damn Air Service is A.W.O.L. Have a drink with me. . . . You enlisted man? Nobody cares here. . . . Warsh over, Sonny. . . . Democracy is shafe for the world."

Andrews was just raising a champagne cocktail to his lips, looking with amusement at the crowd of American officers and civilians who crowded into the small mahogany barroom, when a voice behind him drawled out:

"I'll be damned!"

Andrews turned and saw Henslowe's brown face and small silky mustache. He abandoned his major to his fate.

"God, I'm glad to see you. . . . I was afraid you hadn't been able to work it," . . . said Henslowe slowly, stuttering a little.

"I'm about crazy, Henny, with delight. I just got in a couple of hours ago. . . ." Laughing, interrupting each other, they chattered in broken sentences.

"But how in the name of everything did you get here?"

"With the major?" said Andrews, laughing.

"What the devil?"

"Yes; that major," whispered Andrews in his friend's ear, "rather the worse for wear, asked me to lead him to Henry's Bar and just fed me a cocktail in the memory of Democracy, late defunct. . . . But what are you doing here? It's not exactly . . . exotic."

"I came to see a man who was going to tell me how I could get to Rumania with the Red Cross. . . . But that can wait. . . . Let's get out of here. God, I was afraid you hadn't made it."

"I had to crawl on my belly and lick people's boots to do it. . . . God, it was low! . . . But here I am."

They were out in the street again, walking and gesticulating.

"But 'Libertad, Libertad, allons, ma femme!' as Walt Whitman would have said," shouted Andrews.

"It's one grand and glorious feeling. . . . I've been here three days. My section's gone home; God bless them."

"But what do you have to do?"

"Do? Nothing," cried Henslowe. "Not a blooming bloody goddam thing! In fact, it's no use trying . . . the whole thing is such a mess you couldn't do anything if you wanted to."

"I want to go and talk to people at the Schola Cantorum."

"There'll be time for that. You'll never make anything out of music if you get serious-minded about it."

"Then, last but not least, I've got to get some money from somewhere."

"Now you're talking!" Henslowe pulled a burnt leather pocket book out of the inside of his tunic. "Monaco," he said, tapping the pocket book, which was engraved with a pattern of dull red flowers. He pursed up his lips and pulled out some hundred franc notes, which he pushed into Andrews's hand.

"Give me one of them," said Andrews.

"All or none. . . . They last about five minutes each."

"But it's so damn much to pay back."

"Pay it back—heavens! . . . Here take it and stop your talking. I probably won't have it again, so you'ld better make hay this time. I warn you it'll be spent by the end of the week."

"All right. I'm dead with hunger."

"Let's sit down on the Boulevard and think about where we'll have lunch to celebrate Miss Libertad. . . . But let's not call her that, sounds like Liverpool, Andy, a horrid place."

"How about Freiheit?" said Andrews, as they sat down in basket chairs in the reddish yellow sunlight.

"Treasonable . . . off with your head."

"But think of it, man," said Andrews, "the butchery's over, and you and I and everybody else will soon be human beings again. Human; all too human!"

"No more than eighteen wars going," muttered Henslowe.

"I haven't seen any papers for an age. . . . How do you mean?"

"People are fighting to beat the cats everywhere except on the western front," said Henslowe. "But that's where I come in. The Red Cross sends supply trains to keep them at it. . . . I'm going to Russia if I can work it."

"But what about the Sorbonne?"

"The Sorbonne can go to Ballyhack."

"But, Henny, I'm going to croak on your hands if you don't take me somewhere to get some food."

"Do you want a solemn place with red plush or with salmon pink brocade?"

"Why have a solemn place at all?"

"Because solemnity and good food go together. It's only a religious restaurant that has a proper devotion to the belly. O, I know, we'll go over to Brooklyn."

"Where?"

"To the Rive Gauche. I know a man who insists on calling it Brooklyn. Awfully funny man . . . never been sober in his life. You must meet him."

"Oh, I want to. . . . It's a dog's age since I met anyone new, except you. I can't live without having a variegated crowd about, can you?"

"You've got that right on this boulevard. Serbs, French, English, Americans, Australians, Rumanians, Tcheco-Slovaks; God, is there any uniform that isn't here? . . . I tell you, Andy, the war's been a great thing for the people who knew how to take advantage of it. Just look at their puttees."

"I guess they'll know how to make a good thing of the Peace too."

"Oh, that's going to be the best yet. . . . Come along. Let's be little devils and take a taxi."

"This certainly is the main street of Cosmopolis."

They threaded their way through the crowd, full of uniforms and glitter and bright colors, that moved in two streams up and down the wide sidewalk between the cafés and the boles of the bare trees. They climbed into a taxi, and lurched fast through streets where, in the misty sunlight, grey-green and grey-violet mingled with blues and pale lights as the colors mingle in a pigeon's breast feathers. They passed the leafless gardens of the Tuileries on one side, and the great inner Courts of the Louvre, with their purple mansard roofs and their high chimneys on the other, and saw for a second the river, dull jade green, and the plane trees splotched with brown and cream color along the quais, before they were lost in the narrow brownish-grey streets of the old quarters.

"This is Paris; that was Cosmopolis," said Henslowe.

"I'm not particular, just at present," cried Andrews gaily.

The square in front of the Odéon was a splash of white and the col-lonade a blur of darkness as the cab swerved round the corner and along the edge of the Luxembourg, where, through the black iron fence, many brown and reddish colors in the intricate patterns of leafless twigs opened here and there on statues and balustrades and vistas of misty distances. The cab stopped with a jerk.

"This is the Places des Médicis," said Henslowe.

At the end of a slanting street looking very flat, through the haze, was the dome of the Panthéon. In the middle of the square between the yellow trams and the green low busses, was a quiet pool, where the shadow of horizontals of the house fronts was reflected.

They sat beside the window looking out at the square.

Henslowe ordered.

"Remember how sentimental history books used to talk about prisoners who were let out after years in dungeons, not being able to stand it, and going back to their cells?"

"D'you like sole meunière?"

"Anything, or rather everything! But take it from me, that's all rubbish. Honestly I don't think I've ever been happier in my life. . . . D'you know, Henslowe, there's something in you that is afraid to be happy."

"Don't be morbid. . . . There's only one real evil in the world: being somewhere without being able to get away. . . . I ordered beer. This is the only place in Paris where it's fit to drink."

"And I'm going to every blooming concert . . . Colonne—Lamoureux on Sunday, I know that. . . . The only evil in the world is not to be able to hear music or to make it. . . . These oysters are fit for Lucullus."

"Why not say fit for John Andrews and Bob Henslowe, damn it? . . . Why the ghosts of poor old dead Romans should be dragged in every time a man eats an oyster, I don't see. We're as fine specimens as they were. I swear I shan't let any old turned-to-clay Lucullus outlive me, even if I've never eaten a lamprey."

"And why should you eat a lamp-chimney, Bob?" came a hoarse voice beside them.

Andrews looked up into a round, white face with large grey eyes hidden behind thick steel-rimmed spectacles. Except for the eyes, the face had a vaguely Chinese air.

"Hello, Heinz! Mr. Andrews, Mr. Heineman," said Henslowe.

"Glad to meet you," said Heineman in a jovially hoarse voice. "You guys seem to be overeating, to reckon by the way things are piled up on the table." Through the hoarseness Andrews could detect a faint Yankee tang in Heineman's voice.

"You'ld better sit down and help us," said Henslowe.

"Sure. . . . D'you know my name for this guy?" He turned to Andrews. . . . "Sinbad!"

> "Sinbad was in bad in Tokio and Rome,
>   In bad in Trinidad
>   An' twice as bad at home."

He sang the words loudly, waving a bread stick to keep time.

"Shut up, Heinz, or you'll get us run out of here the way you got us run out of the Olympia that night."

They both laughed.

"An' d'you remember Monsieur Le Guy with his coat?"

"Do I? God!" They laughed till the tears ran down their cheeks. Heineman took off his glasses and wiped them. He turned to Andrews.

"Oh, Paris is the best yet. First absurdity: the Peace Conference and its nine hundred and ninety-nine branches. Second absurdity: spies. Third: American officers A.W.O.L. Fourth: The seven sisters sworn to slay." He broke out laughing again, his chunky body rolling about on the chair.

"What are they?"

"Three of them have sworn to slay Sinbad, and four of them have sworn to slay me. . . . But that's too complicated to tell at lunch time. . . . Eighth: there are the lady relievers, Sinbad's specialty. Ninth: there's Sinbad. . . ."

"Shut up, Heinz, you're getting me maudlin," spluttered Henslowe.

"O Sinbad was in bad all around,"

chanted Heineman. "But no one's given me anything to drink," he said suddenly in a petulant voice. "Garçon, une bouteille de Macon, pour un Cadet de Gascogne. . . . What's the next? It ends with vergogne. You've seen the play, haven't you? Greatest play going. . . . Seen it twice sober and seven other times."

"Cyrano de Bergerac?"

"That's it. Nous sommes les Cadets de Gascogne, rhymes with ivrogne and sans vergogne. . . . You see I work in the Red Cross. . . . You know Sinbad, old Peterson's a brick. . . . I'm supposed to be taking photographs of tubercular children at this minute. . . . The noblest of my professions is that of artistic photographer. . . . Borrowed the photographs from the rickets man. So I have nothing to do for three months and five hundred francs travelling expenses. Oh, children, my only prayer is 'give us this day our red worker's permit' and the Red Cross does the rest." Heineman laughed till the glasses rang on the table. He took off his glasses and wiped them with a rueful air.

"So now I call the Red Cross the Cadets!" cried Heineman, his voice a thin shriek from laughter.

Andrews was drinking his coffee in little sips, looking out of the window at the people that passed. An old woman with a stand of flowers sat on a small cane chair at the corner. The pink and yellow and blue-violet shades of the flowers seemed to intensify the misty straw color and azured grey of the wintry sun and shadow of the streets. A girl in a tight-fitting black dress and black hat stopped at the stand to buy a bunch of pale yellow daisies, and then walked slowly past the window of the restaurant in the direction of the gardens. Her ivory face and slender body and her very dark eyes sent a sudden flush through Andrews's whole frame as he looked at her. The black erect figure disappeared in the gate of the gardens.

Andrews got to his feet suddenly.

"I've got to go," he said in a strange voice. . . . "I just remember a man was waiting for me at the School Headquarters."

"Let him wait."

"Why, you haven't had a liqueur yet," cried Heineman.

"No . . . but where can I meet you people later?"

"Café de Rohan at five . . . opposite the Palais Royal."

"You'll never find it."

"Yes I will," said Andrews.

"Palais Royal metro station," they shouted after him as he dashed out of the door.

He hurried into the gardens. Many people sat on benches in the frail sunlight. Children in bright-colored clothes ran about chasing hoops. A woman paraded a bunch of toy balloons in carmine and green and purple, like a huge bunch of parti-colored grapes inverted above her head. Andrews walked up and down the alleys, scanning faces. The girl had disappeared. He leaned against a grey balustrade and looked down into the empty pond where traces of the explosion of a Bertha still subsisted. He was telling himself that he was a fool. That even if he had found her he could not have spoken to her; just because he was free for a day or two from the army he needn't think the age of gold had come back to earth. Smiling at the thought, he walked across the gardens, wandered through some streets of old houses in grey and white stucco with slate mansard roofs and fantastic complications of chimney-pots till he came out in front of a church with a new classic façade of huge columns that seemed toppling by their own weight.

He asked a woman selling newspapers what the church's name was.

"Mais, Monsieur, c'est Saint Sulpice," said the woman in a surprised tone.

Saint Sulpice. Manon's songs came to his head, and the sentimental melancholy of eighteenth century Paris with its gambling houses in the Palais Royal where people dishonored themselves in the presence of their stern Catonian fathers, and its billets doux written at little gilt tables, and its coaches lumbering in covered with mud from the provinces through the Porte d'Orleans and the Porte de Versailles; the Paris of Diderot and Voltaire and Jean-Jacques, with its muddy streets and its ordinaries where one ate bisques and larded pullets and soufflés; a Paris full of mouldy gilt magnificence, full of pompous ennui of the past and insane hope of the future.

He walked down a narrow, smoky street full of antique shops and old bookshops and came out unexpectedly on the river opposite the statue of Voltaire. The name on the corner was quai Malaquais. Andrews crossed and looked down for a long time at the river. Opposite, behind a lace-work of leafless trees, were the purplish roofs of the Louvre with their high peaks and their ranks and ranks of chimneys; behind him the old houses of the quai and the wing, topped by a balustrade with great grey stone urns of a domed building of which he did not know the name. Barges were coming upstream, the dense green water spuming under their blunt bows, towed by a little black tugboat with its chimney bent back to pass under the bridges. The tug gave a thin shrill whistle. Andrews started walking downstream. He crossed by the bridge at the corner of the Louvre, turned his back on the arch Napoleon built to receive the famous horses from St. Marc's,—a pinkish pastrylike affair— and walked through the Tuileries which were full of people strolling about or sitting in the sun, of doll-like children and nursemaids with elaborate white caps, of fluffy little dogs straining at the ends of leashes. Suddenly a peaceful sleepiness came over him. He sat down in the sun on a bench, watching, hardly seeing them, the people who passed to and fro casting long shadows. Voices and laughter came very softly to his ears above the distant stridency of traffic. From far away he heard for a few moments notes of a military band playing a march. The shadows of the trees were faint blue-grey on the ruddy yellow gravel. Shadows of people kept passing and repassing across them. He felt very languid and happy.

Suddenly he started up; he had been dozing. He asked an old man with a beautifully pointed white beard the way to rue du Faubourg St. Honoré.

After losing his way a couple of times, he walked listlessly up some marble steps where a great many men in khaki were talking. Leaning against the doorpost was Walters. As he drew near Andrews heard him saying to the man next to him:

"Why, the Eiffel tower was the first piece of complete girder construction ever built. . . . That's the first thing a feller who's wide awake ought to see."

"Tell me the Opery's the grandest thing to look at," said the man next it.

"If there's wine an' women there, me for it."

"An' don't forget the song."

"But that isn't interesting like the Eiffel tower is," persisted Walters.

"Say, Walters, I hope you haven't been waiting for me," stammered Andrews.

"No, I've been waiting in line to see the guy about courses. . . . I want to start this thing right."

"I guess I'll see them tomorrow," said Andrews.

"Say have you done anything about a room, Andy? Let's you and me be bunkies."

"All right. . . . But maybe you won't want to room where I do, Walters."

"Where's that? In the Latin Quarter? . . . You bet. I want to see some French life while I am about it."

"Well, it's too late to get a room today."

"I'm going to the 'Y' tonight anyway."

"I'll get a fellow I know to put me up. . . . Then tomorrow, we'll see. Well, so long," said Andrews, moving away.

"Wait. I'm coming with you. . . . We'll walk around town together."

"All right," said Andrews.

The rabbit was rather formless, very fluffy and had a glance of madness in its pink eye with a black center. It hopped like a sparrow along the pavement, emitting a rubber tube from its back, which went up to a bulb in a man's hand which the man pressed to make the rabbit hop. Yet the rabbit had an air of organic completeness. Andrews laughed inordinately when he first saw it. The vendor, who had a basket full of other such rabbits on his arm, saw Andrews laughing and drew timidly near to the table; he had a pink face with little, sensitive lips rather like a real rabbit's, and large frightened eyes of a wan brown.

"Do you make them yourself?" asked Andrews, smiling.

The man dropped his rabbit on the table with a negligent air.

"Oh, oui, Monsieur, d'après la nature."

He made the rabbit turn a somersault by suddenly pressing the bulb hard. Andrews laughed and the rabbit man laughed.

"Think of a big strong man making his living that way," said Walters, disgusted.

"I do it all . . . de matière première au profit de l'accapareur," said the rabbit man.

"Hello, Andy . . . late as hell. . . . I'm sorry," said Henslowe, dropping down into a chair beside them. Andrews introduced Walters, the rabbit man took off his hat, bowed to the company and went off, making the rabbit hop before him along the edge of the curbstone.

"What's happened to Heineman?"

"Here he comes now," said Henslowe.

An open cab had driven up to the curb in front of the café. In it sat Heineman with a broad grin on his face and beside him a woman in a salmon-colored dress, ermine furs and an emerald-green hat. The cab drove off and Heineman, still grinning, walked up to the table.

"Where's the lion cub?" asked Henslowe.

"They say it's got pneumonia."

"Mr. Heineman. Mr. Walters."

The grin left Heineman's face; he said: "How do you do?" curtly, cast a furious glance at Andrews and settled himself in a chair.

The sun had set. The sky was full of lilac and bright purple and carmine. Among the deep blue shadows lights were coming on, primrose-colored street lamps, violet arc lights, ruddy sheets of light poured out of shop windows.

"Let's go inside. I'm cold as hell," said Heineman crossly, and they filed in through the revolving door, followed by a waiter with their drinks.

"I've been in the Red Cross all afternoon, Andy. . . . I think I am going to work that Roumania business. . . . Want to come?" said Henslowe in Andrews's ear.

"If I can get hold of a piano and some lessons and the concerts keep up you won't be able to get me away from Paris with wild horses. No, sir, I want to see what Paris is like. . . . It's going to my head so it'll be weeks before I know what I think about it."

"Don't think about it. . . . Drink," growled Heineman, scowling savagely.

"That's two things I'm going to keep away from in Paris; drink and women. . . . And you can't have one without the other," said Walters.

"True enough. . . . You sure do need them both," said Heineman.

Andrews was not listening to their talk; twirling the stem of his glass of vermouth in his fingers, he was thinking of the Queen of Sheba slipping down from off the shoulders of her elephant, glistening fantastically with jewels in the light of crackling, resinous torches. Music was seeping up through his mind as the water seeps into a hole dug in the sand of the seashore. He could feel all through his body the tension of rhythms and phrases taking form, not quite to be seized as yet, still hovering on the borderland of consciousness. *From the girl at the cross-roads singing under her street-lamp to the patrician pulling roses to pieces from the height of her litter. . . . All the imaginings of your desire. . . .* He thought of the girl with skin like old ivory he had seen in the Place de Medicis. The Queen of Sheba's face was like that now in his imaginings, quiet and inscrutable. A sudden cymbal-clanging of joy made his heart thump hard. He was free now of the imaginings of his desire, to loll all day at café tables watching the tables move in changing patterns before him, to fill his mind and body with a reverberation of all the rhythms of men and women moving in the frieze of life before his eyes; no more like wooden automatons knowing only the motions of the drill manual, but supple and varied, full of force and tragedy.

"For Heaven's sake let's beat it from here. . . . Gives me a pain this place does." Heineman beat his fist on the table.

"All right," said Andrews, getting up with a yawn.

Henslowe and Andrews walked off, leaving Walters to follow them with Heineman.

"We're going to dine at Le Rat qui Danse," said Henslowe, "an awfully funny place. . . . We just have time to walk there comfortably with an appetite."

They followed the long dimly-lighted Rue de Richelieu to the Boulevards, where they drifted a little while with the crowd. The glaring lights seemed to powder the air with gold. Cafés and the tables out-side were crowded. There was an odor of vermouth and coffee and per-fume and cigarette smoke mixed with the fumes of burnt gasoline from taxicabs.

"Isn't this mad?" said Andrews.

"It's always carnival at seven on the Grands Boulevards."

They started climbing the steep streets to Montmartre. At a corner they passed a hard-faced girl with rouge-smeared lips and over-powdered cheeks, laughing on the arm of an American soldier, who had a sallow face and dull-green eyes that glittered in the slanting light of a street-lamp.

"Hello, Stein," said Andrews.

"Who's that?"

"A fellow from our division, got here with me this morning."

"He's got curious lips for a Jew," said Henslowe.

At the fork of two slanting streets, they went into a restaurant that had small windows pasted over with red paper, through which the light came dimly. Inside were crowded oak tables and oak wainscoting with a shelf round the top, on which were shell-cans, a couple of skulls, several cracked majolica plates and a number of stuffed rats. The only people there were a fat woman and a man with long grey hair and beard who sat talking earnestly over two small glasses in the center of the room. A husky-looking waitress with a Dutch cap and apron hovered near the inner door from which came a great smell of fish frying in olive oil.

"The cook here's from Marseilles," said Henslowe, as they settled themselves at a table for four.

"I wonder if the rest of them lost the way," said Andrews.

"More likely old Heinz stopped to have a drink," said Henslowe. "Let's have some hors d'œuvre while we are waiting."

The waitress brought a collection of boat-shaped plates of red salads and yellow salads and green salads and two little wooden tubs with her-rings and anchovies.

Henslowe stopped her as she was going, saying:

"Rien de plus?"

The waitress contemplated the array with a tragic air, her arms folded over her ample bosom.

"Que vouley-vous, Monsieur, c'est l'armistice."

"The greatest fake about all this war business is the peace. I tell you, not till the hors d'œuvre has been restored to its proper abundance and variety will I admit that the war's over."

The waitress tittered.

"Things aren't what they used to be," she said, going back to the kitchen.

Heineman burst into the restaurant at that moment, slamming the door behind him so that the glass rang, and the fat woman and the hairy man started violently in their chairs. He tumbled into a place, grinning broadly.

"And what have you done to Walters?"

Heineman wiped his glasses meticulously.

"Oh, he died of drinking raspberry shrub," he said. . . . "Dee-dong peteet du ving de Bourgogne," he shouted towards the waitress in his nasal French. Then he added: "Le Guy is coming in a minute, I just met him."

The restaurant was gradually filling up with men and women of very various costumes, with a good sprinkling of Americans in uniform and out.

"God, I hate people who don't drink," cried Heineman, pouring out wine. "A man who don't drink just cumbers the earth."

"How are you going to take it in America when they have prohibition?"

"Don't talk about it; here's le Guy. I wouldn't have him know I belong to a nation that prohibits good liquor. . . . Monsieur le Guy, Monsieur Henslowe et Monsieur Andrews," he continued getting up ceremoniously. A little man with twirled mustaches and a small vandyke beard sat down at the fourth place. He had a faintly red nose and little twinkling eyes.

"How glad I am," he said, exposing his starched cuffs with a curious gesture, "to have some one to dine with! When one begins to get old loneliness is impossible. It is only youth that dares think. . . . Afterwards one has only one thing to think about: old age."

"There's always work," said Andrews.

"Slavery. Any work is slavery. What is the use of freeing your intellect if you sell yourself again to the first bidder?"

"Rot!" said Heineman, pouring out from a new bottle.

Andrews had begun to notice the girl who sat at the next table, in front of a pale young soldier in French-blue who resembled her extraordinarily. She had high cheek bones and a forehead in which the modelling of the skull showed through the transparent, faintly-olive skin. Her heavy chestnut hair was coiled carelessly at the back of her head. She spoke very quietly, and pressed her lips together when she smiled. She ate quickly and neatly, like a cat.

The restaurant had gradually filled up with people. The waitress and the patron, a fat man with a wide red sash coiled tightly round his waist, moved with difficulty among the crowded tables. A woman at a table in the corner, with dead white skin and drugged staring eyes, kept laughing hoarsely, leaning her head, in a hat with bedraggled white plumes, against the wall. There was a constant jingle of plates and glasses, and an oily fume of food and women's clothes and wine.

"D'you want to know what I really did with your friend?" said Heineman, leaning towards Andrews.

"I hope you didn't push him into the Seine."

"It was damn impolite. . . . But hell, it was damn impolite of him not to drink. . . . No use wasting time with a man who don't drink. I took him into a café and asked him to wait while I telephoned. I guess he's still waiting. One of the whoreiest cafés on the whole Boulevard Clichy." Heineman laughed uproariously and started explaining it in nasal French to M. le Guy.

Andrews flushed with annoyance for a moment, but soon started laughing. Heineman had started singing again.

> "O, Sinbad was in bad in Tokio and Rome,
> In bad in Trinidad
> And twice as bad at home,
> O, Sinbad was in bad all around!"

Everybody clapped. The white-faced woman in the corner cried "Bravo, Bravo," in a shrill nightmare voice.

Heineman bowed, his big grinning face bobbing up and down like the face of a Chinese figure in porcelain.

"Lui est Sinbad," he cried, pointing with a wide gesture towards Henslowe.

"Give 'em some more, Heinz. Give them some more," said Henslowe, laughing.

> "Big brunettes with long stelets
> On the shores of Italee,
> Dutch girls with golden curls
> Beside the Zuyder Zee . . ."

Everybody cheered again; Andrews kept looking at the girl at the next table, whose face was red from laughter. She had a handkerchief pressed to her mouth, and kept saying in a low voice:

"O qu'il est drôle, celui-là. . . . O qu'il est drôle."

Heineman picked up a glass and waved it in the air before drinking it off. Several people got up and filled it up from their bottles with white wine and red. The French soldier at the next table pulled an army canteen from under his chair and hung it round Heineman's neck.

Heineman, his face crimson, bowed to all sides, more like a Chinese porcelain figure than ever, and started singing in all solemnity this time.

> "Hulas and hulas would pucker up their lips,

> He fell for their ball-bearing hips
> For they were pips . . ."

His chunky body swayed to the ragtime. The woman in the corner kept time with long white arms raised above her head.

"Bet she's a snake charmer," said Henslowe.

> "O, wild woman loved that child
> He would drive the women wild!
> O, Sinbad was in bad all around!"

Heineman waved his arms, pointed again to Henslowe, and sank into his chair saying in the tones of a Shakespearean actor:

"C'est lui Sinbad."

The girl hid her face on the tablecloth, shaken with laughter. Andrews could hear a convulsed little voice saying:

"O qu'il est rigolo. . . ."

Heineman took off the canteen and handed it back to the French soldier.

"Merci, Camarade," he said solemnly.

"Eh bien, Jeanne, c'est temps de ficher le camp," said the French soldier to the girl. They got up. He shook hands with the Americans. Andrews caught the girl's eye and they both started laughing convulsively again. Andrews noticed how erect and supple she walked as his eyes followed her to the door.

Andrews's party followed soon after.

"We've got to hurry if we want to get to the Lapin Agile before closing . . . and I've got to have a drink," said Heineman, still talking in his stagey Shakespearean voice.

"Have you ever been on the stage?" asked Andrews.

"What stage, sir? I'm in the last stages now, sir. . . . I am an artistic photographer and none other. . . . Moki and I are going into the movies together when they decide to have peace."

"Who's Moki?"

"Moki Hadj is the lady in the salmon-colored dress," said Henslowe, in a loud stage whisper in Andrews's ear. "They have a lion cub named Bubu."

"Our first born," said Heineman with a wave of the hand.

The streets were deserted. A thin ray of moonlight, bursting now and then through the heavy clouds, lit up low houses and roughly-cobbled streets and the flights of steps with rare dim lamps bracketed in house walls that led up to the Butte.

There was a gendarme in front of the door of the Lapin Agile. The

street was still full of groups that had just come out, American officers
and Y.M.C.A. women with a sprinkling of the inhabitants of the region.

"Now look, we're late," groaned Heineman in a tearful voice.

"Never mind, Heinz," said Henslowe, "le Guy'll take us to see de
Clocheville like he did last time, n'est pas, le Guy?" Then Andrews heard
him add, talking to a man he had not seen before, "Come along Aubrey,
I'll introduce you later."

They climbed further up the hill. There was a scent of wet gardens in
the air, entirely silent except for the clatter of their feet on the cobbles.
Heineman was dancing a sort of a jig at the head of the procession. They
stopped before a tall cadaverous house and started climbing a rickety
wooden stairway.

"Talk about inside dope. . . . I got this from a man who's actually in
the room when the Peace Conference meets." Andrews heard Aubrey's
voice with a Chicago burr in the r's behind him in the stairs.

"Fine, let's hear it," said Henslowe.

"Did you say the Peace Conference took dope?" shouted Heineman,
whose puffing could be heard as he climbed the dark stairs ahead of
them.

"Shut up, Heinz."

They stumbled over a raised doorstep into a large garret room with a
tile floor, where a tall lean man in a monastic-looking dressing gown of
some brown material received them. The only candle made all their
shadows dance fantastically on the slanting white walls as they moved
about. One side of the room had three big windows, with an occasional
cracked pane mended with newspaper, stretching from floor to ceiling.
In front of them were two couches with rugs piled on them. On the opposite wall was a confused mass of canvases piled one against the other,
leaning helter skelter against the slanting wall of the room.

> "C'est le bon vin, le bon vin,
> C'est la chanson du vin,"

chanted Heineman. Everybody settled themselves on couches. The lanky
man in the brown dressing gown brought a table out of the shadow, put
some black bottles and heavy glasses on it, and drew up a camp stool for
himself.

"He lives that way. . . . They say he never goes out. Stays here and
paints, and when friends come in, he feeds them wine and charges them
double," said Henslowe. "That's how he lives."

The lanky man began taking bits of candle out of a drawer of the table
and lighting them. Andrews saw that his feet and legs were bare below
the frayed edge of the dressing gown. The candle light lit up the men's

flushed faces and the crude banana yellows and arsenic greens of the canvases along the walls, against which jars full of paint brushes cast blurred shadows.

"I was going to tell you, Henny," said Aubrey, "the dope is that the President's going to leave the conference, going to call them all damn blackguards to their faces and walk out, with the band playing the 'Internationale.'"

"God, that's news," cried Andrews.

"If he does that he'll recognize the Soviets," said Henslowe. "Me for the first Red Cross Mission that goes to save starving Russia. . . . Gee, that's great.—I'll write you a postal from Moscow, Andy, if they haven't been abolished as delusions of the bourgeoisie."

"Hell, no. . . . I've got five hundred dollars' worth of Russian bonds that girl Vera gave me. . . . But worth five million, ten million, fifty million if the Czar gets back. . . . I'm backing the little white father," cried Heineman. "Anyway Moki says he's alive; that Savaroff's got him locked up in a suite in the Ritz. . . . And Moki knows."

"Moki knows a damn lot, I'll admit that," said Henslowe.

"But just think of it," said Aubrey, "that means world revolution with the United States at the head of it. What do you think of that?"

"Moki doesn't think so," said Heineman. "And Moki knows."

"She just knows what a lot of reactionary warlords tell her," said Aubrey. "This man I was talking with at the Crillon—I wish I could tell you his name—heard it directly from . . . Well, you know who." He turned to Henslowe, who smiled knowingly. "There's a mission in Russia at this minute making peace with Lenin."

"A goddam outrage!" cried Heineman, knocking a bottle off the table. The lanky man picked up the pieces patiently, without comment.

"The new era is opening, men, I swear it is . . ." began Aubrey. "The old order is dissolving. It is going down under a weight of misery and crime. . . . This will be the first great gesture towards a newer and better world. There is no alternative. The chance will never come back. It is either for us to step courageously forward, or sink into unbelievable horrors of anarchy and civil war. . . . Peace or the dark ages again."

Andrews had felt for some time an uncontrollable sleepiness coming over him. He rolled himself on a rug and stretched out on the empty couch. The voices arguing, wrangling, enunciating emphatic phrases, dinned for a minute in his ears. He went to sleep.

When Andrews woke up he found himself staring at the cracked plaster of an unfamiliar ceiling. For some moments he could not guess where he was. Henslowe was sleeping, wrapped in another rug, on the couch beside him. Except for Henslowe's breathing, there was complete silence. Floods of silvery-grey light poured in through the wide windows, behind which Andrews could see a sky full of bright dove-colored clouds. He sat up carefully. Some time in the night he must have taken off his tunic and boots and puttees, which were on the floor beside the couch. The tables with the bottles had gone and the lanky man was nowhere to be seen.

Andrews went to the window in his stockinged feet. Paris was a slate-grey and dove-color lay spread out like a Turkish carpet, with a silvery band of mist where the river was, out of which the Eiffel Tower stood up like a man wading. Here and there blue smoke and brown spiralled up to lose itself in the faint canopy of brown fog that hung high above the houses. Andrews stood a long while leaning against the window frame, until he heard Henslowe's voice behind him:

"Depuis le jour où je me suis donnée."

"You look like 'Louise.'"

Andrews turned round.

Henslowe was sitting on the edge of the bed with his hair in disorder, combing his little silky mustache with a pocket comb.

"Gee, I have a head," he said. "My tongue feels like a nutmeg grater. . . . Doesn't yours?"

"No. I feel like a fighting cock."

"What do you say we go down to the Seine and have a bath in Benny Franklin's bathtub?"

"Where's that? It sounds grand."

"Then we'll have the biggest breakfast ever."

"That's the right spirit. . . . Where's everybody gone to?"

"Old Heinz has gone to his Moki, I guess, and Aubrey's gone to collect more dope at the Crillon. He says four in the morning when the drunks come home is the prime time for a newspaper man."

"And the Monkish man?"

"Search me."

The streets were full of men and girls hurrying to work. Everything sparkled, had an air of being just scrubbed. They passed bakeries from which came a rich smell of fresh-baked bread. From cafés came whiffs of roasting coffee. They crossed through the markets that were full of heavy carts lumbering to and fro, and women with net bags full of vegetables. There was a pungent scent of crushed cabbage leaves and carrots and wet clay. The mist was raw and biting along the quais, and made the blood come into their cheeks and their hands stiff with cold.

The bathhouse was a huge barge with a house built on it in a lozenge shape. They crossed to it by a little gangplank on which were a few geraniums in pots. The attendant gave them two rooms side by side on the lower deck, painted grey, with steamed over windows, through which Andrews caught glimpses of hurrying green water. He stripped his clothes off quickly. The tub was of copper varnished with some white metal inside. The water flowed in through two copper swans' necks. When Andrews stepped into the hot green water, a little window in the partition flew open and Henslowe shouted in to him:

"Talk about modern conveniences. You can converse while you bathe!"

Andrews scrubbed himself jauntily with a square piece of pink soap, splashing the water about like a small boy. He stood up and lathered himself all over and then let himself slide into the water, which splashed out over the floor.

"Do you think you're a performing seal?" shouted Henslowe.

"It's all so preposterous," cried Andrews, going off into convulsions of laughter. "She has a lion cub named Bubu and Nicolas Romanoff lives in the Ritz, and the Revolution is scheduled for day after tomorrow at twelve noon."

"I'd put it about the first of May," answered Henslowe, amid a sound of splashing. "Gee, it'ld be great to be a people's Commissary. . . . You could go and revolute the grand Llama of Thibet."

"O, it's too deliciously preposterous," cried Andrews, letting himself slide a second time into the bathtub.

II

Two M.P.'s passed outside the window. Andrews watched the yellow pigskin revolver cases until they were out of sight. He felt joyfully secure from them. The waiter, standing by the door with a napkin on his arm, gave him a sense of security so intense it made him laugh. On the marble table before him were a small glass of beer, a notebook full of ruled sheets of paper and a couple of yellow pencils. The beer, the color of topaz in the clear grey light that streamed in through the window, threw a pale yellow glow with a bright center on the table. Outside was the boulevard with a few people walking hurriedly. An empty market wagon passed now and then, rumbling loud. On a bench a woman in a black knitted shawl, with a bundle of newspapers in her knees, was counting sous with loving concentration.

Andrews looked at his watch. He had an hour before going to the Schola Cantorum.

He got to his feet, paid the waiter and strolled down the center of the boulevard, thinking smilingly of pages he had written, of pages he was going to write, filled with a sense of leisurely well-being. It was a grey morning with a little yellowish fog in the air. The pavements were damp, reflected women's dresses and men's legs and the angular outlines of taxicabs. From a flower stand with violets and red and pink carnations irregular blotches of color ran down into the brownish grey of the pavement. Andrews caught a faint smell of violets in the smell of the fog as he passed the flower stand and remembered suddenly that spring was coming. He would not miss a moment of this spring, he told himself; he would follow it step by step, from the first violets. Oh, how fully he must live now to make up for all the years he had wasted in his life.

He kept on walking along the boulevard. He was remembering how he and the girl the soldier had called Jeanne had both kindled with uncontrollable laughter when their eyes had met that night in the restaurant. He wished he could go down the boulevard with a girl like that, laughing through the foggy morning.

He wondered vaguely what part of Paris he was getting to, but was too happy to care. How beautifully long the hours were in the early morning!

At a concert at the Salle Gaveau the day before he had heard Debussy's Nocturnes and Les Sirènes. Rhythms from them were the warp of all his thoughts. Against the background of the grey street and the brownish fog that hung a veil at the end of every vista he began to imagine rhythms of his own, modulations and phrases that grew brilliant and faded, that flapped for a while like gaudy banners above his head through the clatter of the street.

He noticed that he was passing a long building with blank rows of windows, at the central door of which stood groups of American soldiers smoking. Unconsciously he hastened his steps, for fear of meeting an officer he would have to salute. He passed the men without looking at them.

A voice detained him.

"Say, Andrews."

When he turned he saw that a short man with curly hair, whose face, though familiar, he could not place, had left the group at the door and was coming towards him.

"Hello, Andrews. . . . Your name's Andrews, ain't it?"

"Yes." Andrews shook his hand, trying to remember.

"I'm Fuselli. . . . Remember? Last time I saw you you was goin' up to the lines on a train with Chrisfield. . . . Chris we used to call him. . . . At Cosne, don't you remember?"

"Of course I do."

"Well, what's happened to Chris?"

"He's a corporal now," said Andrews.

"Gee he is. . . . I'll be goddamned. . . . They was goin' to make me a corporal once."

Fuselli wore stained olive-drab breeches and badly rolled puttees; his shirt was open at the neck. From his blue denim jacket came a smell of stale grease that Andrews recognised; the smell of army kitchens. He had a momentary recollection of standing in line cold dark mornings and of the sound the food made slopping into mess kits.

"Why didn't they make you a corporal, Fuselli?" Andrews said, after a pause, in a constrained voice.

"Hell, I got in wrong, I suppose."

They were leaning against the dusty house wall. Andrews looked at his feet. The mud of the pavement, splashing up on the wall, made an even dado along the bottom, on which Andrews scraped the toe of his shoe up and down.

"Well, how's everything?" Andrews asked looking up suddenly.

"I've been in a labor battalion. That's how everything is."

"God, that's tough luck!"

Andrews wanted to go on. He had a sudden fear that he would be late. But he did not know how to break away.

"I got sick," said Fuselli grinning. "I guess I am yet. It's a hell of a note the way they treat a feller . . . like he was lower than the dirt."

"Were you at Cosne all the time? That's damned rough luck, Fuselli."

"Cosne sure is a hell of a hole. . . . I guess you saw a lot of fighting. God! you must have been glad not to be in the goddam medics."

"I don't know that I'm glad I saw fighting. . . . Oh, yes, I suppose I am."

"You see, I had it a hell of a time before they found out. Court-martial was damn stiff . . . after the armistice too. . . . Oh, God! why can't they let a feller go home?"

A woman in a bright blue hat passed them. Andrews caught a glimpse of a white over-powdered face; her hips trembled like jelly under the blue skirt with each hard clack of her high heels on the pavement.

"Gee, that looks like Jenny. . . . I'm glad she didn't see me. . . ." Fuselli laughed. "Ought to 'a seen her one night last week. We were so dead drunk we just couldn't move."

"Isn't that bad for what's the matter with you?"

"I don't give a damn now; what's the use?"

"But God; man!" Andrews stopped himself suddenly. Then he said in a different voice; "What outfit are you in now?"

"I'm on the permanent K.P. here," Fuselli jerked his thumb towards the door of the building. "Not a bad job, off two days a week; no drill, good eats. . . . At least you get all you want. . . . But it surely has been hell emptying ash cans and shovelling coal an' now all they've done is dry me up."

"But you'll be goin' home soon now, won't you? They can't discharge you till they cure you."

"Damned if I know. . . . Some guys say a guy never can be cured. . . ."

"Don't you find K.P. work pretty damn dull?"

"No worse than anything else. What are you doin' in Paris?"

"School detachment."

"What's that?"

"Men who wanted to study in the university, who managed to work it."

"Gee, I'm glad I ain't goin' to school again."

"Well, so long, Fuselli."

"So long, Andrews."

Fuselli turned and slouched back to the group of men at the door. Andrews hurried away. As he turned the corner he had a glimpse of Fuselli with his hands in his pockets and his legs crossed leaning against the wall behind the door of the barracks.

III

The darkness, where the rain fell through the vague halos of light round the street lamps, glittered with streaks of pale gold. Andrews's ears were full of the sound of racing gutters and spattering waterspouts, and of the hard unceasing beat of the rain on the pavements. It was after closing time. The corrugated shutters were drawn down, in front of café windows. Andrews's cap was wet; water trickled down his forehead and the sides of his nose, running into his eyes. His feet were soaked and he could feel the wet patches growing on his knees where they received the water running off his overcoat. The street stretched wide and dark ahead of him, with an occasional glimmer of greenish reflection from a lamp. As he walked, splashing with long strides through the rain, he noticed that he was keeping pace with a woman under an umbrella, a slender person who was hurrying with small resolute steps up the boulevard. When he saw her, a mad hope flamed suddenly through him. He remembered a vulgar little theatre and the crude light of a spot light. Through the paint and powder a girl's golden-brown skin had shone with a firm brilliance that made him think of wide sun-scorched uplands, and dancing figures on Greek vases. Since he had seen her two nights ago, he had thought of nothing else. He had feverishly found out her name. "Naya Selikoff!" A mad hope flared through him that this girl he was walking beside was the girl whose slender limbs moved in an endless frieze through his thoughts. He peered at her with eyes blurred with rain. What an ass he was! Of course it couldn't be; it was too early. She was on the stage at this minute. Other hungry eyes were staring at her slenderness, other hands were twitching to stroke her golden-brown skin. Walking under the steady downpour that stung his face and ears and sent a tiny cold trickle down his back, he felt a sudden dizziness of desire come over him. His hands, thrust to the bottom of his coat pockets, clutched convulsively. He felt that he would die, that his pounding blood vessels would burst. The bead curtains of rain rustled and tinkled about him, awakening his nerves, making his skin flash and tingle. In the gurgle of water in gutters and water spouts he could imagine he heard orchestras droning libidinous music. The feverish excitement of his senses began to create frenzied rhythms in his ears:

"O ce pauvre poilu! Qu'il doit etre mouillé" said a small tremulous voice beside him.

He turned.

The girl was offering him part of her umbrella.

"O c'est un Americain!" she said again, still speaking as if to herself.

"Mais ça ne vaut pas la peine."

"Mais oui, mais oui."

He stepped under the umbrella beside her.

"But you must let me hold it."

"Bien."

As he took the umbrella he caught her eye. He stopped still in his tracks.

"But you're the girl at the Rat qui Danse."

"And you were at the next table with the man who sang?"

"How amusing!"

"Et celui-là! O il était rigolo. . . ." She burst out laughing; her head, encased in a little round black hat, bobbed up and down under the umbrella. Andrews laughed too. Crossing the Boulevard St. Germain, a taxi nearly ran them down and splashed a great wave of mud over them. She clutched his arm and then stood roaring with laughter.

"O quelle horreur! Quelle horreur!" she kept exclaiming.

Andrews laughed and laughed.

"But hold the umbrella over us. . . . You're letting the rain in on my best hat," she said again.

"Your name is Jeanne," said Andrews.

"Impertinent! You heard my brother call me that. . . . He went back to the front that night, poor little chap. . . . He's only nineteen . . . he's very clever. . . . O, how happy I am now that the war's over."

"You are older than he?"

"Two years. . . . I am the head of the family. . . . It is a dignified position."

"Have you always lived in Paris?"

"No, we are from Laon. . . . It's the war."

"Refugees?"

"Don't call us that. . . . We work."

Andrews laughed.

"Are you going far?" she asked peering in his face.

"No, I live up here. . . . My name is the same as yours."

"Jean? How funny!"

"Where are you going?"

"Rue Descartes. . . . Behind St. Etienne."

"I live near you."

"But you mustn't come. The concierge is a tigress. . . . Etienne calls her Mme. Clemenceau."

"Who? The saint?"

"No, you silly—my brother. He is a socialist. He's a typesetter at *l'Humanité*."

"Really? I often read *l'Humanité*."

"Poor boy, he used to swear he'd never go in the army. He thought of going to America."

"That wouldn't do him any good now," said Andrews bitterly. "What do you do?"

"I?" a gruff bitterness came into her voice. "Why should I tell you? I work at a dressmaker's."

"Like Louise?"

"You've heard Louise? Oh, how I cried."

"Why did it make you sad?"

"Oh, I don't know. . . . But I'm learning stenography. . . . But here we are!"

The great bulk of the Pantheon stood up dimly through the rain beside them. In front the tower of St. Etienne-du-Mont was just visible. The rain roared about them.

"Oh, how wet I am!" said Jeanne.

"Look, they are giving Louise day after tomorrow at the Opera Comique. . . . Won't you come with me?"

"No, I should cry too much."

"I'll cry too."

"But it's not . . ."

"C'est l'armistice," interrupted Andrews.

They both laughed!

"All right! Meet me at the café at the end of the Boul' Mich' at a quarter past seven. . . . But you probably won't come."

"I swear I will," cried Andrews eagerly.

"We'll see!" She darted away down the street beside St. Etienne-du-Mont. Andrews was left alone amid the seethe of the rain and the tumultuous gurgle of waterspouts. He felt calm and tired.

When he got to his room, he found he had no matches in his pocket.

No light came from the window through which he could hear the hissing clamor of the rain in the court. He stumbled over a chair.

"Are you drunk?" came Walters's voice swathed in bedclothes. "There are matches on the table."

"But where the hell's the table?"

At last his hand, groping over the table, closed on the matchbox.

The match's red and white flicker dazzled him. He blinked his eyes; the lashes were still full of raindrops. When he had lit a candle and set it amongst the music papers upon the table, he tore off his dripping clothes.

"I just met the most charming girl, Walters," Andrews stood naked beside the pile of his clothes, rubbing himself with a towel. "Gee! I was wet. . . . But she was the most charming person I've met since I've been in Paris."

"I thought you said you let the girls alone."

"Whores, I must have said."

"Well! Any girl you could pick up on the street. . . ."

"Nonsense!"

"I guess they are all that way in this damned country. . . . God, it will do me good to see a nice sweet wholesome American girl."

Andrews did not answer. He blew out the light and got into bed.

"But I've got a new job," Walters went on. "I'm working in the school detachment office."

"Why the hell do that? You came here to take courses in the Sorbonne, didn't you?"

"Sure. I go to most of them now. But in this army I like to be in the middle of things, see? Just so they can't put anything over on me."

"There's something in that."

"There's a damn lot in it, boy. The only way is to keep in right and not let the man higher up forget you. . . . Why, we may start fighting again. These damn Germans ain't showin' the right spirit at all . . . after all the President's done for them. I expect to get my sergeantcy out of it anyway."

"Well, I'm going to sleep," said Andrews sulkily.

John Andrews sat at a table outside the Café de Rohan. The sun had just set on a ruddy afternoon, flooding everything with violet-blue light and cold greenish shadow. The sky was bright lilac color, streaked with a few amber clouds. The lights were on in all the windows of the Magazin du Louvre opposite, so that the windows seemed bits of polished glass in the afterglow. In the colonnade of the Palais Royal the shadows were deepening and growing colder. A steady stream of people poured in and out of the Metro. Green buses stuffed with people kept passing. The roar of the traffic and the clatter of footsteps and the grumble of voices swirled like dance music about Andrews's head. He noticed all at once that the rabbit man stood in front of him, a rabbit dangling forgotten at the end of its rubber tube.

"Et ça va bien? le commerce," said Andrews.

"Quietly, quietly," said the rabbit man, distractedly making the rabbit turn a somersault at his feet. Andrews watched the people going into the Metro.

"The gentleman amuses himself in Paris?" asked the rabbit man timidly.

"Oh, yes; and you?"

"Quietly," the rabbit man smiled. "Women are very beautiful at this hour of the evening," he said again in his very timid tone.

"There is nothing more beautiful than this moment of the evening . . . in Paris."

"Or Parisian women." The eyes of the rabbit man glittered.

"Excuse me, sir," he went on. "I must try and sell some rabbits."

"Au revoir," said Andrews holding out his hand.

The rabbit man shook it with sudden vigor and went off, making a rabbit hop before him along the curbstone. He was hidden by the swiftly moving crowds.

In the square, flaring violet arclights were flickering on, lighting up their net-covered globes that hung like harsh moons above the pavement.

Henslowe sat down on a chair beside Andrews.

"How's Sinbad?"

"Sinbad, old boy, is functioning. . . . Aren't you frozen?"

"How do you mean, Henslowe?"

"Overheated, you chump, sitting out here in polar weather."

"No, but I mean. . . . How are you functioning?" said Andrews laughing.

"I'm going to Poland tomorrow."

"How?"

"As guard on a Red Cross supply train. I think you might make it if you want to come, if we beat it right over to the Red Cross before Major Smithers goes. Or we might take him out to dinner."

"But, Henny, I'm staying."

"Why the hell stay in this hole?"

"I like it. I'm getting a better course in orchestration than I imagined existed, and I met a girl the other day, and I'm crazy over Paris."

"If you go and get entangled, I swear I'll beat your head in with a Polish shillaughly. . . . Of course you've met a girl—so have I—lots. We can meet some more in Poland and dance polonaises with them."

"No, but this girl's charming. . . . You've seen her. She's the girl who was with the poilu at the Rat qui Danse the first night I was in Paris. We went to Louise together."

"Must have been a grand sentimental party. . . . I swear. . . . I may run after a Jane now and again but I never let them interfere with the business of existence," muttered Henslowe crossly.

They were both silent.

"You'll be as bad as Heinz with his Moki and the lion cub named Bubu. . . . By the way, it's dead. . . . Well, where shall we have dinner?"

"I'm dining with Jeanne. . . . I'm going to meet her in half an hour. . . . I'm awfully sorry, Henny. We might all dine together."

"A fat chance! No, I'll have to go and find that ass Aubrey, and hear all about the Peace Conference. . . . Heinz can't leave Moki because she's having hysterics on account of Bubu. I'll probably be driven to going to see Berthe in the end. . . . You're a nice one."

"We'll have a grand seeing-off party for you tomorrow, Henny."

"Look! I forgot! You're to meet Aubrey at the Crillon at five tomorrow, and he's going to take you to see Geneviève Rod?"

"Who the hell's Geneviève Rod?"

"Darned if I know. But Aubrey said you'd got to come. She is an intellectual, so Aubrey says."

"That's the last thing I want to meet."

"Well, you can't help yourself. So long!"

Andrews sat a while more at the table outside the café. A cold wind was blowing. The sky was blue-black and the ashen white arc lamps cast a mortuary light over everything. In the Colonnade of the Palais Royal the shadows were harsh and inky. In the square the people were gradually thinning. The lights in the Magazin du Louvre had gone out. From the café behind him, a faint smell of fresh-cooked food began to saturate the cold air of the street.

Then he saw Jeanne advancing across the ash-grey pavement of the square, slim and black under the arc lights. He ran to meet her.

The cylindrical stove in the middle of the floor roared softly. In front of it the white cat was rolled into a fluffy ball in which ears and nose made tiny splashes of pink like those at the tips of the petals of certain white roses. One side of the stove at the table against the window, sat an old brown man with a bright red stain on each cheek bone, who wore formless corduroy clothes, the color of his skin. Holding the small spoon in a knotted hand he was stirring slowly and continuously a liquid that was yellow and steamed in a glass. Behind him was the window with sleet beating against it in the leaden light of a wintry afternoon. The other side of the stove was a zinc bar with yellow bottles and green bottles and a water spigot with a neck like a giraffe's that rose out of the bar beside a varnished wood pillar that made the decoration of the corner, with a terra cotta pot of ferns on top of it. From where Andrews sat on the padded bench at the back of the room the fern fronds made a black lacework against the left-hand side of the window, while against the other was the brown silhouette of the old man's head, and the slant of his cap. The stove hid the door and the white cat, round and symmetrical, formed the center of the visible universe.

On the marble table beside Andrews were some pieces of crisp bread with butter on them, a saucer of damson jam and a bowl with coffee and hot milk from which the steam rose in a faint spiral. His tunic was unbuttoned and he rested his head on his two hands, staring through his fingers at a thick pile of ruled paper full of hastily drawn signs, some in ink and some in pencil, where now and then he made a mark with a pencil. At the other edge of the pile of papers were two books, one yellow and one white with coffee stains on it.

The fire roared and the cat slept and the old brown man stirred and stirred, rarely stopping for a moment to lift the glass to his lips. Occasionally the scratching of sleet upon the windows became audible, or there was a distant sound of dish pans through the door in the back.

The sallow-faced clock that hung above the mirror that backed the bar, jerked out one jingly strike, a half hour. Andrews did not look up. The cat still slept in front of the stove which roared with a gentle singsong. The old brown man still stirred the yellow liquid in his glass. The clock was ticking uphill towards the hour.

Andrews's hands were cold. There was a nervous flutter in his wrists and in his chest. Inside of him was a great rift of light, infinitely vast and infinitely distant. Through it sounds poured from somewhere, so that he trembled with them to his finger tips, sounds modulated into rhythms that washed back and forth and crossed each other like sea waves in a cove, sounds clotted into harmonies.

Behind everything the Queen of Sheba, out of Flaubert, held her fantastic hand with its long, gilded finger nails on his shoulder; and he was leaning forward over the brink of life. But the image was vague, like a shadow cast on the brilliance of his mind.

The clock struck four.

The white fluffy ball of the cat unrolled very slowly. Its eyes were very round and yellow. It put first one leg and then the other out before it on the tiled floor, spreading wide the pinkey-grey claws. Its tail rose up behind it straight as the mast of a ship. With slow processional steps the cat walked towards the door.

The old brown man drank down the yellow liquid and smacked his lips twice, loudly, meditatively.

Andrews raised his head, his blue eyes looking straight before him without seeing anything. Dropping the pencil, he leaned back against the wall and stretched his arms out. Taking the coffee bowl between his two hands, he drank a little. It was cold. He piled some jam on a piece of bread and ate it, licking a little off his fingers afterwards. Then he looked towards the old brown man and said:

"On est bien ici, n'est ce pas, Monsieur Morue?"

"Oui, on est bien ici," said the old brown man in a voice so gruff it seemed to rattle. Very slowly he got to his feet.

"Good. I am going to the barge," he said. Then he called, "Chipette!"

"Oui, m'sieu."

A little girl in a black apron with her hair in two tight pigtails that stood out behind her tiny bullet head as she ran, came through the door from the back part of the house.

"There, give that to your mother," said the old brown man, putting some coppers in her hand.

"Oui, m'sieu."

"You'ld better stay here where it's warm," said Andrews yawning.

"I have to work. It's only soldiers don't have to work," rattled the old brown man.

When the door opened a gust of raw air circled about the wine shop, and a roar of wind and hiss of sleet came from the slush-covered quai outside. The cat took refuge beside the stove, with its back up and its tail waving. The door closed and the old brown man's silhouette, slanted against the wind, crossed the grey oblong of the window.

Andrews settled down to work again.

"But you work a lot a lot, don't you; M'sieu Jean?" said Chipette, putting her chin on the table beside the books and looking up into his eyes with little eyes like black beads.

"I wonder if I do."

"When I'm grown up I shan't work a bit. I'll drive round in a carriage."

Andrews laughed. Chipette looked at him for a minute and then went into the other room carrying away the empty coffee bowl.

In front of the stove the cat sat on its haunches, licking a paw rhythmically with a pink curling tongue like a rose petal.

Andrews whistled a few bars, staring at the cat.

"What d'you think of that, Minet? That's la reine de Saba . . . la reine de Saba."

The cat curled into a ball again with great deliberation and went to sleep.

Andrews began thinking of Jeanne and the thought gave him a sense of quiet well-being. Strolling with her in the evening through the streets full of men and women walking significantly together sent a languid calm through his jangling nerves which he had never known in his life before. It excited him to be with her, but very suavely, so that he forgot that his limbs were swathed stiffly in an uncomfortable uniform, so that his feverish desire seemed to fly out of him until with her body beside him, he seemed to drift effortlessly in the stream of the lives of all the people he passed, so languid from the quiet loves that streamed up about him that the hard walls of his personality seemed to have melted entirely into the mistiness of twilight streets. And for a moment as he thought of it a scent of flowers, heavy with pollen, and sprouting grass and damp moss and swelling sap, seemed to tingle in his nostrils. Sometimes, swimming in the ocean on a rough day, he had felt that same reckless exhilaration when, towards the shore, a huge seething wave had caught him up and sped him forward on its crest. Sitting quietly in the empty wine shop that grey afternoon, he felt his blood grumble and swell in his veins as the new life was grumbling and swelling in the sticky buds of the trees, in the tender green quick under their rough bark, in the little furry animals of the woods and in the sweet-smelling cattle that tramped into mud the lush meadows. In the premonition of spring was a resistless wave of force that carried him and all of them with it tumultuously.

The clock struck five.

Andrews jumped to his feet and still struggling into his overcoat darted out of the door.

A raw wind blew on the square. The river was a muddy grey-green, swollen and rapid. A hoarse triumphant roaring came from it. The sleet had stopped; but the pavements were covered with slush and in the gutters were large puddles which the wind ruffled. Everything,—houses, bridges, river and sky,—was in shades of cold grey-green, broken by one jagged ochre-colored rift across the sky against which the bulk of Notre Dame and the slender spire of the crossing rose dark and purplish. Andrews walked with long strides, splashing through the puddles, until, opposite the low building of the Morgue, he caught a crowded green bus.

Outside the Hotel Crillon were many limousines, painted olive-drab, with numbers in white letters on the doors; the drivers, men with their olive-drab coat collars turned up round their red faces, stood in groups under the portico. Andrews passed the sentry and went through the revolving doors into the lobby, which was vividly familiar. It had the smell he remembered having smelt in the lobbies of New York hôtels,—a smell of cigar smoke and furniture polish. On one side a door led to a big dining room where many men and women were having tea, from which came a smell of pastry and rich food. On the expanse of red carpet in front of him officers and civilians stood in groups talking in low voices. There was a sound of jingling spurs and jingling dishes from the restau-

rant, and near where Andrews stood, shifting his weight from one foot
to the other, sprawled in a leather chair a fat man with a black felt hat
over his eyes and a large watch chain dangling limply over his bulbous
paunch. He cleared his throat occasionally with a rasping noise and spat
loudly into the spittoon beside him.

At last Andrews caught sight of Aubrey, who was dapper with white
cheeks and tortoise shell glasses.

"Come along," he said, seizing Andrews by the arm.

"You are late." Then, he went on, whispering in Andrews's ear as they
went out through the revolving doors: "Great things happened in the
Conference today. . . . I can tell you that, old man."

They crossed the bridge towards the portico of the Chamber of
Deputies with its high pediment and its grey columns. Down the river
they could see faintly the Eiffel Tower with a drift of mist athwart it, like
a section of spider web spun between the city and the clouds.

"Do we have to go to see these people, Aubrey?"

"Yes, you can't back out now. Geneviève Rod wants to know about
American music."

"But what on earth can I tell her about American music?"

"Wasn't there a man named MacDowell who went mad or something?"

Andrews laughed.

"But you know I haven't any social graces. . . . I suppose I'll have to
say I think Foch is a little tin god."

"You needn't say anything if you don't want to. . . . They're very advanced, anyway."

"Oh, rats!"

They were going up a brown-carpeted stair that had engravings on the
landings, where there was a faint smell of stale food and dustpans. At the
top landing Aubrey rang the bell at a varnished door. In a moment a girl
opened it. She had a cigarette in her hand, her face was pale under a mass
of reddish-chestnut hair, her eyes very large, a pale brown, as large as the
eyes of women in those paintings of Artemisias and Berenikes found in
tombs in the Fayum. She wore a plain black dress.

"Enfin!" she said, and held out her hand to Aubrey.

"There's my friend Andrews." She held out her hand to him absently,
still looking at Aubrey.

"Does he speak French? . . . Good. . . . This way."

They went into a large room with a piano where an elderly woman,
with grey hair and yellow teeth and the same large eyes as her daughter,
stood before the fireplace.

"Maman . . . enfin ils arrivent, ces messieurs."

"Geneviève was afraid you weren't coming," Mme. Rod said to

Andrews, smiling. "Monsieur Aubrey gave us such a picture of your playing that we have been excited all day. . . . We adore music."

"I wish I could do something more to the point with it than adore it,"
said Geneviève Rod hastily, then she went on with a laugh: "But I forget. . . . Monsieur Andrews. . . . Monsieur Ronsard." She made a gesture with her hand from Andrews to a young Frenchman in a cut-away
coat, with small mustaches and a very tight vest, who bowed towards
Andrews.

"Now we'll have tea," said Geneviève Rod. "Everybody talks sense
until they've had tea. . . . It's only after tea that anyone is ever amusing."
She pulled open some curtains that covered the door into the adjoining
room.

"I understand why Sarah Bernhardt is so fond of curtains," she said.
"They give an air of drama to existence. . . . There is nothing more
heroic than curtains."

She sat at the head of an oak table where were china platters with vari-
colored pastries, an old pewter kettle under which an alcohol lamp
burned, a Dresden china teapot in pale yellows and greens, and cups and
saucers and plates with a double-headed eagle design in dull vermillion.

"Tout ça," said Geneviève, waving her hand across the table, "c'est
Boche. . . . But we haven't any others, so they'll have to do."

The older woman, who sat beside her, whispered something in her ear
and laughed.

Geneviève put on a pair of tortoise-shell spectacles and starting pouring out tea.

"Debussy once drank out of that cup. . . . It's cracked," she said, handing a cup to John Andrews. "Do you know anything of Moussorgski's
you can play to us after tea?"

"I can't play anything any more. . . . Ask me three months from now."

"Oh, yes, but nobody expects you to do any tricks with it. You can
certainly make it intelligible. That's all I want."

"I have my doubts."

Andrews sipped his tea slowly, looking now and then at Geneviève
Rod who had suddenly begun talking very fast to Ronsard. She held a
cigarette between the fingers of a long thin hand. Her large pale-brown
eyes kept their startled look of having just opened on the world; a little
smile appeared and disappeared maliciously in the curve of her cheek
away from her small firm lips. The older woman beside her kept looking
round the table with a jolly air of hospitality, and showing her yellow
teeth in a smile.

Afterwards they went back to the sitting room and Andrews sat down
at the piano. The girl sat very straight on a little chair beside the piano.
Andrews ran his fingers up and down the keys.

"Did you say you knew Debussy?" he said suddenly.

"I? No; but he used to come to see my father when I was a little girl. . . . I have been brought up in the middle of music. . . . That shows how silly it is to be a woman. There is no music in my head. Of course I am sensitive to it, but so are the tables and chairs in this apartment, after all they've heard."

Andrews started playing Schumann. He stopped suddenly.

"Can you sing?" he said.

"No."

"I'd like to do the *Croses Lyriques*. . . . I've never heard them."

"I once tried to sing *de Soir*," she said.

"Wonderful. Do bring it out."

"But, good Lord, it's too difficult."

"What is the use of being fond of music if you aren't willing to mangle it for the sake of producing it? . . . I swear I'd rather hear a man picking out *Auprès de ma Blonde* on a trombone than Kreisler playing Paganini impeccably enough to make you ill."

"But there is a middle ground."

He interrupted her by starting to play again. As he played without looking at her, he felt that her eyes were fixed on him, that she was standing tensely behind him. Her hand touched his shoulder. He stopped playing.

"Oh, I am dreadfully sorry," she said.

"Nothing. I had finished."

"You were playing something of your own?"

"Have you ever read *La Tentation de Saint Antoine*?" he asked in a low voice.

"Flaubert's?"

"Yes."

"It's not his best work. A very interesting failure though," she said.

Andrews got up from the piano with difficulty, controlling a sudden growing irritation.

"They seem to teach everybody to say that," he muttered.

Suddenly he realized that other people were in the room. He went up to Mme. Rod.

"You must excuse me," he said, "I have an engagement. . . . Aubrey, don't let me drag you away. I am late, I've got to run."

"You must come to see us again."

"Thank you," mumbled Andrews.

Geneviève Rod went with him to the door.

"We must know each other better," she said. "I like you for going off in a huff."

Andrews flushed.

"I was badly brought up," he said, pressing her thin cold hand. "And you French must always remember that we are barbarians. . . . Some are repentant barbarians. . . . I am not."

She laughed, and John Andrews ran down the stairs and out into the grey-blue streets, where the lamps were blooming into primrose color. He had a confused feeling that he had made a fool of himself, which made him writhe with helpless anger. He walked with long strides through the streets of the Rive Gauche full of people going home from work, towards the little wine shop on the Quai de la Tournelle.

It was a Paris Sunday morning. Old women in black shawls were going into the church of St. Etienne-du-Mont. Each time the leather doors opened it let a little whiff of incense out into the smoky morning air. Three pigeons walked about the cobblestones, putting their coral feet one before the other with an air of importance. The pointed façade of the church and its slender tower and cupola cast a bluish shadow on the square in front of it, into which the shadows the old women trailed behind them vanished as they hobbled towards the church. The opposite side of the square and the railing of the Pantheon and its tall brownish-gray flank were flooded with dull orange-colored sunlight.

Andrews walked back and forth in front of the church, looking at the sky and the pigeons and the façade of the Library of Ste. Geneviève, and at the rare people who passed across the end of the square, noting forms and colors and small comical aspects of things with calm delight, savoring everything almost with complacency. His music, he felt, was progressing now that, undisturbed, he lived all day long in the rhythm of it; his mind and his fingers were growing supple. The hard moulds that had grown up about his spirit were softening. As he walked back and forth in front of the church waiting for Jeanne, he took an inventory of his state of mind; he was very happy.

"Eh bien?"

Jeanne had come up behind him. They ran like children hand in hand across the sunny square.

"I have not had any coffee yet," said Andrews.

"How late you must get up! . . . But you can't have any till we get to the Porte Maillot, Jean."

"Why not?"

"Because I say you can't."

"But that's cruelty."

"It won't be long."

"But I am dying with hunger. I will die in your hands."

"Can't you understand? Once we get to the Porte Maillot we'll be far from your life and my life. The day will be ours. One must not tempt fate."

"You funny girl."

The Metro was not crowded. Andrews and Jeanne sat opposite each other without talking. Andrews was looking at the girl's hands, limp on her lap, small overworked hands with places at the tips of the fingers where the skin was broken and scarred, with chipped uneven nails. Suddenly she caught his glance. He flushed, and she said jauntily, "Well, we'll all be rich some day, like princes and princesses in fairy tales."

They both laughed.

As they were leaving the train at the terminus, he put his arm timidly round her waist. She wore no corsets. His fingers trembled at the litheness of the flesh under her clothes. Feeling a sort of terror go through him he took away his arm.

"Now," she said quietly as they emerged into the sunlight and the bare trees of the broad avenue, "you can have all the café-au-lait you want."

"You'll have some too."

"Why be extravagant? I've had my petit déjeuner."

"But I'm going to be extravagant all day. . . . We might as well start now. I don't know exactly why, but I am very happy. We'll eat brioches."

"But, my dear, it's only profiteers who can eat brioches now-a-days."

"You just watch us."

They went into a patisserie. An elderly woman with a lean yellow face and thin hair waited on them, casting envious glances up through her eyelashes as she piled the rich brown brioches on a piece of tissue paper.

"You'll pass the day in the country?" she asked in a little wistful voice as she handed Andrews the change.

"Yes," he said, "how well you guessed."

As they went out of the door they heard her muttering, "Ôla jeunesse, la jeunesse."

They found a table in the sun at a café opposite the gate from which they could watch people and automobiles and carriages coming in and out. Beyond a grass-grown bit of fortifications gave an 1870 look to things.

"How jolly it is at the Porte Maillot!" cried Andrews.

She looked at him and laughed.

"But how gay he is to-day."

"No. I always like it here. It's the spot in Paris where you always feel well. . . . When you go out you have all the fun of leaving town, when you go in you have all the fun of coming back to town. . . . But you aren't eating any brioches?"

"I've eaten one. You eat them. You are hungry."

"Jeanne, I don't think I have ever been so happy in my life. . . . It's almost worth having been in the army for the joy your freedom gives you. That frightful life. . . . How is Etienne?"

"He is in Mayene. He's bored."

"Jeanne, we must live very much, we who are free to make up for all the people who are still . . . bored."

"A lot of good it'll do them," she cried laughing.

"It's funny, Jeanne, I threw myself into the army. I was so sick of being free and not getting anywhere. Now I have learnt that life is to be used, not just held in the hand like a box of bonbons that nobody eats."

She looked at him blankly.

"I mean, I don't think I get enough out of life," he said. "Let's go."

They got to their feet.

"What do you mean?" she said slowly. "One takes what life gives, that is all, there's no choice. . . . But look there's the Malmaison train. . . . We must run."

Giggling and breathless they climbed on the trailer, squeezing themselves on the back platform where everyone was pushing and exclaiming. The car began to joggle its way through Neuilly. Their bodies were pressed together by the men and women about them. Andrews put his arm firmly round Jeanne's waist and looked down at her pale cheek that was pressed against his chest. Her little round black straw hat with a bit of a red flower on it was just under his chin.

"I can't see a thing," she gasped, still giggling.

"I'll describe the landscape," said Andrews. "Why, we are crossing the Seine already."

"Oh, how pretty it must be!"

An old gentleman with a pointed white beard who stood beside them laughed benevolently.

"But don't you think the Seine's pretty?" Jeanne looked up at him impudently.

"Without a doubt, without a doubt. . . . It was the way you said it," said the old gentleman. . . . "You are going to St. Germain?" he asked Andrews.

"No, to Malmaison."

"Oh, you should go to St. Germain. M. Reinach's prehistoric museum is there. It is very beautiful. You should not go home to your country without seeing it."

"Are there monkeys in it?" asked Jeanne.

"No," said the old gentleman turning away.

"I adore monkeys," said Jeanne.

The car was going along a broad empty boulevard with trees and grass plots and rows of low store-houses and little dilapidated rooming houses along either side. Many people had got out and there was plenty of room, but Andrews kept his arm round the girl's waist. The constant contact with her body made him feel very languid.

"How good it smells!" said Jeanne.

"It's the spring."

"I want to lie on the grass and eat violets. . . . Oh, how good you were to bring me out like this, Jean. You must know lots of fine ladies you could have brought out, because you are so well educated. How is it you are only an ordinary soldier?"

"Good God! I wouldn't be an officer."

"Why? It must be rather nice to be an officer."

"Does Etienne want to be an officer?"

"But he's a socialist, that's different."

"Well, I suppose I must be a socialist too, but let's talk of something else."

Andrews moved over to the other side of the platform. They were passing little villas with gardens on the road where yellow and pale-purple crocuses bloomed. Now and then there was a scent of violets in the moist air. The sun had disappeared under soft purplish-grey clouds. There was occasionally a rainy chill in the wind.

Andrews suddenly thought of Geneviève Rod. Curious how vividly he remembered her face, her wide, open eyes and her way of smiling without moving her firm lips. A feeling of annoyance went through him. How silly of him to go off rudely like that! And he became very anxious to talk to her again; things he wanted to say to her came to his mind.

"Well, are you asleep?" said Jeanne tugging at his arm. "Here we are." Andrews flushed furiously.

"Oh, how nice it is here, how nice it is here!" Jeanne was saying.

"Why, it is eleven o'clock," said Andrews.

"We must see the palace before lunch," cried Jeanne, and she started running up a lane of linden trees, where the fat buds were just bursting into little crinkling fans of green. New grass was sprouting in the wet ditches on either side. Andrews ran after her, his feet pounding hard in the moist gravel road. When he caught up to her he threw his arms round her recklessly and kissed her panting mouth. She broke away from him and strode demurely arranging her hat.

"Monster," she said, "I trimmed this hat specially to come out with you and you do your best to wreck it."

"Poor little hat," said Andrews, "but it is so beautiful today, and you are very lovely, Jeanne."

"The great Napoleon must have said that to the Empress Josephine and you know what he did to her," said Jeanne almost solemnly.

"But she must have been awfully bored with him long before."

"No," said Jeanne, "that's how women are."

They went through big iron gates into the palace grounds.

Later they sat at a table in the garden of a little restaurant. The sun, very pale, had just showed itself, making the knives and forks and the white wine in their glasses gleam faintly. Lunch had not come yet. They sat looking at each other silently. Andrews felt weary and melancholy. He could think of nothing to say. Jeanne was playing with some tiny white daisies with pink tips to their petals, arranging them in circles and crosses on the table-cloth.

"Aren't they slow?" said Andrews.

"But it's nice here, isn't it?" Jeanne smiled brilliantly. "But how glum he looks now." She threw some daisies at him. Then, after a pause, she added mockingly: "It's hunger, my dear. Good Lord, how dependent men are on food!"

Andrews drank down his wine at a gulp. He felt that if he could only make an effort he could lift off the stifling melancholy that was settling down on him like a weight that kept growing heavier.

A man in khaki, with his face and neck scarlet, staggered into the garden dragging beside him a mud-encrusted bicycle. He sank into an iron chair, letting the bicycle fall with a clatter at his feet.

"Hi, hi," he called in a hoarse voice.

A waiter appeared and contemplated him suspiciously. The man in khaki had hair as red as his face, which was glistening with sweat. His shirt was torn, and he had no coat. His breeches and puttees were invisible for mud.

"Gimme a beer," croaked the man in khaki.

The waiter shrugged his shoulders and walked away.

"Il demande une bière," said Andrews.

"Mais Monsieur. . . ."

"I'll pay. Get it for him."

The waiter disappeared.

"Thankee, Yank," roared the man in khaki.

The waiter brought a tall narrow yellow glass. The man in khaki took it from his hand, drank it down at a draught and handed back the empty glass. Then he spat, wiped his mouth on the back of his hand, got with difficulty to his feet and shambled towards Andrews's table.

"Oi presoom the loidy and you don't mind, Yank, if Oi parley wi' yez a bit. Do yez?"

"No, come along; where did you come from?"

The man in khaki dragged an iron chair behind him to a spot near the table. Before sitting down he bobbed his head in the direction of Jeanne with an air of solemnity tugging at the same time at a lock of his red hair. After some fumbling he got a red-bordered handkerchief out of his pocket and wiped his face with it, leaving a long black smudge of machine oil on his forehead.

"Oi'm a bearer of important secret messages, Yank," he said, leaning back in the little iron chair. "Oi'm a despatch-rider."

"You look all in."

"Not a bit of it. Oi just had a little hold up, that's all, in a woodland lake. Some buggers tried to do me in."

"What d'you mean?"

"Oi guess they had a little information . . . that's all. Oi'm carryin' important messages from our headquarters in Rouen to your president. Oi was goin' through a bloody thicket past this side. Oi don't know how you pronounce the bloody town. . . . Oi was on my bike making about thoity for the road was all a-murk when Oi saw four buggers standing acrost the road . . . lookter me suspicious-like, so Oi jus' jammed the juice into the boike and made for the middle 'un. He dodged all right. Then they started shootin' and a bloody bullet buggered the boike. . . . It was bein' born with a caul that saved me. . . . Oi picked myself up outer the ditch an lost 'em in the woods. Then Oi got to another bloody town and commandeered this old sweatin' machine. . . . How many kills is there to Paris, Yank?"

"Fifteen or sixteen, I think,"

"What's he saying, Jean?"

"Some men tried to stop him on the road. He's a despatch rider."

"Isn't he ugly? Is he English?"

"Irish."

"You bet you, miss; Hirlanday; that's me. . . . You picked a good looker this toime, Yank. But wait till Oi git to Paree. Oi clane up a good hundre' pound on this job in bonuses. What part d'ye come from, Yank?"

"Virginia. I live in New York."

"Oi been in Detroit; goin' back there to git in the automoebile business soon as Oi clane up a few more bonuses. Europe's dead an stinkin', Yank. Ain't no place for a young fellow. It's dead an stinkin', that's what it is."

"It's pleasanter to live here than in America. . . . Say, d'you often get held up that way?"

"Ain't happened to me before, but it has to pals o' moine."

"Who d'you think it was?"

"Oi dunno; 'Uns or some of these bloody secret agents round the Peace Conference. . . . But Oi got to go; that despatch won't keep."

"All right. The beer's on me."

"Thank ye, Yank." The man got to his feet, shook hands with Andrews and Jeanne, jumped on the bicycle and rode out of the garden to the road, threading his way through the iron chairs and tables.

"Wasn't he a funny customer?" cried Andrews, laughing. "What a wonderful joke things are!"

The waiter arrived with the omelette that began their lunch.

"Gives you an idea of how the old lava's bubbling in the volcano. There's nowhere on earth a man can dance so well as on a volcano."

"But don't talk that way," said Jeanne laying down her knife and fork. "It's terrible. We will waste our youth to no purpose. Our fathers enjoyed themselves when they were young. . . . And if there had been no war we should have been so happy, Etienne and I. My father was a small manufacturer of soap and perfumery. Etienne would have had a splendid situation. I should never have had to work. We had a nice house. I should have been married. . . ."

"But this way, Jeanne, haven't you more freedom?"

She shrugged her shoulders. Later she burst out:

"But what's the good of freedom? What can you do with it? What one wants is to live well and have a beautiful house and be respected by people. Oh, life was so sweet in France before the war."

"In that case it's not worth living," said Andrews in a savage voice, holding himself in.

They went on eating silently. The sky became overcast. A few drops splashed on the table-cloth.

"We'll have to take coffee inside," said Andrews.

"And you think it is funny that people shoot at a man on a motorcycle going through a wood. All that seems to me terrible, terrible," said Jeanne.

"Look out. Here comes the rain!"

They ran into the restaurant through the first hissing sheet of the shower and sat at a table near a window watching the rain drops dance and flicker on the green iron tables. A scent of wet earth and the mushroom-like odor of sodden leaves came in borne on damp gusts through the open door. A waiter closed the glass doors and bolted them.

"He wants to keep out the spring. He can't," said Andrews.

They smiled at each other over their coffee cups. They were in sympathy again.

When the rain stopped they walked across wet fields by a foot path full of little clear puddles that reflected the blue sky and the white- and amber-tinged clouds where the shadows were light purplish-grey. They walked slowly arm in arm, pressing their bodies together. They were very tired, they did not know why and stopped often to rest leaning against the damp boles of trees. Beside a pond pale blue and amber and silver from the reflected sky, they found under a big beech tree a patch of wild violets, which Jeanne picked greedily, mixing them with the little crimson-tipped daisies in the tight bouquet. At the suburban railway station, they sat silent, side by side on a bench, sniffing the flowers now and then, so sunk in languid weariness that they could hardly summon strength to climb into a seat on top of a third class coach, which was crowded with people coming home from a day in the country. Everybody had violets and crocuses and twigs with buds on them. In people's stiff, citified clothes lingered a smell of wet fields and sprouting woods. All the girls shrieked and threw their arms round the men when the train went through a tunnel or under a bridge. Whatever happened, everybody laughed. When the train arrived in the station, it was almost with reluctance that they left it, as if they felt that from that moment their work-a-day lives began again. Andrews and Jeanne walked down the platform without touching each other. Their fingers were stained and sticky from touching buds and crushing young sappy leaves and grass stalks. The air of the city seemed dense and unbreatheable after the scented moisture of the fields.

They dined at a little restaurant on the Quai Voltaire and afterwards walked slowly towards the Place St. Michel, feeling the wine and the warmth of the food sending new vigor into their tired bodies. Andrews had his arm round her shoulder and they talked in low intimate voices, hardly moving their lips, looking long at the men and women they saw sitting twined in each other's arms on benches, at the couples of boys and girls that kept passing them, talking slowly and quietly, as they were, bodies pressed together as theirs were.

"How many lovers there are," said Andrews.

"Are we lovers?" asked Jeanne with a curious little laugh.

"I wonder. . . . Have you ever been crazily in love, Jeanne?"

"I don't know. There was a boy in Laon named Marcelin. But I was a little fool then. The last news of him was from Verdun."

"Have you had many . . . like I am?"

"How sentimental we are," she cried laughing.

"No. I wanted to know. I know so little of life," said Andrews.

"I have amused myself, as best I could," said Jeanne in a serious tone. "But I am not frivolous. . . . There have been very few men I have liked. . . . So I have had few friends . . . do you want to call them lovers? But lovers are what married women have on the stage. . . . All that sort of thing is very silly."

"Not so very long ago," said Andrews, "I used to dream of being romantically in love, with people climbing up the ivy on castle walls, and fiery kisses on balconies in the moonlight."

"Like at the Opéra Comique," cried Jeanne laughing.

"That was all very silly. But even now, I want so much more of life than life can give."

They leaned over the parapet and listened to the hurrying swish of the river, now soft and now loud, where the reflections of the lights on the opposite bank writhed like golden snakes.

Andrews noticed that there was someone beside them. The faint, greenish glow from the lamp on the quai enabled him to recognize the lame boy he had talked to months ago on the Butte.

"I wonder if you'll remember me," he said.

"You are the American who was in the Restaurant, Place du Terte, I don't remember when, but it was long ago."

They shook hands.

"But you are alone," said Andrews.

"Yes, I am always alone," said the lame boy firmly. He held out his hand again.

"Au revoir," said Andrews.

"Good luck!" said the lame boy. Andrews heard his crutch tapping on the pavement as he went away along the quai.

"Jeanne," said Andrews, suddenly, "you'll come home with me, won't you?"

"But you have a friend living with you."

"He's gone to Brussels. He won't be back till tomorrow."

"I suppose one must pay for one's dinner," said Jeanne maliciously.

"Good God, no." Andrews buried his face in his hands. The singsong of the river pouring through the bridges filled his ears. He wanted desperately to cry. Bitter desire that was like hatred made his flesh tingle, made his hands ache to crush her hands in them.

"Come along," he said gruffly.

"I didn't mean to say that," she said in a gentle, tired voice. "You know, I'm not a very nice person." The greenish glow of the lamp lit up the contour of one of her cheeks as she tilted her head up, and glimmered in her eyes. A soft sentimental sadness suddenly took hold of Andrews; he felt as he used to feel when, as a very small child, his mother used to tell him Br' Rabbit stories, and he would feel himself drifting helplessly on the stream of her soft voice, narrating, drifting towards something unknown and very sad, which he could not help.

They started walking again, past the Pont Neuf, towards the glare of the Place St. Michel. Three names had come into Andrews's head, "Arsinoë, Berenike, Artimisia." For a little while he puzzled over them, and then he remembered that Geneviève Rod had the large eyes and the wide, smooth forehead and the firm little lips the women had in the portraits that were sewn on the mummy cases in the Fayum. But those patrician women of Alexandria had not had chestnut hair with a glimpse of burnished copper in it; they might have dyed it, though!

"Why are you laughing?" asked Jeanne.

"Because things are so silly."

"Perhaps you mean people are silly," she said, looking up at him out of the corners of her eyes.

"You're right."

They walked in silence till they reached Andrews's door.

"You go up first and see that there's no one there," said Jeanne in a business-like tone.

Andrews's hands were cold. He felt his heart thumping while he climbed the stairs.

The room was empty. A fire was ready to light in the small fireplace. Andrews hastily tidied up the table and kicked under the bed some soiled clothes that lay in a heap in a corner. A thought came to him: how like his performances in his room at college when he had heard that a relative was coming to see him.

He tiptoed downstairs.

"Bien. Tu peux venir, Jeanne," he said.

She sat down rather stiffly in the straight-backed armchair beside the fire.

"How pretty the fire is," she said.

"Jeanne, I think I'm crazily in love with you," said Andrews in an excited voice.

"Like at the Opéra Comique." She shrugged her shoulders. "The room's nice," she said. "Oh, but, what a big bed!"

"You're the first woman who's been up here in my time, Jeanne. . . . Oh, but this uniform is frightful."

Andrews thought suddenly of all the tingling bodies constrained into the rigid attitudes of automatons in uniforms like this one; of all the hideous farce of making men into machines. Oh, if some gesture of his could only free them all for life and freedom and joy. The thought drowned everything else for the moment.

"But you pulled a button off," cried Jeanne laughing hysterically. "I'll just have to sew it on again."

"Never mind. If you knew how I hated them."

"What white skin you have, like a woman's. I suppose that's because you are blond," said Jeanne.

The sound of the door being shaken vigorously woke Andrews. He got up and stood in the middle of the floor for a moment without being able to collect his wits. The shaking of the door continued, and he heard Walters's voice crying "Andy, Andy." Andrews felt shame creeping up through him like nausea. He felt a passionate disgust towards himself and Jeanne and Walters. He had an impulse to move furtively as if he had stolen something. He went to the door and opened it a little.

"Say, Walters, old man," he said, "I can't let you in. . . . I've got a girl with me. I'm sorry. . . . I thought you wouldn't get back till tomorrow."

"You're kidding, aren't you?" came Walters's voice out of the dark hall.

"No." Andrews shut the door decisively and bolted it again.

Jeanne was still asleep. Her black hair had come undone and spread over the pillow. Andrews pulled the covers up about her carefully.

Then he got into the other bed, where he lay awake a long time, staring at the ceiling.

IV

People walking along the boulevard looked curiously through the railing at the line of men in olive-drab that straggled round the edge of the courtyard. The line moved slowly, past a table where an officer and two enlisted men sat poring over big lists of names and piles of palely tinted banknotes and silver francs that glittered white. Above the men's heads a thin haze of cigarette smoke rose into the sunlight. There was a sound of voices and of feet shuffling on the gravel. The men who had been paid went off jauntily, the money jingling in their pockets.

The men at the table had red faces and tense, serious expressions. They pushed the money into the soldiers' hands with a rough jerk and pronounced the names as if they were machines clicking.

Andrews saw that one of the men at the table was Walters; he smiled and whispered "Hello" as he came up to him. Walters kept his eyes fixed on the list.

While Andrews was waiting for the man ahead of him to be paid, he heard two men in the line talking.

"Wasn't that a hell of a place? D'you remember the lad that died in the barracks one day?"

"Sure, I was in the medicks there too. There was a hell of a sergeant in that company tried to make the kid get up, and the loot came and said he'd court-martial him, an' then they found out that he'd cashed in his checks."

"What'd 'ee die of?"

"Heart failure, I guess. I dunno, though, he never did take to the life."

"No. That place Cosne was enough to make any guy cash in his checks."

Andrews got his money. As he was walking away, he strolled up to the two men he had heard talking.

"Were you fellows in Cosne?"

"Sure."

"Did you know a fellow named Fuselli?"

"I dunno. . . ."

"Sure, you do," said the other man. "You remember Dan Fuselli, the little wop thought he was goin' to be corporal."

"He had another think comin'." They both laughed.

Andrews walked off, vaguely angry. There were many soldiers on the Boulevard Montparnasse. He turned into a side street, feeling suddenly furtive and humble, as if he would hear any minute the harsh voice of a sergeant shouting orders at him.

The silver in his breeches pocket jingled with every step.

Andrews leaned on the balustrade of the balcony, looking down into the square in front of the Opéra Comique. He was dizzy with the beauty of the music he had been hearing. He had a sense somewhere in the distances of his mind of the great rhythm of the sea. People chattered all about him on the wide, crowded balcony, but he was only conscious of the blue-grey mistiness of the night where the lights made patterns in green-gold and red-gold. And compelling his attention from everything else, the rhythm swept through him like sea waves.

"I thought you'ld be here," said Geneviève Rod in a quiet voice beside him.

Andrews felt strangely tongue-tied.

"It's nice to see you," he blurted out, after looking at her silently for a moment.

"Of course you love *Pelléas*."

"It is the first time I've heard it."

"Why haven't you been to see us? It's two weeks. . . . We've been expecting you."

"I didn't know . . . Oh, I'll certainly come. I don't know anyone at present I can talk music to."

"You know me."

"Anyone else, I should have said."

"Are you working?"

"Yes. . . . But this hinders frightfully." Andrews yanked at the front of his tunic. "Still, I expect to be free very soon. I'm putting in an application for discharge."

"I suppose you will feel you can do so much better. . . . You will be much stronger now that you have done your duty."

"No . . . by no means."

"Tell me, what was that you played at our house?"

"'The Three Green Riders on Wild Asses,'" said Andrews smiling.

"What do you mean?"

"It's a prelude to the 'Queen of Sheba,'" said Andrews. "If you didn't

think the same as M. Emile Faguet and everyone else about St. Antoine,
I'd tell you what I mean."

"That was very silly of me. . . . But if you pick up all the silly things
people say accidentally . . . well, you must be angry most of the time."

In the dim light he could not see her eyes. There was a little glow on
the curve of her cheek coming from under the dark of her hat to her
rather pointed chin. Behind it he could see other faces of men and
women crowded on the balcony talking, lit up crudely by the gold glare
that came out through the French windows from the lobby.

"I have always been tremendously fascinated by the place in La
Tentation where the Queen of Sheba visited Antoine, that's all," said
Andrews gruffly.

"Is that the first thing you've done? It made me think a little of
Borodine."

"The first that's at all pretentious. It's probably just a steal from everything I've ever heard."

"No, it's good. I suppose you had it in your head all through those
dreadful and glorious days at the front. . . . Is it for piano or orchestra?"

"All that's finished is for piano. I hope to orchestrate it eventually. . .
. Oh, but it's really silly to talk this way. I don't know enough. . . . I need
years of hard work before I can do anything. . . . And I have wasted so
much time. . . . That is the most frightful thing. One has so few years of
youth!"

"There's the bell, we must scuttle back to our seats. Till the next in-
termission." She slipped through the glass doors and disappeared.
Andrews went back to his seat very excited, full of unquiet exultation.
The first strains of the orchestra were pain, he felt them so acutely.

After the last act they walked in silence down a dark street, hurrying
to get away from the crowds of the Boulevards.

When they reached the Avenue de l'Opéra, she said:

"Did you say you were going to stay in France?"

"Yes, indeed, if I can. I am going tomorrow to put in an application
for discharge in France."

"What will you do then?"

"I shall have to find a job of some sort that will let me study at the
Schola Cantorum. But I have enough money to last a little while."

"You are courageous."

"I forgot to ask you if you would rather take the Métro."

"No; let's walk."

They went under the arch of the Louvre. The air was full of a fine wet
mist, so that every street lamp was surrounded by a blur of light.

"My blood is full of the music of Debussy," said Geneviève Rod,
spreading out her arms.

"It's no use trying to say what one feels about it. Words aren't much good, anyway, are they?"

"That depends."

They walked silently along the quais. The mist was so thick they could not see the Seine, but whenever they came near a bridge they could hear the water rustling through the arches.

"France is stifling," said Andrews, all of a sudden. "It stifles you very slowly, with beautiful silk bands. . . . America beats your brains out with a policeman's billy."

"What do you mean?" she asked, letting pique chill her voice.

"You know so much in France. You have made the world so neat. . . ."

"But you seem to want to stay here," she said with a laugh.

"It's that there's nowhere else. There is nowhere except Paris where one can find out things about music, particularly. . . . But I am one of those people who was not made to be contented."

"Only sheep are contented."

"I think I have been happier this month in Paris than ever before in my life. It seems six, so much has happened in it."

"Poissac is where I am happiest."

"Where is that?"

"We have a country house there, very old and very tumbledown. They say that Rabelais used to come to the village. But our house is from later, from the time of Henri Quatre. Poissac is not far from Tours. An ugly name, isn't it? But to me it is very beautiful. The house has orchards all round it, and yellow roses with flushed centers poke themselves in my window, and there is a little tower like Montaigne's."

"When I get out of the army, I shall go somewhere in the country and work and work."

"Music should be made in the country, when the sap is rising in the trees."

"'D'après nature,' as the rabbit man said."

"Who's the rabbit man?"

"A very pleasant person," said Andrews, bubbling with laughter. "You shall meet him some day. He sells little stuffed rabbits that jump, outside the Café de Rohan."

"Here we are. . . . Thank you for coming home with me."

"But how soon. Are you sure it is the house? We can't have got there as soon as this."

"Yes, it's my house," said Geneviève Rod laughing. She held out her hand to him and he shook it eagerly. The latchkey clicked in the door.

"Why don't you have a cup of tea with us here tomorrow?" she said.

"With pleasure."

The big varnished door with its knocker in the shape of a ring closed

behind her. Andrews walked away with a light step, feeling jolly and ex-
hilarated.

As he walked down the mist-filled quai towards the Place St. Michel,
his ears were filled with the lisping gurgle of the river past the piers of
the bridges.

Walters was asleep. On the table in his room was a card from Jeanne.
Andrews read the card holding it close to the candle.

"How long it is since I saw you!" it read. "I shall pass the Café de
Rohan Wednesday at seven, along the pavement opposite the Magazin
du Louvre."

It was a card of Malmaison.

Andrews flushed. Bitter melancholy throbbed through him. He
walked languidly to the window and looked out into the dark court. A
window below his spilled a warm golden haze into the misty night,
through which he could make out vaguely some pots of ferns standing
on the wet flagstones. From somewhere came a dense smell of hyacinths.
Fragments of thought slipped one after another through his mind. He
thought of himself washing windows long ago at training camp, and remembered the way the gritty sponge scraped his hands. He could not
help feeling shame when he thought of those days. "Well, that's all over
now," he told himself. He wondered, in a half-irritated way, about
Geneviève Rod. What sort of a person was she? Her face, with its wide
eyes and pointed chin and the reddish-chestnut hair, unpretentiously
coiled above the white forehead, was very vivid in his mind, though
when he tried to remember what it was like in profile, he could not. She
had thin hands, with long fingers that ought to play the piano well.
When she grew old would she be yellow-toothed and jolly, like her
mother? He could not think of her old; she was too vigorous; there was
too much malice in her passionately-restrained gestures. The memory of
her faded, and there came to his mind Jeanne's overworked little hands,
with callous places, and the tips of the fingers grimy and scarred from
needlework. But the smell of hyacinths that came up from the mist-filled
courtyard was like a sponge wiping all impressions from his brain. The
dense sweet smell in the damp air made him feel languid and melancholy.

He took off his clothes slowly and got into bed. The smell of the hyacinths came to him very faintly, so that he did not know whether or not
he was imagining it.

The major's office was a large white-painted room, with elaborate
mouldings and mirrors in all four walls, so that while Andrews waited,
cap in hand, to go up to the desk, he could see the small round major
with his pink face and bald head repeated to infinity in two directions in
the grey brilliance of the mirrors.

"What do you want?" said the major, looking up from some papers he was signing.

Andrews stepped up to the desk. On both sides of the room a skinny figure in olive-drab, repeated endlessly, stepped up to endless mahogany desks, which faded into each other in an endless dusty perspective.

"Would you mind O.K.-ing this application for discharge, Major?"

"How many dependents?" muttered the major through his teeth, poring over the application.

"None. It's for discharge in France to study music."

"Won't do. You need an affidavit that you can support yourself, that you have enough money to continue your studies. You want to study music, eh? D'you think you've got talent? Needs a very great deal of talent to study music."

"Yes, sir. . . . But is there anything else I need except the affidavit?"

"No. . . . It'll go through in short order. We're glad to release men. . . . We're glad to release any man with a good military record. . . . Williams!"

"Yes, sir."

A sergeant came over from a small table by the door.

"Show this man what he needs to do to get discharged in France."

Andrews saluted. Out of the corner of his eye he saw the figures in the mirror, saluting down an endless corridor.

When he got out on the street in front of the great white building where the major's office was, a morose feeling of helplessness came over him. There were many automobiles of different sizes and shapes, limousines, runabouts, touring cars, lined up along the curb, all painted olive-drab and neatly stencilled with numbers in white. Now and then a personage came out of the white marble building, puttees and Sam Brown belt gleaming, and darted into an automobile, or a noisy motorcycle stopped with a jerk in front of the wide door to let out an officer in goggles and mud-splattered trench coat, who disappeared immediately through revolving doors. Andrews could imagine him striding along halls, where from every door came an imperious clicking of typewriters, where papers were piled high on yellow varnished desks, where sallow-faced clerks in uniform loafed in rooms, where the four walls were covered from floor to ceiling with card catalogues. And every day they were adding to the paper, piling up more little drawers with index cards. It seemed to Andrews that the shiny white marble building would have to burst with all the paper stored up within it, and would flood the broad avenue with avalanches of index cards.

"Button yer coat," snarled a voice in his ear.

Andrews looked up suddenly. An M.P. with a raw-looking face in which was a long sharp nose, had come up to him.

Andrews buttoned up his overcoat and said nothing.

"Ye can't hang around here this way," the M.P. called after him.

Andrews flushed and walked away without turning his head. He was stinging with humiliation; an angry voice inside him kept telling him that he was a coward, that he should make some futile gesture of protest. Grotesque pictures of revolt flamed through his mind, until he remembered that when he was very small, the same tumultuous pride had seethed and ached in him whenever he had been reproved by an older person. Helpless despair fluttered about within him like a bird beating against the wires of a cage. Was there no outlet, no gesture of expression, would he have to go on this way day after day, swallowing the bitter gall of indignation, that every new symbol of his slavery brought to his lips?

He was walking in an agitated way across the Jardin des Tuileries, full of little children and women with dogs on leashes and nursemaids with starched white caps, when he met Geneviève Rod and her mother. Geneviève was dressed in pearl grey, with an elegance a little too fashionable to please Andrews. Mme. Rod wore black. In front of them a black and tan terrier ran from one side to the other, on nervous little legs that trembled like steel springs.

"Isn't it lovely this morning?" cried Geneviève.

"I didn't know you had a dog."

"Oh, we never go out without Santo, a protection to two lone women, you know," said Mme. Rod, laughing. "Viens, Santo, dis bon jour au Monsieur."

"He usually lives at Poissac," said Geneviève.

The little dog barked furiously at Andrews, a shrill bark like a child squalling.

"He knows he ought to be suspicious of soldiers. . . . I imagine most soldiers would change with him if they had a chance. . . . Viens Santo, viens Santo. . . . Will you change lives with me, Santo?"

"You look as if you'd been quarrelling with somebody," said Geneviève Rod lightly.

"I have, with myself. . . . I'm going to write a book on slave psychology. It would be very amusing," said Andrews in a gruff, breathless voice.

"But we must hurry, dear, or we'll be late to the tailor's," said Mme. Rod. She held out her black-gloved hand to Andrews.

"We'll be in at tea time this afternoon. You might play me some more of the 'Queen of Sheba,'" said Geneviève.

"I'm afraid I shan't be able to, but you never can tell. . . . Thank you."

He was relieved to have left them. He had been afraid he would burst out into some childish tirade. What a shame old Henslowe hadn't come back yet. He could have poured out all his despair to him; he had often enough before; and Henslowe was out of the army now. Wearily

Andrews decided that he would have to start scheming and intriguing again as he had schemed and intrigued to come to Paris in the first place. He thought of the white marble building and the officers with shiny puttees going in and out, and the typewriters clicking in every room, and the understanding of his helplessness before all that complication made him shiver.

An idea came to him. He ran down the steps of a métro station. Aubrey would know someone at the Crillon who could help him.

But when the train reached the Concorde station, he could not summon the will power to get out. He felt a harsh repugnance to any effort. What was the use of humiliating himself and begging favors of people? It was hopeless anyway. In a fierce burst of pride a voice inside of him was shouting that he, John Andrews, should have no shame, that he should force people to do things for him, that he, who lived more acutely than the rest, suffering more pain and more joy, who had the power to express his pain and his joy so that it would impose itself on others, should force his will on those around him. "More of the psychology of slavery," said Andrews to himself, suddenly smashing the soap-bubble of his egoism.

The train had reached the Porte Maillot.

Andrews stood in the sunny boulevard in front of the métro station, where the plane trees were showing tiny gold-brown leaves, sniffing the smell of a flower-stall in front of which a woman stood, with a deft abstracted gesture tying up bunch after bunch of violets. He felt a desire to be out in the country, to be away from houses and people. There was a line of men and women buying tickets for St. Germain; still indecisive, he joined it, and at last, almost without intending it, found himself jolting through Neuilly in the green trailer of the electric car, that waggled like a duck's tail when the car went fast.

He remembered his last trip on that same car with Jeanne, and wished mournfully that he might have fallen in love with her, that he might have forgotten himself and the army and everything in crazy, romantic love.

When he got off the car at St. Germain, he had stopped formulating his thoughts; soggy despair throbbed in him like an infected wound.

He sat for a while at the café opposite the château looking at the light red walls and the strong stone-bordered windows and the jaunty turrets and chimneys that rose above the classic balustrade with its big urns on the edge of the roof. The park, through the tall iron railings, was full of russet and pale lines, all mist of new leaves. Had they really lived more vividly, the people of the Renaissance? Andrews could almost see men with plumed hats and short cloaks and elaborate brocaded tunics swaggering with a hand at the sword hilt, about the quiet square in front of the gate of the château. And he thought of the great, sudden wind of freedom that had blown out of Italy, before which dogmas and slaveries had crumbled to dust. In contrast, the world today seemed pitifully arid. Men seemed to have shrunk in stature before the vastness of the mechanical contrivances they had invented. Michael Angelo, da Vinci, Aretino, Cellini; would the strong figures of men ever so dominate the world again? Today everything was congestion, the scurrying of crowds; men had become ant-like. Perhaps it was inevitable that the crowds should sink deeper and deeper in slavery. Whichever won, tyranny from above, or spontaneous organization from below, there could be no individuals.

He went through the gates into the park, laid out with a few flower beds where pansies bloomed; through the dark ranks of elm trunks, was brilliant sky, with here and there a moss-green statue standing out against it. At the head of an alley he came out on a terrace. Beyond the strong curves of the pattern of the iron balustrade was an expanse of country, pale green, falling to blue towards the horizon, patched with pink and slate-colored houses and carved with railway tracks. At his feet the Seine shone like a curved sword blade.

He walked with long strides along the terrace, and followed a road that turned into the forest, forgetting the monotonous tread mill of his thoughts, in the flush that the fast walking sent through his whole body, in the rustling silence of the woods, where the moss on the north side of the boles of the trees was emerald, and where the sky was soft grey through a lavender lacework of branches. The green gnarled woods made him think of the first act of *Pelléas*. With his tunic unbuttoned and his shirt open at the neck and his hands stuck deep in his pockets, he went along whistling like a school boy.

After an hour he came out of the woods on a highroad, where he found himself walking beside a two-wheeled cart, that kept pace with him exactly, try as he would to get ahead of it. After a while, a boy leaned out:

"Hey, l'Américain, vous voulez monter?"

"Where are you going?"

"Conflans-Ste.-Honorine."

"Where's that?"

The boy flourished his whip vaguely towards the horse's head.

"All right," said Andrews.

"These are potatoes," said the boy, "make yourself comfortable."

Andrews offered him a cigarette, which he took with muddy fingers. He had a broad face, red cheeks and chunky features. Reddish-brown hair escaped spikily from under a mud-spattered beret.

"Where did you say you were going?"

"Conflans-Ste.-Honorine. Silly all these saints, aren't they?"

Andrews laughed.

"Where are you going?" the boy asked.

"I don't know. I was taking a walk."

The boy leaned over to Andrews and whispered in his ear:
"Deserter?"

"No. . . . I had a day off and wanted to see the country."

"I just thought, if you were a deserter, I might be able to help you. Must be silly to be a soldier. Dirty life. . . . But you like the country. So do I. You can't call this country. I'm not from this part; I'm from Brittany. There we have real country. It's stifling near Paris here, so many people, so many houses."

"It seems mighty fine to me."

"That's because you're a soldier. Better than barracks, hein? Dirty life that. I'll never be a soldier. I'm going into the navy. Merchant marine, and then if I have to do service I'll do it on the sea."

"I suppose it is pleasanter."

"There's more freedom. And the sea. . . . We Bretons, you know, we all die of the sea or of liquor."

They laughed.

"Have you been long in this part of the country?" asked Andrews.

"Six months. It's very dull, this farming work. I'm head of a gang in a fruit orchard, but not for long. I have a brother shipped on a sailing vessel. When he comes back to Bordeaux, I'll ship on the same boat."

"Where to?"

"South America, Peru; how should I know?"

"I'd like to ship on a sailing vessel," said Andrews.

"You would? It seems very fine to me to travel, and see new countries. And perhaps I shall stay over there."

"Where?"

"How should I know? If I like it, that is. . . . Life is very bad in Europe."

"It is stifling, I suppose," said Andrews slowly, "all these nations, all these hatreds, but still . . . it is very beautiful. Life is very ugly in America."

"Let's have something to drink. There's a bistro!"

The boy jumped down from the cart and tied the horse to a tree. They went into a small wine shop with a counter and one square oak table.

"But won't you be late?" said Andrews.

"I don't care. I like talking, don't you?"

"Yes, indeed."

They ordered wine of an old woman in a green apron, who had three yellow teeth that protruded from her mouth when she spoke.

"I haven't had anything to eat," said Andrews.

"Wait a minute." The boy ran out to the cart and came back with a canvas bag, from which he took half a loaf of bread and some cheese.

"My name's Marcel," the boy said when they had sat for a while sipping wine.

"Mine is Jean . . . Jean André."

"I have a brother named Jean, and my father's name is André. That's pleasant, isn't it?"

"But it must be a splendid job, working in a fruit orchard," said Andrews, munching bread and cheese.

"It's well paid; but you get tired of being in one place all the time. It's not as it is in Brittany. . . ." Marcel paused. He sat, rocking a little on the stool, holding on to the seat between his legs. A curious brilliance came into his grey eyes. "There," he went on in a soft voice, "it is so quiet in the fields, and from every hill you look at the sea. . . . I like that, don't you?" he turned to Andrews, with a smile.

"You are lucky to be free," said Andrews bitterly. He felt as if he would burst into tears.

"But you will be demobilized soon; the butchery is over. You will go home to your family. That will be good, hein?"

"I wonder. It's not far enough away. Restless!"

"What do you expect?"

A fine rain was falling. They climbed in on the potato sacks and the horse started a jog trot; its lanky brown shanks glistened a little from the rain.

"Do you come out this way often?" asked Marcel.

"I shall. It's the nicest place near Paris."

"Some Sunday you must come and I'll take you round. The Castle is very fine. And then there is Malmaison, where the great Emperor lived with the Empress Joséphine."

Andrews suddenly remembered Jeanne's card. This was Wednesday. He pictured her dark figure among the crowd of the pavement in front of the Café de Rohan. Of course it had to be that way. Despair, so helpless as to be almost sweet, came over him.

"And girls," he said suddenly to Marcel, "are they pretty round here?"

Marcel shrugged his shoulders.

"It's not women that we lack, if a fellow has money," he said.

Andrews felt a sense of shame, he did not exactly know why.

"My brother writes that in South America the women are very brown and very passionate," added Marcel with a wistful smile. "But travelling and reading books, that's what I like. . . . But look, if you want to take the train back to Paris. . . ." Marcel pulled up the horse to a standstill. "If you want to take the train, cross that field by the foot path and keep right along the road to the left till you come to the river. There's a ferryman. The town's Herblay, and there's a station. . . . And any Sunday before noon I'll be at 3 rue des Evèques, Reuil. You must come and we'll take a walk together."

They shook hands, and Andrews strode off across the wet fields. Something strangely sweet and wistful that he could not analyse lingered in his mind from Marcel's talk. Somewhere, beyond everything, he was conscious of the great free rhythm of the sea.

Then he thought of the Major's office that morning, and of his own skinny figure in the mirrors, repeated endlessly, standing helpless and humble before the shining mahogany desk. Even out here in these fields where the wet earth seemed to heave with the sprouting of new growth, he was not free. In those office buildings, with white marble halls full of the clank of officers' heels, in index cards and piles of typewritten papers, his real self, which they had power to kill if they wanted to, was in his name and his number, on lists with millions of other names and other numbers. This sentient body of his, full of possibilities and hopes and desires, was only a pale ghost that depended on the other self, that suffered for it and cringed for it. He could not drive out of his head the picture of himself, skinny, in an ill-fitting uniform, repeated endlessly in the two mirrors of the Major's white-painted office.

All of a sudden, through bare poplar trees, he saw the Seine.

He hurried along the road, splashing now and then in a shining puddle, until he came to a landing place. The river was very wide, silvery, streaked with pale-green and violet, and straw-color from the evening sky. Opposite were bare poplars and behind them clusters of buff-colored houses climbing up a green hill to a church, all repeated upside down in the color-streaked river. The river was very full, and welled up above its banks, the way the water stands up above the rim of a glass filled too full. From the water came an indefinable rustling, flowing sound that rose and fell with quiet rhythm in Andrews's ears.

Andrews forgot everything in the great wave of music that rose impetuously through him, poured with the hot blood through his veins, with the streaked colors of the river and the sky through his eyes, with the rhythm of the flowing river through his ears.

V

"So I came without," said Andrews, laughing.

"What fun!" cried Geneviève. "But anyway they couldn't do anything to you. Chartres is so near. It's at the gates of Paris."

They were alone in the compartment. The train had pulled out of the station and was going through suburbs where the trees were in leaf in the

gardens, and fruit trees foamed above the red brick walls, among the box-
like villas.

"Anyway," said Andrews, "it was an opportunity not to be missed."

"That must be one of the most amusing things about being a soldier,
avoiding regulations. I wonder whether Damocles didn't really enjoy his
sword, don't you think so?"

They laughed.

"But mother was very doubtful about my coming with you this way.
She's such a dear, she wants to be very modern and liberal, but she always gets frightened at the last minute. And my aunt will think the
world's end has come when we appear."

They went through some tunnels, and when the train stopped at
Sèvres, had a glimpse of the Seine valley, where the blue mist made a
patina over the soft pea-green of new leaves. Then the train came out on
wide plains, full of the glaucous shimmer of young oats and the golden-
green of fresh-sprinkled wheat fields, where the mist on the horizon was
purplish. The train's shadow, blue, sped along beside them over the grass
and fences.

"How beautiful it is to go out of the city this way in the early morning! . . . Has your aunt a piano?"

"Yes, a very old and tinkly one."

"It would be amusing to play you all I have done at the 'Queen of
Sheba.' You say the most helpful things."

"It is that I am interested. I think you will do something some day."

Andrews shrugged his shoulders.

They sat silent, their ears filled up by the jerking rhythm of wheels
over rails, now and then looking at each other, almost furtively. Outside,
fields and hedges and patches of blossom, and poplar trees faintly powdered with green, unrolled, like a scroll before them, behind the flicker
of telegraph poles and the festooned wires on which the sun gave glints
of red copper. Andrews discovered all at once that the coppery glint on
the telegraph wires was the same as the glint in Geneviève's hair.
"Berenike, Artemisia, Arsinoë," the names lingered in his mind. So that
as he looked out of the window at the long curves of the telegraph wires
that seemed to rise and fall as they glided past, he could imagine her face,
with its large, pale brown eyes and its small mouth and broad smooth
forehead, suddenly stilled into the encaustic painting on the mummy case
of some Alexandrian girl.

"Tell me," she said, "when did you begin to write music?"

Andrews brushed the light, disordered hair off his forehead.

"Why, I think I forgot to brush my hair this morning," he said. "You
see, I was so excited by the idea of coming to Chartres with you."

They laughed.

"But my mother taught me to play the piano when I was very small," he went on seriously. "She and I lived alone in an old house belonging to her family in Virginia. How different all that was from anything you have ever lived. It would not be possible in Europe to be as isolated as we were in Virginia. . . . Mother was very unhappy. She had led a dreadfully thwarted life . . . that unrelieved hopeless misery that only a woman can suffer. She used to tell me stories, and I used to make up little tunes about them, and about anything. The great success," he laughed, "was, I remember, to a dandelion. . . . I can remember so well the way Mother pursed up her lips as she leaned over the writing desk. . . . She was very tall, and as it was dark in our old sitting room, had to lean far over to see. . . . She used to spend hours making beautiful copies of tunes I made up. My mother is the only person who has ever really had any importance in my life. . . . But I lack technical training terribly."

"Do you think it is so important?" said Geneviève, leaning towards him to make herself heard above the clatter of the train.

"Perhaps it isn't. I don't know."

"I think it always comes sooner or later, if you feel intensely enough."

"But it is so frightful to feel all you want to express getting away beyond you. An idea comes into your head, and you feel it grow stronger and stronger and you can't grasp it; you have no means to express it. It's like standing on a street corner and seeing a gorgeous procession go by without being able to join it, or like opening a bottle of beer and having it foam all over you without having a glass to pour it into."

Geneviève burst out laughing.

"But you can drink from the bottle, can't you?" she said, her eyes sparkling.

"I'm trying to," said Andrews.

"Here we are. There's the cathedral. No, it's hidden," cried Geneviève.

They got to their feet. As they left the station, Andrews said:

"But after all, it's only freedom that matters. When I'm out of the army! . . . "

"Yes, I suppose you are right . . . for you that is. The artist should be free from any sort of entanglement."

"I don't see what difference there is between an artist and any other sort of workman," said Andrews savagely.

"No, but look."

From the square where they stood, above the green blur of a little park, they could see the cathedral, creamy yellow and rust color, with the sober tower and the gaudy tower, and the great rose window between, the whole pile standing nonchalantly, knee deep in the packed roofs of the town.

They stood shoulder to shoulder, looking at it without speaking.

In the afternoon they walked down the hill towards the river, that flowed through a quarter of tottering, peak-gabled houses and mills, from which came a sound of grinding wheels. Above them, towering over gardens full of pear trees in bloom, the apse of the cathedral bulged against the pale sky. On a narrow and very ancient bridge they stopped and looked at the water, full of a shimmer of blue and green and grey from the sky and from the vivid new leaves of the willow trees along the bank.

Their senses glutted with the beauty of the day and the intricate magnificence of the cathedral, languid with all they had seen and said, they were talking of the future with quiet voices.

"It's all in forming a habit of work," Andrews was saying. "You have to be a slave to get anything done. It's all a question of choosing your master, don't you think so?"

"Yes. I suppose all the men who have left their imprint on people's lives have been slaves in a sense," said Geneviève slowly. "Everyone has to give up a great deal of life to live anything deeply. But it's worth it." She looked Andrews full in the eyes.

"Yes, I think it's worth it," said Andrews. "But you must help me. Now I am like a man who has come up out of a dark cellar. I'm almost too dazzled by the gorgeousness of everything. But at least I am out of the cellar."

"Look, a fish jumped," cried Geneviève.

"I wonder if we could hire a boat anywhere. . . . Don't you think it'ld be fun to go out in a boat?"

A voice broke in on Geneviève's answer:

"Let's see your pass, will you?"

Andrews turned round. A soldier with a round brown face and red cheeks stood beside him on the bridge. Andrews looked at him fixedly. A little zigzag scar above his left eye showed white on his heavily tanned skin.

"Let's see your pass," the man said again; he had a high pitched, squeaky voice.

Andrews felt the blood thumping in his ears.

"Are you an M.P.?"

"Yes."

"Well I'm in the Sorbonne Detachment."

"What the hell's that?" said the M.P., laughing thinly.

"What does he say?" asked Geneviève, smiling.

"Nothing. I'll have to go see the officer and explain," said Andrews in a breathless voice. "You go back to your Aunt's and I'll come as soon as I've arranged it."

"No, I'll come with you."

"Please go back. It may be serious. I'll come as soon as I can," said Andrews harshly.

She walked up the hill with swift decisive steps, without turning round.

"Tough luck, buddy," said the M.P. "She's a good-looker. I'd like to have a half-hour with her myself."

"Look here. I'm in the Sorbonne School Detachment in Paris, and I came down here without a pass. Is there anything I can do about it?"

"They'll fix you up, don't worry," cried the M.P. shrilly. "You ain't a member of the General Staff in disguise, are ye? School Detachment! Gee, won't Bill Huggis laugh when he hears that? You pulled the best one yet, buddy. . . . But come along," he added in a confidential tone. "If you come quiet I won't put the handcuffs on ye."

"How do I know you're an M.P.?"

"You'll know soon enough."

They turned down a narrow street between grey stucco walls leprous with moss and water stains.

At a chair inside the window of a small wine shop a man with a red M.P. badge sat smoking. He got up when he saw them pass and opened the door with one hand on his pistol holster.

"I got one bird, Bill," said the man, shoving Andrews roughly in the door.

"Good for you, Handsome; is he quiet?"

"Um." Handsome grunted.

"Sit down there. If you move you'll git a bullet in your guts." The M.P. stuck out a square jaw; he had a sallow skin, puffy under the eyes that were grey and lustreless.

"He says he's in some goddam School Detachment. First time that's been pulled, ain't it?"

"School Detachment. D'you mean an O.T.C?" Bill sank laughing into his chair by the window, spreading his legs out over the floor.

"Ain't that rich?" said Handsome, laughing shrilly again.

"Got any papers on ye? Ye must have some sort of papers."

Andrews searched his pockets. He flushed.

"I ought to have a school pass."

"You sure ought. Gee, this guy's simple," said Bill, leaning far back in the chair and blowing smoke through his nose.

"Look at his dawg-tag, Handsome."

The man strode over to Andrews and jerked open the top of his tunic. Andrews pulled his body away.

"I haven't got any on. I forgot to put any on this morning."

"No tag, no insignia."

"Yes, I have, infantry."

"No papers. . . . I bet he's been out a hell of a time," said Handsome meditatively.

"Better put the cuffs on him," said Bill in the middle of a yawn.

"Let's wait a while. When's the loot coming?"

"Not till night."

"Sure?"

"Yes. Ain't no train."

"How about a side car?"

"No, I know he ain't comin'," snarled Bill.

"What d'you say we have a little liquor, Bill? Bet this bloke's got money. You'll set us up to a glass o' cognac, won't you, School Detachment?"

Andrews sat very stiff in his chair, staring at them.

"Yes," he said, "order up what you like."

"Keep an eye on him, Handsome. You never can tell what this quiet kind's likely to pull off on you."

Bill Huggis strode out of the room with heavy steps. In a moment he came back swinging a bottle of cognac in his hand.

"Tole the Madame you'd pay, Skinny," said the man as he passed Andrews's chair. Andrews nodded.

The two M.P.'s drew up to the table beside which Andrews sat. Andrews could not keep his eyes off them. Bill Huggis hummed as he pulled the cork out of the bottle.

> "It's the smile that makes you happy,
> It's the smile that makes you sad."

Handsome watched him, grinning.

Suddenly they both burst out laughing.

"An' the damn fool thinks he's in a school battalion," said Handsome in his shrill voice.

"It'll be another kind of a battalion you'll be in, Skinny," cried Bill Huggis. He stifled his laughter with a long drink from the bottle.

He smacked his lips.

"Not so goddam bad," he said. Then he started humming again:

> "It's the smile that makes you happy,
> It's the smile that makes you sad."

"Have some, Skinny?" said Handsome, pushing the bottle towards Andrews.

"No, thanks," said Andrews.

"Ye won't be gettin' good cognac where yer goin', Skinny, not by a damn sight," growled Bill Huggis in the middle of a laugh.

"All right, I'll take a swig." An idea had suddenly come into Andrews's head.

"Gee, the bastard kin drink cognac," cried Handsome.

"Got enough money to buy us another bottle?"

Andrews nodded. He wiped his mouth absently with his handkerchief; he had drunk the raw cognac without tasting it.

"Get another bottle, Handsome," said Bill Huggis carelessly. A purplish flush had appeared in the lower part of his cheeks. When the other man came back, he burst out laughing.

"The last cognac this Skinny guy from the school detachment'll git for many a day. Better drink up strong, Skinny. . . . They don't have that stuff down on the farm. . . . School Detachment; I'll be goddamned!" He leaned back in his chair, shaking with laughter.

Handsome's face was crimson. Only the zigzag scar over his eye remained white. He was swearing in a low voice as he worked the cork out of the bottle.

Andrews could not keep his eyes off the men's faces. They went from one to the other, in spite of him. Now and then, for an instant, he caught a glimpse of the yellow and brown squares of the wall paper and the bar with a few empty bottles behind it.

He tried to count the bottles; "one, two, three . . . " but he was staring in the lustreless grey eyes of Bill Huggis, who lay back in his chair, blowing smoke out of his nose, now and then reaching for the cognac bottle, all the while humming faintly, under his breath:

> "It's the smile that makes you happy,
> It's the smile that makes you sad."

Handsome sat with his elbows on the table, and his chin in his beefy hands. His face was flushed crimson, but the skin was softly moulded, like a woman's.

The light in the room was beginning to grow grey.

Handsome and Bill Huggis stood up. A young officer, with clearly-marked features and a campaign hat worn a little on one side, came in, stood with his feet wide apart in the middle of the floor.

Andrews went up to him.

"I'm in the Sorbonne Detachment, Lieutenant, stationed in Paris."

"Don't you know enough to salute?" said the officer, looking him up and down. "One of you men teach him to salute," he said slowly.

Handsome made a step towards Andrews and hit him with his fist between the eyes. There was a flash of light and the room swung round, and there was a splitting crash as his head struck the floor. He got to his feet. The fist hit him in the same place, blinding him, the three figures and the bright oblong of the window swung round. A chair crashed down with him, and a hard rap in the back of his skull brought momentary blackness.

"That's enough, let him be," he heard a voice far away at the end of a black tunnel.

A great weight seemed to be holding him down as he struggled to get up, blinded by tears and blood. Rending pains darted like arrows through his head. There were handcuffs on his wrists.

"Git up," snarled a voice.

He got to his feet, faint light came through the streaming tears in his eyes. His forehead flamed as if hot coals were being pressed against it.

"Prisoner, attention!" shouted the officer's voice. "March!"

Automatically, Andrews lifted one foot and then the other. He felt in his face the cool air of the street. On either side of him were the hard steps of the M.P.'s. Within him a nightmare voice was shrieking, shrieking.

PART SIX

UNDER THE WHEELS

I

The uncovered garbage cans clattered as they were thrown one by one into the truck. Dust, and a smell of putrid things, hung in the air about the men as they worked. A guard stood by with his legs wide apart, and his rifle-butt on the pavement between them. The early mist hung low, hiding the upper windows of the hospital. From the door beside which the garbage cans were ranged came a thick odor of carbolic. The last garbage can rattled into place on the truck, the four prisoners and the guard clambered on, finding room as best they could among the cans, from which dripped bloody bandages, ashes, and bits of decaying food, and the truck rumbled off towards the incinerator, through the streets of Paris that sparkled with the gaiety of early morning.

The prisoners wore no tunics; their shirts and breeches had dark stains of grease and dirt; on their hands were torn canvas gloves. The guard was a sheepish, pink-faced youth, who kept grinning apologetically, and had trouble keeping his balance when the truck went round corners.

"How many days do they keep a guy on this job, Happy?" asked a boy with mild blue eyes and a creamy complexion, and reddish curly hair.

"Damned if I know, kid; as long as they please, I guess," said the bull-necked man next him, who had a lined prize fighter's face, with a heavy protruding jaw. Then, after looking at the boy for a minute, with his face twisted into an astonished sort of grin, he went on: "Say, kid, how in hell did you git here? Robbin' the cradle, Oi call it, to send you here, kid."

"I stole a Ford," the boy answered cheerfully.

"Like hell you did!"

"Sold it for five hundred francs."

Happy laughed, and caught hold of an ash can to keep from being thrown out of the jolting truck.

"Kin ye beat that, guard?" he cried. "Ain't that somethin'?"

The guard sniggered.

"Didn't send me to Leavenworth 'cause I was so young," went on the kid placidly.

"How old are you, kid?" asked Andrews, who was leaning against the driver's seat.

"Seventeen," said the boy, blushing and casting his eyes down.

"He must have lied like hell to git in this goddam army," boomed the deep voice of the truck driver, who had leaned over to spit a long squirt of tobacco juice.

The truck driver jammed the brakes on. The garbage cans banged against each other.

The Kid cried out in pain: "Hold your horses, can't you? You nearly broke my leg."

The truck driver was swearing in a long string of words.

"Goddam these dreamin', skygazin' sons of French bastards. Why don't they get out of your way? Git out an' crank her up, Happy."

"Guess a feller'd be lucky if he'd break his leg or somethin'; don't you think so, Skinny?" said the fourth prisoner in a low voice.

"It'll take mor'n a broken leg to git you out o' this labor battalion, Hoggenback. Won't it, guard?" said Happy, as he climbed on again.

The truck jolted away, trailing a haze of cinder dust and a sour stench of garbage behind it. Andrews noticed all at once that they were going down the quais along the river. Notre Dame was rosy in the misty sunlight, the color of lilacs in full bloom. He looked at it fixedly a moment, and then looked away. He felt very far from it, like a man looking at the stars from the bottom of a pit.

"My mate, he's gone to Leavenworth for five years," said the Kid when they had been silent some time listening to the rattle of the garbage cans as the trucks jolted over the cobbles.

"Helped yer steal the Ford, did he?" asked Happy.

"Ford nothin'! He sold an ammunition train. He was a railroad man. He was a mason, that's why he only got five years."

"I guess five years in Leavenworth's enough for anybody," muttered Hoggenback, scowling. He was a square-shouldered dark man, who always hung his head when he worked.

"We didn't meet up till we got to Paris; we was on a hell of a party together at the Olympia. That's where they picked us up. Took us to the Bastille. Ever been in the Bastille?"

"I have," said Hoggenback.

"Ain't no joke, is it?"

"Christ!" said Hoggenback. His face flushed a furious red. He turned away and looked at the civilians walking briskly along the early morning streets, at the waiters in shirt sleeves swabbing off the café tables, at the women pushing handcarts full of bright-colored vegetables over the cobblestones.

"I guess they ain't nobody gone through what we guys go through with," said Happy. "It'ld be better if the ole war was still a' goin', to my way o' thinkin'. They'd chuck us into the trenches then. Ain't so low as this."

"Look lively," shouted the truck driver, as the truck stopped in a dirty yard full of cinder piles. "Ain't got all day. Five more loads to get yet."

The guard stood by with angry face and stiff limbs; for he feared there were officers about, and the prisoners started unloading the garbage cans; their nostrils were full of the stench of putrescence; between their lips was a gritty taste of cinders.

The air in the dark mess shack was thick with steam from the kitchen at one end. The men filed past the counter, holding out their mess kits, into which the K.P.'s splashed the food. Occasionally someone stopped to ask for a larger helping in an ingratiating voice. They ate packed together at long tables of roughly planed boards, stained from the constant spilling of grease and coffee and still wet from a perfunctory scrubbing. Andrews sat at the end of a bench, near the door through which came the glimmer of twilight, eating slowly, surprised at the relish with which he ate the greasy food, and at the exhausted contentment that had come over him almost in spite of himself. Hoggenback sat opposite him.

"Funny," he said to Hoggenback, "it's not really as bad as I thought it would be."

"What d'you mean, this labor battalion? Hell, a feller can put up with anything; that's one thing you learn in the army."

"I guess people would rather put up with things than make an effort to change them."

"You're goddam right. Got a butt?"

Andrews handed him a cigarette. They got to their feet and walked out into the twilight, holding their mess kits in front of them. As they were washing their mess kits in a tub of greasy water, where bits of food floated in a thick scum, Hoggenback suddenly said in a low voice:

"But it all piles up, Buddy; some day there'll be an accountin'. D'you believe in religion?"

"No."

"Neither do I. I come of folks as done their own accountin'. My father an' my gran'father before him. A feller can't eat his bile day after day, day after day."

"I'm afraid he can, Hoggenback," broke in Andrews. They walked towards the barracks.

"Goddam it, no," cried Hoggenback aloud. "There comes a point where you can't eat yer bile any more, where it don't do no good to cuss. Then you runs amuck."

Hanging his head he went slowly into the barracks.

Andrews leaned against the outside of the building, staring up at the sky. He was trying desperately to think, to pull together a few threads of his life in this moment of respite from the nightmare. In five minutes the bugle would din in his ears, and he would be driven into the barracks. A tune came to his head that he played with eagerly for a moment, and then, as memory came to him, tried to efface with a shudder of disgust.

> "There's the smile that makes you happy,
> There's the smile that makes you sad."

It was almost dark. Two men walked slowly by in front of him.

"Sarge, may I speak to you?" came a voice in a whisper.

The sergeant grunted.

"I think there's two guys trying to break loose out of here."

"Who? If you're wrong it'll be the worse for you, remember that."

"Surley an' Watson. I heard 'em talkin' about it behind the latrine."

"Damn fools."

"They was sayin' they'd rather be dead than keep up this life."

"They did, did they?"

"Don't talk so loud, Sarge. It wouldn't do for any of the fellers to know I was talkin' to yer. Say, Sarge . . . " the voice became whining, "don't you think I've nearly served my time down here?"

"What do I know about that? 'Tain't my job."

"But, Sarge, I used to be company clerk with my old outfit. Don't ye need a guy round the office?"

Andrews strode past them into the barracks. Dull fury possessed him. He took off his clothes and got silently into his blankets.

Hoggenback and Happy were talking beside his bunk.

"Never you mind," said Hoggenback, "somebody'll get that guy sooner or later."

"Git him, nauthin'! The fellers in that camp was so damn skeered they jumped if you snapped yer fingers at 'em. It's the discipline. I'm tellin' yer, it gits a feller in the end," said Happy.

Andrews lay without speaking, listening to their talk, aching in every muscle from the crushing work of the day.

"They court-martialled that guy, a feller told me," went on Hoggenback. "An' what d'ye think they did to him? Retired on half pay. He was a major."

"Gawd, if Oi iver git out o' this army, Oi'll be so goddam glad," began Happy. Hoggenback interrupted:

"That you'll forgit all about the raw deal they gave you, an' tell every-body how fine ye liked it."

Andrews felt the mocking notes of the bugle outside stabbing his ears. A non-com's voice roared: "Quiet," from the end of the building, and the lights went out. Already Andrews could hear the deep breathing of men asleep. He lay awake, staring into the darkness, his body throbbing with the monotonous rhythms of the work of the day. He seemed still to hear the sickening whine in the man's voice as he talked to the sergeant outside in the twilight. "And shall I be reduced to that?" he was asking himself.

Andrews was leaving the latrine when he heard a voice call softly, "Skinny."

"Yes," he said.

"Come here, I want to talk to you." It was the Kid's voice. There was no light in the ill-smelling shack that served for a latrine. Outside they could hear the guard humming softly to himself as he went back and forth before the barracks door.

"Let's you and me be buddies, Skinny."

"Sure," said Andrews.

"Say, what d'you think the chance is o' cuttin' loose?"

"Pretty damn poor," said Andrews.

"Couldn't you just make a noise like a hoop an' roll away?"

They giggled softly.

Andrews put his hand on the boy's arm.

"But, Kid, it's too risky. I got in this fix by taking a risk. I don't feel like beginning over again, and if they catch you, it's desertion. Leavenworth for twenty years, or life. That'ld be the end of everything."

"Well, what the hell's this?"

"Oh, I don't know; they've got to let us out some day."

"Sh . . . sh. . . ."

Kid put his hand suddenly over Andrews's mouth. They stood rigid, so that they could hear their hearts pounding.

Outside there was a brisk step on the gravel. The sentry halted and saluted. The steps faded into the distance, and the sentry's humming began again.

"They put two fellers in the jug for a month for talking like we are. . . . In solitary," whispered Kid.

"But, Kid, I haven't got the guts to try anything now."

"Sure you have, Skinny. You an' me's got more guts than all the rest of 'em put together. God, if people had guts, you couldn't treat 'em like they were curs. Look, if I can ever get out o' this, I've got a hunch I can make a good thing writing movie scenarios. I want to get on in the world, Skinny."

"But, Kid, you won't be able to go back to the States."

"I don't care. New Rochelle's not the whole world. They got the movies in Italy, ain't they?"

"Sure. Let's go to bed."

"All right. Look, you an' me are buddies from now on, Skinny."

Andrews felt the Kid's hand press his arm.

In his dark, airless bunk, in the lowest of three tiers, Andrews lay awake a long time, listening to the snores and the heavy breathing about him. Thoughts fluttered restlessly in his head, but in his blank hopelessness he could only frown and bite his lips, and roll his head from side to side on the rolled-up tunic he used for a pillow, listening with desperate attention to the heavy breathing of the men who slept above him and beside him.

When he fell asleep he dreamed that he was alone with Geneviève Rod in the concert hall of the Schola Cantorum, and that he was trying desperately hard to play some tune for her on the violin, a tune he kept forgetting, and in the agony of trying to remember, the tears streamed down his cheeks. Then he had his arms round Geneviève's shoulders and was kissing her, kissing her, until he found that it was a wooden board he was kissing, a wooden board on which was painted a face with broad forehead and great pale brown eyes, and small tight lips, and all the while a boy who seemed to be both Chrisfield and the Kid kept telling him to run or the M.P.'s would get him. Then he sat frozen in icy terror with a bottle in his hand, while a frightful voice behind him sang very loud:

"There's the smile that makes you happy,
There's the smile that makes you sad."

The bugle woke him, and he sat up with such a start that he hit his head hard against the bunk above him. He lay back cringing from the pain like a child. But he had to hurry desperately to get his clothes on in time for roll call. It was with a feeling of relief that he found that mess was not ready, and that men were waiting in line outside the kitchen shack, stamping their feet and clattering their mess kits as they moved about through the chilly twilight of the spring morning. Andrews found he was standing behind Hoggenback.

"How's she comin', Skinny?" whispered Hoggenback, in his low mysterious voice.

"Oh, we're all in the same boat," said Andrews with a laugh.

"Wish it'ld sink," muttered the other man. "D'ye know," he went on after a pause, "I kinder thought an edicated guy like you'ld be able to keep out of a mess like this. I wasn't brought up without edication, but I guess I didn't have enough."

"I guess most of 'em can; I don't see that it's much to the point. A man suffers as much if he doesn't know how to read and write as if he had a college education."

"I dunno, Skinny. A feller who's led a rough life can put up with an awful lot. The thing is, Skinny, I might have had a commission if I hadn't been so damned impatient. . . . I'm a lumberman by trade, and my dad's cleaned up a pretty thing in war contracts jus' a short time ago. He could have got me in the engineers if I hadn't gone off an' enlisted."

"Why did you?"

"I was restless-like. I guess I wanted to see the world. I didn't care about the goddam war, but I wanted to see what things was like over here."

"Well, you've seen," said Andrews, smiling.

"In the neck," said Hoggenback, as he pushed out his cup for coffee.

In the truck that was taking them to work, Andrews and the Kid sat side by side on the jouncing backboard and tried to talk above the rumble of the exhaust.

"Like Paris?" asked the Kid.

"Not this way," said Andrews.

"Say, one of the guys said you could parlay French real well. I want you to teach me. A guy's got to know languages to get along in this country."

"But you must know some."

"Bedroom French," said the Kid, laughing.

"Well?"

"But if I want to write a movie scenario for an Eytalian firm, I can't just write 'voulay-vous couchezavecmoa' over and over again."

"But you'll have to learn Italian, Kid."

"I'm goin' to. Say, ain't they taking us a hell of a ways today, Skinny?"

"We're goin' to Passy Wharf to unload rock," said somebody in a grumbling voice.

"No, it's cement . . . cement for the stadium we're presentin' the French Nation. Ain't you read in the 'Stars and Stripes' about it?"

"I'd present 'em with a swift kick, and a hell of a lot of other people, too."

"So we have to sweat unloadin' ce-ment all day," muttered Hoggenback, "to give these goddam frawgs a stadium."

"If it weren't that it'ld be somethin' else."

"But, ain't we got folks at home to work for?" cried Hoggenback. "Mightn't all this sweat be doin' some good for us? Building a stadium! My gawd!"

"Pile out there. . . . Quick!" rasped a voice from the driver's seat.

Through the haze of choking white dust, Andrews got now and then a glimpse of the grey-green river, with its tugboats sporting their white cockades of steam and their long trailing plumes of smoke, and its blunt-nosed barges and its bridges, where people walked jauntily back and forth, going about their business, going where they wanted to go. The bags of cement were very heavy, and the unaccustomed work sent racking pains through his back. The biting dust stung under his finger nails, and in his mouth and eyes. All the morning a sort of refrain went through his head: "People have spent their lives . . . doing only this. People have spent their lives doing only this." As he crossed and recrossed the narrow plank from the barge to the shore, he looked at the black water speeding seawards and took extraordinary care not to let his foot slip. He did not know why, for one-half of him was thinking how wonderful it would be to drown, to forget in eternal black silence the hopeless struggle. Once he saw the Kid standing before the sergeant in charge in an attitude of complete exhaustion, and caught a glint of his blue eyes as he looked up appealingly, looking like a child begging out of a spanking. The sight amused him, and he said to himself: "If I had pink cheeks and cupid's bow lips, I might be able to go through life on my blue eyes"; and he pictured the kid, a fat, cherubic old man, stepping out of a white limousine, the way people do in the movies, and looking about him with those same mild blue eyes. But soon he forgot everything in the agony of the heavy cement bags bearing down on his back and hips.

In the truck on the way back to the mess the Kid, looking fresh and smiling among the sweating men, like ghosts from the white dust, talking hoarsely above the clatter of the truck, sidled up very close to Andrews.

"D'you like swimmin', Skinny?"

"Yes. I'd give a lot to get some of this cement dust off me," said Andrews, without interest.

"I once won a boy's swimmin' race at Coney," said the Kid.

Andrews did not answer.

"Were you in the swimmin' team or anything like that, Skinny, when you went to school?"

"No. . . . It would be wonderful to be in the water, though. I used to swim way out in Chesapeake Bay at night when the water was phosphorescent."

Andrews suddenly found the Kid's blue eyes, bright as flames from excitement, staring into his.

"God, I'm an ass," he muttered.

He felt the Kid's fist punch him softly in the back. "Sergeant said they was goin' to work us late as hell tonight," the Kid was saying aloud to the men round him.

"I'll be dead if they do," muttered Hoggenback.

"An' you a lumberjack!"

"It ain't that. I could carry their bloody bags two at a time if I wanted ter. A feller gets so goddam mad, that's all; so goddam mad. Don't he, Skinny?" Hoggenback turned to Andrews and smiled.

Andrews nodded his head.

After the first two or three bags Andrews carried in the afternoon, it seemed as if every one would be the last he could possibly lift. His back and thighs throbbed with exhaustion; his face and the tips of his fingers felt raw from the biting cement dust.

When the river began to grow purple with evening, he noticed that two civilians, young men with buff-colored coats and canes, were watching the gang at work.

"They says they's newspaper reporters, writing up how fast the army's being demobilized," said one man in an awed voice.

"They come to the right place."

"Tell 'em we're leavin' for home now. Loadin' our barracks bags on the steamer.

The newspaper men were giving out cigarettes. Several men grouped round them. One shouted out:

"We're the guys does the light work. Blackjack Pershing's own pet labor battalion."

"They like us so well they just can't let us go."

"Damn jackasses," muttered Hoggenback, as, with his eyes to the ground, he passed Andrews. "I could tell 'em some things'd make their goddam ears buzz."

"Why don't you?"

"What the hell's the use? I ain't got the edication to talk up to guys like that."

The sergeant, a short, red-faced man with a mustache clipped very short, went up to the group round the newspaper men.

"Come on, fellers, we've got a hell of a lot of this cement to get in before it rains," he said in a kindly voice; "the sooner we get it in, the sooner we get off."

"Listen to that bastard, ain't he juss too sweet for pie when there's company?" muttered Hoggenback on his way from the barge with a bag of cement.

The Kid brushed past Andrews without looking at him.

"Do what I do, Skinny," he said.

Andrews did not turn round, but his heart started thumping very fast. A dull sort of terror took possession of him. He tried desperately to summon his will power, to keep from cringing, but he kept remembering the way the room had swung round when the M.P. had hit him, and heard again the cold voice of the lieutenant saying: "One of you men teach him how to salute."

Time dragged out interminably.

At last, coming back to the edge of the wharf, Andrews saw that there were no more bags in the barge. He sat down on the plank, too exhausted to think. Blue-grey dusk was closing down on everything. The Passy bridge stood out, purple against a great crimson afterglow.

The Kid sat down beside him, and threw an arm trembling with excitement round his shoulders.

"The guard's lookin' the other way. They won't miss us till they get to the truck. . . . Come on, Skinny," he said in a low, quiet voice.

Holding on to the plank, he let himself down into the speeding water. Andrews slipped after him, hardly knowing what he was doing. The icy water closing about his body made him suddenly feel awake and vigorous. As he was swept by the big rudder of the barge, he caught hold of the Kid, who was holding on to a rope. They worked their way without speaking round to the outer side of the rudder. The swift river tugging savagely at them made it hard to hold on.

"Now they can't see us," said the Kid between clenched teeth. "Can you work your shoes an' pants off?"

Andrews started struggling with one boot, the Kid helping to hold him up with his free hand.

"Mine are off," he said. "I was all fixed." He laughed, though his teeth were chattering.

"All right. I've broken the laces," said Andrews.

"Can you swim under water?"

Andrews nodded.

"We want to make for that bunch of barges the other side of the bridge. The barge people'll hide us."

"How d'ye know they will?"

The Kid had disappeared.

Andrews hesitated a moment, then let go his hold and started swimming with the current for all his might.

At first he felt strong and exultant, but very soon he began to feel the icy grip of the water bearing him down; his arms and legs seemed to stiffen. More than against the water, he was struggling against paralysis within him, so that he thought that every moment his limbs would go rigid. He came to the surface and gasped for air. He had a second's glimpse of figures, tiny like toy soldiers, gesticulating wildly on the deck of the barge. The report of a rifle snapped through the air. He dove again, without thinking, as if his body were working independently of his mind.

The next time he came up, his eyes were blurred from the cold. There was a taste of blood in his mouth. The shadow of the bridge was just above him. He turned on his back for a second. There were lights on the bridge.

A current swept him past one barge and then another. Certainty possessed him that he was going to be drowned. A voice seemed to sob in his ears grotesquely: "And so John Andrews was drowned in the Seine, drowned in the Seine, in the Seine."

Then he was kicking and fighting in a furious rage against the coils about him that wanted to drag him down and away. The black side of a barge was slipping up stream beside him with lightning speed. How fast those barges go, he thought. Then suddenly he found that he had hold of a rope, that his shoulders were banging against the bow of a small boat, while in front of him, against the dull purple sky, towered the rudder of the barge. A strong warm hand grasped his shoulder from behind, and he was being drawn up and up, over the bow of the boat that hurt his numbed body like blows, out of the clutching coils of the water.

"Hide me, I'm a deserter," he said over and over again in French. A brown and red face with a bristly white beard, a bulbous, mullioned sort of face, hovered over him in the middle of a pinkish mist.

II

"Oh, qu'il est propre! Oh, qu'il a la peau blanche!" Women's voices were shrilling behind the mist. A coverlet that felt soft and fuzzy against his skin was being put about him. He was very warm and torpid. But somewhere in his thoughts a black crawling thing like a spider was trying to reach him, trying to work its way through the pinkish veils of torpor. After a long while he managed to roll over, and looked about him.

"Mais reste tranquille," came the woman's shrill voice again.

"And the other one? Did you see the other one?" he asked in a choked whisper.

"Yes, it's all right. I'm drying it by the stove," came another woman's voice, deep and growling, almost like a man's.

"Maman's drying your money by the stove. It's all safe. How rich they are, these Americans!"

"And to think that I nearly threw it overboard with the trousers," said the other woman again.

John Andrews began to look about him. He was in a dark low cabin. Behind him, in the direction of the voices, a yellow light flickered. Great dishevelled shadows of heads moved about on the ceiling. Through the close smell of the cabin came a warmth of food cooking. He could hear the soothing hiss of frying grease.

"But didn't you see the Kid?" he asked in English, dazedly trying to pull himself together, to think coherently. Then he went on in French in a more natural voice:

"There was another one with me."

"We saw no one. Rosaline, ask the old man," said the older woman.

"No, he didn't see anyone," came the girl's shrill voice. She walked over to the bed and pulled the coverlet round Andrews with an awkward gesture. Looking up at her, he had a glimpse of the bulge of her breasts and her large teeth that glinted in the lamplight, and very vague in the shadow, a mop of snaky, disordered hair.

"Qu'il parle bien français," she said, beaming at him.

Heavy steps shuffled across the cabin as the older woman came up to the bed and peered in his face.

"Il va mieux," she said, with a knowing air.

She was a broad woman with a broad flat face and a swollen body swathed in shawls. Her eyebrows were very bushy, and she had thick grey whiskers that came down to a point on either side of her mouth, as well as a few bristling hairs on her chin. Her voice was deep and growling, and seemed to come from far down inside her huge body.

Steps creaked somewhere, and the old man looked at him through spectacles placed on the end of his nose. Andrews recognized the irregular face full of red knobs and protrusions.

"Thanks very much," he said.

All three looked at him silently for some time. Then the old man pulled a newspaper out of his pocket, unfolded it carefully, and fluttered it above Andrews's eyes. In the scant light Andrews made out the name: "Libertaire."

"That's why," said the old man, looking at Andrews fixedly, through his spectacles.

"I'm a sort of a socialist," said Andrews.

"Socialists are good-for-nothings," snarled the old man, every red protrusion on his face seeming to get redder.

"But I have great sympathy for anarchist comrades," went on Andrews, feeling a certain liveliness of amusement go through him and fade again.

"Lucky you caught hold of my rope, instead of getting on to the next barge. He'd have given you up for sure. Sont des royalistes, ces salauds-la."

"We must give him something to eat; hurry, Maman. . . . Don't worry, he'll pay, won't you, my little American?"

Andrews nodded his head.

"All you want," he said.

"No, if he says he's a comrade, he shan't pay, not a sou," growled the old man.

"We'll see about that," cried the old woman, drawing her breath in with an angry whistling sound.

"It's only that living's so dear nowadays," came the girl's voice.

"Oh, I'll pay anything I've got," said Andrews peevishly, closing his eyes again.

He lay a long while on his back without moving.

A hand shoved in between his back and the pillow roused him. He sat up. Rosaline was holding a bowl of broth in front of him that steamed in his face.

"Mange ça," she said.

He looked into her eyes, smiling. Her rusty hair was neatly combed. A bright green parrot with a scarlet splash in its wings, balanced itself unsteadily on her shoulder, looking at Andrews out of angry eyes, hard as gems.

"Il est jaloux, coco," said Rosaline, with a shrill little giggle.

Andrews took the bowl in his two hands and drank some of the scalding broth.

"It's too hot," he said, leaning back against the girl's arm.

The parrot squawked out a sentence that Andrews did not understand. Andrews heard the old man's voice answer from somewhere behind him: "Nom de Dieu!"

The parrot squawked again.

Rosaline laughed.

"It's the old man who taught him that," she said. "Poor Coco, he doesn't know what he's saying."

"What does he say?" asked Andrews.

"'Les bourgeois à la lanterne, nom de dieu!' It's from a song," said Rosaline. "Oh, qu'il est malin, ce Coco!"

Rosaline was standing with her arms folded beside the bunk. The parrot stretched out his neck and rubbed it against her cheek, closing and unclosing his gem-like eyes. The girl formed her lips into a kiss, and murmured in a drowsy voice:

"Tu m'aimes, Coco, n'est-ce pas, Coco? Bon Coco."

"Could I have something more, I'm awfully hungry," said Andrews.

"Oh, I was forgetting," cried Rosaline, running off with the empty bowl.

In a moment she came back without the parrot, with the bowl in her hand full of a brown stew of potatoes and meat.

Andrews ate it mechanically, and handed back the bowl.

"Thank you," he said, "I am going to sleep."

He settled himself into the bunk. Rosaline drew the covers up about him and tucked them in round his shoulders. Her hand seemed to linger a moment as it brushed past his cheek. But Andrews had already sunk into a torpor again, feeling nothing but the warmth of the food within him and a great stiffness in his legs and arms.

When he woke up the light was grey instead of yellow, and a swish-ing sound puzzled him. He lay listening to it for a long time, wondering what it was. At last the thought came with a sudden warm spurt of joy that the barge must be moving.

He lay very quietly on his back, looking up at the faint silvery light on the ceiling of the bunk, thinking of nothing, with only a vague dread in the back of his head that someone would come to speak to him, to ques-tion him.

After a long time he began to think of Geneviève Rod. He was hav-ing a long conversation with her about his music, and in his imagination she kept telling him that he must finish the "Queen of Sheba," and that she would show it to Monsieur Gibier, who was a great friend of a cer-tain concert director, who might get it played. How long ago it must be since they had talked about that. A picture floated through his mind of himself and Geneviève standing shoulder to shoulder looking at the Cathedral at Chartres, which stood up nonchalantly, above the tumul-tuous roofs of the town, with its sober tower and its gaudy towers and the great rose windows between. Inexorably his memory carried him forward, moment by moment, over that day, until he writhed with shame and revolt. Good god! Would he have to go on all his life re-membering that? "Teach him how to salute," the officer had said, and Handsome had stepped up to him and hit him. Would he have to go on all his life remembering that?

"We tied up the uniform with some stones, and threw it overboard," said Rosaline, jabbing him in the shoulder to draw his attention.

"That was a good idea."

"Are you going to get up? It's nearly time to eat. How you have slept."

"But I haven't anything to put on," said Andrews, laughing, and waved a bare arm above the bedclothes.

"Wait, I'll find something of the old man's. Say, do all Americans have skin so white as that? Look."

She put her brown hand, with its grimed and broken nails, on Andrews's arm, that was white with a few silky yellow hairs.

"It's because I'm blond," said Andrews. "There are plenty of blond Frenchmen, aren't there?"

Rosaline ran off giggling, and came back in a moment with a pair of corduroy trousers and a torn flannel shirt that smelt of pipe tobacco.

"That'll do for now," she said. "It's warm today for April. Tonight we'll buy you some clothes and shoes. Where are you going?"

"By God, I don't know."

"We're going to Havre for cargo." She put both hands to her head and began rearranging her straggling rusty-colored hair. "Oh, my hair," she said, "it's the water, you know. You can't keep respectable-looking on these filthy barges. Say, American, why don't you stay with us a while? You can help the old man run the boat."

He found suddenly that her eyes were looking into his with trembling eagerness.

"I don't know what to do," he said carelessly. "I wonder if it's safe to go on deck."

She turned away from him petulantly and led the way up the ladder.

"Oh, v'là le camarade," cried the old man who was leaning with all his might against the long tiller of the barge. "Come and help me."

The barge was the last of a string of four that were describing a wide curve in the midst of a reach of silvery river full of glittering patches of pale, pea-green lavender, hemmed in on either side by frail blue roots of poplars. The sky was a mottled luminous grey with occasional patches, the color of robins' eggs. Andrews breathed in the dank smell of the river and leaned against the tiller when he was told to, answering the old man's curt questions.

He stayed with the tiller when the rest of them went down to the cabin to eat. The pale colors and the swishing sound of the water and the blue-green banks slipping by and unfolding on either hand, were as soothing as his deep sleep had been. Yet they seemed only a veil covering other realities, where men stood interminably in line and marched with legs made all the same length on the drill field, and wore the same clothes and cringed before the same hierarchy of polished belts and polished puttees and stiff-visored caps, that had its homes in vast offices crammed with index cards and card catalogues; a world full of the tramp of marching, where cold voices kept saying:—"Teach him how to salute." Like a bird in a net, Andrews's mind struggled to free itself from the obsession.

Then he thought of his table in his room in Paris, with its piled sheets of ruled paper, and he felt he wanted nothing in the world except to work. It would not matter what happened to him if he could only have time to weave into designs the tangled skein of music that seethed through him as the blood seethed through his veins.

There he stood, leaning against the long tiller, watching the blue-green poplars glide by, here and there reflected in the etched silver mirror of the river, feeling the moist river wind flutter his ragged shirt, thinking of nothing.

After a while the old man came up out of the cabin, his face purplish, puffing clouds of smoke out of his pipe.

"All right, young fellow, go down and eat," he said.

Andrews lay flat on his belly on the deck, with his chin resting on the back of his two hands. The barge was tied up along the river bank among many other barges. Beside him, a small fuzzy dog barked furiously at a yellow mongrel on the shore. It was nearly dark, and through the pearly mist of the river came red oblongs of light from the taverns along the bank. A slip of a new moon, shrouded in haze, was setting behind the poplar trees. Amid the round of despairing thoughts, the memory of the Kid intruded itself. He had sold a Ford for five hundred francs, and gone on a party with a man who'd stolen an ammunition train, and he wanted to write for the Italian movies. No war could down people like that. Andrews smiled, looking into the black water. Funny, the Kid was dead, probably, and he, John Andrews, was alive and free. And he lay there moping, still whimpering over old wrongs. "For God's sake be a man!" he said to himself. He got to his feet.

At the cabin door, Rosaline was playing with the parrot.

"Give me a kiss, Coco," she was saying in a drowsy voice, "just a little kiss. Just a little kiss for Rosaline, poor little Rosaline."

The parrot, which Andrews could hardly see in the dusk, leaned towards her, fluttering his feathers, making little clucking noises.

Rosaline caught sight of Andrews.

"Oh, I thought you'd gone to have a drink with the old man," she cried.

"No. I stayed here."

"D'you like it, this life?"

Rosaline put the parrot back on his perch, where he swayed from side to side, squawking in protest: "Les bourgeois à la lanterne, nom de dieu!"

They both laughed.

"Oh, it must be a wonderful life. This barge seems like heaven after the army."

"But they pay you well, you Americans."

"Seven francs a day."

"That's luxury, that."

"And be ordered around all day long!"

"But you have no expenses. . . . It's clear gain. . . . You men are funny. The old man's like that too. . . . It's nice here all by ourselves, isn't it, Jean?"

Andrews did not answer. He was wondering what Geneviève Rod would say when she found out he was a deserter.

"I hate it. . . . It's dirty and cold and miserable in winter," went on Rosaline. "I'd like to see them at the bottom of the river, all these barges. . . . And Paris women, did you have a good time with them?"

"I only knew one. I go very little with women."

"All the same, love's nice, isn't it?"

They were sitting on the rail at the bow of the barge. Rosaline had sidled up so that her leg touched Andrews's leg along its whole length.

The memory of Geneviève Rod became more and more vivid in his mind. He kept thinking of things she had said, of the intonations of her voice, of the blundering way she poured tea, and of her pale-brown eyes wide open on the world, like the eyes of a woman in an encaustic painting from a tomb in the Fayoum.

"Mother's talking to the old woman at the Creamery. They're great friends. She won't be home for two hours yet," said Rosaline.

"She's bringing my clothes, isn't she?"

"But you're all right as you are."

"But they're your father's."

"What does that matter?"

"I must go back to Paris soon. There is somebody I must see in Paris."

"A woman?"

Andrews nodded.

"But it's not so bad, this life on the barge. I'm just lonesome and sick of the old people. That's why I talk nastily about it. . . . We could have good times together if you stayed with us a little."

She leaned her head on his shoulder and put a hand awkwardly on his bare forearm.

"How cold these Americans are!" she muttered, giggling drowsily.

Andrews felt her hair tickle his cheek.

"No, it's not a bad life on the barge, honestly. The only thing is, there's nothing but old people on the river. It isn't life to be always with old people. . . . I want to have a good time."

She pressed her cheek against his. He could feel her breath heavy in his face.

"After all, it's lovely in summer to drowse on the deck that's all warm with the sun, and see the trees and the fields and the little houses slipping by on either side . . . If there weren't so many old people. . . . All the boys go away to the cities. . . . I hate old people; they're so dirty and slow. We mustn't waste our youth, must we?"

Andrews got to his feet.

"What's the matter?" she cried sharply.

"Rosaline," Andrews said in a low, soft voice, "I can only think of going to Paris."

"Oh, the Paris woman," said Rosaline scornfully. "But what does that matter? She isn't here now."

"I don't know. . . . Perhaps I shall never see her again anyway," said Andrews.

"You're a fool. You must amuse yourself when you can in this life. And you a deserter. . . . Why, they may catch you and shoot you any time."

"Oh, I know, you're right. You're right. But I'm not made like that, that's all."

"She must be very good to you, your little Paris girl."

"I've never touched her."

Rosaline threw her head back and laughed raspingly.

"But you aren't sick, are you?" she cried.

"Probably I remember too vividly, that's all. . . . Anyway, I'm a fool, Rosaline, because you're a nice girl."

There were steps on the plank that led to the shore. A shawl over her head and a big bundle under her arm, the old woman came up to them, panting wheezily. She looked from one to the other, trying to make out their faces in the dark.

"It's a danger . . . like that . . . youth," she muttered between hard short breaths.

"Did you find the clothes?" asked Andrews in a casual voice.

"Yes. That leaves you forty-five francs out of your money, when I've taken out for your food and all that. Does that suit you?"

"Thank you very much for your trouble."

"You paid for it. Don't worry about that," said the old woman. She gave him the bundle. "Here are your clothes and the forty-five francs. If you want, I'll tell you exactly what each thing cost."

"I'll put them on first," he said, with a laugh.

He climbed down the ladder into the cabin.

Putting on new, unfamiliar-shaped clothes made him suddenly feel strong and joyous. The old woman had bought him corduroy trousers, cheap cloth shoes, a blue cotton shirt, woollen socks, and a second-hand black serge jacket. When he came on deck she held up a lantern to look at him.

"Doesn't he look fine, altogether French?" she said.

Rosaline turned away without answering. A little later she picked up the perch and carried the parrot, that swayed sleepily on the crosspiece, down the ladder.

"Les bourgeois à la lanterne, nom de dieu!" came the old man's voice singing on the shore.

"He's drunk as a pig," muttered the old woman. "If only he doesn't fall off the gang plank."

A swaying shadow appeared at the end of the plank, standing out against the haze of light from the houses behind the poplar trees.

Andrews put out a hand to catch him as he reached the side of the barge. The old man sprawled against the cabin.

"Don't bawl me out, dearie," he said, dangling an arm round Andrews's neck, and a hand beckoning vaguely towards his wife. "I've found a comrade for the little American."

"What's that?" said Andrews sharply. His mouth suddenly went dry with terror. He felt his nails pressing into the palms of his cold hands.

"I've found another American for you," said the old man in an important voice. "Here he comes." Another shadow appeared at the end of the gangplank.

"Les bourgeois à la lanterne, nom de dieu!" shouted the old man.

Andrews backed away cautiously towards the other side of the barge. All the little muscles of his thighs were trembling. A hard voice was saying in his head: "Drown yourself, drown yourself. Then they won't get you."

The man was standing on the end of the plank. Andrews could see the contour of the uniform against the haze of light behind the poplar trees.

"God, if I only had a pistol," he thought.

"Say, Buddy, where are you?" came an American voice.

The man advanced towards him across the deck.

Andrews stood with every muscle taut.

"Gee! You've taken off your uniform. . . . Say, I'm not an M.P. I'm A.W.O.L. too. Shake." He held out his hand.

Andrews took the hand doubtfully, without moving from the edge of the barge.

"Say, Buddy, it's a damn fool thing to take off your uniform. Ain't you got any? If they pick you up like that it's life, Kid."

"I can't help it. It's done now."

"Gawd, you still think I'm an M.P., don't yer? . . . I swear I ain't. Maybe you are. Gawd, it's hell, this life. A feller can't put his trust in nobody."

"What division are you from?"

"Hell, I came to warn you this bastard frawg's got soused an' has been blabbin' in the gin mill there how he was an anarchist an' all that, an' how he had an American deserter who was an anarchist an' all that, an' I said to myself: 'That guy'll git nabbed if he ain't careful,' so I cottoned up to the old frawg an' said I'd go with him to see the camarade, an' I think we'd better both of us make tracks out o' this berg."

"It's damn decent. I'm sorry I was so suspicious. I was scared green when I first saw you."

"You were goddam right to be. But why did yous take yer uniform off?"

"Come along, let's beat it. I'll tell you about that."

Andrews shook hands with the old man and the old woman. Rosaline had disappeared.

"Goodnight. . . . Thank you," he said, and followed the other man across the gangplank.

As they walked away along the road they heard the old man's voice roaring:

"Les bourgeois à la lanterne, nom de dieu!"

"My name's Eddy Chambers," said the American.

"Mine's John Andrews."

"How long 've you been out?"

"Two days."

Eddy let the air out through his teeth in a whistle.

"I got away from a labor battalion in Paris. They'd picked me up in Chartres without a pass."

"Gee, I've been out a month an' more. Was you infantry too?"

"Yes. I was in the School Detachment in Paris when I was picked up. But I never could get word to them. They just put me to work without a trial. Ever been in a labor battalion?"

"No, thank Gawd, they ain't got my number yet."

They were walking fast along a straight road across a plain under a clear star-powdered sky.

"I been out eight weeks yesterday. What'd you think o' that?" said Eddy.

"Must have had plenty of money to go on."

"I've been flat fifteen days."

"How d'you work it?"

"I dunno. I juss work it though. . . . Ye see, it was this way. The gang I was with went home when I was in hauspital, and the damn skunks put me in class A and was goin' to send me to the Army of Occupation. Gawd, it made me sick, goin' out to a new outfit where I didn't know anybody, an' all the rest of my bunch home walkin' down Water Street with brass bands an' reception committees an' girls throwing kisses at 'em an' all that. Where are yous goin'?"

"Paris."

"Gee, I wouldn't. Risky."

"But I've got friends there. I can get hold of some money."

"Looks like I hadn't got a friend in the world. I wish I'd gone to that goddam outfit now. . . . I ought to have been in the engineers all the time, anyway."

"What did you do at home?"

"Carpenter."

"But gosh, man, with a trade like that you can always make a living anywhere."

"You're goddam right, I could, but a guy has to live underground, like a rabbit, at this game. If I could git to a country where I could walk around like a man, I wouldn't give a damn what happened. If the army ever moves out of here an' the goddam M.P.'s, I'll set up in business in one of these here little towns. I can parlee pretty well. I'd juss as soon marry a French girl an' git to be a regular frawg myself. After the raw deal they've given me in the army, I don't want to have nothin' more to do with their damn country. Democracy!"

He cleared his throat and spat angrily on the road before him.

They walked on silently. Andrews was looking at the sky, picking out constellations he knew among the glittering masses of stars.

"Why don't you try Spain or Italy?" he said after a while.

"Don't know the lingo. No, I'm going to Scotland."

"But how can you get there?"

"Crossing on the car ferries to England from Havre. I've talked to guys has done it."

"But what'll you do when you do get there?"

"How should I know? Live around best I can. What can a feller do when he don't dare show his face in the street?"

"Anyway, it makes you feel as if you had some guts in you to be out on your own this way," cried Andrews boisterously.

"Wait till you've been at it two months, boy, and you'll think what I'm tellin' yer. . . . The army's hell when you're in it; but it's a hell of a lot worse when you're out of it, at the wrong end."

"It's a great night, anyway," said Andrews.

"Looks like we ought to be findin' a haystack to sleep in."

"It'ld be different," burst out Andrews, suddenly, "if I didn't have friends here."

"Oh, you've met up with a girl, have you?" asked Eddy ironically.

"Yes. The thing is we really get along together, besides all the rest."

Eddy snorted.

"I bet you ain't ever even kissed her," he said. "Gee, I've had buddies has met up with that friendly kind. I know a guy married one, an' found out after two weeks."

"It's silly to talk about it. I can't explain it. . . . It gives you confidence in anything to feel there's someone who'll always understand anything you do."

"I s'pose you're goin' to git married."

"I don't see why. That would spoil everything."

Eddy whistled softly.

They walked along briskly without speaking for a long time, their steps ringing on the hard road, while the dome of the sky shimmered above their heads. And from the ditches came the singsong shrilling of toads. For the first time in months Andrews felt himself bubbling with a spirit of joyous adventure. The rhythm of the three green horsemen that was to have been the prelude to the Queen of Sheba began rollicking through his head.

"But, Eddy, this is wonderful. It's us against the universe," he said in a boisterous voice.

"You wait," said Eddy.

When Andrews walked by the M.P. at the Gare-St. Lazare, his hands were cold with fear. The M.P. did not look at him. He stopped on the crowded pavement a little way from the station and stared into a mirror in a shop window. Unshaven, with a check cap on the side of his head and his corduroy trousers, he looked like a young workman who had been out of work for a month.

"Gee, clothes do make a difference," he said to himself.

He smiled when he thought how shocked Walters would be when he turned up in that rig, and started walking with leisurely stride across Paris, where everything bustled and jingled with early morning, where from every café came a hot smell of coffee, and fresh bread steamed in the windows of the bakeries. He still had three francs in his pocket. On a side street the fumes of coffee roasting attracted him into a small bar. Several men were arguing boisterously at the end of the bar. One of them turned a ruddy, tow-whiskered face to Andrews, and said:

"Et toi, tu vas chômer le premier mai?"

"I'm on strike already," answered Andrews laughing.

The man noticed his accent, looked at him sharply a second, and turned back to the conversation, lowering his voice as he did so. Andrews drank down his coffee and left the bar, his heart pounding. He could not help glancing back over his shoulder now and then to see if he was being followed. At a corner he stopped with his fists clenched and leaned a second against a house wall.

"Where's your nerve. Where's your nerve?" He was saying to himself.

He strode off suddenly, full of bitter determination not to turn round again. He tried to occupy his mind with plans. Let's see, what should he do? First he'd go to his room and look up old Henslowe and Walters. Then he would go to see Geneviève. Then he'd work, work, forget everything in his work, until the army should go back to America and there should be no more uniforms on the streets. And as for the future, what did he care about the future?

When he turned the corner into the familiar street where his room was, a thought came to him. Suppose he should find M.P.'s waiting for him there? He brushed it aside angrily and strode fast up the sidewalk, catching up to a soldier who was slouching along in the same direction, with his hands in his pockets and eyes on the ground. Andrews stopped suddenly as he was about to pass the soldier and turned. The man looked up. It was Chrisfield.

Andrews held out his hand.

Chrisfield seized it eagerly and shook it for a long time.

"Jesus Christ! Ah thought you was a Frenchman, Andy. . . . Ah guess you got yer dis-charge then. God, Ah'm glad."

"I'm glad I look like a Frenchman, anyway. . . . Been on leave long, Chris?"

Two buttons were off the front of Chrisfield's uniform; there were streaks of dirt on his face, and his puttees were clothed with mud. He looked Andrews seriously in the eyes, and shook his head.

"No. Ah done flew the coop, Andy," he said in a low voice.

"Since when?"

"Ah been out a couple o' weeks. Ah'll tell you about it, Andy. Ah was comin' to see you now. Ah'm broke."

"Well look, I'll be able to get hold of some money tomorrow. . . . I'm out too."

"What d'ye mean?"

"I haven't got a discharge. I'm through with it all. I've deserted."

"God damn! That's funny that you an' me should both do it, Andy. But why the hell did you do it?"

"Oh, it's too long to tell here. Come up to my room."

"There may be fellers there. Ever been at the Chink's?"

"No."

"I'm stayin' there. There're other fellers who's A.W.O.L. too. The Chink's got a gin mill."

"Where is it."

"Eight, rew day Petee Jardings."

"Where's that?"

"Way back of that garden where the animals are."

"Look, I can find you there tomorrow morning, and I'll bring some money."

"Ah'll wait for ye, Andy, at nine. It's a bar. Ye won't be able to git in without me, the kids is pretty scared of plainclothes men."

"I think it'll be perfectly safe to come up to my place now."

"Naw, Ah'm goin' to git the hell out of here."

"But Chris, why did you go A.W.O.L.?"

"Oh, Ah doan know. . . . A guy who's in the Paris detachment got yer address for me."

"But, Chris, did they say anything to him about me?"

"No, nauthin'."

"That's funny. . . . Well, Chris, I'll be there tomorrow, if I can find the place."

"Man, you've got to be there."

"Oh, I'll turn up," said Andrews with a smile.

They shook hands nervously.

"Say, Andy," said Chrisfield, still holding on to Andrews's hand, "Ah went A.W.O.L. 'cause a sergeant . . . God damn it; it's weighin' on ma mind awful these days. . . . There's a sergeant that knows."

"What you mean?"

"Ah told ye about Anderson. . . . Ah know you ain't tole anybody,

Andy." Chrisfield dropped Andrews's hand and looked at him in the face with an unexpected sideways glance. Then he went on through clenched teeth: "Ah swear to Gawd Ah ain't tole another livin' soul. . . . An' the sergeant in Company D knows."

"For God's sake, Chris, don't lose your nerve like that."

"Ah ain't lost ma nerve. Ah tell you that guy knows." Chrisfield's voice rose, suddenly shrill.

"Look, Chris, we can't stand talking out here in the street like this. It isn't safe."

"But mebbe you'll be able to tell me what to do. You think, Andy. Mebbe, tomorrow, you'll have thought up somethin' we can do. . . . So long."

Chrisfield walked away hurriedly. Andrews looked after him a moment, and then went in through the court to the house where his room was.

At the foot of the stairs an old woman's voice startled him.

"Mais, Monsieur André, que vous avez l'air étrange; how funny you look dressed like that."

The concierge was smiling at him from her cubbyhole beside the stairs. She sat knitting with a black shawl round her head, a tiny old woman with a hooked bird-like nose and eyes sunk in depressions full of little wrinkles, like a monkey's eyes.

"Yes, at the town where I was demobilized, I couldn't get anything else," stammered Andrews.

"Oh, you're demobilized, are you? That's why you've been away so long. Monsieur Valters said he didn't know where you were. . . . It's better that way, isn't it?"

"Yes," said Andrews, starting up the stairs.

"Monsieur Valters is in now," went on the old woman, talking after him. "And you've got in just in time for the first of May."

"Oh, yes, the strike," said Andrews, stopping half-way up the flight.

"It'll be dreadful," said the old woman. "I hope you won't go out. Young folks are so likely to get into trouble . . . Oh, but all your friends have been worried about your being away so long."

"Have they?'" said Andrews. He continued up the stairs.

"Au revoir, Monsieur."

"Au revoir, Madame."

III

"No, nothing can make me go back now. It's no use talking about it."

"But you're crazy, man. You're crazy. One man alone can't buck the system like that, can he, Henslowe?"

Walters was talking earnestly, leaning across the table beside the lamp. Henslowe, who sat very stiff on the edge of a chair, nodded with compressed lips. Andrews lay at full length on the bed, out of the circle of light.

"Honestly, Andy," said Henslowe with tears in his voice, "I think you'd better do what Walters says. It's no use being heroic about it."

"I'm not being heroic, Henny," cried Andrews, sitting up on the bed. He drew his feet under him, tailor fashion, and went on talking very quietly. "Look. . . . It's a purely personal matter. I've got to a point where I don't give a damn what happens to me. I don't care if I'm shot, or if I live to be eighty. . . . I'm sick of being ordered round. One more order shouted at my head is not worth living to be eighty . . . to me. That's all. For God's sake let's talk about something else."

"But how many orders have you had shouted at your head since you got in this School Detachment? Not one. You can put through your discharge application probably . . ." Walters got to his feet, letting the chair crash to the floor behind him. He stopped to pick it up. "Look here; here's my proposition," he went on. "I don't think you are marked A.W.O.L. in the School office. Things are so damn badly run there. You can turn up and say you've been sick and draw your back pay. And nobody'll say a thing. Or else I'll put it right up to the guy who's top sergeant. He's a good friend of mine. We can fix it up on the records some way. But for God's sake don't ruin your whole life on account of a little stubbornness, and some damn fool anarchistic ideas or other a feller like you ought to have had more sense than to pick up. . . ."

"He's right, Andy," said Henslowe in a low voice.

"Please don't talk any more about it. You've told me all that before," said Andrews sharply. He threw himself back on the bed and rolled over towards the wall.

They were silent a long time. A sound of voices and footsteps drifted up from the courtyard.

"But, look here, Andy," said Henslowe nervously stroking his moustache. "You care much more about your work than any abstract idea of asserting your right of individual liberty. Even if you don't get caught. . . . I think the chances of getting caught are mighty slim if you use your head. . . . But even if you don't, you haven't enough money to live for long over here, you haven't. . . ."

"Don't you think I've thought of all that? I'm not crazy, you know. I've figured up the balance perfectly sanely. The only thing is, you fellows can't understand. Have you ever been in a labor battalion? Have you ever had a man you'd been chatting with five minutes before deliberately knock you down? Good God, you don't know what you are talking about, you two. . . . I've got to be free, now. I don't care at what cost. Being free's the only thing that matters."

Andrews lay on his back talking towards the ceiling.

Henslowe was on his feet, striding nervously about the room.

"As if anyone was ever free," he muttered.

"All right, quibble, quibble. You can argue anything away if you want to. Of course, cowardice is the best policy, necessary for survival. The man who's got most will to live is the most cowardly . . . go on." Andrews's voice was shrill and excited, breaking occasionally like a half-grown boy's voice.

"Andy, what on earth's got hold of you? . . . God, I hate to go away this way," added Henslowe after a pause.

"I'll pull through all right, Henny. I'll probably come to see you in Syria, disguised as an Arab sheik." Andrews laughed excitedly.

"If I thought I'd do any good, I'd stay. . . . But there's nothing I can do. Everybody's got to settle their own affairs, in their own damn fool way. So long, Walters."

Walters and Henslowe shook hands absently.

Henslowe came over to the bed and held out his hand to Andrews.

"Look, old man, you will be as careful as you can, won't you? And write me care American Red Cross, Jerusalem. I'll be damned anxious, honestly."

"Don't you worry, we'll go travelling together yet," said Andrews, sitting up and taking Henslowe's hand.

They heard Henslowe's steps fade down the stairs and then ring for a moment on the pavings of the courtyard.

Walters moved his chair over beside Andrews's bed.

"Now, look, let's have a man-to-man talk, Andrews. Even if you want to ruin your life, you haven't a right to. There's your family, and haven't you any patriotism? . . . Remember, there is such a thing as duty in the world."

Andrews sat up and said in a low, furious voice, pausing between each word:

"I can't explain it. . . . But I shall never put a uniform on again. . . . So for Christ's sake shut up."

"All right, do what you goddam please; I'm through with you." Walters suddenly flashed into a rage. He began undressing silently. Andrews lay a long while flat on his back in the bed, staring at the ceiling, then he too undressed, put the light out, and got into bed.

The rue des Petits-Jardins was a short street in a district of warehouses. A grey, windowless wall shut out the light along all of one side. Opposite was a cluster of three old houses leaning together as if the outer ones were trying to support the beetling mansard roof of the center house. Behind them rose a huge building with rows and rows of black windows.

When Andrews stopped to look about him, he found the street completely deserted. The ominous stillness that had brooded over the city during all the walk from his room near the Pantheon seemed here to culminate in sheer desolation. In the silence he could hear the light padding noise made by the feet of a dog that trotted across the end of the street. The house with the mansard roof was number eight. The front of the lower storey had once been painted in chocolate-color, across the top of which was still decipherable the sign: "Charbon, Bois. Lhomond." On the grimed window beside the door, was painted in white: "Débit de Boissons."

Andrews pushed on the door, which opened easily. Somewhere in the interior a bell jangled, startlingly loud after the silence of the street. On the wall opposite the door was a speckled mirror with a crack in it, the shape of a star, and under it a bench with three marble-top tables. The zinc bar filled up the third wall. In the fourth was a glass door pasted up with newspapers. Andrews walked over to the bar. The jangling of the bell faded to silence. He waited, a curious uneasiness gradually taking possession of him. Anyways, he thought, he was wasting his time; he ought to be doing something to arrange his future. He walked over to the street door. The bell jangled again when he opened it. At the same moment a man came out through the door the newspapers were pasted over. He was a stout man in a dirty white shirt stained to a brownish color round the armpits and caught in very tightly at the waist by the broad elastic belt that held up his yellow corduroy trousers. His face was flabby, of a greenish color; black eyes looked at Andrews fixedly through barely open lids, so that they seemed long slits above the cheekbones. "That's the Chink," thought Andrews.

"Well," said the man, taking his place behind the bar with his legs far apart.

"A beer, please," said Andrews.

"There isn't any."

"A glass of wine then."

The man nodded his head, and keeping his eyes fastened on Andrews all the while, strode out of the door again.

A moment later, Chrisfield came out, with rumpled hair, yawning, rubbing an eye with the knuckles of one fist.

"Lawsie, Ah juss woke up, Andy. Come along in back."

Andrews followed him through a small room with tables and benches, down a corridor where the reek of ammonia bit into his eyes, and up a staircase littered with dirt and garbage. Chrisfield opened a door directly on the stairs, and they stumbled into a large room with a window that gave on the court. Chrisfield closed the door carefully, and turned to Andrews with a smile.

"Ah was right smart 'askeered ye wouldn't find it, Andy."

"So this is where you live?"

"Um hum, a bunch of us lives here."

A wide bed without coverings, where a man in olive-drab slept rolled in a blanket, was the only furniture of the room.

"Three of us sleeps in that bed," said Chrisfield.

"Who's that?" cried the man in the bed, sitting up suddenly.

"All right, Al, he's a buddy o' mine," said Chrisfield. "He's taken off his uniform."

"Jesus, you got guts," said the man in the bed.

Andrews looked at him sharply. A piece of towelling, splotched here and there with dried blood, was wrapped round his head, and a hand, swathed in bandages, was drawn up to his body. The man's mouth took on a twisted expression of pain as he let his head gradually down to the bed again.

"Gosh, what did you do to yourself?" cried Andrews.

"I tried to hop a freight at Marseilles."

"Needs practice to do that sort o' thing," said Chrisfield, who sat on the bed, pulling his shoes off. "Ah'm goin' to git back to bed, Andy. Ah'm juss dead tired. Ah chucked cabbages all night at the market. They give ye a job there without askin' no questions."

"Have a cigarette." Andrews sat down on the foot of the bed and threw a cigarette towards Chrisfield. "Have one?" he asked Al.

"No. I couldn't smoke. I'm almost crazy with this hand. One of the wheels went over it. . . . I cut what was left of the little finger off with a razor." Andrews could see the sweat rolling down his cheek as he spoke.

"Christ, that poor beggar's been havin' a time, Andy. We was 'askeert to get a doctor, and we all didn't know what to do."

"I got some pure alcohol an' washed it in that. It's not infected. I guess it'll be all right."

"Where are you from, Al?" asked Andrews.

"'Frisco. Oh, I'm goin' to try to sleep. I haven't slept a wink for four nights."

"Why don't you get some dope?"

"Oh, we all ain't had a cent to spare for anythin', Andy."

"Oh, if we had kale we could live like kings—not," said Al in the middle of a nervous little giggle.

"Look, Chris," said Andrews, "I'll halve with you. I've got five hundred francs."

"Jesus Gawd, man, don't kid about anything like that."

"Here's two hundred and fifty. . . . It's not so much as it sounds."

Andrews handed him five fifty-franc notes.

"Say, how did you come to bust loose?" said Al, turning his head towards Andrews.

"I got away from a labor battalion one night. That's all."

"Tell me about it, buddy. I don't feel my hand so much when I'm talking to somebody. . . . I'd be home now if it wasn't for a gin mill in Alsace. Say, don't ye think that big headgear they sport up there is awful good looking? Got my goat every time I saw one. . . . I was comin' back from leave at Grenoble, an' I went through Strasburg. Some town. My outfit was in Coblenz. That's where I met up with Chris here. Anyway, we was raisin' hell round Strasburg, an' I went into a gin mill down a flight of steps. Gee, everything in that town's plumb picturesque, just like a kid I used to know at home whose folks were Eytalian used to talk about when he said how he wanted to come overseas. Well, I met up with a girl down there, who said she'd just come down to a place like that to look for her brother who was in the foreign legion."

Andrews and Chrisfield laughed.

"What you laughin' at?" went on Al in an eager taut voice. "Honest to Gawd. I'm goin' to marry her if I ever get out of this. She's the best little girl I ever met up with. She was waitress in a restaurant, an' when she was off duty she used to wear that there Alsatian costume. . . . Hell, I just stayed on. Every day, I thought I'd go away the next day. . . . Anyway, the war was over. I warn't a damn bit of use. . . . Hasn't a fellow got any rights at all? Then the M.P.'s started cleanin' up Strasburg after A.W.O.L.'s, an' I beat it out of there, an' Christ, it don't look as if I'd ever be able to get back."

"Say, Andy," said Chrisfield, suddenly, "let's go down after some booze."

"All right."

"Say, Al, do you want me to get you anything at the drug store?"

"No. I won't do anythin' but lay low and bathe it with alcohol now and then, against infection. Anyways, it's the first of May. You'll be crazy to go out. You might get pulled. They say there's riots going on."

"Gosh, I forgot it was the first of May," cried Andrews. "They're running a general strike to protest against the war with Russia and . . ."

"A guy told me," interrupted Al, in a shrill voice, "there might be a revolution."

"Come along, Andy," said Chris from the door.

On the stairs Andrews felt Chrisfield's hand squeezing his arm hard.

"Say, Andy," Chris put his lips close to Andrews's ear and spoke in a rasping whisper. "You're the only one that knows . . . you know what. You an' that sergeant. Doan you say anythin' so that the guys here kin ketch on, d'ye hear?"

"All right, Chris, I won't, but man alive, you oughtn't to lose your nerve about it. You aren't the only one who ever shot an . . . "

"Shut yer face, d'ye hear?" muttered Chrisfield savagely.

They went down the stairs in silence. In the room next to the bar they found the Chink reading a newspaper.

"Is he French?" whispered Andrews.

"Ah doan know what he is. He ain't a white man, Ah'll wager that," said Chris, "but he's square."

"D'you know anything about what's going on?" asked Andrews in French, going up to the Chink.

"Where?" The Chink got up, flashing a glance at Andrews out of the corners of his slit-like eyes.

"Outside, in the streets, in Paris, anywhere where people are out in the open and can do things. What do you think about the revolution?"

The Chink shrugged his shoulders.

"Anything's possible," he said.

"D'you think they really can overthrow the army and the government in one day, like that?"

"Who?" broke in Chrisfield.

"Why, the people, Chris, the ordinary people like you and me, who are tired of being ordered round, who are tired of being trampled down by other people just like them, who've had the luck to get in right with the system."

"D'you know what I'll do when the revolution comes?" broke in the Chink with sudden intensity, slapping himself on the chest with one hand. "I'll go straight to one of those jewelry stores, rue Royale, and fill my pockets and come home with my hands full of diamonds."

"What good'll that do you?"

"What good? I'll bury them back there in the court and wait. I'll need them in the end. D'you know what it'll mean, your revolution? Another system! When there's a system there are always men to be bought with diamonds. That's what the world's like."

"But they won't be worth anything. It'll only be work that is worth anything."

"We'll see," said the Chink.

"D'you think it could happen, Andy, that there'd be a revolution, an' there wouldn't be any more armies, an' we'd be able to go round like we are civilians? Ah doan think so. Fellers like us ain't got it in 'em to buck the system, Andy."

"Many a system's gone down before; it will happen again."

"They're fighting the Garde Républicaine now before the Gare de l'Est," said the Chink in an expressionless voice. "What do you want down here? You'ld better stay in the back. You never know what the police may put over on us."

"Give us two bottles of vin blank, Chink," said Chrisfield.

"When'll you pay?"

"Right now. This guy's given me fifty francs."

"Rich, are you?" said the Chink with hatred in his voice, turning to Andrews. "Won't last long at that rate. Wait here."

He strode into the bar, closing the door carefully after him. A sudden jangling of the bell was followed by a sound of loud voices and stamping feet. Andrews and Chrisfield tiptoed into the dark corridor, where they stood a long time, waiting, breathing the foul air that stung their nostrils with the stench of plaster-damp and rotting wine. At last the Chink came back with three bottles of wine.

"Well, you're right," he said to Andrews. "They are putting up barricades on the Avenue Magenta."

On the stairs they met a girl sweeping. She had untidy hair that straggled out from under a blue handkerchief tied under her chin, and a pretty-colored fleshy face. Chrisfield caught her up to him and kissed her, as he passed.

"We all calls her the dawg-faced girl," he said to Andrews in explanation. "She does our work. Ah like to had a fight with Slippery over her yisterday. . . . Didn't Ah, Slippery?"

When he followed Chrisfield into the room, Andrews saw a man sitting on the window ledge smoking. He was dressed as a second lieutenant, his puttees were brilliantly polished, and he smoked through a long, amber cigarette-holder. His pink nails were carefully manicured.

"This is Slippery, Andy," said Chrisfield. "This guy's an ole buddy o' mine. We was bunkies together a hell of a time, wasn't we, Andy?"

"You bet we were."

"So you've taken your uniform off, have you? Mighty foolish," said Slippery. "Suppose they nab you?"

"It's all up now anyway. I don't intend to get nabbed," said Andrews.

"We got booze," said Chrisfield.

Slippery had taken dice from his pocket and was throwing them meditatively on the floor between his feet, snapping his fingers with each throw.

"I'll shoot you one of them bottles, Chris," he said.

Andrews walked over to the bed. Al was stirring uneasily, his face flushed and his mouth twitching.

"Hello," he said. "What's the news?"

"They say they're putting up barricades near the Gare de l'Est. It may be something."

"God, I hope so. God, I wish they'd do everything here like they did in Russia; then we'd be free. We couldn't go back to the States for a while, but there wouldn't be no M.P.'s to hunt us like we were criminals.

. . . I'm going to sit up a while and talk." Al giggled hysterically for a moment.

"Have a swig of wine?" asked Andrews.

"Sure, it may set me up a bit; thanks." He drank greedily from the bottle, spilling a little over his chin.

"Say, is your face badly cut up, Al?"

"No, it's just scotched, skin's off; looks like beefsteak, I reckon. . . . Ever been to Strasburg?"

"No."

"Man, that's the town. And the girls in that costume. . . . Whee!"

"Say, you're from San Francisco, aren't you?"

"Sure."

"Well, I wonder if you knew a fellow I knew at training camp, a kid named Fuselli from 'Frisco?"

"Knew him! Jesus, man, he's the best friend I've got. . . . Ye don't know where he is now, do you?"

"I saw him here in Paris two months ago."

"Well, I'll be damned. . . . God, that's great!" Al's voice was staccato from excitement. "So you knew Dan at training camp? The last letter from him was 'bout a year ago. Dan'd just got to be corporal. He's a damn clever kid, Dan is, an' ambitious too, one of the guys always makes good. . . . Gawd, I'd hate to see him this way. D'you know, we used to see a hell of a lot of each other in 'Frisco, an' he always used to tell me how he'd make good before I did. He was goddam right, too. Said I was too soft about girls. . . . Did ye know him real well?"

"Yes. I even remember that he used to tell me about a fellow he knew who was called Al. . . . He used to tell me about how you two used to go down to the harbor and watch the big liners come in at night, all aflare with lights through the Golden Gate. And he used to tell you he'd go over to Europe in one, when he'd made his pile."

"That's why Strasburg made me think of him," broke in Al, tremendously excited. "'Cause it was so picturesque like. . . . But honest, I've tried hard to make good in this army. I've done everything a feller could. An' all I did was to get into a cushy job in the regimental office. . . . But Dan, Gawd, he may even be an officer by this time."

"No, he's not that," said Andrews. "Look here, you ought to keep quiet with that hand of yours."

"Damn my hand. Oh, it'll heal all right if I forget about it. You see, my foot slipped when they shunted a car I was just climbing into, an' . . . I guess I ought to be glad I wasn't killed. But, gee, when I think that if I hadn't been a fool about that girl I might have been home by now. . . ."

"The Chink says they're putting up barricades on the Avenue Magenta."

"That means business, kid!"

"Business nothin'," shouted Slippery from where he and Chrisfield leaned over the dice on the tile floor in front of the window. "One tank an' a few husky Senegalese'll make your goddam socialists run so fast they won't stop till they get to Dijon. . . . You guys ought to have more sense." Slippery got to his feet and came over to the bed, jingling the dice in his hand. "It'll take more'n a handful o' socialists paid by the Boches to break the army. If it could be broke, don't ye think people would have done it long ago?"

"Shut up a minute. Ah thought Ah heard somethin'," said Chrisfield suddenly, going to the window.

They held their breath. The bed creaked as Al stirred uneasily in it.

"No, warn't anythin'; Ah'd thought Ah'd heard people singin'."

"The Internationale," cried Al.

"Shut up," said Chrisfield in a low gruff voice.

Through the silence of the room they heard steps on the stairs.

"All right, it's only Smiddy," said Slippery, and he threw the dice down on the tiles again.

The door opened slowly to let in a tall, stoop-shouldered man with a long face and long teeth.

"Who's the frawg?" he asked in a startled way, with one hand on the door knob.

"All right, Smiddy; it ain't a frawg; it's a guy Chris knows. He's taken his uniform off."

"'Lo, buddy," said Smiddy, shaking Andrews's hand. "Gawd, you look like a frawg."

"That's good," said Andrews.

"There's hell to pay," broke out Smiddy breathlessly. "You know Gus Evans and the little black-haired guy goes 'round with him? They been picked up. I seen 'em myself with some M.P.'s at Place de la Bastille. An' a guy I talked to under the bridge where I slep' last night said a guy'd tole him they were goin' to clean the A.W.O.L.'s out o' Paris if they had to search through every house in the place."

"If they come here they'll git somethin' they ain't lookin' for," muttered Chrisfield.

"I'm goin' down to Nice; getting too hot around here," said Slippery. "I've got travel orders in my pocket now."

"How did you get 'em?"

"Easy as pie," said Slippery, lighting a cigarette and puffing affectedly towards the ceiling. "I met up with a guy, a second loot, in the Knickerbocker Bar. We gets drunk together, an' goes on a party with two girls I know. In the morning I get up bright an' early, and now I've got five thousand francs, a leave slip and a silver cigarette case, an' Lootenant

J. B. Franklin's runnin' around sayin' how he was robbed by a Paris whore, or more likely keepin' damn quiet about it. That's my system."

"But, gosh darn it, I don't see how you can go around with a guy an' drink with him, an' then rob him," cried Al from the bed.

"No different from cleaning a guy up at craps."

"Well?"

"An' suppose that feller knew that I was only a bloody private. Don't you think he'd have turned me over to the M.P.'s like winkin'?"

"No, I don't think so," said Al. "They're juss like you an me, skeered to death they'll get in wrong, but they won't light on a feller unless they have to."

"That's a goddam lie," cried Chrisfield. "They like ridin' yer. A doughboy's less'n a dawg to 'em. Ah'd shoot anyone of 'em lake Ah'd shoot a nigger."

Andrews was watching Chrisfield's face; it suddenly flushed red. He was silent abruptly. His eyes met Andrews's eyes with a flash of fear.

"They're all sorts of officers, like they're all sorts of us," Al was insisting.

"But you damn fools, quit arguing," cried Smiddy. "What the hell are we goin' to do? It ain't safe here no more, that's how I look at it."

They were silent.

At last Chrisfield said:

"What you goin' to do, Andy?"

"I hardly know. I think I'll go out to St. Germain to see a boy I know there who works on a farm to see if it's safe to take a job there. I won't stay in Paris. Then there's a girl here I want to look up. I must see her." Andrews broke off suddenly, and started walking back and forth across the end of the room.

"You'd better be damn careful; they'll probably shoot you if they catch you," said Slippery.

Andrews shrugged his shoulders.

"Well, I'd rather be shot than go to Leavenworth for twenty years, Gawd! I would," cried Al.

"How do you fellers eat here?" asked Slippery.

"We buy stuff an' the dawg-faced girl cooks it for us."

"Got anything for this noon?"

"I'll go see if I can buy some stuff," said Andrews. "It's safer for me to go out than for you."

"All right, here's twenty francs," said Slippery, handing Andrews a bill with an offhand gesture.

Chrisfield followed Andrews down the stairs. When they reached the passage at the foot of the stairs, he put his hand on Andrews's shoulder and whispered:

"Say, Andy, d'you think there's anything in that revolution business? Ah hadn't never thought they could buck the system thataway."

"They did in Russia."

"Then we'd be free, civilians, like we all was before the draft. But that ain't possible, Andy; that ain't possible, Andy."

"We'll see," said Andrews, as he opened the door to the bar.

He went up excitedly to the Chink, who sat behind the row of bottles along the bar.

"Well, what's happening?"

"Where?"

"By the Gare de l'Est, where they were putting up barricades?"

"Barricades!" shouted a young man in a red sash who was drinking at a table. "Why, they tore down some of the iron guards round the trees, if you call that barricades. But they're cowards. Whenever the cops charge they run. They're dirty cowards."

"D'you think anything's going to happen?"

"What can happen when you've got nothing but a bunch of dirty cowards?"

"What d'you think about it?" said Andrews, turning to the Chink.

The Chink shook his head without answering. Andrews went out.

When he came back he found Al and Chrisfield alone in their room. Chrisfield was walking up and down, biting his finger nails. On the wall opposite the window was a square of sunshine reflected from the opposite wall of the Court.

"For God's sake beat it, Chris. I'm all right," Al was saying in a weak, whining voice, his face twisted up by pain.

"What's the matter?" cried Andrews, putting down a large bundle.

"Slippery's seen a M.P. nosin' around in front of the gin mill."

"Good God!"

"They've beat it. . . . The trouble is Al's too sick. . . . Honest to gawd, Ah'll stay with you, Al."

"No. If you know somewhere to go, beat it, Chris. I'll stay here with Al and talk French to the M.P.'s if they come. We'll fool 'em somehow." Andrews felt suddenly amused and joyous.

"Honest to gawd, Andy, Ah'd stay if it warn't that that sergeant knows," said Chrisfield in a jerky voice.

"Beat it, Chris. There may be no time to waste."

"So long, Andy." Chrisfield slipped out of the door.

"It's funny, Al," said Andrews, sitting on the edge of the bed and unwrapping the package of food, "I'm not a damn bit scared any more. I think I'm free of the army, Al. . . . How's your hand?"

"I dunno. Oh, how I wish I was in my old bunk at Coblenz. I warn't made for buckin' against the world this way. . . . If we had old Dan with

us. . . . Funny that you know Dan. . . . He'd have a million ideas for gettin' out of this fix. But I'm glad he's not here. He'd bawl me out so, for
not havin' made good. He's a powerful ambitious kid, is Dan."

"But it's not the sort of thing a man can make good in, Al," said
Andrews slowly. They were silent. There was no sound in the courtyard,
only very far away the clatter of a patrol of cavalry over cobblestones. The
sky had become overcast and the room was very dark. The mouldy plaster peeling off the walls had streaks of green in it. The light from the
courtyard had a greenish tinge that made their faces look pale and dead,
like the faces of men that have long been shut up between damp prison
walls.

"And Fuselli had a girl named Mabe," said Andrews.

"Oh, she married a guy in the Naval Reserve. They had a grand wed-
ding," said Al.

IV

"At last I've got to you!"

John Andrews had caught sight of Geneviève on a bench at the end of
the garden under an arbor of vines. Her hair flamed bright in a splotch
of sun as she got to her feet. She held out both hands to him.

"How good-looking you are like that," she cried.

He was conscious only of her hands in his hands and of her pale-
brown eyes and of the bright sun-splotches and the green shadows fluttering all about them.

"So you are out of prison," she said, "and demobilized. How wonderful! Why didn't you write? I have been very uneasy about you. How
did you find me here?"

"Your mother said you were here."

"And how do you like it, my Poissac?"

She made a wide gesture with her hand. They stood silent a moment,
side by side, looking about them. In front of the arbor was a parterre of
rounded box-bushes edging beds where disorderly roses hung in clusters
of pink and purple and apricot-color. And beyond it a brilliant emerald
lawn full of daisies sloped down to an old grey house with, at one end,
a squat round tower that had an extinguisher-shaped roof. Beyond the
house were tall, lush-green poplars, through which glittered patches of
silver-grey river and of yellow sand banks. From somewhere came a
drowsy scent of mown grass.

"How brown you are!" she said again. "I thought I had lost you. . . .
You might kiss me, Jean."

The muscles of his arms tightened about her shoulders. Her hair flamed in his eyes. The wind that rustled through broad grape-leaves made a flutter of dancing light and shadow about them.

"How hot you are with the sun!" she said. "I love the smell of the sweat of your body. You must have run very hard, coming here."

"Do you remember one night in the spring we walked home from *Pelleas and Melisande*? How I should have liked to have kissed you then, like this!" Andrews's voice was strange, hoarse, as if he spoke with difficulty.

"There is the château *très froid et très profond*," she said with a little laugh.

"And your hair. *Je les tiens dans les doits, je les tiens dans la bouche. . . . Toute ta chevelure, toute ta chevelure, Mélisande, est tombée de la tour. . . .'* D'you remember?"

"How wonderful you are."

They sat side by side on the stone bench without touching each other.

"It's silly," burst out Andrews excitedly. "We should have faith in our own selves. We can't live a little rag of romance without dragging in literature. We are drugged with literature so that we can never live at all, of ourselves."

"Jean, how did you come down here? Have you been demobilized long?"

"I walked almost all the way from Paris. You see, I am very dirty."

"How wonderful! But I'll be quiet. You must tell me everything from the moment you left me in Chartres."

"I'll tell you about Chartres later," said Andrews gruffly. "It has been superb, one of the biggest weeks in my life, walking all day under the sun, with the road like a white ribbon in the sun over the hills and along river banks, where there were yellow irises blooming, and through woods full of blackbirds, and with the dust in a little white cloud round my feet, and all the time walking towards you, walking towards you."

"And *la Reine de Saba,* how is it coming?"

"I don't know. It's a long time since I thought of it. . . . You have been here long?"

"Hardly a week. But what are you going to do?"

"I have a room overlooking the river in a house owned by a very fat woman with a very red face and a tuft of hair on her chin. . . ."

"Madame Boncour."

"Of course. You must know everybody. . . . It's so small."

"And you're going to stay here a long time?"

"Almost forever, and work, and talk to you; may I use your piano now and then?"

"How wonderful!"

Geneviève Rod jumped to her feet. Then she stood looking at him, leaning against one of the twisted stems of the vines, so that the broad leaves fluttered about her face. A white cloud, bright as silver, covered the sun, so that the hairy young leaves and the wind-blown grass of the lawn took on a silvery sheen. Two white butterflies fluttered for a second about the arbor.

"You must always dress like that," she said after a while.

Andrews laughed.

"A little cleaner, I hope," he said. "But there can't be much change. I have no other clothes and ridiculously little money."

"Who cares for money?" cried Geneviève. Andrews fancied he detected a slight affectation in her tone, but he drove the idea from his mind immediately.

"I wonder if there is a farm round here where I could get work."

"But you couldn't do the work of a farm labourer," cried Geneviève, laughing.

"You just watch me."

"It'll spoil your hands for the piano."

"I don't care about that; but all that's later, much later. Before anything else I must finish a thing I am working on. There is a theme that came to me when I was first in the army, when I was washing windows at the training camp."

"How funny you are, Jean! Oh, it's lovely to have you about again. But you're awfully solemn today. Perhaps it's because I made you kiss me."

"But, Geneviève, it's not in one day that you can unbend a slave's back, but with you, in this wonderful place . . . Oh, I've never seen such sappy richness of vegetation! And think of it, a week's walking first across those grey rolling uplands, and then at Blois down into the haze of richness of the Loire. . . . D'you know Vendôme? I came by a funny little town from Vendôme to Blois. You see, my feet. . . . And what wonderful cold baths I've had on the sand banks of the Loire. . . . No, after a while the rhythm of legs all being made the same length on drill fields, the hopeless caged dullness will be buried deep in me by the gorgeousness of this world of yours!"

He got to his feet and crushed a leaf softly between his fingers.

"You see, the little grapes are already forming. . . . Look up there," she said as she brushed the leaves aside just above his head. "These grapes here are the earliest; but I must show you my domain, and my cousins and the hen yard and everything."

She took his hand and pulled him out of the arbor. They ran like children, hand in hand, round the box-bordered paths.

"What I mean is this," he stammered, following her across the lawn. "If I could once manage to express all that misery in music, I could shove it far down into my memory. I should be free to live my own existence, in the midst of this carnival of summer."

At the house she turned to him. "You see the very battered ladies over the door," she said. "They are said to be by a pupil of Jean Goujon."

"They fit wonderfully in the landscape, don't they? Did I ever tell you about the sculptures in the hospital where I was when I was wounded?"

"No, but I want you to look at the house now. See, that's the tower; all that's left of the old building. I live there, and right under the roof there's a haunted room I used to be terribly afraid of. I'm still afraid of it. . . . You see this Henri Quatre part of the house was just a fourth of the house as planned. This lawn would have been the court. We dug up foundations where the roses are. There are all sorts of traditions as to why the house was never finished."

"You must tell me them."

"I shall later; but now you must come and meet my aunt and my cousins."

"Please, not just now, Geneviève. . . . I don't feel like talking to anyone except you. I have so much to talk to you about."

"But it's nearly lunch time, Jean. We can have all that after lunch."

"No, I can't talk to anyone else now. I must go and clean myself up a little anyway."

"Just as you like. . . . But you must come this afternoon and play to us. Two or three people are coming to tea. . . . It would be very sweet of you, if you'ld play to us, Jean."

"But can't you understand? I can't see you with other people now."

"Just as you like," said Geneviève, flushing, her hand on the iron latch of the door.

"Can't I come to see you tomorrow morning? Then I shall feel more like meeting people, after talking to you a long while. You see, I . . ." He paused with his eyes on the ground. Then he burst out in a low, passionate voice: "Oh, if I could only get it out of my mind . . . those tramping feet, those voices shouting orders."

His hand trembled when he put it in Geneviève's hand. She looked in his eyes calmly with her wide brown eyes.

"How strange you are today, Jean! Anyway, come back early tomorrow."

She went in the door. He walked round the house, through the carriage gate, and went off with long strides down the road along the river that led under linden trees to the village.

Thoughts swarmed teasingly through his head, like wasps about a rotting fruit. So at last he had seen Geneviève, and had held her in his arms and kissed her. And that was all. His plans for the future had never gone beyond that point. He hardly knew what he had expected, but in all the sunny days of walking, in all the furtive days in Paris, he had thought of nothing else. He would see Geneviève and tell her all about himself; he would unroll his life like a scroll before her eyes. Together they would piece together the future. A sudden terror took possession of him. She had failed him. Floods of denial seethed through his mind. It was that he had expected so much; he had expected her to understand him without explanation, instinctively. He had told her nothing. He had not even told her he was a deserter. What was it that had kept him from telling her? Puzzle as he would, he could not formulate it. Only, far within him, the certainty lay like an icy weight: she had failed him. He was alone. What a fool he had been to build his whole life on a chance of sympathy? No. It was rather this morbid playing at phrases that was at fault. He was like a touchy old maid, thinking imaginary results. "Take life at its face value," he kept telling himself. They loved each other anyway, somehow; it did not matter how. And he was free to work. Wasn't that enough?

But how could he wait until tomorrow to see her, to tell her everything, to break down all the silly little barriers between them, so that they might look directly into each other's lives?

The road turned inland from the river between garden walls at the entrance to the village. Through half-open doors Andrews got glimpses of neatly-cultivated kitchen-gardens and orchards where silver-leaved boughs swayed against the sky. Then the road swerved again into the village, crowded into a narrow paved street by the white and cream-colored houses with green or grey shutters and pale, red-tiled roofs. At the end, stained golden with lichen, the mauve-grey tower of the church held up its bells against the sky in a belfry of broad pointed arches. In front of the church Andrews turned down a little lane towards the river again, to come out in a moment on a quay shaded by skinny acacia trees. On the corner house, a ramshackle house with roofs and gables projecting in all directions, was a sign: "Rendezvous de la Marine." The room he stepped into was so low, Andrews had to stoop under the heavy brown beams as he crossed it. Stairs went up from a door behind a worn billiard table in the corner. Mme. Boncour stood between Andrews and the stairs. She was a flabby, elderly woman with round eyes and a round, very red face and a curious smirk about the lips.

"Monsieur payera un petit peu d'advance, n'est-ce pas, Monsieur?"

"All right," said Andrews, reaching for his pocketbook. "Shall I pay you a week in advance?"

The woman smiled broadly.

"Si Monsieur désire. . . . It's that life is so dear nowadays. Poor people like us can barely get along."

"I know that only too well," said Andrews.

"Monsieur est étranger . . ." began the woman in a wheedling tone, when she had received the money.

"Yes. I was only demobilized a short time ago."

"Aha! Monsieur est démobilisé. Monsieur remplira la petite feuille pour la police, n'est-ce pas?"

The woman brought from behind her back a hand that held a narrow printed slip.

"All right. I'll fill it out now," said Andrews, his heart thumping.

Without thinking what he was doing, he put the paper on the edge of the billiard table and wrote: "John Brown, aged 23. Chicago, Ill., Etats-Unis. Musician. Holder of passport No. 1,432,286."

"Merci, Monsieur. A bientôt, Monsieur. Au revoir, Monsieur."

The woman's singing voice followed him up the rickety stairs to his room. It was only when he had closed the door that he remembered that he had put down for a passport number his army number. "And why did I write John Brown as a name?" he asked himself.

> "John Brown's body lies a-mouldering in the grave,
>   But his soul goes marching on.
>   Glory, glory, hallelujah!
>   But his soul goes marching on."

He heard the song so vividly that he thought for an instant someone must be standing beside him singing it. He went to the window and ran his hand through his hair. Outside the Loire rambled in great loops towards the blue distance, silvery reach upon silvery reach, with here and there the broad gleam of a sand bank. Opposite were poplars and fields patched in various greens rising to hills tufted with dense shadowy groves. On the bare summit of the highest hill a windmill waved lazy arms against the marbled sky.

Gradually John Andrews felt the silvery quiet settle about him. He pulled a sausage and a piece of bread out of the pocket of his coat, took a long swig of water from the pitcher on his washstand, and settled himself at the table before the window in front of a pile of ruled sheets of music paper. He nibbled the bread and the sausage meditatively for a long while, then wrote "Arbeit und Rhythmus" in a large careful hand at the top of the paper. After that he looked out of the window without moving, watching the plumed clouds sail like huge slow ships against the slate-blue sky. Suddenly he scratched out what he had written and scrawled above it: "*The Body and Soul of John Brown.*" He got to his feet and walked about the room with clenched hands.

"How curious that I should have written that name. How curious that I should have written that name!" he said aloud.

He sat down at the table again and forgot everything in the music that possessed him.

The next morning he walked out early along the river, trying to occupy himself until it should be time to go to see Geneviève. The memory of his first days in the army, spent washing windows at the training camp, was very vivid in his mind. He saw himself again standing naked in the middle of a wide, bare room, while the recruiting sergeant measured and prodded him. And now he was a deserter. Was there any sense to it all? Had his life led in any particular direction, since he had been caught haphazard in the treadmill, or was it all chance? A toad hopping across a road in front of a steam roller.

He stood still, and looked about him. Beyond a clover field was the river with its sand banks and its broad silver reaches. A boy was wading far out in the river catching minnows with a net. Andrews watched his quick movements as he jerked the net through the water. And that boy, too, would be a soldier; the lithe body would be thrown into a mould to be made the same as other bodies, the quick movements would be standardized into the manual at arms, the inquisitive, petulant mind would be battered into servility. The stockade was built; not one of the sheep would escape. And those that were not sheep? They were deserters; every rifle muzzle held death for them; they would not live long. And yet other nightmares had been thrown off the shoulders of men. Every man who stood up courageously to die loosened the grip of the nightmare.

Andrews walked slowly along the road, kicking his feet into the dust like a schoolboy. At a turning he threw himself down on the grass under some locust trees. The heavy fragrance of their flowers and the grumbling of the bees that hung drunkenly on the white racemes made him feel very drowsy. A cart passed, pulled by heavy white horses; an old man with his back curved like the top of a sunflower stalk hobbled after, using the whip as a walking stick. Andrews saw the old man's eyes turned on him suspiciously. A faint pang of fright went through him; did the old man know he was a deserter? The cart and the old man had already disappeared round the bend in the road. Andrews lay a long while listening to the jingle of the harness thin into the distance, leaving him again to the sound of the drowsy bees among the locust blossoms.

When he sat up, he noticed that through a break in the hedge beyond the slender black trunks of the locusts, he could see rising above the trees the extinguisher-shaped roof of the tower of Geneviève Rod's house. He remembered the day he had first seen Geneviève, and the boyish awkwardness with which she poured tea. Would he and Geneviève ever find a moment of real contact? All at once a bitter thought came to him. "Or is it that she wants a tame pianist as an ornament to a clever young woman's drawing room?" He jumped to his feet and started walking fast towards the town again. He would go to see her at once and settle all that forever. The village clock had begun to strike; the clear notes vibrated crisply across the fields: ten.

Walking back to the village he began to think of money. His room was twenty francs a week. He had in his purse a hundred and twenty-four francs. After fishing in all his pockets for silver, he found three francs and a half more. A hundred and twenty-seven francs fifty. If he could live on forty francs a week, he would have three weeks in which to work on the "Body and Soul of John Brown." Only three weeks; and then he must find work. In any case he would write Henslowe to send him money if he had any; this was no time for delicacy; everything depended on his having money. And he swore to himself that he would work for three weeks, that he would throw the idea that flamed within him into shape on paper, whatever happened. He racked his brains to think of someone in America he could write to for money. A ghastly sense of solitude possessed him. And would Geneviève fail him too?

Geneviève was coming out by the front door of the house when he reached the carriage gate beside the road.

She ran to meet him.

"Good morning. I was on my way to fetch you."

She seized his hand and pressed it hard.

"How sweet of you!"

"But, Jean, you're not coming from the village."

"I've been walking."

"How early you must get up!"

"You see, the sun rises just opposite my window, and shines in on my bed. That makes me get up early."

She pushed him in the door ahead of her. They went through the hall to a long high room that had a grand piano and many old high-backed chairs, and in front of the French windows that opened on the garden, a round table of black mahogany littered with books. Two tall girls in muslin dresses stood beside the piano.

"These are my cousins. . . . Here he is at last. Monsieur Andrews, ma cousine Berthe et ma cousine Jeanne. Now you've got to play to us; we are bored to death with everything we know."

"All right. . . . But I have a great deal to talk to you about later," said Andrews in a low voice.

Geneviève nodded understandingly.

"Why don't you play us *La Reine de Saba,* Jean?"

"Oh, do play that," twittered the cousins.

"If you don't mind, I'd rather play some Bach."

"There's a lot of Bach in that chest in the corner," cried Geneviève. "It's ridiculous; everything in the house is jammed with music."

They leaned over the chest together, so that Andrews felt her hair brush against his cheek, and the smell of her hair in his nostrils. The cousins remained by the piano.

"I must talk to you alone soon," whispered Andrews.

"All right," she said, her face reddening as she leaned over the chest. On top of the music was a revolver.

"Look out, it's loaded," she said, when he picked it up.

He looked at her inquiringly. "I have another in my room. You see Mother and I are often alone here, and then, I like firearms. Don't you?"

"I hate them," muttered Andrews.

"Here's tons of Bach."

"Fine. . . . Look, Geneviève," he said suddenly, "lend me that revolver for a few days. I'll tell you why I want it later."

"Certainly. Be careful, because it's loaded," she said in an offhand manner, walking over to the piano with two volumes under each arm. Andrews closed the chest and followed her, suddenly bubbling with gaiety. He opened a volume haphazard.

"To a friend to dissuade him from starting on a journey," he read. "Oh, I used to know that."

He began to play, putting boisterous vigor into the tunes. In a pianissimo passage he heard one cousin whisper to the other:

"Qu'il a l'air intéressant."

"Farouche, n'est-ce pas? Genre révolutionnaire," answered the other cousin, tittering. Then he noticed that Mme. Rod was smiling at him. He got to his feet.

"Mais ne vous dérangez pas," she said.

A man with white flannel trousers and tennis shoes and a man in black with a pointed grey beard and amused grey eyes had come into the room, followed by a stout woman in hat and veil, with long white cotton gloves on her arms. Introductions were made. Andrews's spirits began to ebb. All these people were making strong the barrier between him and Geneviève. Whenever he looked at her, some well-dressed person stepped in front of her with a gesture of politeness. He felt caught in a ring of well-dressed conventions that danced about him with grotesque gestures of politeness. All through lunch he had a crazy desire to jump to his feet and shout: "Look at me; I'm a deserter. I'm under the wheels of your system. If your system doesn't succeed in killing me, it will be that much weaker, it will have less strength to kill others." There was talk about his demobilization, and his music, and the Schola Cantorum. He felt he was being exhibited. "But they don't know what they're exhibiting," he said to himself with a certain bitter joy.

After lunch they went out into the grape arbor, where coffee was brought. Andrews sat silent, not listening to the talk, which was about Empire furniture and the new taxes, staring up into the broad sunsplotched leaves of the grape vines, remembering how the sun and shade had danced about Geneviève's hair when they had been in the arbor alone the day before, turning it all to red flame. Today she sat in shadow, and her hair was rusty and dull. Time dragged by very slowly.

At last Geneviève got to her feet.

"You haven't seen my boat," she said to Andrews. "Let's go for a row. I'll row you about."

Andrews jumped up eagerly.

"Make her be careful, Monsieur Andrews, she's dreadfully imprudent," said Madame Rod.

"You were bored to death," said Geneviève, as they walked out on the road.

"No, but those people all seemed to be building new walls between you and me. God knows there are enough already."

She looked him sharply in the eyes a second, but said nothing.

They walked slowly through the sand of the river edge, till they came to an old flat-bottomed boat painted green with an orange stripe, drawn up among the reeds.

"It will probably sink; can you swim?" she asked, laughing.

Andrews smiled, and said in a stiff voice:

"I can swim. It was by swimming that I got out of the army."

"What do you mean?"

"When I deserted."

"When you deserted?"

Geneviève leaned over to pull on the boat. Their heads almost touching, they pulled the boat down to the water's edge, then pushed it half out on to the river.

"And if you are caught?"

"They might shoot me; I don't know. Still, as the war is over, it would probably be life imprisonment, or at least twenty years."

"You can speak of it as coolly as that?"

"It is no new idea to my mind."

"What induced you to do such a thing?"

"I was not willing to submit any longer to the treadmill."

"Come, let's go out on the river."

Geneviève stepped into the boat and caught up the oars.

"Now push her off, and don't fall in," she cried.

The boat glided out into the water. Geneviève began pulling on the oars slowly and regularly. Andrews looked at her without speaking.

"When you're tired, I'll row," he said after a while.

Behind them the village, patched white and buff-color and russet and pale red with stucco walls and steep, tiled roofs, rose in an irregular pyramid to the church. Through the wide pointed arches of the belfry they could see the bells hanging against the sky. Below in the river the town was reflected complete, with a great rift of steely blue across it where the wind ruffled the water.

The oars creaked rhythmically as Geneviève pulled on them.

"Remember, when you are tired," said Andrews again after a long pause.

Geneviève spoke through clenched teeth:

"Of course, you have no patriotism."

"As you mean it, none."

They rounded the edge of a sand bank where the current ran hard. Andrews put his hands beside her hands on the oars and pushed with her. The bow of the boat grounded in some reeds under willows.

"We'll stay here," she said, pulling in the oars that flashed in the sun as she jerked them, dripping silver, out of the water.

She clasped her hands round her knees and leaned over towards him.

"So that is why you want my revolver. . . . Tell me all about it, from Chartres," she said, in a choked voice.

"You see, I was arrested at Chartres and sent to a labor battalion, the equivalent for your army prison, without being able to get word to my commanding officer in the School Detachment. . . ." He paused.

A bird was singing in the willow tree. The sun was under a cloud; beyond the long pale green leaves that fluttered ever so slightly in the wind, the sky was full of silvery and cream-colored clouds, with here and there a patch the color of a robin's egg. Andrews began laughing softly.

"But, Geneviève, how silly those words are, those pompous, efficient words: detachment, battalion, commanding officer. It would have all happened anyway. Things reached the breaking point; that was all. I could not submit any longer to the discipline. . . . Oh, those long Roman words, what millstones they are about men's necks! That was silly, too; I was quite willing to help in the killing of Germans, I had no quarrel with, out of curiosity or cowardice. . . . You see, it has taken me so long to find out how the world is. There was no one to show me the way."

He paused as if expecting her to speak. The bird in the willow tree was still singing.

Suddenly a dangling twig blew aside a little so that Andrews could see him—a small grey bird, his throat all puffed out with song.

"It seems to me," he said very softly, "that human society has been always that, and perhaps will be always that: organizations growing and stifling individuals, and individuals revolting hopelessly against them, and at last forming new societies to crush the old societies and becoming slaves again in their turn. . . ."

"I thought you were a socialist," broke in Geneviève sharply, in a voice that hurt him to the quick, he did not know why.

"A man told me at the labor battalion," began Andrews again, "that they'd tortured a friend of his there once by making him swallow lighted cigarettes; well, every order shouted at me, every new humiliation before the authorities, was as great an agony to me. Can't you understand?" His voice rose suddenly to a tone of entreaty.

She nodded her head. They were silent. The willow leaves shivered in a little wind. The bird had gone.

"But tell me about the swimming part of it. That sounds exciting."

"We were working unloading cement at Passy—cement to build the stadium the army is presenting to the French, built by slave labor, like the pyramids."

"Passy's where Balzac lived. Have you ever seen his house there?"

"There was a boy working with me, the Kid, 'le gosse,' it'ld be in French. Without him, I should never have done it. I was completely crushed. . . . I suppose that he was drowned. . . . Anyway, we swam under water as far as we could, and, as it was nearly dark, I managed to get on a barge, where a funny anarchist family took care of me. I've never heard of the Kid since. Then I bought these clothes that amuse you so, Geneviève, and came back to Paris to find you, mainly."

"I mean as much to you as that?" whispered Geneviève.

"In Paris, too. I tried to find a boy named Marcel, who worked on a farm near St. Germain. I met him out there one day. I found he'd gone to sea. . . . If it had not been that I had to see you, I should have gone straight to Bordeaux or Marseilles. They aren't too particular who they take as a seaman now."

"But in the army didn't you have enough of that dreadful life, always thrown among uneducated people, always in dirty, foul-smelling surroundings, you, a sensitive person, an artist? No wonder you are almost crazy after years of that." Geneviève spoke passionately, with her eyes fixed on his face.

"Oh, it wasn't that," said Andrews with despair in his voice. "I rather like the people you call low. Anyway, the differences between people are so slight. . . ." His sentence trailed away. He stopped speaking, sat stirring uneasily on the seat, afraid he would cry out. He noticed the hard shape of the revolver against his leg.

"But isn't there something you can do about it? You must have friends," burst out Geneviève. "You were treated with horrible injustice. You can get yourself reinstated and properly demobilised. They'll see you are a person of intelligence. They can't treat you as they would anybody."

"I must be, as you say, a little mad, Geneviève," said Andrews. "But now that I, by pure accident, have made a gesture, feeble as it is, towards human freedom, I can't feel that . . . Oh, I suppose I'm a fool. . . . But there you have me, just as I am, Geneviève."

He sat with his head drooping over his chest, his two hands clasping the gunwales of the boat. After a long while Geneviève said in a dry little voice:

"Well, we must go back now; it's time for tea."

Andrews looked up. There was a dragon fly poised on the top of a reed, with silver wings and a long crimson body.

"Look just behind you, Geneviève."

"Oh, a dragon fly! What people was it that made them the symbol of life? It wasn't the Egyptians. O, I've forgotten."

"I'll row," said Andrews.

The boat was hurried along by the current. In a very few minutes they had pulled it up on the bank in front of the Rods' house.

"Come and have some tea," said Geneviève.

"No, I must work."

"You are doing something new, aren't you?"

Andrews nodded.

"What's its name?"

"The Soul and Body of John Brown."

"Who's John Brown?"

"He was a madman who wanted to free people. There's a song about him."

"It is based on popular themes?"

"Not that I know of. . . . I only thought of the name yesterday. It came to me by a very curious accident."

"You'll come tomorrow?"

"If you're not too busy."

"Let's see, the Boileaus are coming to lunch. There won't be anybody at tea time. We can have tea together alone."

He took her hand and held it, awkward as a child with a new playmate.

"All right, at about four. If there's nobody there, we'll play music," he said.

She pulled her hand from him hurriedly, made a curious formal gesture of farewell, and crossed the road to the gate without looking back. There was one idea in his head, to get to his room and lock the door and throw himself face down on the bed. The idea amused some distant part of his mind. That had been what he had always done when, as a child, the world had seemed too much for him. He would run upstairs and lock the door and throw himself face downward on the bed. "I wonder if I shall cry?" he thought.

Madame Boncour was coming down the stairs as he went up. He backed down and waited. When she got to the bottom, pouting a little, she said:

"So you are a friend of Mme. Rod, Monsieur?"

"How did you know that?"

A dimple appeared near her mouth in either cheek.

"You know, in the country, one knows everything," she said.

"Au revoir," he said, starting up the stairs.

"Mais, Monsieur. You should have told me. If I had known I should not have asked you to pay in advance. Oh, never. You must pardon me, Monsieur."

"All right."

"Monsieur est Américain? You see I know a lot." Her puffy cheeks shook when she giggled. "And Monsieur has known Mme. Rod et Mlle. Rod a long time. An old friend. Monsieur is a musician."

"Yes. Bon soir." Andrews ran up the stairs.

"Au revoir, Monsieur." Her chanting voice followed him up the stairs. He slammed the door behind him and threw himself on the bed.

When Andrews awoke next morning, his first thought was how long he had to wait that day to see Geneviève. Then he remembered their talk of the day before. Was it worth while going to see her at all, he asked himself. And very gradually he felt cold despair taking hold of him. He felt for a moment that he was the only living thing in a world of dead machines; the toad hopping across the road in front of a steam roller. Suddenly he thought of Jeanne. He remembered her grimy, overworked fingers lying in her lap. He pictured her walking up and down in front of the Café de Rohan one Wednesday night, waiting for him. In the place of Geneviève, what would Jeanne have done? Yet people were always alone, really; however much they loved each other, there could be no real union. Those who rode in the great car could never feel as the others felt; the toads hopping across the road. He felt no rancour against Geneviève.

These thoughts slipped from him while he was drinking the coffee and eating the dry bread that made his breakfast; and afterwards, walking back and forth along the river bank, he felt his mind and body becoming as if fluid, and supple, trembling, bent in the rush of his music like a poplar tree bent in a wind. He sharpened a pencil and went up to his room again.

The sky was cloudless that day. As he sat at his table the square of blue through the window and the hills topped by their windmill and the silver-blue of the river, were constantly in his eyes. Sometimes he wrote notes down fast, thinking nothing, feeling nothing, seeing nothing; other times he sat for long periods staring at the sky and at the windmill, vaguely happy, playing with unexpected thoughts that came and vanished, as now and then a moth fluttered in the window to blunder about the ceiling beams, and, at last, to disappear without his knowing how.

When the clock struck twelve, he found he was very hungry. For two days he had eaten nothing but bread, sausage and cheese. Finding Madame Boncour behind the bar downstairs, polishing glasses, he ordered dinner of her. She brought him a stew and a bottle of wine at once, and stood over him watching him eat it, her arms akimbo and the dimples showing in her huge red cheeks.

"Monsieur eats less than any young man I ever saw," she said.

"I'm working hard," said Andrews, flushing.

"But when you work you have to eat a great deal, a great deal."

"And if the money is short?" asked Andrews with a smile. Something in the steely searching look that passed over her eyes for a minute startled him.

"There are not many people here now, Monsieur, but you should see it on a market day. . . . Monsieur will take some dessert?"

"Cheese and coffee."

"Nothing more? It's the season of strawberries."

"Nothing more, thank you."

When Madame Boncour came back with the cheese, she said:

"I had Americans here once, Monsieur. A pretty time I had with them, too. They were deserters. They went away without paying, with the gendarmes after them I hope they were caught and sent to the front, those good-for-nothings."

"There are all sorts of Americans," said Andrews in a low voice. He was angry with himself because his heart beat so.

"Well, I'm going for a little walk. Au revoir, Madame."

"Monsieur is going for a little walk. Amusez-vous bien, Monsieur. Au revoir, Monsieur," Madame Boncour's singsong tones followed him out.

A little before four Andrews knocked at the front door of the Rods' house. He could hear Santo, the little black and tan, barking inside. Madame Rod opened the door for him herself.

"Oh, here you are," she said. "Come and have some tea. Did the work go well to-day?"

"And Geneviève?" stammered Andrews.

"She went out motoring with some friends. She left a note for you. It's on the tea-table."

He found himself talking, making questions and answers, drinking tea, putting cakes into his mouth, all through a white dead mist.

Geneviève's note said:

"Jean:—I'm thinking of ways and means. You must get away to a neutral country. Why couldn't you have talked it over with me first, before cutting off every chance of going back. I'll be in tomorrow at the same time.

"Bien à vous. G. R."

"Would it disturb you if I played the piano a few minutes, Madame Rod?" Andrews found himself asking all at once.

"No, go ahead. We'll come in later and listen to you."

It was only as he left the room that he realized he had been talking to the two cousins as well as to Madame Rod.

At the piano he forgot everything and regained his mood of vague joyousness. He found paper and a pencil in his pocket, and played the theme that had come to him while he had been washing windows at the top of a stepladder at training camp arranging it, modelling it, forgetting everything, absorbed in his rhythms and cadences. When he stopped work it was nearly dark. Geneviève Rod, a veil round her head, stood in the French window that led to the garden.

"I heard you," she said. "Go on."

"I'm through. How was your motor ride?"

"I loved it. It's not often I get a chance to go motoring."

"Nor is it often I get a chance to talk to you alone," cried Andrews bitterly.

"You seem to feel you have rights of ownership over me. I resent it. No one has rights over me." She spoke as if it were not the first time she had thought of the phrase.

He walked over and leaned against the window beside her.

"Has it made such a difference to you, Geneviève, finding out that I am a deserter?"

"No, of course not," she said hastily.

"I think it has, Geneviève. . . . What do you want me to do? Do you think I should give myself up? A man I knew in Paris has given himself up, but he hadn't taken his uniform off. It seems that makes a difference. He was a nice fellow. His name was Al, he was from San Francisco. He had nerve, for he amputated his own little finger when his hand was crushed by a freight car."

"Oh, no, no. Oh, this is so frightful. And you would have been a great composer. I feel sure of it."

"Why, would have been? The stuff I'm doing now's better than any of the dribbling things I've done before, I know that."

"Oh, yes, but you'll need to study, to get yourself known."

"If I can pull through six months, I'm safe. The army will have gone. I don't believe they extradite deserters."

"Yes, but the shame of it, the danger of being found out all the time."

"I am ashamed of many things in my life, Geneviève. I'm rather proud of this."

"But can't you understand that other people haven't your notions of individual liberty?"

"I must go, Geneviève."

"You must come in again soon."

"One of these days."

And he was out in the road in the windy twilight, with his music papers crumpled in his hand. The sky was full of tempestuous purple clouds; between them were spaces of clear claret-colored light, and here and there a gleam of opal. There were a few drops of rain in the wind that rustled the broad leaves of the lindens and filled the wheat fields with waves like the sea, and made the river very dark between rosy sand banks. It began to rain. Andrews hurried home so as not to drench his only suit. Once in his room he lit four candles and placed them at the corners of his table. A little cold crimson light still filtered in through the rain from the afterglow, giving the candles a ghostly glimmer. Then he lay on his bed, and staring up at the flickering light on the ceiling, tried to think.

"Well, you're alone now, John Andrews," he said aloud, after a half-hour, and jumped jauntily to his feet. He stretched himself and yawned. Outside the rain pattered loudly and steadily. "Let's have a general accounting," he said to himself. "It'll be easily a month before I hear from old Howe in America, and longer before I hear from Henslowe, and already I've spent twenty francs on food. Can't make it this way. Then, in real possessions, I have one volume of Villon, a green book on counterpoint, a map of France torn in two, and a moderately well-stocked mind."

He put the two books on the middle of the table before him, on top of his disorderly bundle of music papers and notebooks. Then he went on, piling his possessions there as he thought of them. Three pencils, a fountain pen. Automatically he reached for his watch, but he remembered he'd given it to Al to pawn in case he didn't decide to give himself up, and needed money. A toothbrush. A shaving set. A piece of soap. A hairbrush and a broken comb. Anything else? He groped in the musette that hung on the foot of the bed. A box of matches. A knife with one blade missing, and a mashed cigarette. Amusement growing on him every minute, he contemplated the pile. Then, in the drawer, he remembered, was a clean shirt and two pairs of soiled socks. And that was all, absolutely all. Nothing saleable there. Except Geneviève's revolver. He pulled it out of his pocket. The candlelight flashed on the bright nickel. No, he might need that; it was too valuable to sell. He pointed it towards himself. Under the chin was said to be the best place. He wondered if he would pull the trigger when the barrel was pressed against his chin. No, when his money gave out he'd sell the revolver. An expensive death for a starving man. He sat on the edge of the bed and laughed.

Then he discovered he was very hungry. Two meals in one day; shocking! He said to himself. Whistling joyfully, like a schoolboy, he strode down the rickety stairs to order a meal of Madame Boncour.

It was with a strange start that he noticed that the tune he was whistling was:

> "John Brown's body lies a-mouldering in the grave,
>   But his soul goes marching on."

The lindens were in bloom. From a tree beside the house great gusts of fragrance, heavy as incense, came in through the open window. Andrews lay across the table with his eyes closed and his cheek in a mass of ruled papers. He was very tired. The first movement of the "Soul and Body of John Brown" was down on paper. The village clock struck two. He got to his feet and stood a moment looking absently out of the window. It was a sultry afternoon of swollen clouds that hung low over the river. The windmill on the hilltop opposite was motionless. He seemed to hear Geneviève's voice the last time he had seen her, so long ago. "You would have been a great composer." He walked over to the table and turned over some sheets without looking at them. "Would have been." He shrugged his shoulders. So you couldn't be a great composer and a deserter too in the year 1919. Probably Geneviève was right. But he must have something to eat.

"But how late it is," expostulated Madame Boncour, when he asked for lunch.

"I know it's very late. I have just finished a third of the work I'm doing."

"And do you get paid a great deal, when that is finished?" asked Madame Boncour, the dimples appearing in her broad cheeks.

"Some day, perhaps."

"You will be lonely now that the Rods have left."

"Have they left?"

"Didn't you know? Didn't you go to say goodby? They've gone to the seashore. . . . But I'll make you a little omelette."

"Thank you."

When Madame Boncour came back with the omelette and fried potatoes, she said to him in a mysterious voice:

"You didn't go to see the Rods as often these last weeks."

"No."

Madame Boncour stood staring at him, with her red arms folded round her breasts, shaking her head.

When he got up to go upstairs again, she suddenly shouted:

"And when are you going to pay me? It's two weeks since you have paid me."

"But, Madame Boncour, I told you I had no money. If you wait a day or two, I'm sure to get some in the mail. It can't be more than a day or two."

"I've heard that story before."

"I've even tried to get work at several farms round here."

Madame Boncour threw back her head and laughed, showing the blackened teeth of her lower jaw.

"Look here," she said at length, "after this week, it's finished. You either pay me, or . . . And I sleep very lightly, Monsieur." Her voice took on suddenly its usual sleek singsong tone.

Andrews broke away and ran upstairs to his room.

"I must fly the coop tonight," he said to himself. But suppose then letters came with money the next day. He writhed in indecision all the afternoon.

That evening he took a long walk. In passing the Rods' house he saw that the shutters were closed. It gave him a sort of relief to know that Geneviève no longer lived near him. His solitude was complete, now.

And why, instead of writing music that would have been worth while if he hadn't been a deserter, he kept asking himself, hadn't he tried long ago to act, to make a gesture, however feeble, however forlorn, for other people's freedom? Half by accident he had managed to free himself from the treadmill. Couldn't he have helped others? If he only had his life to live over again. No; he had not lived up to the name of John Brown.

It was dark when he got back to the village. He had decided to wait one more day.

The next morning he started working on the second movement. The lack of a piano made it very difficult to get ahead, yet he said to himself that he should put down what he could, as it would be long before he found leisure again.

One night he had blown out his candle and stood at the window watching the glint of the moon on the river. He heard a soft heavy step on the landing outside his room. A floorboard creaked, and the key turned in the lock. The step was heard again on the stairs. John Andrews laughed aloud. The window was only twenty feet from the ground, and there was a trellis. He got into bed contentedly. He must sleep well, for tomorrow night he would slip out of the window and make for Bordeaux.

Another morning. A brisk wind blew, fluttering Andrews's papers as he worked. Outside the river was streaked blue and silver and slate-colored. The windmill's arms waved fast against the piled clouds. The scent of the lindens came only intermittently on the sharp wind. In spite of himself, the tune of "John Brown's Body" had crept in among his ideas. Andrews sat with a pencil at his lips, whistling softly, while in the back of his mind a vast chorus seemed singing:

> "John Brown's body lies a-mouldering in the grave,
>   But his soul goes marching on.
>   Glory, glory, hallelujah!
>   But his soul goes marching on."

If one could only find freedom by marching for it, came the thought. All at once he became rigid, his hands clutched the table edge.

There was an American voice under his window:

"D'you think she's kiddin' us, Charley?"

Andrews was blinded, falling from a dizzy height. God, could things repeat themselves like that? Would everything be repeated? And he seemed to hear voices whisper in his ears: "One of you men teach him how to salute."

He jumped to his feet and pulled open the drawer. It was empty. The woman had taken the revolver. "It's all planned, then. She knew," he said aloud in a low voice.

He became suddenly calm.

A man in a boat was passing down the river. The boat was painted bright green; the man wore a curious jacket of burnt-brown color, and held a fishing pole.

Andrews sat in his chair again. The boat was out of sight now, but there was the windmill turning, turning against the piled white clouds.

There were steps on the stairs.

Two swallows, twittering, curved past the window, very near, so that Andrews could make out the markings on their wings and the way they folded their legs against their pale-grey bellies.

There was a knock.

"Come in," said Andrews firmly.

"I beg yer pardon," said a soldier with his hat, that had a band, in his hand. "Are you the American?"

"Yes."

"Well, the woman down there said she thought your papers wasn't in very good order." The man stammered with embarrassment.

Their eyes met.

"No, I'm a deserter," said Andrews.

The M.P. snatched for his whistle and blew it hard. There was an answering whistle from outside the window.

"Get your stuff together."

"I have nothing."

"All right, walk downstairs slowly in front of me."

Outside the windmill was turning, turning, against the piled white clouds of the sky.

Andrews turned his eyes towards the door. The M.P. closed the door after them, and followed on his heels down the steps.

On John Andrews's writing table the brisk wind rustled among the broad sheets of paper. First one sheet, then another, blew off the table, until the floor was littered with them.